"C'mere," Jack whispered, leaning forward.

Katherine's eyes widened and she cut her gaze toward the open door. "Jack, stop. We mustn't."

His look grew hungry. Amused. "Oh, but we must," he answered.

In a state of near panic, Katherine practically lunged forward and let her lips graze Jack's. "There. Now go away."

"You call that a kiss? That'll never do," he said. "If you can say 'there' after a puny little peck like that, I think we'd better have a lesson. I'm good at lessons." He moved closer.

Katherine teetered for a moment between fear of what might happen if she did—and what would happen if she didn't....

Dear Reader,

This month, Silhouette Romance brings you six wonderful new love stories—guaranteed to keep your summer sizzling! Starting with a terrific FABULOUS FATHER by Arlene James. A *Mail-order Brood* was not what Leon Paradise was expecting when he asked Cassie Esterbridge to be his wife. So naturally the handsome rancher was shocked when he discovered that his mail-order bride came with a ready-made family!

Favorite author Suzanne Carey knows the kinds of stories Romance readers love. And this month, Ms. Carey doesn't disappoint. *The Male Animal* is a humorous tale of a couple who discover love—in the midst of their divorce.

The fun continues as Marie Ferrarella brings us another delightful tale from her Baby's Choice series—where matchmaking babies bring together their unsuspecting parents.

In an exciting new trilogy from Sandra Steffen, the Harris brothers vow that no woman will ever tie them down. But their WEDDING WAGER doesn't stand a chance against love. This month, a confirmed bachelor suddenly becomes a single father—and a more-than-willing groom—in *Bachelor Daddy*.

Rounding out the month, Jeanne Rose combines the thrill of the chase with the excitement of romance in *Love on the Run*. And *The Bridal Path* is filled with secrets—and passion—as Alaina Hawthorne spins a tale of love under false pretenses.

I hope you'll join us in the coming months for more great books from Elizabeth August, Kasey Michaels and Helen Myers.

Until then—

Happy Reading!

Anne Canadeo
Senior Editor

Please address questions and book requests to:
Silhouette Reader Service
U.S.: 3010 Walden Ave., P.O. Box 1325, Buffalo, NY 14269
Canadian: P.O. Box 609, Fort Erie, Ont. L2A 5X3

THE BRIDAL PATH

Alaina Hawthorne

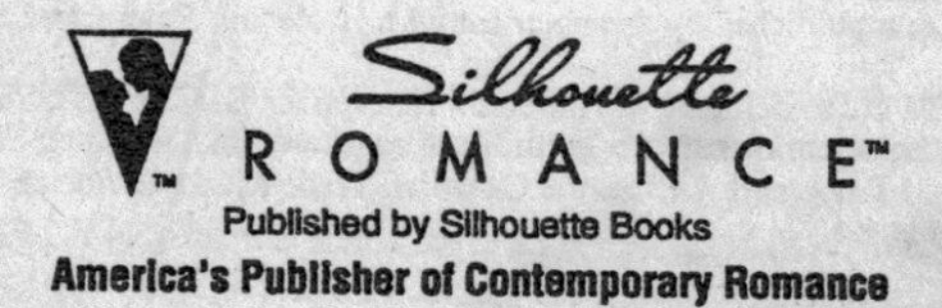

Special thanks to Betty Gyenes, Pat Kay, Elaine Kimberley and Heather MacAllister, my dear friends, whose encouragement and patience made this possible.

To Doug and Kitty. Wish you were here.

SILHOUETTE BOOKS

ISBN 0-373-19029-8

THE BRIDAL PATH

This edition published by arrangement with Harlequin Enterprises B. V.

Printed in U.S.A.

Books by Alaina Hawthorne

Silhouette Romance

Out of the Blue #672
The Bridal Path #1029

ALAINA HAWTHORNE,

a native Texan, has been writing fiction and nonfiction since she was a teenager. Her first Silhouette Romance won the Romance Writers of America RITA Award for Best First Book. She lives in Houston with Sallie, her rottweiler, and loves hearing from her readers.

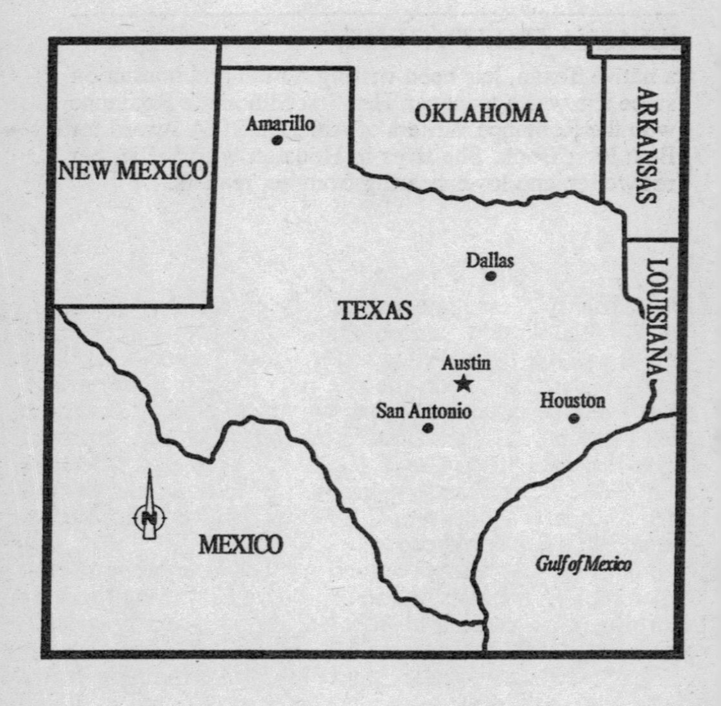
NEW MEXICO
Amarillo
OKLAHOMA
ARKANSAS
Dallas
TEXAS
LOUISIANA
Austin
San Antonio
Houston
N
MEXICO
Gulf of Mexico

Chapter One

As Katherine Hanshaw stepped into David Wiley's office, her stomach slowly, nauseously turned. She wasn't really afraid; she liked Mr. Wiley and was fairly certain he liked her. After all, he'd been the one who hired her almost five years ago when she had to drop out of college. At that time jobs in Houston, Texas, had been pretty scarce, but he'd hired her as an entry-level teller and promised advancement if she was willing to work hard. Katherine *had* worked hard and, true to his word, he'd eventually had her promoted to senior bookkeeper.

But there was always something ominous about being called into your boss's office, especially first thing Monday morning. The look on his face wasn't particularly encouraging, either. He looked worried. And a little scared.

He glanced up and ran a hand through his thinning brown hair. "Ah, Katherine, won't you take a seat," he muttered and nodded toward a maroon leather guest chair. "Thanks for coming down so quickly."

"Of course, Mr. Wiley." *As if I wouldn't drop everything when the bank vice president sends for me.* She sat, crossed her legs at the ankle and waited for him to finish reading the file that lay open on his desk. It took a little effort to resist the impulse to ask if she'd done something wrong.

In a few moments, he removed his glasses and pinched the bridge of his nose. "Katherine," he began. "I'll come right to the point. We'd like you to take a bookkeeping job outside the bank."

She was completely taken aback. "I'm being laid off?"

Wiley gave her a startled look. "Oh, no. Nothing like that. You see, the bank holds the note on Blazingbrook Farm—a riding stable up on Highway 290, and the owner, Jack Fitzpatrick, is a good man, but he's had some setbacks in the past few years. His note balloons in September, and we're concerned that he's not going to be able to make it."

Katherine twisted in her chair. "I've never worked with foreclosures, Mr. Wiley," she said, hating the thought of it.

His eyes widened slightly. "Oh, we don't want to take the property back. Just the opposite. We'd like to help him keep it."

"I—I don't understand what you . . . how I—"

"I guess I'm not being very clear, am I?" He leaned forward again. "We want to know exactly how bad things are at the stable, and we've found out that Fitzpatrick is advertising for summer help. He's running a summer program that involves having a dozen or so teenagers work and live at the stable all summer, and since he's a bachelor he needs a chaperon—a single, young woman who can live and work at the stable. But his ad says the job involves some bookkeeping." He paused. "That's why we think you'd be the perfect person for the job. We're sure Fitzpatrick will, too."

Katherine sat motionless for a moment. Something in Mr. Wiley's smooth explanation wasn't quite coming together. "But why doesn't someone from the bank just ask him if he needs an extension? Or offer some kind of help with his note?"

With scarcely any hesitation at all, Mr. Wiley began to speak. Katherine had the distinct impression he was quoting from a speech he'd memorized. "There are several factors at work here," he said. "One faction on the board wants very much to take the property back and develop it commercially. But there is also another...ah, concern, that supports Fitzpatrick's ownership of the stable. Fitzpatrick is only aware of the group that wants to turn Blazingbrook into condominiums." He cleared his throat and shifted his look away. "The upshot of all this is that he would never trust help from anyone at Farm and Home." He began to pick at his fingernails. "That's why, if you agree to help out, you'll only be able to mention the name of the bank's parent, Worldcorps." Almost as an afterthought, he added, "That's what's listed on your résumé."

Katherine frowned. "Résumé? What résumé?"

He pushed the file toward her, and she leaned forward and took it. Katherine read its contents with a growing sense of unease. "Mr. Wiley, this is a beautiful letter of recommendation from you, but it sort of exaggerates my experience, don't you think?" She looked up at him. "I only did that one job for the legal department and this makes it sound as if I know all about tax work. And here, on the curriculum vitae, I was only a dorm counselor for a semester, but this implies that I—"

"Katherine," he interrupted, and smiled tightly, "I'm sure you'll agree that there is not one single falsehood in that résumé. We've merely accentuated the positive. I'm sorry if the wording disappoints you, but we are very eager to place someone at Blazingbrook, and we're certain you'd be perfect. As a matter of fact, we forwarded several résumés, and just as we thought, yours is the only one that received a positive response."

Katherine felt it again—a kind of weightless nausea. "So without telling me you sent my résumé to... Wait a minute. Response? What kind of response?"

Wiley spread his hands out on his desk and spoke smoothly—glibly. "I'm sorry there wasn't time to tell you, but I had no choice. If you decide to do this for us, you'll have an interview out at the stable today." He glanced at his watch. "In about two hours, actually."

Katherine felt her eyes widening in horror. "*Two hours?* Mr. Wiley, this really . . . disturbs me. I just can't walk away from my job here. We've got a closing in two weeks and Dean and Mary can't do it alone. What about my section reports? And if I change jobs I'll lose my benefits, my seniority. What about insurance? And my anniversary with the bank is in July, and I'm supposed to get five more vacation days and—"

"Wait a minute, wait a minute," he interrupted, holding up his hand. "I'll take care of any staffing problems in your section, and of course you'll keep all your benefits because you'll remain on the books as an outside auditor. If Fitzpatrick offers you the job and you take it, we'll make up the difference in your salary." He paused and lowered his voice. "There will also be a nice bonus for you at the end of summer."

Katherine wanted very much to keep her thoughts orderly and organized, but Wiley's request had caught her off balance. "I'm sorry, Mr Wiley, you know I'd like to cooperate, but I just don't think I can. You said I'd have to live at the stable and I've just signed another lease on my apartment—"

"All that will be taken care of. The bank will arrange the termination of your lease and the moving and storage of your things." Then he slid his gaze away. "There is another thing you might want to think about, Katherine. I've always thought of you as such a willing, bright and capable employee and, as you know, the economy in Houston is always unpredictable. If you do this for us, I can guarantee your immunity from any layoff that might occur in the future."

Katherine took a slow, deep breath. Wiley's tone also implied that if she *didn't* do what he asked, she'd be the first one out the door if there were a cutback in staff. Rumors of layoffs circulated at the bank constantly. Everyone stayed nervous. If she were laid off, she'd lose all her benefits. And what about her car? The bank carried the note. She could just imagine how understanding they'd be about her missing a payment or two. Katherine clamped her lips together.

She wished she'd been more diligent about saving; that way she wouldn't feel so cornered.

Part of her wanted to slap the folder shut, smack it down on the desk and march out—the part of her that didn't have to worry about rent, health insurance, car notes and charge-account bills. She wrestled her outrage under control, but she didn't dare look Wiley in the face. She knew he'd see exactly what she was thinking. Instead, she looked at her lap where her hands lay balled into fists.

"Mr. Wiley, I don't know anything about horses. I've never been around large animals. I've worked here since I quit college and you know very well—"

"You don't have to know anything about horses. You just have to be able to work well with people. And we both know you can do that, don't we? You've certainly proven yourself as a team player here." He paused. "At least up until now," he added. Slyly, Katherine thought.

"What makes you so sure he'll hire me?"

"No one can be *sure,* of course, but I have great confidence in you. In fact, I'm positive the only way he wouldn't hire someone with your qualifications would be if you deliberately sabotaged your interview." He smiled. A knowing, foxy smile.

Katherine's blood rushed furiously through her, and she had the most horrible constriction in her throat. If only she had time to think, time to weigh her options. Time to figure out exactly what was going on here—if the bank *really* wanted to help this Fitzpatrick guy keep his stable. For a long moment she listened to the ticking of the clock. She looked at it, at the hands sweeping relentlessly round and round.

"I need your answer now, Katherine."

She winced. Office sounds penetrated the door—copying machines, the clicking of keyboards, someone in heels walking briskly on the parquet floor outside. Katherine liked those sounds. She liked the gray snakeskin pumps and matching dove-colored suit she wore. She liked the little name plate on her desk. She'd even envisioned the day when she would have a nice big name plate and a door of her own. "You said the job entails bookkeeping?"

"That's right."

She looked straight into Wiley's watery blue eyes. "Will the bank expect me to provide copies of his books?" Job or no job, there were some things she was simply unwilling to do.

"Not necessarily." He rested his elbows on his desk and steepled his fingers. "You see, apparently Fitzpatrick makes money selling show horses. If we knew when he had an animal available, we might be able to bring that fact to the attention of people with plenty of capital for that type of investment."

Well, well, well, Katherine thought. Don't we sound altruistic. Almost philanthropic. And if the possibility of being fired weren't being dangled over her head like the Sword of Damocles she might even have admired the sentiment.

"How soon does he want someone to start?"

Wiley fidgeted with the paper clips on his desk. "Almost immediately. Or that's what we believe." He rocked back in his chair.

Katherine pressed her lips together. No matter what protest she presented, David Wiley would already have some oily response prepared. She had no choice. If she wanted to keep her job, she'd have to do what he asked. "Well, I suppose I'd better get started if I don't want to be late for my interview. And, by the way, just in case he asks, why do I want to quit my job at... Worldcorps to take a job at a stable?" Just this once she let a hint of sarcasm creep into her tone.

He ignored it. "We knew we could count on you," he said as he practically lunged over the desk to snatch the folder back. "Now, this is what you can say without having to lie at all...."

Two hours and seventeen minutes later, Katherine commenced the hand-over-hand maneuver necessary to corner her neat little car. A faded sign confirmed that she was finally on Blazingbrook Drive, the road Wiley said would dead-end into the yard of the jumping horse stable. Live oaks and elms arched over the drive in a dappling canopy and whitewashed paddock boards flanked her on both sides.

Gravel flew from the spinning tires and rattled against the undercarriage. Katherine hated the sound. She'd sped nearly all the way out of Houston, and despite Mr. Wiley's concise directions she'd completely missed the turnoff. Twice. The whole way out she'd teetered between helpless rage and apprehension.

After all, what right had these people to force her to take this stupid assignment? She had her own life: friends, ballet class, guitar lessons, finches to feed. She also figured the reason Wiley waited so long to tell her about the interview was to put more pressure on her—to wait until the last possible moment so she wouldn't have time to think it out. But in the end she had no choice. She needed her job.

Now that the decision had been made, her immediate problem was arriving on time and convincing Jack Fitzpatrick to hire her. One of the last things Wiley told her was that this Fitzpatrick guy was a fanatic about punctuality. And now, to add to her anxiety, she was already more than fifteen minutes late for the interview.

Whitewashed fence boards blurred into pale lines as her car clattered down the road and finally reached a break in the fence line. Slowing momentarily, she downshifted and braced herself to whip around the sharp corner. Then she saw the sign painted in stern, red foot-high letters.

Caution. Slow. Show Horses.

Katherine scowled and applied the brakes. They squealed. Gleefully. Finally, she saw a wide, shell-topped parking lot set in the midst of the paddocks. Pecan trees and silver maples partially obscured the looming arch of a barn painted red oxide. Through the trailing branches of a stand of ancient willows, she saw the white columns of a two-story colonial house. The one thing she didn't see was a place to park.

Cars, trucks and horse trailers were angled into every available space. The knot between her shoulder blades increased to the size of a fist—and tightened. She halted her car and prepared to shove the gearshift into reverse when she thought she saw an opening. It was almost too good to be true—right next to the portable building with the Office shingle. She gunned the engine and aimed at the gap. She had to swing out a little to get around an ugly battered red pickup truck and barely slowed down as she once again whipped her car through the turn. It was going to be a squeeze—the building on one side, the huge truck on the other, the legs sticking out from under the pickup.

The legs sticking out from under the pickup...

Katherine gasped and slammed on the brakes as soon as the thought registered. A giant, invisible vise closed around her rib cage. Had she hit the brakes in time? *Surely I didn't...I couldn't have...* The car slid to a stop, and before the engine muttered into silence she shoved the door open and leaped out. "Please let him be all right. Please. Please," she prayed.

As soon as she reached the front of the car, she saw that the legs weren't crushed. In fact, they were two long muscular legs that thrashed enthusiastically as their owner struggled out from under the pickup. Katherine's heart hammered so loudly in her ears that she barely heard the sound of tearing material and the lively, colorful language emanating from beneath the truck. "Are you all right? I didn't see you when I turned in just now."

Katherine couldn't quite understand all the words of his answer, but she had no trouble at all comprehending his meaning. As the angry torrent abated slightly, a tanned, blunt-fingered hand appeared from under the truck and slapped around the bumper. Buttons flew as, in one smooth motion, a tall man yanked himself from beneath the truck to stand glowering over her. His shirt, freed of its buttons, flapped wildly around the man's lean torso as if frantic to escape. A sheen of perspiration glistened on his tanned skin, and cables of muscle etched a pattern on his chest.

Katherine gasped slightly. The impression was leather stretched over stainless steel. He wasn't too much over six feet tall, but at barely five foot four, she had to crane her head back awkwardly to look up into his eyes—lambent, tiger-gold eyes crackling with fury. An old scar ran jaggedly down one temple and sent a pale tentacle searching over one cheekbone.

Katherine had never seen anyone so livid in her life. A vein throbbed ominously at his temple, and his neck and shoulders fairly bristled with angry tension. He appeared to be gathering himself to launch into a hostile tirade, and she flinched at the prospect of being the object of that temper.

Her own pulse hammered at her temples. As a matter of fact, now that he stood in front of her, instead of slowing down, her heart seemed to race even more wildly than before even though he was obviously unhurt. She cleared her throat. "I'm so sorry. I just didn't see—"

"Did you even look?"

His amber eyes hardened to a furious yellow and a tendon jumped on the side of his jaw.

"Well, of course I did. But I was in such a hurry..." *The interview*. Reflexively she stole a look at her watch.

"Am I keeping you from something?" he asked snappishly, then muttered something unintelligible under his breath—something that sounded suspiciously like "stupid woman driver."

That did it. Katherine's nerves were already raw, and she wasn't about to let anyone else push her around. Not today, anyway. She felt a blush of anger rising in her cheeks and fought to hold her temper. Drawing herself up to her full height, she planted one hand on her hip and pointed a carefully painted fingernail at him. "Listen, mister, I have an appointment to keep, but before I go I'd like to point out that what just happened is every bit as much your fault as mine. In fact, you're pretty lucky I saw you in time to stop. From now on, if I were you, I'd do my mechanic work in a garage and not on the blind side of a parked car."

She glared up without blinking and concentrated on making her chin jut forcefully. His gaze narrowed, and he studied her through bright, hard eyes. The man had obviously spent hours in the sun because he had a pattern of squint lines at the corners of his eyes, and even his eyebrows were sunbleached. His hair was a warm brown that had faded at the temples to the color of wheat. He scowled at Katherine, then took a deep breath. She braced herself for the tirade she knew he was about to unleash at her.

Instead of a stream of abuse, however, only a disgusted sigh broke from his lips. "Oh, hell. I suppose you're right."

Katherine clutched at her aplomb. "Excuse me?"

The angry stance softened. "I said, 'You are right,'" he slowly enunciated. "But I don't have to like it." Taking a casual step toward her, he slowly wiped his right hand on the seat of his pants—an act Katherine found alarmingly sensual. "Jack Fitzpatrick," he said, and thrust his freshly dried hand toward her.

Katherine automatically reached out to accept his proffered hand. Realization dawned. *Jack Fitzpatrick.*

Her hand snapped back almost reflexively to cover her mouth. "Oh, no," she whispered against her fingers as she gazed, stricken, into his widening eyes.

Mr. Fitzpatrick looked down at his palm, then turned his hand over and studied the back where the sun had bleached the fine hair almost white. He looked back up at her, and his face screwed into a wry expression. Realization flickered in his eyes. "You must be Katherine Hanshaw."

Katherine nodded bleakly. "Mr. Fitz—"

"You're late," he said quietly.

"I know. I'm so sorry, but I—"

"And didn't you see the sign? You're not supposed to drive through here like a bat out of hell. There are kids and horses everywhere."

"Mr. Fitzpatrick, I—"

"Well, Ms. Hanshaw," he said briskly, "thanks very much for coming all the way out here. You have excellent references and just the experience I thought I was looking for. Too bad I didn't have a chance to interview you for the job." At this point he stopped and made a show of swatting at the dust clinging to his jeans. "You see, I have a riding lesson to give, but first I have to go change my shirt. Good luck with your job hunting."

He turned on his heel and strode toward the house, his ruined shirt a flapping accusation. Despair settled like lead in Katherine's stomach as she watched him walk away. When Mr. Wiley phoned to see how the interview went, Fitzpatrick would tell him she'd arrived late, driven recklessly through the stable and then tried to run him down. Wiley would assume she'd done it deliberately. A tidal wave of hopelessness welled up inside her, but then something snapped. *I can't make things any worse, so what the hell?* "Mr. Fitzpatrick, may I speak with you just a minute?"

He didn't stop but glanced over his shoulder and slowed enough to let her catch up. With his lips pressed in a tight line he raised one eyebrow. "Yes?"

Nerves and the unaccustomed awkwardness of running across a lawn in three-inch pumps left Katherine breathless. "Mr. Fitzpatrick, I know I was late and I know I should have driven more cautiously—"

"Glad we agree on that," he said flatly. "Goodbye now. Drive carefully."

Katherine took a deep breath. "Mr. Fitzpatrick, I really need this job. As a matter of fact, I'm almost desperate to have this job. If you'd just let me explain what happened—"

Finally he stopped walking and faced her. "I'm sorry to hear that, Ms. Hanshaw, but I have to have someone reliable. I've got a dozen or so girls here. If you can't be on time for an interview, not to mention almost running over my—"

"But, Mr. Fitzpatrick, I guarantee you I take my responsibilities seriously, almost obsessively. If you hire me you'll have a dependable, hardworking employee." She thought she might be getting to him. There seemed to be a softening at the corners of his mouth, and his stance definitely seemed less hostile. If she didn't know better, she'd almost swear he was enjoying himself rather than trying to discourage an unsuitable applicant. "My experience includes working in situations just like this. And my experience in finance also proves..." She racked her brain for something meaningful her experience proved, but the grueling morning had seriously impaired her ability to think on her feet. She let her shoulders slump. "At least interview me, Mr. Fitzpatrick," she said. She wanted to sound convincing and earnest without groveling. "You won't be sorry. I guarantee it."

He folded his arms across his chest, glanced at his watch and gave her a doubtful look. Katherine felt sure she saw something flicker behind those golden irises. Maybe amusement. Maybe something warmer. He was obviously thinking... weighing and counterweighing. Oddly, instead of feeling inadequate under that powerful scrutiny, Katherine felt a kind of thrill surge through her. For a moment she almost thought she was trembling. *For Pete's sake, get hold of yourself or he'll see how... how nervous you are. He'll know something's up.*

"Ms. Hanshaw—"

"Katherine. Please call me Katherine."

"Katherine," he said slowly, almost as if tasting something for the first time. "I'm not trying to be unreasonable, but I—"

At that moment a commotion erupted at the barn.

Katherine swung around in time to see a flame-colored horse lunge through the double doors, then whip around when he slammed to the end of his lead line. Grasping the other end of the nylon lead was quite possibly the prettiest girl Katherine had ever seen. Her white-blond hair flew behind her like a wind-torn cloud, and her huge eyes flashed with emotion. Even at a distance, Katherine could see that she had perfect skin and a wide, passionate mouth. At first Katherine thought the girl must be terrified of the plunging animal, but then she realized the girl wasn't frightened at all. She was furious.

"Whoa!" she shouted, giving the line a savage yank. "You pig!" she shouted. "I said *whoa!*"

The snorting animal halted, his nostrils flaring. He faced the girl standing almost beneath him and pawed the ground twice. The girl reached up, snatched the lead line where it clipped to the halter under the horse's jaw and gave it another yank. The animal's head bounced and his eyes rolled, but he stood still, his wild eyes swiveling in agitation.

The girl glanced from Jack to Katherine and narrowed her eyes. Her chest rose as she took an enormous breath and set her shoulders angrily. Then she stalked toward them, with the horse prancing gingerly at her side. The animal looked dangerous, and Katherine took a step back to stand slightly behind Jack.

"Jack," the girl said, and halted a few feet in front of them. "I need to talk to you right now." She ignored Katherine. "I don't care how great he's supposed to be, I'm not ever riding this piece of junk again." The horse, lips twitching tentatively, extended his nose toward Jack. "Don't," the girl snapped, and smacked him across the cheek with the lead line. Snorting in shock, the horse threw his head up and crouched back on his haunches.

"He bites," she spat out. "He kicked Bingo. He can't pick up his leads, he hangs over fences and . . . and I'm just not ever getting on this . . . this *thing* again. You'll just have to call Sonny and tell him he can come right back here and take it away." Then she clamped her pretty lips together and glared at him. Katherine could have been a fence post for all the attention the girl paid her.

Despite her appalling behavior, Jack only folded his arms across his chest and gave the girl an indulgent smile. "Having a bad day?" he asked impassively.

The child almost sputtered with fury. Her hands clenched and opened and her lips quivered as she visibly groped for a reply. Obviously she couldn't think of anything suitably devastating, because instead of speaking she gave Jack a venomous look, whirled on her heel and stalked off toward the barn, the agitated animal plunging alongside her. On the long walk back to the stable she occasionally gave the horse's lead a yank. He bounced along beside her, unfazed and unrepentant.

Katherine tried to keep her expression calm. The girl had ignored her. Deliberately. Disdainfully. Obviously the spoiled child was a wealthy client—much too important to the business to get the chilling setdown she deserved for her rudeness. Cutting her eyes toward Jack, Katherine caught him gazing at her, his mouth quirked in an enigmatic expression. She raised her eyebrows.

I'll never be able to keep my mouth shut, she thought. There was no way she could docilely endure the kind of treatment Jack had just swallowed. Still, if she wanted this job she'd have to show a little diplomacy.

"Well," she said, clearing her throat expressively. "What an *interesting* little girl. She certainly doesn't care for that horse very much, does she?"

"No," he answered, his expression unreadable. "She does seem a little disappointed."

Irritation skittered up Katherine's spine and set her jaw on edge. How could a grown man allow a child to speak to him that way? "That's all?" she asked, straining to keep the incredulity out of her voice. "You mean that's normal behavior for that child when she's disappointed? I'd hate to see what happens when she gets . . . miffed."

"Yeah. Pretty bad, wasn't it?" he said and looked back toward the barn.

Katherine followed his gaze. The girl stood just outside the barn doors, one hand grasping the horse's halter, the other planted on her hip. Her striking eyes were narrowed and her lips were pressed together in an ugly line. As soon as her eyes met Katherine's, she jutted her jaw, whirled and disappeared inside, dragging the animal with her.

"I think her behavior is more than *pretty bad,*" Katherine replied. "That's one of the rudest displays I've ever seen. In fact, I don't think I'd have been nearly as patient as you were. Who is that little terror?"

Jack sighed. "The little terror's name is Theodora. She prefers to be called Teddie, though." He looked down at Katherine. "She's my daughter."

Chapter Two

Jack gazed down at Katherine Hanshaw without speaking. Had he not been so irritated, he might have laughed. The look on her face was priceless: huge aquamarine eyes widening in horror and that full, pretty mouth dropping open. Then she licked her lips, and something knotted in his stomach.

"Mr. Fitzpatrick, I..."

"Yes," he said slowly and raised one eyebrow in his best skeptical and disapproving look. When he did, she seemed to lose her train of thought. Her mouth closed and she gripped her purse until her knuckles whitened.

"I apologize," she said quietly. "I'm sure that sounded awfully insensitive of me—"

"Yes, it did. Didn't it?" He let his brow drop back into place, then crossed his arms—still gazing down at her. "Now I suppose you've realized you made a harsh and premature judgment and you want to take it all back. Right?"

She appeared more miserable than ever as she looked away. He could almost see the tiny presence inside her head jumping up and down and shouting, *Yes. Just say yes. Say anything.* Instead she sighed and shook her head slightly.

"Actually, I don't want to take it back. I still think your daughter behaved rudely. To both of us. But I didn't mean . . . I—"

"At least you're honest," he interrupted. Honesty was something he appreciated. After the way he'd been lied to and nearly robbed, honesty was something he demanded from the people he worked with, his family, even the kids at the barn.

"Mr. Fitzpatrick," she began again, as she looked up at him with despair filling her eyes. "You see, when she called you Jack I assumed—"

"All the girls call me Jack," he said. "Teddie does it to fit in."

She squared her shoulders and took a deep breath, obviously gathering her courage. He would have liked to observe this moment with amused detachment, but at the moment he felt neither amused nor detached. His favorite shirt had just been turned into a shop rag, he dreaded giving Spoiled Rotten Roberts his stupid private lesson and Teddie had just delivered another of her award-winning performances in front of his *former* best hope for the summer chaperon's job. To top that off, the former best hope had shown up late and nearly run him down. Between her and his daughter, he wasn't sure who he wanted to pounce on more.

Katherine cleared her throat and took a deep breath before her words came tumbling out. "I do want to apologize for speaking unkindly." She looked up at him intently, and once again he felt that punch to his middle. She really was pretty—all that thick, honey-colored hair hanging loose past her shoulders. And the freckles sprinkled over the bridge of her nose made her look sexy and innocent at the same time. Not to mention those enormous Caribbean blue eyes.

"Believe me," she said earnestly. "If I hadn't been so upset I would never have said such a thing. I'm having such a horrible day, and I realize that I'm making things worse every minute, but I still want very much to interview for this job. I really need it. Really."

Jack started to reply brusquely, but then she blinked those huge liquid eyes. If he didn't know better he'd almost think she was batting her long feathery lashes at him. Hah. As if that sort of thing would have any effect.

He rolled one aching shoulder and regarded her with what he hoped was an impassive look. He was certain the look would have been much more convincingly impassive had his belly behaved and not knotted up on him like that. He hated the feeling. It reminded him of being in an elevator that suddenly drops three floors. This is nuts, he thought. I don't even know her. I don't have time for this. This is probably the most important summer of my entire career.

He glanced toward the barn just in time to see Teddie pretending to ignore them while loitering at the open doors. Her shoulders were stiff and she had her face set in his least favorite expression—the one you couldn't quite smack her for but couldn't disregard, either. Actually, he'd never smacked Teddie, but there had been plenty of times when he'd wanted to. Especially lately. Sometime in the past year or so his spirited and affectionate little girl had been replaced by this moody, volatile, demanding . . . *person*.

She had been in an especially foul mood ever since he'd told her he couldn't afford to finance her latest hare-brained scheme—something to do with the modeling classes her grandfather had given her. She furiously resented Jack's spending the money to hire a summer chaperon and refused to acknowledge that without a summer program there wouldn't be a Blazingbrook for much longer. Then she said Jack should pay her to be a chaperon, despite the fact that she was only thirteen. Then, of course, Brooks stuck his interfering nose and fat wallet into the picture and made another of his grandstand offers to pay for everything. As usual, at the thought of his former father-in-law, a black fury rumbled through Jack. No good stewing about that now, he thought, and with effort he forced his thoughts back to the present.

Katherine Hanshaw still gazed earnestly up at him with those tragic blue-green eyes. Teddie glared at him from the barn. He sighed. These two ought to be marooned together, he thought. They deserve each other.

Then an idea struck him. Of course. He smiled and motioned for Teddie to join them. Quickly. She scowled, jammed her hands into her pockets and approached with what he would call a defiant saunter.

"Katherine," he said, and glanced down at her. "I won't be able to finish this interview right now. But here's Teddie. Teddie, you left in such a hurry I didn't get a chance to introduce you two. Katherine, my daughter, Teddie. Teddie, this is Katherine Hanshaw. I told you about her."

This was great. They eyed each other like two wild animals meeting across a very small watering hole. Each extended a reluctant hand. To Katherine's credit, she did offer a smile with hers. Teddie, of course, didn't reciprocate. Jack beamed at both of them. A few moments alone with Teddie should be enough to send Miss Eyelashes here careering back down Blazingbrook Road in that silly little Italian sports car she nearly mashed him with. Not having to interview her would be a relief; she seemed so earnest. So eager. Why would a woman like that want a job like this? he wondered momentarily. Something about her gave him an ache right under his sternum, and he already had enough problems. "Teddie, I want you to show Katherine around the barns and the house while I give Harvey his lesson. Katherine, if you can stay after Teddie shows you around, we'll finish our talk. How's that? Good. Now you two better get started."

Teddie once again whirled on her heel and stalked off toward the barn. She's getting really good at making that look spontaneous, Jack thought. Katherine, being a bit shorter and wearing street shoes, was having to really stride out to keep up. Taking such big steps showed off her pretty calves, hips and... hips. Gymnastics, he thought. Must be. No, come to think of it, I'd say ballet. Years, probably. She looked completely out of place at the stable. Tailored business suit and sexy shoes. He liked the shoes, though. She and her shoes would be completely at home in the Sponsors' Box at a big charity show. Or the polo grounds. As he watched them disappear into the barn, he felt his smile fade. Too bad. He'd probably never see her again.

That would be the best thing, he thought. He needed someone to help make life run smoother and easier this summer. Somehow "smoother" and "easier" were two words that didn't leap to mind when he thought of having that blonde in his house. Too bad, but Katherine just wouldn't do. Too fragile. Too pretty. Pretty? You see, he berated himself, you're already thinking about her the wrong way. Hell, she was interviewing for a job as a *chaperon*.

He'd seen what happened when trainers got involved with pretty stable hands. At best, people in the industry snickered behind their hands and rolled their eyes in amused pity. At worst, there was talk of coercion and harassment. In every instance reputations were ruined and businesses damaged. That wasn't going to happen to him. After one last glance at the barn, he turned away and walked briskly toward the house. He had almost put everything back together and nothing, *nothing* was going to stand in the way of getting Blazingbrook back on its feet. Nothing.

"Nothing, I said."

"Teddie," Katherine repeated, doing her best to keep her tone even. "There's obviously something bothering you, but if it's not me, would you mind walking a little slower?"

She didn't answer the question but shot Katherine a hostile glare as she led the way through the barn and down the aisles of stalls. The horses hung their heads over the half doors and wobbled their ears invitingly or dozed with tails swishing at glossy flanks.

"This is the tack room," Teddie said, and paused in front of an open door. Inside Katherine saw saddles, bridles, buggy whips and undefinable bits of harness and hardware hanging from rows of hooks on the walls. Against the far wall were two or three long, low benches, and Katherine saw stained rags and tins of saddle soap stacked neatly on the worn wood. She thought she caught Teddie staring thoughtfully at her from the corner of her eye, but when she turned, the girl was looking down the row of stalls and biting her lip.

"Would you like to see the rest of the horses?" she asked. Almost sweetly.

Katherine smiled. "Sure. How many are there?"

"Oh, about thirty more in this barn. There are three other barns, an outdoor schooling ring, an indoor ring for bad weather and then the hunt field. I know," she said, and tilted her head. "We'll go see Pandora and Phoenix." Then she smiled again, but it didn't bring any warmth to her face.

Well, Katherine thought, this is a little better. She relaxed and breathed deeply as she walked down the freshly swept aisle. The barn smelled of new wood shavings, hay, grain and the woodsy, dusky scent of the animals. High overhead, ceiling fans circulated the warm air and sent stray wisps of hay scudding down the corridor in front of them like golden stick insects. An aisle or two over, a horse squealed angrily and then the sound of a board kicked by a steel-shod hoof reverberated around them.

"It's close to snack time," Teddie explained and once again flashed her brilliant smile. "They're all pigs," she said giving the nearest horse an affectionate pat. "They live to eat."

"I know the feeling," Katherine murmured, silently wondering at Teddie's sudden warmth.

"You?" Teddie said, giving Katherine an exaggerated once-over. "But you're *so* petite."

"It's a constant struggle," Katherine replied, cautiously pleased by Teddie's obvious attempt to be friendly. "I'm so short I subsist only on greens when what I really want to do is fling myself on the all-you-can-eat pizza buffet."

"We *live* on diets here," Teddie replied, and tossed her head, sending a cloud of silver-blond hair tumbling over her shoulders. "It's hard enough for the horses to clear the jumps without our big bottoms weighing them down any more than necessary. And wait until you see our assorted backsides crammed into tan stretch-twill jodphurs. Not a pretty sight!"

"I hardly believe that," Katherine said, eyeing Teddie's lithe, athletic build. "You're so tall and slim. You could be a model."

Teddie's jaw fell and she stared momentarily, startled and bright eyed, straight at Katherine. For an instant Katherine saw something desperate flicker through Teddie's expression, but the look quickly disappeared to be replaced by a closed look. For a few moments they walked through the barn in silence.

Teddie didn't speak again but led the way down the aisles to a quiet part of the barn. They passed several empty stalls before they stopped at a huge square box stall. Inside stood what was obviously an aged mare. Her gray coat had turned completely white in places and her eyes were milky. A guttural nicker rattled her nostrils when Teddie pushed the door open.

"Hello, Pan," she crooned and groped in her pocket. She drew out two small carrots and fed one to the mare while she scratched her ears and under her mane. "This is Pandora," she said softly to no one in particular. "She's *my* horse."

Katherine didn't know what to say. She didn't know anything about hunters and jumpers, but she'd just seen enough sleek, gorgeous animals to let her know that this was a very old, very nearly spent horse. From her delicate lines and huge eyes, however, even Katherine could tell that she'd once been a beautiful, elegant animal. But now? Well... "I just assumed that all the horses that belonged to the stable belonged to you, too."

Teddie didn't look up. "Oh, gosh, no. Most of the horses here are privately owned. We own about fifteen lesson horses and the rest are horses my dad buys to train and then sell. Pandora is mine, though." Teddie dropped her head against the mare and wrapped her arms around her neck. "She was my mother's horse," she murmured. "My mom died when I was seven. Pan's all that I have left of her."

"Oh." Her mother's horse. How sad. In awkward, painful moments such as this Katherine knew there was very little to say, but something from the heart never hurts. She reached up and gently stroked the mare's quivering nose.

The velvety muzzle was as soft as moleskin and Pandora's warm breath brushed gently over her fingers. "I'm awfully sorry."

Teddie straightened up. Her face was pale and her eyes bright and hard. "Yeah," she said. "Me too." Giving Pandora another pat, she stepped out of the stall and clipped a webbing gate into the heavy metal eyes screwed into the doorjamb. Then, as if thinking better of it, she pulled the heavy wooden door closed. Pandora lifted her head to look between the bars at the top of the door.

"No more carrots for you," Teddie said tenderly. "You'll get fat."

Then she faced Katherine. "This," she said, pointing at the stall next to Pandora's, "is my father's horse, Phoenix. He's a stallion." She took a few steps down the aisle to the sliding door. "The rest of the male horses in the barn are geldings. That means they've been, um, fixed. Phoenix is the only one who can still make mares pregnant. Did you see the mare and colt in the front paddock, Fox and Ishmael? Ishmael is Phoenix's colt."

"Why is he way over here? All by himself?"

Teddie gave Katherine a wary look. "Well," she said slowly. "He doesn't like the other male horses, geldings or not. And they're afraid of him. He also makes the mares, ah, high-strung so we just keep him over here. Pandora keeps him company because she's older and steady."

"Ah," Katherine said.

"Come see him," Teddie said sweetly. "He's pretty impressive."

Katherine stepped up to the heavy wooden door and looked through the brass bars. In the corner stood a black horse, glistening haunches turned toward them. The creature was undoubtedly the most masculine animal Katherine had ever seen. His ebony neck was heavy with muscle, and a cascade of blue-black mane tumbled over his thick, powerful shoulders. His back was broad and creased deeply down the center. He was by far the tallest and largest of all the horses Katherine had seen. He stood, head down and hip cocked, facing the corner. He ignored them.

Teddie bumped her hip against the door, making it rattle on its rollers. The stallion tipped his head slightly toward them, showing a cloudy white eye. His ears swiveled forward, then back.

"What's wrong with his eye?" Katherine asked. "Is he blind?"

Teddie laughed a little. Harshly. "Good heavens, no. That's a scar. Here, look." She grabbed the bars of the door and shook them until the door clattered. In the next stall Pandora gave a startled snort and the stallion whipped his head around to reveal a long, jagged strip of white, like a streak of melted lightning, running down the center of his face. It ran over one eye, staining it white, and slid off the hard angles of his face midway between his eyes and cup-shaped nostrils. The stallion's unscarred eye was as black as his coat and completely unfathomable. He faced them with his ears flattened against his head and his nostrils narrowed to slits.

"See," Teddie said. "He sees just fine."

For one moment the stallion regarded them balefully, then turned back to the wall, a sullen, brooding monarch.

"Would you like to make friends with him?" Teddie asked. The look on her face was so eager that Katherine hated to disappoint the girl, despite her own apprehension.

"Well," Katherine said, "I—I suppose so."

"Good," Teddie replied, her eyes glowing. "I saved a carrot. Horses just *love* carrots." Sure enough, she still had one of the small slightly limp vegetables she had pulled out of her pocket in Pandora's stall. "Now you stand right here," she said quietly. For an instant Katherine thought she heard a quaver in Teddie's voice and she glanced at her. Teddie didn't meet her gaze but fidgeted with the catch on the heavy sliding door. Inside the stall, Phoenix curved his neck slightly and regarded the two of them through an ominous, faded eye.

"I'll just pull this open," Teddie said. The webbing gate was already clipped to its hooks across the open doorway. Just inside the gate a black rubber water bucket hung on the wall, and beyond it Katherine saw the wooden feed box. A few dusty corn kernels lay forgotten in the straw and wood shavings.

"Hold the carrot out," Teddie said. "Good—a little farther. Stick your arm as far into the stall as you can. Yeah, that's it. Now wave it back and forth like you're trying to get his attention." She moved aside to let Katherine stand alone in the stall doorway. "Hooo, horse," Teddie said gruffly and tapped on the metal bars of the stall door with one of her rings. Ting. Ting. Ting. "Horse, hey. Wave the carrot, Katherine." Then she once again grabbed the bars of the door and shook it.

Phoenix exploded.

Instantaneously the stallion transformed from a quiet if morose animal to a bellowing avalanche of plunging midnight flesh. He flung himself toward the stall door screaming in rage—mouth agape and black lips drawn back to reveal huge yellow teeth. His ears had flattened hideously against his long bullet-shaped head and his nostrils were pinched into slits giving him a reptilian, almost dragonlike, look. Katherine caught a glimpse of his gunmetal-colored belly and saw the flash of his steel shoes as his front hooves came slicing through the air toward her.

She shrieked, threw her arms up and flung herself away as hard as she could. She tumbled backward across the aisle until the wooden wall opposite Phoenix's stall struck her high up between the shoulders and the nape of her neck. Points of lights swam momentarily through her blackened vision as she slid down the rough wood. As she sat slumped against the wall, trembling and trying to gather her thoughts, she heard two sounds: the door to the stall sliding closed and barely smothered giggling.

For several long, head-spinning moments she sat motionless. The ache up in her shoulders began to fade and the rush of adrenaline passed, leaving in its wake a sad and painful shock. Tears stung her eyes and the back of her throat, and she groped at the hem of her skirt. One of her shoes was missing and a fat runner was snaking up the outside of her left leg. Slowly her vision cleared and her banging heart beat more slowly. She saw a pair of slender, blue-jeaned legs approach. "You okay?" There was no warmth in the question.

Katherine didn't trust her voice. She was fighting tears and the aftermath of sudden panic. She could hear Phoenix stamping and snorting in his stall. Just as she levered herself up, she heard approaching footsteps and then a masculine voice. "What the . . . What's going on here? Are you all right, Katherine?"

Katherine glanced up to see Jack just rounding the corner. As he walked toward her, he extended his hands, but she was already scrambling to her feet and motioned him away. Her emotions were now more clearly in focus.

She was livid.

Jack stopped in front of her, hands on his hips. He glared from Katherine to Teddie. "I said," he repeated, "what's going on here? Teddie?"

Katherine didn't dare look Jack in the face. She wanted to strangle his daughter and was sure he'd be able to tell. Instead she looked down at her skirt and in the most even tone she could manage, she said, "Teddie was just introducing me to your horse. I guess he's not used to strangers." Standing awkwardly on one foot, she looked up and down the aisle for her missing shoe. Then she glanced furtively at Jack. He had Teddie riveted in his gaze.

"What did you do?"

Katherine had heard the expression about all the color draining from someone's face but she'd never seen it demonstrated until that moment. Teddie's eyes widened in horror and then she dropped her head to stare at her boots. "I...it was an accident. I was trying to...to..." Her voice trailed off.

Katherine thought he'd been as furious as possible when she'd nearly run over his legs. The emotion she'd seen earlier was almost mellow compared to what she saw now. His eyes were fairly glittering and the fist planted on his hip shook with fury. A twinge of pity for Teddie skittered through her. Briefly.

"Apologize," he snapped.

"I'm sorry," Teddie said, her eyes never meeting Katherine's.

"Apology accepted," Katherine said evenly.

"Get into the house," Jack said, his voice still dangerously low. "Wait for me in your room."

"Dad, I—"

"To your room, Teddie, and I mean now."

The girl had to pass in between Katherine and her father, and it appeared that she tried to make herself small as she scuttled between the two adults. Jack's scathing gaze followed her until she disappeared around a corner. Then he turned toward Katherine.

"Are you all right? What happened?"

Katherine told him and watched his growing consternation. She related the story as dispassionately as she could but her throat began to tighten and her voice grew strained. "And then you came around the corner, and...and..." She had to stop. Between fear, anger, hurt feelings and bruised pride, she was losing control of her voice.

"Katherine, I apologize again. She's never done anything like this before. I can't imagine what's gotten into her. I'm glad Harvey didn't show for his lesson or you might have left before I found out what she did. What can I do to make up for this?"

Katherine glared up at him. "You can consider me for this job."

His jaw fell and he appeared totally taken aback. "What? You mean you'd still want to work here? After this?"

"Nothing has changed, Mr. Fitzpatrick. I told you that I need this job and I still do." She knew her voice was quavering. Hell, she was shaking all over. Between humiliation, fear and absolute fury at what Teddie had done, she was surprised she didn't shake her fillings loose. But if this stupid incident helped her get this job, she wouldn't complain. Much. She stared up into his amber eyes and tried to keep her own from filling.

His expression was easy enough to read: incredulity mixed with slight amusement, temporarily simmering anger and maybe just a tinge of admiration. He sighed. "Well," he replied, "I'll show you the office and explain the rest of the job to you, if you're really serious."

"I am, Mr. Fitzpatrick."

"Please call me Jack. Everyone does."

"Thank you. Jack," she said. Absurdly she felt more like crying than ever. She needed to distract herself before she started blubbering and blew it again. "You don't see my shoe anywhere, do you?"

His expression immediately hardened. "Where were you standing when it . . . when you—"

"I was standing right in front of that horse's stall. The door was open and . . . oh, my gosh. Do you think it's . . ."

"Oh, hell," Jack said. "I'll look."

Then, just as if there were no danger at all, he pushed the heavy door open, unclipped the webbing gate and stepped inside.

The hair on Katherine's neck rose. "Jack, be careful. He's awfully . . ."

Before she could finish what she said, Phoenix whipped around to face Jack. His ears swiveled forward and he arched his neck. He took one mincing step, and for an instant his ears flattened back and he parted his lips, showing his teeth. The animal would strike Jack, cripple or kill him and she would be utterly helpless. "Please be careful," she whispered. Her voice sounded like a strangled croak. Jack didn't seem to hear her. He reached casually toward the stallion and grabbed the animal's halter.

"You old monster," he said gently. "Have you been scaring the ladies again?" Then he ran a hand absently along Phoenix's thick jaw and scratched beneath his throat. While casually stroking his horse, he kicked through the straw bedding Katherine could barely stand to watch. He leaned over.

"Here we go," Jack said, and cast a rueful glance over his shoulder. "The heel is loose, I think."

Katherine tried not to clench her teeth. "Those are . . . *were* my best shoes."

"They'll be fixed. Or replaced," he said evenly. "If not today, tomorrow for sure."

Then he casually turned and unclipped the gate. Katherine's stomach still churned even after he'd refastened the gate and pulled the heavy sliding door closed. "How can you turn your back on him like that?" she asked. "He would have trampled me if I hadn't jumped out of the way."

Jack's mouth quirked. "Oh, Phoenix and I are old friends. We established who's who in this relationship a good while back." Then he grinned. "I try not to forget who's boss." He handed her the shoe. "I'm really sorry about this. You're going to have to hobble all the way back to the house and across the yard and through the parking lot."

"Oh, well," she said, as she leaned over and slipped off her remaining shoe. "My hose are already ruined. If this is the worst thing that ever happens to me, I'll count myself lucky." This whole thing might turn out to be a blessing in disguise, she thought. What a great opportunity to show him how good-natured she could be, how congenial, how easy to work with. At this point she was willing to use almost any tactic available to increase her chances of getting hired. For a rueful moment she thought she'd never tried so desperately to get a job she didn't want.

They walked through the barn and back out into the blazing sunlight. Jack didn't cut across the parking lot, but instead walked around to the back of the house in order to keep on the grass. As they approached the rear of the house, Katherine saw two girls lounging on patio recliners by the pool. When they climbed up the stairs of the deck, Jack introduced Paula Philbin, a chubby redheaded teenager with waist-length pigtails, and Judy Tuttle, whose short, dark hair set off her fair, perfect skin and mahogany-colored eyes. When she stood, Katherine noted with envy her tall, lithe figure.

Judy smiled as she took Katherine's hand. "You must be the one interviewing for the chaperon job." Then her eyes fell to Katherine's stocking feet. "What happened to your—"

"Teddie," Jack said flatly. He didn't smile.

Judy shaded her eyes with her hand. "I thought she looked upset when she went into the house."

"I'll bet she did," he said. "Well, Katherine," he said, turning to face her. "Shall we go on in?"

"Sure," she replied. "Nice to meet you both."

The girls murmured pleasantries as Jack led Katherine across the deck and through a squeaky screen door. The enormous kitchen had a green-and-white linoleum tile floor, and a long, heavily scarred banquet-length table stood in front of a row of open windows. Through swaying gauze curtains she saw a deep porch crowded with wicker chairs and an old glider swing. The house was completely quiet.

"Jack, if you want to speak with Teddie before we get started, I don't mind waiting."

He turned to face her. "Oh," he replied with a tight smile, "I think it would be better for both Teddie and me if I wait for a while before I go up." He motioned toward a hallway. "The office is through here."

As Jack led Katherine through the quiet house she noticed the decor—or lack of it. She also noticed that every available surface and inch of wall space was crammed with some type of equine photograph or memento. There were dozens of photographs of horses jumping, riders sitting astride horses while accepting ribbons or trophies or both. Other clutter also echoed the equestrian theme—ribbons, trophies, riding boots, velveteen hard hats, short riding whips and assorted bits of harness Katherine didn't recognize all jumbled in homey disarray on the end tables, cushions and threadbare carpet.

Jack led the way through the tangle of furniture and down a dark wood-paneled hallway. Here again, photographs hung haphazardly on every available inch of wall space. The office was a converted library with a fireplace flanked by walls of bookshelves. Picture windows opened onto the rolling paddocks beside the house. He motioned for Katherine to take the chair behind the desk and he pulled another up beside her.

"This is how the barn works," he began. "Blazingbrook is a hunter-and-jumper stable. We give lessons, board horses and buy and sell prospects—horses we think have show-ring potential. I've been doing this all my life. I started riding when I was five and turned professional when I was seventeen. I've represented the United States in international events, and except for a few years after I had an accident, I've ridden and shown horses for almost thirty years."

For a fleeting moment Katherine wondered if the accident was the "setback" Mr. Wiley had mentioned.

"Blaize, Teddie's mother, and I opened Blazingbrook. She rode competitively, too, and we worked together here. While she and I were married, there wasn't a need to hire a summer chaperon. Blaize took care of that. After my accident there wasn't a summer program anymore. This is the first year I've started it again."

For a fleeting moment Katherine wondered what he'd meant by "while we were married." Teddie said her mother had died, but she didn't mention that her parents had been divorced. Jack straightened for a moment and rubbed his back.

"Over the next week about a dozen teenage girls will move in. They work on stable management, they get intensive lessons and we travel to about ten A-rated horse shows all around the state. You won't have to go to horse shows because plenty of parents go and help supervise. Here's a schedule."

He handed Katherine a sheet of paper with the heading, "Texas Hunter and Jumper Association." She glanced at it just long enough to see that the shows were spread all over the state and occurred about every other weekend throughout the summer.

Jack rocked back in his chair. "Most of the girls have been coming here for years. Like Judy—you know, you met her at the pool. She's been a student of mine since she was ten and she's in college now."

He leaned forward again and riffled the stacks of paper on the desk. "Where's the damn . . . I have a list of the girls' names somewhere," he muttered. While he searched, he spoke distractedly. "The upstairs has been turned into a dormitory. You have your own room at the head of the landing." He paused for a moment and glanced at Katherine. "The parents expect the girls to be chaperoned like the daughters of Spanish royalty," he said wryly. "And, believe me, they'll scrutinize every move we make. I'm afraid that means your social life will be pretty well zeroed out for most of the summer. No late nights. No, you know—"

"Oh, that's no problem," Katherine said. "I'm not seeing anyone."

Jack smiled broadly. "Good, good," he said. "Besides generally riding herd on the girls... who, by the way, start arriving Friday, you'll be responsible for some bookkeeping, travel arrangements and writing checks—you know, office stuff. Any problem with that? Great. Judy helped me write an outline of everything that you'd be doing. It's pretty basic stuff. I know my notes aren't the best, but I think you'll be able to..." He leaned close to shuffle through the papers again.

Katherine was once more struck by his lean toughness. He'd missed a spot shaving where the scar snaked over his cheekbone. Fine, sand-colored stubble contrasted with his dark skin and his hair was heavy and thick. He could use a haircut, she thought, and found herself having to suppress an urge to run her fingers behind his neck and pull it out of his collar.

"Oh, yeah. Here it is. See," he said, and glanced at her. For a moment, just when his eyes caught hers, she was certain his pupils enlarged. The bright gold of his irises retreated as the dark circle grew, taking light in, taking her in. Katherine realized she wasn't breathing and parted her lips. His gaze fell to her mouth and she felt as if she had been released. His brows came together and he looked back at the desk. "Where was I? Oh, yes. The outline." For the briefest instant he hesitated. "What do you think? Any questions?"

Katherine suddenly felt extremely awkward. She knew she should say how confident she felt and how eagerly she anticipated hearing from him, then offer a businesslike handshake and walk crisply away. It was hard to feel crisp and businesslike without shoes and with bits of hay clinging to your ravaged hosiery. It was even harder to feel crisp with him sitting so close. He didn't make her feel businesslike at all. In fact, whenever she looked at him she felt off balance. Well, she thought, you better fake some crispness. "I—I don't have any questions about the work, Jack," she said. "But I would like to say that I think I'd do a good job for you."

He fixed her with an intent look. "One more thing. Why do you want this job? After all, with your experience you must be making at least three times what I can pay."

"Well," she said, despising the quaver in her voice. "I found out my job with . . . with Worldcorps is definitely going to change in the fall, and I thought that rather than spending the whole summer waiting for them to lower the boom on me, I'd do something different—you know, less stressful—while I decide where I want to go next." As Wiley had said, it wasn't really a lie.

He gazed at her thoughtfully for a moment. "You have the best experience and recommendations of anyone who applied. If you're still interested, after all you've been through today, I'd like to offer you this position."

For the first time since she'd been called to David Wiley's office that morning, the knot between Katherine's shoulders loosened. The chair felt suddenly so comfortable; the desk seemed just the right size. "I'm still interested."

"Well, Katherine," Jack said, offering her his hand. "I guess you've got a job."

Chapter Three

Tuesday morning, David Wiley called an informal meeting in his office and announced to everyone in Katherine's section that she was leaving on a temporary and highly confidential assignment. Mary Williams eyed her with sudden curiosity mixed with apprehension.

"But we're closing in two weeks. How can I reach you?" she asked. "I mean, if I have questions about the closing? Dean hasn't done one alone either, so—"

Mr. Wiley cleared his throat. "We're bringing Dan Landry up in Katherine's absence," he said smoothly.

Mary closed her mouth and looked unhappily at Katherine.

Katherine smiled sympathetically and shrugged. She couldn't say where she was going because Mr. Wiley had warned her not to in case word got back to those who wanted to foreclose on Blazingbrook.

For the next two days Katherine worked feverishly to clear her desk and make sure all her accounts were in order. As Wiley had promised, Worldcorps had arranged to box and store all her furniture, and the apartment manager agreed to collect her mail and forward it to the stable weekly. She didn't even have to relinquish her phone number; instead, calls were automatically forwarded to an answering machine.

Thursday morning, Katherine once again drove into the parking lot of Blazingbrook Farm. This time she wore her hair tied back in a ponytail; it felt odd to be going to work dressed in jeans, sneakers and a T-shirt. Strange, but nice. Well, she thought, at least it'll be nice not to worry about dry cleaning and panty hose for a while.

When she pulled into the shell-topped parking lot, she saw Jack leaning against the paddock fence and watching Fox and Ishmael, the chestnut mare and her gangly black colt. Had Katherine not known better, she would have sworn he was just loitering at the pen and waiting for her to appear. He strode up smiling as Katherine at a snail's pace, backed her car up to the sidewalk leading to the house. "I'm not late, am I?"

He shook his head. "Not at all. Need help getting your things in?"

Katherine shielded her eyes with her hands. It wasn't even nine but the sun reflected mercilessly off the powdery-white oyster-shell surface. "Thanks, but I can handle it. It's just some clothes and my birds."

"All right, then. I'm on my way to Austin to look at a horse, but I'll be back this evening. Judy's probably in the house with some of the girls. She'll introduce you to everyone. If they're not inside, they'll be around the pool."

Katherine felt a slight uneasiness. She pressed her lips together and glanced toward the house. "Is Teddie around? You know she and I still need to talk."

Jack's expression filled with irritation and he looked away. "You'll find her in her room. She's grounded for two weeks, and I told her to wait until you spoke with her to start her chores."

"I'll go right up, then."

Jack ran a hand distractedly through his thick hair. "If you want me to wait, I'll be glad to."

"No," Katherine replied. "I'm sure everything will be fine." She hoped she sounded more convinced than she felt.

"Good. I'll give you the grand tour of the grounds later on. Maybe after dinner. Or tomorrow, for sure."

"I'd like that," Katherine replied. "This is a beautiful place," she said, gazing at the line of ancient willows flanking the walkway to the house.

"Do you really like it?" Jack said.

"Of course. Who wouldn't?"

He pressed his lips together for a moment. "You'd be surprised. Anyway, I love it. Well, I'd better go now if I'm going to get to Austin and back before dinner. Mrs. Gomez will skin me alive if I'm late. Thanks."

He lifted his hand, then turned and walked to his truck—the rusting, one-ton heap he'd been lying under the day Katherine had pulled into the driveway. The sight of that pickup reminded her of the inauspicious start to her interview and caused her to flush. When he reached the truck, he lifted his right hand and smacked the hood with his palm. "Out! Out! Out!" he shouted, whacking the hood with each word. "I'm leaving, so get out." He glanced over his shoulder at Katherine and rolled his eyes. "Can you believe I have to do this?"

Katherine gave him what she knew was an incredulous look. "But what are you doing?"

"Damn cats," he muttered, shaking his head and banging away on a rusty quarter panel.

"What?"

Instead of replying, he leaned over and put his ear down close to the truck's grill. "I don't hear anything. That's a good sign." Then he popped open the hood. "Ahh," he said triumphantly. "Come here, you." He reached down inside the engine compartment where Katherine couldn't see. "Oh, damn."

"What's going on?" she asked.

He glanced at her, his expression devilish. "Keep an eye out for oncoming chaperons, will you." Then he dropped on the ground and shouldered his way under the truck. A streak of calico flew out and across the lawn. Out tumbled a slower, smaller streak of gray. Followed by a black. A silver.

Jack scrambled back out from under the truck and dusted his jeans off. "Paisley keeps moving her blasted kittens all over the place. This heap seems to be her favorite hiding place."

"Is that what you were doing on Monday?"

"Yeah," he replied, giving his jeans a final swat. "The day I was almost a victim of death by chaperon."

Katherine valiantly tried not to laugh. "I thought you were doing...you know, mechanic stuff."

"Listen," he said. "My dignity was already suffering by the time I got out from under that heap. I wasn't about to tell you I was kitten hunting. It just isn't...well, macho. Not nearly as manly as adjusting carburetors or manifolds or...whatever."

Katherine couldn't help laughing. "Kitten rescue. Who'd have thought it? Wait till I tell the girls."

"You better not. If you snitch on me, I'll get you back. I'm bigger, you know." He made a threatening feint with his lean shoulders.

She threw her head back. "You don't scare me."

Something inside her twinged. A distant voice. A tiny accusation. It was nothing she could easily identify, but suddenly she couldn't meet his gaze, and an awkward awareness crept up her shoulders and balled itself in a tingly mass between her breasts. Her smile faded and she looked away. "I—I guess I'll get my things now."

"Okay," he said quietly. "See you later."

Katherine watched as he pulled away and then took out the covered cage where Pete, Phoebe and Sallie were flitting and chirping miserably. She didn't try to carry any clothes just yet but decided to go ahead and have her talk with Teddie first. In the house, she introduced herself to Mrs. Gomez, the cook and made her way upstairs. Since Jack had showed her around the house on Monday, she knew where her room was. And Teddie's. After setting the birds on the little chest of drawers in her room, she walked down the hall and rapped lightly on Teddie's door. She heard a quavery "Come in," turned the handle and stepped inside.

Teddie looked up. Katherine was totally unprepared for the utterly desolate, red-eyed teenager gazing miserably at her. Teddie's slender hands clutched the arms of her chair in a grip that made her knuckles whiten. Instead of the brittle slender beauty of earlier that week, she now appeared to be just a pathetically thin, unhappy little girl.

"Where's my dad?"

"Gone to Austin to look at a horse, he said."

Teddie's lips parted and her eyes enlarged to panic-filled saucers. Her gaze ricocheted around the room as if she desperately sought an escape route. Katherine felt a twinge of pity. "We didn't get off to a very good start, did we?"

"Not very," Teddie mumbled, her eyes still cutting left, then right.

"I'm going to be completely honest with you, Teddie. What you did Monday was mean. You scared me. You also hurt me and you hurt my feelings." She walked to the chair beside Teddie's and sat down.

Teddie gaze began to climb. "I'm sorry about Phoenix. I didn't mean to hurt anyone. To hurt you, I mean." She leveled a red-eyed glare at Katherine. "I admit that I did want to scare you away, though. You see, if my dad didn't have to pay a chaperon he could..." Then her shoulders fell and she seemed to shrink deeper into her chair. "Oh, what's the use? I just can't stand anyone else around who wants to push me around or spy on me—"

"Hold on, Teddie. Why don't you give me a chance before you decide we're not going to get along. I'm not here to bully you or to spy or anything like that. I just need a job for the summer. Really."

Teddie stared at Katherine's eyes for a few long heartbeats, then she seemed to deflate even more, to grow smaller and less rigid in her chair. "Oh."

"There *is* one more thing. The shoe your father's horse ruined has to be repaired, and I expect you to pay for it."

The girl nodded. "How much is it?"

"Replacing the heel will cost a little more than twenty dollars." Actually, the shoes had been irreparably damaged and would cost nearly five times that much to replace, but Katherine knew Teddie would never be able to afford that. She thought she was being extremely generous. Then she saw Teddie's reaction.

The girl's head dropped and her mouth opened, but no sound came out. Her shoulders caved in and then her lip began to tremble. She was trying not to cry.

Katherine crossed to her. "What is it? What's wrong?"

Teddie could hardly answer. She raised a contorted, tear-streaked face. Her eyes streamed, and her nose was running. "Twenty dollars," she said through racking sobs. "It's so...so much money."

Katherine winced. "It's a lot of money to me, too, Teddie. Those were my best shoes."

Teddie stared dully, then blinked as if assimilating new evidence. "I'm sorry," she said, and shoved a strand of liquid platinum hair behind one perfect, shell-shaped ear. "Couldn't we work out something else instead of money? I mean, couldn't I work it off...or something? You see I'm saving...I've been saving for a long time to pay for...to buy something. Jack won't let me take money from my grandfather, and since I only get ten dollars a week..." Her voice trailed off, and her eyes pleaded.

Teddie's obvious misery dragged at Katherine's heart, but she knew weakening would ultimately hurt more than it helped. "I'm sorry, Teddie, but this is one thing that I can't agree to. You'll have to pay for what you ruined."

Teddie looked down. She appeared totally defeated. "Okay. I understand," she said softly. Her shoulders sagged.

Sadness and guilt churned in Katherine's mind, but she knew giving in would also be wrong. "One more thing, Teddie..."

The girl looked up, suspicion hardening her watery eyes.

"Do you think we could declare a truce?" Katherine knew it would be asking too much too soon to expect more.

There was a slight softening in Teddie's look, not warmth, but at least she didn't seem quite as guarded or hostile. "Sure," she said and smiled. Bleakly. "Truce. Can I bring you the money later? After dinner."

"Of course." Katherine stood and left the room. She knew she felt every bit as miserable as Teddie. Later, when she was placing the last of her things in the chest of drawers a white envelope slid under her door. Katherine opened the flap. Inside were several limp bills and a note. In rather loopy, childish penmanship Teddie had written a note on pale pink stationery. "I'm sorry for what I did. I'm glad you get to work here. Teddie F."

During the day, five more girls arrived and Katherine spent several hours helping them unpack and settle in. The girls introduced her to their horses and patiently taught her the names of the huge jumps set up in the indoor ring. After that, she spent part of the afternoon going over Jack's books and trying to learn his system. He'd said he'd been "a little casual" in his office procedures. The truth was his receipts for months were crammed into assorted envelopes or shoe boxes or held together in clumps with rubber bands. Total chaos. Katherine did what she could and then gave up until he could sit with her and explain it all.

As he had said, Jack returned just before dinner. When they all sat down, there were eleven of them, and at least six more would arrive by Saturday. Katherine didn't want to mention the state of his ledgers in front of the girls, so she decided to wait until the following morning.

Lights out came at nine o'clock for the younger girls, and the seniors got an extra half hour, but no one complained. After the last of the girls vacated the bathroom, Katherine waited for almost thirty minutes for the water to get hot again. It never did, and so after hissing and blustering through a brief, chilly shower, she dressed for bed, turned off her lamp and opened the curtains to let in the moonlight.

The rolling lawns were bathed in silver, and beneath the waving trees purple shadows pooled on the ground. She rested her forehead lightly on the glass. The faint hum of the filter motor from the swimming pool rose from the backyard, and the occasional hunting call of a nighthawk wove itself into the fabric of the navy night. She was just turning to slip into her bed when a glimmer caught her eye.

"What?" she murmured to herself and squinted out the window. Across the lawn, she was certain she had seen a light. Yes, right there—coming from the indoor ring behind the main barn. Katherine stood watching for a moment and wondered what could be going on at the late hour. In moments she thought she caught a flash of movement. She blinked, rubbed her eyes and waited. Again, a flash of movement. It was unmistakable. Someone was riding after lights-out.

Katherine pursed her lips. She wondered if she should do a bed check to discover the culprit by elimination. But what if she woke all the girls, got everyone stirred up? She could just imagine a whole troop of giggling, eye-rolling teenagers gathered at the windows waiting for one of their companions to get hauled back inside for a good dressing down. With my luck, she thought morosely, it would be Teddie out there, and she's supposed to be grounded. Oh, for Pete's sake, I *am* the chaperon. This is my job.

With a sigh of irritation, Katherine plopped back on the bed and dragged on jeans, a T-shirt and her sandals. She pulled the door shut and winced at the echoing creak her feet made on the hall floorboards. As she approached the ring, the thud of hooves became unmistakable. Then she rounded the corner.

The jumps looked different at night. Under the high fluorescent lights the painted rails seemed more jewel toned, the white standards more pristine. In the center of the ring loomed a huge plywood wall painted to imitate red brick. It seemed incredibly real and solid. Rustic gates, wishing-well standards and old-fashioned stiles all scattered at angles beneath the hangar-like roof. Around the far corner galloped Phoenix, his black neck arched and his mouth dripping foam as he champed his bit. He turned in a tight figure eight and disappeared around the far side of the wall.

Katherine stopped at the railing and leaned on her elbows until the stallion reappeared. He was sweating and his breath huffed with every stride. Riding the stallion, wearing jeans and a plain white T-shirt was Jack. When he saw her, he pulled the horse to a stop. "Hi."

"Hi. I saw the light and I thought... I just came to see who was out here."

"Sometimes I ride late at night. Phoenix cuts up so bad I usually try to wait until the ring is empty to work him. It just saves headaches."

Although Katherine knew nothing about horsemanship, she could see Jack was alert, on guard. He held his hands high and his legs clamped firmly around the stallion's barrel. Even when he spoke, he gazed in concentration directly between Phoenix's ears. There was no relaxed reassurance, none of Jack's customary swagger, to the way he handled the animal. She also saw that although Jack was obviously challenged by Phoenix, he also seemed somehow at home.

Although she was certain Jack was in complete control, somehow being outside the ring and having the stout wooden rail between herself and the stallion seemed a good idea. She wasn't even sure she wanted to watch Jack ride. "Well, since everything's okay, I guess I'll head back in."

"Why don't you stay for a while?"

She hesitated. Phoenix pawed the ground restively and ground his bit between his powerful jaws. The sound set Katherine's teeth on edge. "Maybe I ought to get back inside. Like I said, I—"

"Really, Katherine. Don't go. I'm not going to be too long. He just needs a little stretch." Phoenix switched legs and raked the ground with his other ebony foreleg. "Stop that," Jack commanded, scowling down at his horse. He looked expectantly back at Katherine. "If you're not too tired, when I'm through we'll have a cup of coffee."

"I don't know, Jack. It's awfully late and sometimes coffee keeps me awake."

"Decaf."

Katherine smiled. *He really wants me to wait for him.* She felt a swirling delight. "Okay."

"Good. This won't take any time."

Katherine didn't discern any movement on Jack's part, but he must have squeezed with his legs because the stallion immediately moved forward at a canter. His legs cut through the thick night air like gleaming scimitars, and his long tail floated behind him like blackened, tattered clothing.

Katherine eased up onto the rail. She let her legs dangle and her heels drummed faintly on the wooden railing as she studied the jumps. They were huge. One was so wide that Katherine could easily have driven a car between its standards. Then Jack circled the ring showing Phoenix the fences—an obvious prelude to jumping. Her heart began to slam in her chest. On his next pass by her, Jack gave her a wink. "I know what you're thinking," he called. "I can see it in your face."

He turned in a tight circle and pointed the stallion toward the enormous square oxer situated directly in front of her. "You're saying to yourself, 'What an incredible animal.'" Phoenix arched over the fence like a black rainbow, his head thrust forward and knees curled almost to his chin. When he landed he bucked once. Powerfully. Jack seemed completely oblivious to it.

"You're saying to yourself, 'What an amazing, athletic creature....'"

Wheel. Gallop. Soar.

"You're wondering how much work it takes to achieve this kind of perfection."

Turn. Leap.

"Yes. I can just see it your eyes. You're saying, 'He's magnificent. And come to think of it, that horse isn't bad, either.'"

Chapter Four

Katherine's legs froze in midswing and she let both heels thump against the wooden rails. "You know, Jack," she said, doing her best to keep a straight face, "I'm afraid I'm going to have to go inside, after all. It's getting pretty deep out here and I'm just wearing sandals."

He laughed and pulled the stallion to a stop directly in front of her. When the horse took a step in her direction, Katherine hastily swung around and dropped to the ground outside the ring. Jack regarded her solemnly. "So you still haven't forgiven him."

"He scares me." She looked up at him and smiled sheepishly. "Even more than the nice ones do."

He gave her a thoughtful look. "So you're not too crazy about horses at all?"

"I don't know. I like Pandora. But I've never been around horses before. My parents weren't very, you know, outdoorsy."

"You've never ridden a horse?"

"Not once. Not even a pony ride."

"Would you like to?"

Katherine looked away. "I don't know. I—I'm not very—"

"Wait a minute." Jack vaulted off and landed lightly in the ring. "Why don't you try now, just for a minute. I'll hold on to him the whole time. He'll just walk. I promise."

Katherine gave Jack and the horse a skeptical look. "I don't know. I don't think so."

He looked eager and excited. "Come on, Katherine. You'll love it. I know. You get on and I'll ride behind you. We'll ride double."

"Won't he mind the extra weight?"

"Nah. Well, I don't know. How much do you weigh?" His eyes gleamed with humor.

"Don't be rude. I'm thinking."

The invitation enticed her. To be able to gallop across moonlight-silvered fields on horseback. All that power beneath you waiting for your command. Phoenix regarded her with a huge, liquid eye. Somehow with Jack to control him he seemed more noble than dangerous.

"What do I do?"

Jack beamed. "Just a second." He ran up the stirrup iron, unbuckled the girth, slipped the saddle off and sat it on the rail. Then he resituated the saddle pad in the middle of the horse's back.

Katherine gazed dubiously from the horse to the man. Without the saddle Phoenix again loomed huge and unpredictable. "What? No saddle?"

Jack smiled at her. "Not with two of us. Here, it'll be okay. Just hop over the rail and put your knee in here." He cupped his hands and threaded his fingers together. "I'll give you a leg up and then I'll swing up behind you."

Katherine eased over the rail. Her sandals looked ridiculously out of place; her toes pink, wiggly and vulnerable. "You know, I'm not really dressed for this..."

She walked up, steadied herself with a hand on Jack's shoulder and put her knee in his hands. "Actually, it might be better if I—"

"Grab a handful of his mane to steady yourself. Right there. That's it." He lifted her easily and suddenly the horse's back was beneath her.

"I'm not really... Oh." She was riding Phoenix. She was riding horseback. The heat of the animal's enormous body seeped through the sheepskin saddle pad and surged through her thighs. A thrill rolled through her and she nearly shuddered. Phoenix champed his bit and shook his head. So warm. So powerful. His mane was a midnight thatch hanging down on one side of his neck, not split and hanging over both as she'd thought. She held on to it and rolled the thick, coarse hairs between her fingers. With her other hand she tentatively patted the animal. His powerful neck extended far in front of her and his ears flicked forward, then back. He curved his head around to nose her leg.

"He's not going to bite me, is he?"

Jack smiled. "He wouldn't dare. Now lean way forward and over to the right. That's it."

He stood on the ground at Phoenix's left foreleg and grabbed a handful of mane. "Hold on." And with one smooth motion, he swung up and seated himself behind her.

The stallion grunted and shifted to the side. Katherine gasped.

"Easy," Jack said. His words caught in Katherine's hair and warmed her nape. "Walk. Walk."

Jack slipped his arms around her, and his body leaned against her. "Take the reins like this," he said. "I'll hold them with you. Just like I am. Thumbs up. See? Nothing to it."

The stallion moved forward, his head swaying gently from side to side with each step. Even through the thick sheepskin pad Katherine still felt the bunch and extension of his muscles, the ponderous stretch and roll as he walked around the ring. She didn't want to accidentally pull on the horse's mouth and . . . well, irritate him or anything, so she held the leather reins gingerly. "Is this right?" she asked.

"Perfect," he murmured.

Jack's arms enclosed hers, and she was struck by the contrast.

Dark. Fair.

Absently, she wondered if he noticed the same thing. As he easily, almost casually, guided the horse, the tendons and sinews in his arms rose and fell like the cables of a powerful but silent machine. He wore some kind of sports watch, and the springy hair on his wrists and forearms was bleached almost white. Prominent knuckles strained against the dark skin and his hands were broad and weathered.

Angles. Curves.

With every powerful stride Phoenix took, Jack's body touched hers slightly—the flat muscles of his chest barely grazing her shoulder blades. An awareness of him shivered all along her back: the legs curving directly behind hers, the strong, taut stomach that never quite nested itself in the small of her back. Katherine was suddenly aware of the intimacy of their position. Heat rose from the horse's body and enveloped them. His hooves thudded quietly into the sawdust, and his shoes quietly clicked on little pebbles in the footing.

Summer smells and night smells drifted around her—the acrid, woodsy smell of the horse, the grass bruised by countless hooves, distant night flowers and some scent Jack wore that hovered just beyond perception. Cedar, maybe. Brandy, leather, saddle soap. She wanted to lean back against him and breathe it in, fix it in her mind so she would be sure to recognize it and call it up with this memory. Level with her eyes, his strong chin loomed just to her left. She saw his mouth curve into a smile.

Male. Female.

"Like it?" His voice was sonorous, rumbling. She felt it through her back.

"Yes."

"Me too."

Katherine found herself hypnotized by the rolling of the horse's gait. Her eyelids drifted down a little. Jack's breath seem to gather itself into her hair and slide down her nape into her shirt. Invisible fingers brushed between her shoulder blades, slid down into the hollow of her spine and swirled there dreamily.

She stole a glance to her right. To her left. Such broad shoulders. You didn't usually notice because he wasn't what you'd call muscle-bound. More lean and sinewy. A little weather-beaten. But here, seated in front of him on the enormous stallion and tucked right up close like this...well, you just couldn't miss it. And with his arms reaching around her, well, if she weren't his employee she'd be tempted to lean back into that broad, hard chest and—

"Jack?"

Katherine whipped around toward the voice, bumping her head against Jack's chin. "Sorry."

"Hermes," he said. "There you are. I was just giving Katherine a ride."

For an instant Katherine was certain she heard an irritated edge in Jack's voice. Hermes, the head groom, looked confused as he gazed from Jack to Katherine and back. "You want me to come back later, Jack?"

"No. We're all through now," he replied.

Jack reined Phoenix in, and when he did his arms closed around her briefly—the suggestion of an embrace. Then he slid off and landed lightly in the sawdust. "Down on this side. That's it—just swing your leg over and I'll spot you."

When she landed in the ring, Jack's hands closed on her waist to steady her. Her sandals sank in the footing and the grainy sawdust rasped between her toes. When she turned to thank him for the ride, they stood so close that she still felt the same shimmering awareness she had when they rode together. Only now the closeness—the connected feeling—embarrassed her. With Hermes waiting at the other end of the ring, it almost seemed she'd been caught doing something, well, wrong. Like teenagers who linger on the front porch until someone flips on a light.

Warmth rolled up her neck and she knew her fair skin would be darkening. "Oh, would you look at that," she said as she dropped her gaze. "My sandals are...my toes are all...I guess I'll have to go take another cold shower." *Cold shower? What on earth will he think you're thinking?* The warmth surging up her neck intensified to blazing heat.

Jack stepped backward, and under his breath Katherine was almost certain she heard him murmur, "Me too."

When he stepped away to walk the stallion toward Hermes, she stole a glance at him. Ramrod straight. A little bit of male swagger. Broad, broad shoulders. Narrow hips. Nice, round . . . *Stop that.*

When Jack handed the bridle to Hermes, the stallion extended his long, ebony head as if breathing in the man's scent. His lips worked, and for an instant Katherine thought he was going to bite, but at the last minute must have thought better of it. Jack grasped the reins, pulled the stallion's head against his chest and rubbed behind the twitching ears. The horse tipped his head slightly and pinched his eyes shut. Again, his lips worked irritably as he grudgingly endured the affection.

Although Jack's face was in profile Katherine could see his expression. He smiled. Lost for a moment in happy distraction. *He loves that horse.* She wrinkled her nose.

As they walked away from the ring and back toward the house, the night closed around them. Once again Katherine felt a heightened awareness that made every night sound seem more intimate—the quiet rhythm of their steps, the faint, metallic click as Jack's spur buckles brushed against his boots. When his elbow casually brushed against hers, a thrill of sensation raised the flesh all along her arm. She mentally groped for something engaging to say—some thoughtful question. Maybe an intelligent observation. Nothing occurred to her. What's going on? she wondered. Why do I feel so keyed up? What if he thinks I'm awkward? Or too dumb to make conversation?

When he opened the back door for her, he murmured a polite "After you." The creak of the door seemed to reverberate around Katherine as she stepped into the darkened house, and their footsteps echoed furtively in the quiet kitchen. Katherine hoped they didn't wake up any of the girls. It was well past eleven and the house seemed nestled into itself for the night. Faint, homey noises surrounded them—the hum of the refrigerator, the distant groan of old boards settling, the rasp of the sand on Jack's boots against the linoleum. A dim light from over the sink made their shadows dance thin and blue-gray on walls.

Jack glanced up at the clock. "I didn't realize it was so late, and I don't want to keep you up unless you—"

"Yes," Katherine said. "I really should go on up now."

Jack's face was shadowed, but even in the dimness Katherine saw a certain focusing in his look. There was something unmistakable about the way his eyes locked on to hers. She felt his attention, his awareness and concentration on her face. Her mouth. Her lips. *My God, he wants to kiss me.* For a moment she forgot to breathe.

And I—I want to kiss him, too. Images tumbled through her mind—his strong, straight mouth angling across hers. Powerful arms pressing her against him. Burying her fingers in that thick hair and feeling the warm rasp of his cheeks against her throat as she folded her arms around his torso. *Wait a minute. What are you thinking? You're supposed to be the chaperon, for Pete's sake.* He moved closer.

Katherine felt dizzy. Her mouth dropped open and she let the air rush in through her lips. She forced herself to look away—toward the archway leading out of the kitchen. "Good night, then." Her voice fell softly in the gloom. The sound didn't seem to break the silence but rather to blend and meld with the intimacy of the moment.

"Yes, well." He cleared his throat. "I guess I'd better go lock up."

Katherine backed away, not daring to look at him. "See you in the morning," she murmured as she walked away. She felt his gaze against her back until she disappeared around the corner.

Two weeks later Jack walked briskly through the house, whistling and thumping his palm with the butt of a short riding crop. He had once dreaded this time of the month—the bills, the deposits, juggling the notes and trying to keep enough cash in his account to buy feed and decent prospects, but now he had Katherine. What a godsend.

At first she'd been pretty cross about the state of his books. He smiled at the memory of her sitting on the floor surrounded by little piles of receipts and check stubs, a legal pad beside her—honey-colored hair piled on her head and ballpoint pens stuck through the golden twist. There had been unreconciled bank statements. Lots of them. She had gradually become more and more frustrated with him, and eventually she'd brandished a freshly sharpened number-two pencil at him and ordered him out.

Actually he had never liked the paperwork side of the business, the tedium and gloom of it. Since there was always such bad news, he'd learned quite a few creative ways to put it off. Now things were different. In only two weeks she had created a filing system, straightened out his ledgers, consolidated some old loans and balanced the checkbook. Hell, there was even cash in the Petty Cash box.

The house seemed different with her around, too. Before there had always been a sort of film over everything—despite his efforts and the occasional magnanimous gesture from Mrs. Gomez, who was only supposed to cook. Pictures hung straight, things just generally seemed to be more "picked up" with Katherine there. And everything had been done efficiently. Cheerfully.

All the girls, even Teddie, loved her. A couple of nights a week, Katherine would sit in the living room and play her guitar and they'd all sing. He'd even joined in until they told him he couldn't anymore. They called his singing donkey noises, but he was sure they were just teasing.

When he strode into the office Katherine glanced up and smiled at him. He grinned. "Hello, boss."

"You're in a good mood," she said, tipping her head slightly. Her eyes, that amazing ocean blue, sparkled. She seemed glad to see him.

Jack felt it again—that punch to his middle. He took a deep breath. "Yeah, I am in a good mood. Are we all set for the Junction show?"

She leaned back in her chair and her pink cotton tank shirt pulled across her body, accentuating every firm contour. The punch to his middle radiated through his torso and concentrated itself in an alarming escalation just below his belt. He sat quickly on the edge of her desk and realized she was answering his question and he hadn't been listening. He dragged his gaze upward to her face.

"...hotel room, stalls and hay are all taken care of. How about chaperons?"

Jack picked up one of her pencils and drummed the eraser on her desk. "Meg's folks are going and Keelie's. Judy'll be there, too, so we've got plenty. What'll you do without us?"

She gave him a sassy smile. "I guess I'll just have to muddle through as best I can. It's hard to imagine—just me, the remote control to the television and all that hot water. All to myself. No boom boxes. No phone messages—"

"Stop. Stop," he said. "If I didn't have three horses to show, I might call myself in sick."

"You can't," she said smugly. "You're the coach." Then she tipped her head to the side and gave him an odd look. "You...you have three horses to show? Are they for sale?"

"They will be soon. They're all pretty good. You saw Teddie riding Mountain the other day." As Jack explained the prospects for each horse, Katherine seemed to grow nervous or agitated. She scribbled the name of each animal on her pad and made little stars and dollars signs. Odd, he thought. After the thorough going-over she'd given his books she certainly knew every intimate detail of his business. I guess she knows how important this is, he told himself.

In less than three months he'd have to have enough money to meet his note or he'd lose everything—this time for good. That must be it, he thought. She's just naturally a little embarrassed because she knows how important this is. That made him smile. He liked the fact that she cared. He knew it was more than just integrity and friendly concern for his business. She liked him. He could tell. Maybe, in September when all this was behind them, they could even . . . He stood suddenly. Best not to think of that now. He'd save that until later.

For the next few weeks Katherine concentrated on learning the stable routine. Every morning Jack, Katherine and the girls all met around the table for chore assignments and brief lessons on stable management. The major horse shows had started, and now Katherine had almost every other weekend off. Since so many parents attended the shows, she didn't have to chaperon.

Then on Wednesday morning, her fourth week at Blazingbrook, Katherine awoke to the sound of rain drumming against her windows. Looking out, she saw a flat, leaden sky and water standing in silver puddles across the sodden fields. She dressed quickly and joined the others in the kitchen. When Jack looked up and saw her he smiled.

"Morning," he said. "Here. Sit next to me. I want you to see how we do the rotation for feeding the horses."

When she sat next to him, he leaned closer and angled his notes for her to see. As soon as she leaned toward him she felt it—the quickening, the heightened awareness. She was certain that intangible parts of her were reaching toward him—like invisible metal shavings straining toward a magnet. She remembered their late-night ride, his arms wrapped around her, his broad chest warm and unyielding against her back. Jack leaned closer, and Katherine suddenly had the feeling that he'd read her mind or somehow interpreted the subtle signals she knew she was emanating.

"What a nasty day," he said, and glanced at the girls sitting around the table. "Since you all want to go to the mall, I'll hay the big barn for you, but you still have to get the stalls done before you leave." The girls lounged over their bowls of cereal and murmured or nodded in sleepy agreement. After Jack read off a list of stable duties, Paula and Kimmie Spears slipped into rain slickers and went puddle-hopping across the sodden yard.

Katherine stood at the door watching them and listening to their high-spirited yelps. She turned to Jack. "Can I help you give hay to the horses?"

He glanced up with a look of delighted surprise. "Do you really want to?"

"Sure. I'd love to." She wanted very much to spend more time with him, even if that meant lugging bales of hay through the barn. More and more she found herself just wanting to be around him. He worked so hard; he drove himself so mercilessly day and night, but it seemed when she was with him, he relaxed. Sometimes, after he'd had a good laugh with her and the girls, the lines etched around his eyes would smooth out a little. If only she knew more about him—but he didn't speak about the past at all, and she was reluctant to ask any of the girls.

Since she assumed giving the horses hay would be backbreaking and tedious, she wasn't prepared for the simple delight waiting for her in the cathedral-like hayloft. She followed Jack up a winding wrought-iron stairway and emerged into the loft through a hole in the roof. He flipped a switch and a row of dusty light bulbs flicked on, illuminating a square castle of golden hay standing in the center of the loft. Huge beams, as thick as railroad ties, crisscrossed the cobwebbed ceiling that towered over them. Besides the central stack, along each wall yellow bales lay in groups like little bunkers.

Jack walked to the first stack. "Watch your step," he said quietly. "See? There's a square hole cut out over each stall. You pull a section of hay off each bale, like this. These are called flakes." The stalks of dried grass rustled and he separated them. "And then you drop it down here. About this much for each horse."

Beneath their feet the horse nickered and pawed impatiently, obviously knowing a golden feast was about to drop from heaven. All along the rows of stalls, Katherine heard the animals grunting, nickering and kicking impatiently. "Nothing to it," she said.

She thoroughly enjoyed the chore. She liked the hollow sound of her footsteps thumping on the floorboards and the sweet smell of the hay, like dried sunshine. Looking down on the gleaming backs of the horses and hearing their greedy, grateful crunching sounds made her feel knowledgeable and important to the workings of Blazingbrook. She had finished her side of the barn—twenty horses—when she met Jack. They faced each other, the enormous castle of hay on one side and hay doors on the other.

"You want to see something pretty?" he asked.

Rain drummed faintly on the tin roof and the companionable sounds of the horses rustled beneath them. Katherine felt warm and flushed from exertion and simple happiness. "Sure."

"Wait here," he said.

She heard the thump of his booted feet fading toward the stairs. Then the lights went out. Katherine gasped.

"It's okay," Jack called, his voice echoing in the loft. "This'll only take a second."

Gray light seeped in through the rough seams in the boards and soon she could discern the outline of the doors and the faint, looming shape of the hay stacked behind her. Jack's footsteps grew louder. "I want you to see this view," he said softly in the gloom.

He pushed the hay door and it rumbled as he shoved it open. Almost beneath her feet, the rolling expanse of Blazingbrook Farm stretched out toward a swaying forest of cedar and pine. Blanchard Creek winked up at them and glittered like a liquid jewel despite the heavy sky.

This side of the property didn't front on any highway, and the magnificent, jagged Houston skyline loomed far, far in the distance like the Emerald City in *The Wizard of Oz* movie. To Katherine it seemed that they could have been looking out over a virgin forest in a different world. Just beneath them the empty paddocks showed a network of trails where the impatient horses had paced, waiting to be led to warm stalls and full feed boxes. The brightly painted jumps in the hunt field looked small, like toys set up and abandoned by a careless, giant child.

"It's beautiful," Katherine said softly. An ache of wanting squeezed in her chest. She could look out over this landscape every day of her life. Warmth bloomed behind her, and she knew Jack was standing close, looking over her shoulder.

"Beautiful," he murmured, and the warm rush of his breath whispered against her neck.

Knowing he stood so close brought her nerves to screaming attention. An urgency deep inside her, something elemental, demanded that she turn around. Claim him now.

Intuition, innuendo—every moment they'd spent together insisted it was what he wanted. What they both wanted. A warm hand rested lightly on her shoulder. That warmth surged through her body and called up more power.

He said nothing. She dropped her head to the side and rested her cheek on his hand. His arm wrapped around her waist and pulled her toward him, pressing her against the length of his body.

With a groan she turned around and wound her arms around his neck. She barely had time to see the hot look of joy burning in his eyes before his mouth dropped on hers.

Chapter Five

Katherine wanted to open her eyes but she was afraid. Afraid that the arms holding her, the warm mouth moving across hers might be only a fantasy. One part of her acutely registered every nuance—his touch, his mouth, his distant moan—willing it into memory. Another part of her spiraled away in a kind of delirious joy.

Jack was kissing her.

Outside, the storm gathered itself and flung gusts of wind at the barn. The wind changed and rushed through the open doors, sending handfuls of loose hay scudding across the floor. The rain smell—water and iron and ozone—filled the loft and cut into the warm scent of horses, hay and leather until finally the sky broke open and sent a cold sheet of rain slapping through the door. Then they were laughing and clinging to each other, hands exploring faces, lips, hair, until he pulled her down onto the sweet, whispering hay.

His lips moved over hers again. Tasting. Teasing. He leaned away from her and smiled. "You don't know how many times I've thought of kissing you," he said as he smoothed a strand of hair away from her face. "I can't believe this is finally happening. That we're together this way."

"I know," she murmured, as she reached up and trailed her fingers over his cheek.

His gaze held her. "You've thought of this, too, haven't you? I can see it in your eyes."

Katherine couldn't tell him how she felt. She could only show him. Tangling her fingers in the thickness of his hair, she urged his face down to hers. Jack sighed into her mouth and she accepted him—the heat of his stomach pressed against hers, the planes and angles of his shoulders, his arms. But then a distant accusation intruded: what are you doing? What are you thinking?

As if instantly aware of the subtle change in her, the intensity of his embrace changed. His mouth left hers and trailed down the side of her face. His teeth grazed her neck; his warm breath slid into her hair and stayed there, warming her. He groaned. "What are we going to do?"

Katherine squeezed her eyes closed. "First," she said softly, "we'd better sit up."

In answer, he buried his face in the hollow of her neck. Katherine released a shaky breath. For one more precious moment she held him, trying to commit to memory the feel of his body, the smell of his hair and skin and clothes. Finally he rolled away, sat up and rested his elbows on his knees. He dropped his head into his hands and plowed his fingers through his hair.

Katherine gathered her legs underneath her and leaned forward to brush away the bits of hay clinging to his shirt. She spent one delicious moment awash in the joy of this simple intimacy, then rested her cheek against his back. "What happens now?"

He turned and once again pulled her into an embrace. Tender. Powerful. "I don't know. I just know I have to...to be with you. To spend time alone with you."

"I feel the same way, but the girls...my job. I mean—"

"I know this..." With a simple eloquent gesture he summed up what was beginning between them. "This comes at an awkward time and place for both of us. Publicly having an affair with my girls' chaperon would probably close Blazingbrook for good, not to mention—"

"We can't have a secret affair, Jack. I couldn't sneak around even—"

"Of course not. That's not what I meant." He scowled and picked up a stalk of hay while the base rumble of distant thunder shook the barn. Jack folded the wisp of straw and flung it at the open doors. The rain droned steadily on the roof. "There's only one thing we can do."

Although he wasn't looking at her she nodded. "I know."

"We have to stop now, as well as we can. We can't let this happen—until September, I mean. It won't be easy, but I just don't see any other way."

"You're right." Katherine tried to smile. "But we'll get to know each other in other ways. It won't be so bad."

He moved a little closer and took her hand, smoothing it into his palm and studying it as if trying to memorize the shape of her fingers. He sighed. "We'd better get back."

"I suppose so."

Jack stood and held his hands out to her. She took them, and when he pulled her up he held her against his chest for one long moment. "Give me a good long hug," he said softly. "I need one that'll last until September."

"In September," she said as she clung to him, "I'd like to meet you here. In this same place..."

He tipped her head back. "It's a date." His gaze roamed her face. Fell to her mouth. He squeezed his eyes closed. "But now," he said huskily, "we'd better get back." They walked silently past the golden mountain of hay, and at the head of the stairs he paused to flip the lights back on.

"I've got to go back and close the doors," he said. "You go on down and I'll finish up here and see you back in the house. Later." They didn't kiss again. She knew this time they might not be able to stop. But just before she turned to go the look of tender hunger in his eyes swirled through her like a caress that stayed with her for hours.

For Katherine, the rest of the day passed like a happy dream. Several times she touched her lips and tried to recall every moment of what had happened in the loft. His touch. All he'd said. Once, though, a niggling thought shouldered into her happy reverie. What would Jack say if he knew she wasn't being completely honest about what brought her to Blazingbrook?

She shook the thought off. At the end of the summer she resolved to tell him everything, no matter what the consequences. Surely he would understand. After all, no matter what first brought her to the stable, her intentions had always been honorable. But for now, September was an eternity away and she had work to do. She shoved her misgivings to the back of her mind and returned to the office.

Slowly Katherine became accustomed to the constant drumroll of footsteps on the stairway, the dueling boom boxes, incessant blow dryers and ceaseless jangling of the telephone. Saturday was always the busiest day of the week at the stable. At eight-thirty the third Saturday morning in June, she clutched her clipboard against her chest as she hurried from the large barn to the outdoor ring where the intermediate lesson was just getting started.

Besides the regular boarders, every other weekend dozens of children drove out from Houston for group lessons. Jack taught only the advanced riders and a few private lessons while the best of the advanced riders like Teddie or Judy taught the others. Katherine's duties included making sure the parents had signed releases and paid for the classes.

Dust hung in the air and tickled her nose. The muffled thump of horse hooves was punctuated by an occasional ringing click as one or another of the animals would overstride and clip his own steel shoes. Katherine counted the riders, checked her receipts one last time and then readjusted her sun hat.

Teddie waited just at the gate surrounded by the mounted children of the beginner group, and Katherine saw that she was holding the reins of a pale, tired-looking horse. The girl sitting astride the old mare was saucer eyed with fear. Katherine walked up slowly and stroked the horse's cheek.

"Hi, Teddie. Isn't this Pandora?"

"Yeah," Teddie said, and patted the mare. She nodded up at Pandora's rider. "And this is Suzanne Sifara. Her dad works for my grandfather. Pan's helping Suzanne today, aren't you, Pan?"

Pandora appeared much more relaxed and confident than Suzanne did. "You know, Suzanne, Pandora is what you call an honest horse. She never bucks. Never refuses. Even when she's tired."

Suzanne appeared to unfreeze a little and blinked. "Really?"

"Really," Teddie said.

Suzanne loosened her stranglehold on the mare's mane long enough to lean down and pat her gingerly.

"You know," Teddie murmured, glancing at Katherine. "Every time she sees me she nickers. When I come home from school and Pandora is waiting for me by the gate, it's like my mom is still alive. Like she's waiting for me to tell her about my day."

Katherine didn't know what to say, but the flying dust seemed suddenly to burn her throat and eyes. With a brief, thoughtful smile Teddie walked out to the center of the ring, clapped her hands and began calling instructions to her pupils. "Now don't everybody bunch up. That's good. Sit up straight, Pattie. Why does everybody look so serious? We're having fun, aren't we?"

Katherine walked over to the indoor ring where Jack was schooling the advanced riders. Whenever she visited the ring Jack always had her come and stand with him while he gave the lesson. Even after seeing dozens of jumping sessions, Katherine still found them beautiful but terrifying. She waited until the horses cantered by to join Jack in the center of the ring. As soon as he saw her he grinned broadly.

When she took her place next to him he leaned toward her slightly. "Do you think it would blow our cover if I kissed your socks off right now?"

Katherine knew her eyes had grown huge. "But, Jack, you... I—"

He winked. "Yeah, I guess you're right." While Katherine tried to think of a suitable threat of retaliation to mutter to him, he turned back to face the galloping riders.

"Okay, Paula, trot that in-and-out and canter down over this hog's back."

Katherine glanced around the ring. She knew the hog's back was the huge arrangement of poles and standards with the center part of the barrier higher than the front and back. She resisted the urge to squeeze her eyes shut and forced herself to watch as Paula urged her horse, Swain, into a trot.

A light sheen glistened on the neck and shoulders of the big, handsome gray gelding. His ears pricked forward as he approached the first jump. The in-and-out consisted of two small jumps with room for only one stride between the "in" and the "out" portions—rather like jumping into a little pen and then jumping out the other side. He hopped it easily and landed in a canter. When he rounded on the hog's back, his head came up and he gathered speed. Katherine clutched her clipboard and held her breath; the jump was higher than her shoulders. Swain closed the distance in four thundering strides and then, at the last minute, he hunkered down on his haunches, ducked his head and slid to a stop. Paula went flying over his ears and crashed into the poles, demolishing the jump.

"Oh, my God," Katherine said, as she dropped everything she held and ran with Jack to where Paula was clambering out from the tangle of lumber and standards. The girl had gamely hung on to the bridle, and Swain pranced nervously at the end of the reins. Jack appeared concerned but not frightened.

"You okay?" he asked.

Paula reached up and adjusted the chin strap of her hard hat. "Yeah, fine." She smiled a little sheepishly. "Only bruised my pride. Everything else is pretty well padded."

Jack gave her a leg up back on the horse and Katherine helped him reset the fence. She didn't mention it, but she knew she had seen the sheen of tears in Paula's eyes. She felt certain Jack must have seen it as well.

"That's called refusing," he said. "It's premeditated cowardice on the horse's part. If you're riding in a class and your horse refuses, it costs you three faults. If the rider falls off, it's automatic disqualification. Our friend, Swain, seems to refuse often. And well." The lines around Jack's eyes seemed a little more deeply etched when he and Katherine took their places back in the center of the ring. "Okay. One more time," he called.

Swain refused. Paula flew.

He once again helped her up, but when she remounted he whispered something to her and she walked her horse out of the ring. She had been excused from the lesson.

The other girls had exchanged meaningful, sympathetic looks. Jack, his face thunderous with anger, whirled on Katherine. "You see," he said, gesturing furiously at Paula's dejected, retreating figure. "She's not ready for an animal like Swain. It's just too much horse for her. But would her father listen to me? No. *Nothing but the best for my daughter.*"

He continued the tirade to himself while he reset the jump. "I'd like to put his big fat backside on that horse sometime." He kicked the base of the jump back square. "That's the problem with some people. Half of them don't want to spend time with their kids. They just want to lob wads of money at them. As if that's any substitute for real concern."

Katherine knew at some point he'd stopped talking about Paula and Swain, but she didn't think it was a good time to ask what had him so adamant. The rest of the lesson went well, but an hour later Jack still remained irritated and preoccupied. When he had excused the girls from the ring, he turned to Katherine. "I've got to work one of the other horses. Did you say there was something we needed to talk about?"

Katherine nodded. "The books, Jack. You're going to have to help me sort out some of this. What I'm seeing in the ledger just can't be right."

He glanced at his watch. "Okay. Why don't we plan to meet in the office at about eleven?" A trace of his customary devilment returned to his eyes. "That'll give me time to think of someone to blame it on." He left the ring without looking back. Walking stiffly, Katherine thought.

She checked her watch. Since the last of the morning lessons had started, she could retreat to the coolness of the house and tackle the bookkeeping. The checks and cash she'd collected would have to be deposited and then there was invoicing and countless minor jobs. She sighed and shoved a limp tendril of hair back under her hat and walked toward the back porch.

After studying Jack's books, she had come to understand the intricacies of stable economics. Apparently the cost of boarding the horses, which she had at first thought enormous, was barely enough to cover the overhead. The real profit came from buying and selling horses. Jack would spot a talented prospect, buy the horse cheaply and then—after some hard work and careful training—turn around and sell the animal at a profit. There were now several horses that as soon as Jack offered them for sale, Katherine intended to phone Mr. Wiley so he could alert the investors he'd mentioned.

She opened the back door and pulled her hat off, letting her damp hair tumble down. She sighed, grateful to momentarily escape the heat and dust. After helping herself to a soda, she looked into the living room. Judy and some of the other girls were sprawled on the floor and furniture watching a video. Paula, apparently none the worse for her falls, sat with them. On her way to the office, Katherine paused to study some of the photographs on the wall.

Just at the arched doorway leading back through to the kitchen, she noticed a picture of a much younger Teddie astride a fat white pony. On one side of the pony stood Jack, holding a cotton lead rope; on the other, a laughing blond woman was frozen in the act of dragging from her face a wind-tossed lock of hair. The woman was Hollywood beautiful—leggy, perfect teeth, enormous gray eyes and long, heavy sun-streaked hair. Jack wore the mildly bored, indulgent look young fathers often wear when forced to pose. Judy walked up and looked over her shoulder.

"Blaize," she said simply. "Teddie's mom."

"I thought so," Katherine murmured. "I see where Teddie gets her looks. What a beautiful family they made."

"Well, at least to look at," Judy muttered.

Katherine felt too awkward to ask for an explanation, but instead stood back and scanned the dozens of photographs hanging on the closest wall. "I don't see any recent pictures of Jack. There's plenty of Teddie. And I see you there, Judy. Twice. No, three...wow, you're everywhere. Paula, too. But there're no more of Jack."

"Well," Judy said, tilting her head back and squinting at the wall, "the most recent ones are usually in the office and he did lose three or four years after the accident."

"Accident?"

Judy looked blankly at her. "Oh, I guess you don't know. I just assume everyone does. Jack had a riding accident seven or eight years ago. He was in the hospital for months and months, and then in a wheelchair for a solid year." She frowned as if trying to remember. "And then he had to use crutches off and on for a long time after that." She shifted uncomfortably from foot to foot. "That's why he went so long without a summer program. He lost all his business."

Paula came to join them and the three of them walked through to the kitchen and sat at the long table. "It happened at the Christmas Show in San Antonio," Paula said in a conspiratorial whisper.

"Oh, it did not," Judy said. "It was at Austin, the last show of the summer. I was there. It was just horrible. Anyway, it was years before he was strong enough to ride competitively again." She paused. "It wasn't soon enough, though."

"Soon enough for what?" Katherine asked.

"For who, you mean," Paula said with a scowl. "Blaize couldn't stand it. Having to run the stable, take care of Teddie and Jack and do the books and all the jobs that Jack had been doing. She couldn't hack it."

"Oh, Paula, it wasn't all her fault," Judy said with exasperation. "Teddie was only five or six years old and Mr. Brooks—Blaize's dad—swore he wouldn't help out at all as long as Blaize lived with Jack. He promised all sorts of things if she'd just move back into his house and bring Teddie." She made a hopeless gesture with her hands. "She just couldn't stand up to him with Jack flat on his back. She was at her father's within a year. And then she died. I don't think she ever saw Jack out of his wheelchair."

"How tragic," Katherine said. "But what kind of man is Mr. Brooks? How could he do that to his flesh and blood? To Jack?"

Judy shrugged. "I don't know him very well. Every other weekend he comes in his Rolls—"

"Did you say Rolls?" Katherine asked, trying to keep the incredulity from her voice.

"Oh, yeah," Judy continued. "He's really loaded. Anyway, he comes by a lot to pick up Teddie, but he and Jack never speak. They hated each other from day one. Brooks thought Jack was just another horse-show Romeo out to get his beautiful daughter and her daddy's money. Then when Jack was nineteen he and Blaize eloped. She was barely eighteen, and Brooks tried to force her to annul it, but as it turned out, she came back from the honeymoon pregnant. Pretty soon they bought this place and it went okay for a few years."

Judy stopped and took a quick drink of her soda. "Teddie was only five or so when Jack got hurt. Anyway, it was a couple of years after the accident and he was still rehabilitating when Blaize went to Colorado with her new boyfriend. They were both killed in a car crash and things really turned ugly."

"How could they get worse?" Katherine asked.

Judy's voice dropped. "Mr. Brooks tried to convince the courts that Jack wasn't a fit parent. You know. Destitute. Disabled. He tried to get custody of Teddie."

Katherine's jaw dropped. "How horrible. But obviously it didn't work."

Judy shook her head and leaned back in her chair. "There was a long, nasty court battle, but Jack won." She leaned forward again and said quietly, "He had a terrible time getting the lawyers he wanted to represent him because he didn't have the kind of money Brooks had. My dad was one of his lawyers, and I understand Jack is still making payments. Between being flat on his back half the time and all that court stuff, he nearly lost the stable."

Katherine shook her head. "Isn't that sad. I think it's terrible for all of them."

Judy pursed her lips. "Well, Miss Teddie sometimes uses it to her advantage, but it's hard to blame her. I understand that Brooks just showers her with gifts Jack won't let her bring home. Jack blames almost all of Teddie's brattiness on Brooks. It's a mess."

"Yeah," Paula echoed. "A big mess."

Katherine turned the soda can between her fingers. "I guess there wasn't any kind of settlement."

"Oh, no. Not in this business. Magic Knight, the horse Jack was riding, belonged to Colonel Sheppeck then. When Jack was trying to keep Blaize happy, he took all sorts of dangerous chances. He had a reputation for riding anything. Magic Knight is a perfect example. He was extraordinary—one of those rare animals that teeters on that fine line between brilliance and madness, but he wasn't ready for the kind of class Jack was riding him in. He had all the talent in the world but at the time he wasn't much more than a colt."

At that moment the screen door creaked open and Jack strode in, smiling. "Oh, no, Judy, you're not talking horses at her, are you?"

A slight flush colored her face but she managed to give him a sassy smile. "Well, of course I am. I thought the rule was that we could only discuss two topics: horses and how wonderful you are."

Jack smiled broadly. "Oh, yes. That rule. I've been meaning to shorten it. Who wants to talk about horses, anyway?"

"Everybody lift your feet," Paula said drily.

"Show some respect, rotten kid," Jack said and faked a swipe at her. "Katherine, pay no attention to these two. And plug your ears before your thinking is hopelessly contaminated."

Still chuckling, he pulled out the chair next to Katherine's and sat down. He smiled and under the table she felt n unmistakable heat against her thigh. Her insides did a low roll, and again she felt the beginnings of a blush. *Maybe he doesn't realize he's touching me.* But how could e not have been aware that the entire length of his lean, nuscled leg was pressed against hers, causing eddies of sen-ation to swirl up her thigh and meet in a stormy vortex be-ween her legs. *How can he do this?* He's teasing me, she hought. Or maybe he doesn't feel the way I do. The look on is face was inscrutable. She parted her lips to make it eas-er to breathe.

His face was so close to hers that she could see the motes f color floating in the golden wheel of his irises. She'd ever seen eyes like his. A fire-colored kaleidoscope—flax, mber, gold. Hypnotic. His smile slipped away, but his lips emained parted.

This is against the rules, she thought. We agreed that we vouldn't do anything like this. Such contact just makes it arder. *Harder.* The pressure against her leg seemed to in-rease. No, no, I mean more difficult. Good grief, she hought, how am I going to keep from touching him?

At that moment the back door banged open and Hermes urst into the kitchen. He spoke in rapid, staccato Spanish nd gesticulated wildly. Behind him. Toward the barns.

The only word Katherine understood at all was "Phoe-ix," but from the old man's tone and the fear on his face, Katherine was certain something had gone terribly wrong in he stable. Jack's face darkened and he stood so abruptly hat his chair crashed backward and clattered on the floor. The two men were halfway to the door when he shouted over is shoulder.

"Call Dr. Sherwood, Katherine. Tell him Phoenix has ttacked Fox and her colt." By the time the door banged hut, he was sprinting across the lawn with Hermes trailing ehind him.

There was a moment of stunned silence. "Ishmael," Judy aid. The legs of her chair shrieked on the linoleum, then she nd Paula were racing out the door behind the men.

Katherine ran to the office. Dr. Sherwood's number was posted by the phone and Katherine jabbed it out. Time crawled.

"Why?" she muttered. "Why would a stallion attack a harmless colt? His own baby." After what seemed an interminable time, the veterinarian answered. Katherine told him all she knew, and he promised to be there in twenty minutes.

Katherine found Jack and the others clustered around Fox in the paddock closest to the big barn. Sweat poured down the mare's face and shoulders and veins protruded on her neck. Every few moments she lashed out with one of her back hooves, striking at nothing. Jack held her halter and snubbed her close to his chest.

Ishmael stood quivering by her side and appeared to be trying to melt into her. Great long strips of hair had been gouged away from his back, and on the crest of his little neck was an ugly pattern of raw, elliptical bite marks. Fox grunted and kicked again—this time forward—a "cow kick."

With a jolt Katherine realized she was trying to kick Ishmael. "What happened?" she asked. "What's wrong with her?"

Judy turned toward her. "Hermes was moving Phoenix into the aisle to clean his stall and he got away. He jumped into the paddock with Fox—she's in season. Anyway, she tried to fight him and Ishmael kept getting in the way. Phoenix roughed them both up real bad." Her voice dropped. "Hermes says he picked Ishmael up by the neck and threw him. Now Fox is so weirded out she doesn't want to have anything to do with him."

Katherine didn't know what to say. Jack had one arm around the mare's neck and the other over her nose as he pulled her head downward. "Bring Ishmael here, Hermes. *Aqui, por favor.*"

When Ishmael's face was close to Fox's, the mare's ears flattened and she lunged forward trying to bite him. The foal cringed and gave a pathetic, high-pitched whinny of terror and despair.

"No good. No good," Jack said. "You'd better take him inside." He snatched Fox's face up close to his. "You stupid cow," he said. "Don't you recognize your own baby?"

"Why is she doing that?" Katherine asked.

"She's just scared stupid," Judy answered. "That happens sometimes."

"Will she snap out of it?"

Judy shrugged. "Sometimes they do. Sometimes not."

A few moments later Dr. Sherwood arrived and drove his huge van right up to the paddock. After examining both horses, he said neither was injured badly—bruised, shaken and traumatized, but still sound. He gave both horses tranquilizers, but nothing would induce Fox to accept her colt.

Phoenix was unhurt.

Dr. Sherwood left some vitamins, instructions for weaning the foal and a jar of salve for his surface wounds. Most pathetic of all was the desperation with which Ishmael flung himself at the stall boards separating him from his mother. Jack said he'd hoped having them close would induce her to take her colt back, but he finally had to order Fox moved to another barn.

"Why did he do it?" Katherine asked Jack, as they walked back to the house with the girls. "Why did he attack Ishmael? His own colt?"

"Ishmael got in the way."

"That's it? That's why he almost murdered that baby—"

"Katherine," Jack said, in an exasperated voice. "That isn't Trigger or Mr. Ed in that stall. Phoenix is a real stallion. It didn't matter that it was Ishmael. It could have been a water buffalo or a kitten and it still wouldn't have made any difference to him. Nothing could have stood between him and Fox. She was his."

"Well," Katherine said icily. "Well, if that's the way it is, I think you should get rid of him."

"That's exactly what I intend to do," Jack replied evenly. He stopped for a moment and let the girls pass by them on their way to the house. "I'm sure you've seen from the books that I have a pretty big . . . huge, in fact, balloon note due in September. Phoenix is the horse I expect to bail me out of this mess once and for all. Actually," he said, as he smiled ruefully, "By the end of the summer he's going to sell for enough to raise Blazingbrook from its proverbial ashes." He rubbed his chin. "If he doesn't, I'll be riding him to the not so proverbial poorhouse."

Katherine scowled, "And good riddance," she said under her breath. She detested the stallion and knowing he was for sale comforted her. "But if he's so wonderful, why wait until the end of the summer to sell him?"

Jack paused. "Well, I... he's got to be campaigned. You know, shown quite a bit so the people who have big money to spend on show horses will get interested." He glanced away from her and raked his fingers through his hair. "By the end of the summer, plenty of people will have seen him. At Austin, the last show of the summer, there's a certain class at that show..." He paused for a moment and gazed back toward the barn. "Anyway, there's a class at this show that should show everyone what he can do. Phoenix has international potential."

When he casually mentioned the estimated price he'd get for the horse, Katherine had to ask him to repeat it. Twice. A nice home cost less. Judy yelled from the back porch that Jack had a call waiting, so he ran ahead. Katherine walked more slowly and tried to sort out her thoughts. There was obviously more to this than Jack was telling her.

And following her all the way back to the house, floating sadly in the heavy air, came the anguished sound of Ishmael calling his mother. She never answered.

Chapter Six

At eleven-thirty the following Wednesday morning, Jack sauntered into the office. "How'd it go?" he asked.

Katherine looked up and smiled ruefully at him. "It sure took longer than I thought it would. I just finished with the show secretary five minutes ago."

"Any problem?" Jack asked.

Katherine shrugged. "Nothing serious. If I knew more it wouldn't have been any trouble at all, but when she started asking about tack stalls and hay and signing up for feed, I was pretty lost."

Jack's face clouded. "Judy didn't help you?"

Katherine drummed her pencil lightly on the blotter. "She couldn't. The, em, you know. The horseshoe guy..."

"The farrier?"

"Of course. The farrier showed up and she had to go help hold horses while he... did his thing."

Jack grinned, obviously amused at Katherine's choice of words. "Do you know how his thing went?"

Katherine faked a swipe at him. "Oh, you. If you're going to torment the help, you can just leave."

Jack dodged her halfhearted swat easily. "Tormenting the help is my new favorite pastime." He winced, rolled his shoulders and stretched, pulling the fabric of his shirt taut across his chest. "I like it better than tormenting animals and small children." He stifled a yawn. "Any trouble with the hotel reservations?"

Katherine hesitated. She was still a little dazed from the effect of the tightened material across Jack's body.

"Um, no. Not really. Is there some reason there should have been?"

"Well, one of the oldest tricks in the book is to cancel someone else's hotel reservations and stable space. The horse-show secretary would be on to it, but hotel clerks will just give all your rooms up, and when you pull into town late at night for a big show, sometimes you don't have any place to sleep."

"That's mean!" Katherine exclaimed. "What a disappointment for the kids."

Jack shrugged. "That's business. For a lot of people horse shows are a big-money game. Some people think that you should do whatever you can get away with to increase your chances of winning." He smiled. "Once Sonny Sheppeck canceled all our hotel reservations at the Junction show. All the hotels filled up by the time we got there, so we had to sleep four to a stall, including the horse."

"Really?"

He nodded. "Yeah. Someday I'll tell you what I did to retaliate."

There was something about the glimmer in his eyes that made Katherine uncomfortable. "I'm not sure I want to know."

"Oh, don't worry about it. Sonny and I are still friends." He dropped his gaze and picked up the chipped mug Katherine used for a pen holder. "So," he said quietly, "you're sure you don't want to go with us?"

He seemed wistful and a quiet thrill warmed Katherine. *He's going to miss me.* "Well, I wish I could—"

"I bet you do," he said derisively. "Almost four days of no teenagers—"

Katherine dropped her gaze. "If you needed me to chaperon I'd go of course, but since there are so many parents going..."

"Yeah," Jack said as he replaced the cup. "There are plenty of volunteers around early in the season, but by the end of July, that'll taper off. I'll really need you then, but I'm glad you can have a little time to yourself." His voice dropped, and he picked at a spot on his jeans. "So, what will you do?"

"Oh," Katherine replied. "I'll stay busy. I have my guitar lesson on Saturday, of course. I'll have lunch with my girlfriends. Hang on the phone." She studied his hand. She wanted to reach out and rest her hand on his, just there where it lay on his thigh. The jeans were pale—almost white—from years of washing, and she knew Jack's long, flat muscles would make a warm and unyielding contrast with the old soft cloth. Thinking about it made her cheeks warm, and she dragged her gaze toward safer territory.

"I'll phone," Jack said softly.

"When?" Katherine blurted out. Then she felt a rush of embarrassment and looked away. "I—I mean, so I can be sure to be around just in case you...you need me to—" She looked up expecting to see amusement, but instead his eyes were even more wistful than his voice had been.

"I'll phone every day. If you're not around, I'll call back until you are."

They shared a smile and a moment of perfect accord.

"I better get back out there," Jack said. But instead of getting up he glanced over his shoulder toward the doorway, then turned back. He leaned forward and tilted his head. "C'm 'ere," he whispered.

Katherine's eyes widened and she cut her gaze toward the open door. "Jack, stop. We mustn't," she hissed.

His look grew hungry. Amused. "Oh, but we must," he answered. He was practically stalking her across the desk, the muscles of his forearms and shoulders defined sharply beneath his knit shirt. He began to push away her neat stacks of paper. The carefully arranged pens. The blotter.

In a state of near panic Katherine practically lunged forward and let her lips graze Jack's. "There. Now go away."

"You call that a kiss? That'll never do," he said. "If you can say 'There' after a puny little peck like that, I think we'd better have a lesson. I'm good at lessons." He moved closer.

Katherine teetered for a moment between fear of what would happen if she did and what would happen if she didn't.

She did. Closing her eyes, she leaned toward him and let her lips touch his. Firm. Warm. Perfect. Delicious warmth erupted at her throat when she felt his fingers trace the line of her jaw. He tasted good, like hot food made to be eaten outdoors. His touch reminded her of the way the sun made her skin draw and tingle when she lay out by the pool. She opened her mouth to him and his tongue teased hers, urging her to come closer.

In her stomach, butterflies erupted like a whirlwind, and she finally tore herself away. "Jack," she gasped. Although she only said his name, she knew her eyes spoke volumes.

His eyes were cloudy with desire. "Satan, get behind me," he muttered drawing his hand across his forehead. He stood abruptly and flinched when his boots met the floor with a solid thud. "I'd better get out of here before you have to...before I..." He left the sentence unfinished, but turned at the door. "We'll put a bookmark right here, and come back to this later."

Katherine smiled. Weakly. "In September," she said as firmly as she could.

One corner of his mouth quirked. "Right."

Katherine lowered herself back into her chair and watched him until he disappeared through the door. She listened until she heard the back door bang shut. She brought her fingers to her mouth and smiled against them. "I'll never make it until September," she said quietly. It's a good thing he's going to be gone for four days, she thought. My heart rate should just about be back to normal by then.

The thought was sobering. Four days without Jack. That was the only unpleasant aspect of having the time to herself—the fact that she wouldn't be seeing him until Sunday. As the thoughts flitted through her mind, she pursed her lips in determination.

While Jack and the girls were gone, there were plenty of things she needed to accomplish. Earlier that week she'd left a message for David Wiley, telling him Jack was taking three horses that he intended to sell to the show. If one of the bank's anonymous buyers appeared at the show and bought them, Katherine would be truly convinced that the bank really wanted to support Jack's ownership of Blazingbrook. If none of the horses sold and it turned out Wiley was deceiving her, well, she'd deal with that later.

What if they're really trying to take the barn away from him? Maybe I should tell Jack the truth about how I came to be here? But then, she thought, what if there really were silent investors at the bank trying to help him and she ruined it by telling him what she knew? Katherine rubbed her temples. She would just have to wait and see.

Since the house was quiet, she decided to go upstairs and lie down for a little while before the lessons ended. She hummed to herself as she walked up the steps, enjoying the quiet before the lunchtime stampede began, but just as she reached the top of the stairs she paused. A disturbing sound echoed quietly from the landing. Someone was crying. Hard. Muffled sobs and the choking gasps of some awful grief filled the hallway.

Katherine passed her own door and stopped at Teddie's room. There was no mistaking it. She was crying as if her heart were broken. Katherine rapped lightly on the door. "Teddie? Teddie, it's Katherine. May I come in?"

The sobs abated momentarily, but no one answered.

"Teddie?"

The door opened and the girl stood aside, head down, silver hair stringy and disheveled. She didn't meet Katherine's eyes.

Katherine touched her lightly on the shoulder. "What is it, sweetheart? Are you hurt?"

Teddie shrugged, and took a long, shuddering breath. "I didn't think anyone was in the house," she said, her voice high and strained. "I—I was just finishing up packing for the show."

Katherine reached out and stroked Teddie's hair behind her perfect ear. "I heard you crying."

As soon as Katherine's words were out, Teddie's shoulders caved in and she raised her hands to cover her face.

"What is it? What's wrong?" Katherine looked helplessly around the room, searching for some clue to what had the girl so distraught. A half-packed leather suitcase lay open on the bed beside a matching garment bag, and by the bed stood Teddie's black handmade riding boots—silent, elegant sentinels. "Is it the show? Are you nervous or... something? What is it?"

Teddie looked up, her expression furious and tormented. "I don't want to go to the stupid horse show. I hate horse shows. I *hate* them. I wish I never had to go again. Ever."

For several long moments Katherine was aware only of the quiet rush of her own breath and Teddie's quivering gasps as she fought her tears. "I thought...I know everyone thinks that you love horses—"

"I *do* love horses," Teddie said vehemently, shoving her hands through her hair. "Pandora especially, but I hate horse shows. They make me sick."

"Have you talked to your dad about this?"

Teddie gasped and looked up so suddenly she startled Katherine. "No," she almost shouted. "And you mustn't, either. Promise me you won't say—"

"Easy, Teddie, of course I won't—"

"Promise me."

She looked so desperate and stricken that Katherine didn't hesitate. "Of course I promise not to say anything about it. But why haven't *you* told him?"

Teddie swallowed hard. "Jack is trying real hard to get the barn back on its feet and he needs me to help. With the horses. With the lessons and all, you know. I can't tell him I hate the business. It would hurt his feelings. It would mess up everything between us."

"Teddie, I don't think that's right—"

"Oh, yes it is," she said fiercely. "You don't know him. You don't know how important the stable is to him. It's all he cares about."

Katherine pushed Teddie's hair away from her face. "But that's just not true, Teddie. Your father loves you very much. I'm sure if he knew that going to horse shows made you so unhappy he'd do something different. I just know it."

Rather than seeming reassured, Teddie once again buried her face in her hands. "It's not just the stupid horse shows. It's..." She didn't finish her sentence but instead walked over to her dressing table and opened the lap drawer. When she turned around, she held out a heavy white envelope. "Look."

Katherine took the envelope. "But, Teddie, this is wonderful news. This says you're a finalist in the *Panache* magazine teen model search. You're one of only ten out of... well, it says thousands of entrants." She looked up. "Why are you sad? Does your dad know? Is it a secret about the contest or something? Do I—"

"I can't finish the contest," she blurted out, her voice cracking. "You have to have a professional composite and I can't afford it. I don't have three hundred extra dollars and my dad doesn't, either. And he won't let my grandfather pay for it, so that's out. I don't know what I'm going to do."

"Sweetheart, I'm sorry to be so ignorant, but what's a composite?"

Teddie swiped at her eyes with the heel of her hand. "It's a collage of photographs that shows you wearing different outfits. You know, doing different looks—sporty, sophisticated, evening. There's a great photographer in town, too, and the agency gave me a list of hair and makeup people, but it costs hundreds of dollars."

She wrung her hands and her voice became thinner and higher pitched as she spoke. "I'm going to be a model someday. All the girls in my modeling class and the teacher, too—they all say I've got what it takes. But the classes and the competitions cost a lot, and my dad won't take help because he thinks modeling is just a whim."

"Wait, Teddie. I'm sure there's something we can do. How about a loan? Won't your dad let your grandfather loan you the money? With the understanding that it would be paid back."

Teddie shook her head miserably. "My dad has a real thing about money and my grandfather. Jack hates him. The only reason he let Granddad pay for my modeling classes is because it was a Christmas present. Even then he had to check it out and make sure it wasn't too much money."

Katherine racked her brain for a solution. "You can't earn the money somehow?"

Teddie's shoulders slumped in dejection. "I've been trying, but I just can't save fast enough." She looked earnestly into Katherine's eyes. "I know I would be able to make a bunch of money being a model. And there's a big cash prize that I'd get for winning." Her eyes filled. "I could help my dad out if I win, but I can't do anything without a composite."

"Teddie," Katherine said. "This is something you really need to talk to your dad about. I'm just positive if he knew—"

"No!" She responded forcefully. "I can't." Her eyes grew huge as she fixed a horrified gaze on Katherine. "You're not going to tell, are you? You promised."

"Of course I won't," Katherine said, as she fended off a growing uneasiness. More secrets to keep. She frowned and thought for a moment. "Well, isn't there another way you can get the money for your composite? Something you could sell?"

Teddie sank down on the edge of her bed and gazed at her lap. Her voice dropped to a murmur. "The only thing I own that I could sell is Pandora."

Her mother's horse.

The girl's shoulders rose then fell. "I've been thinking about it... selling her, I mean." Her voice fell so low that Katherine could barely hear her. "But she's all I have left of my mom."

Katherine sat down. "Oh, Teddie, I don't think it would be a good idea to sell Pandora. You love her so much. Don't you even want to try to talk to your father about this? At least give him a chance. All this pretending and hiding your feelings is going to come out in another way." As she said the words she felt a twinge of guilt because she hadn't been exactly honest with Jack, either.

Teddie merely clamped her jaw. "I know my dad. He would never understand." She looked up, her face white. "I don't think I can talk about this anymore. I need to finish packing since we're leaving so early in the morning."

Helplessness dragged at Katherine as she walked across the room. She turned at the door. "If you want to talk any-time, I'm just down the hall." The girl nodded, but Kath-erine knew she wouldn't take her up on the offer. Katherine walked back to her own room and closed the door. What she wanted to do was march downstairs immediately, find Jack and tell him everything Teddie had said.

But she had promised.

Well, she thought, there's got to be a way I can let him know and still keep my word to Teddie. She spent the rest of the day working in the office and thinking up subtle ways to let Jack know that something serious was bothering his daughter. At dinner that evening Katherine sat in the center of the long table between a couple of the youngest girls. They had seemed a little homesick, and Katherine wanted to give them some attention. Teddie was unusually quiet and only picked at her food, but Jack didn't seem to notice. He was his usual gregarious self: joking, teasing, popping questions about horse care or competitive strategy. Kath-erine wanted to shout at him, but she had decided on a plan.

Much later, after all the girls had showered and gone to bed, Katherine stood at her window looking toward the barns and the back of the stable property. As soon as she saw a flash of movement in the indoor ring, she slipped quietly down the stairs. When she reached the railing, she stopped and leaned on her elbows until Jack appeared around the far end of the ring. He wasn't working the Phoenix, though. Katherine recognized Paula's horse,

Swain—the one who had stopped in front of the jump and sent the girl flying over his head. The gray gelding was sweating and his breath huffed with every stride. Obviously he'd been worked hard.

When Jack saw her he pulled the horse to a stop. "Hello, gorgeous."

Katherine felt suddenly shy. "Hi. I saw the light and I thought I'd come see you."

Jack smiled broadly. "Lucky me." He dropped the reins on the horses' neck and rested one broad hand on his thigh. "Now how long is it until September?"

Katherine smiled. "About two months, I believe."

Jack frowned. "Actually it's fifty-three days and—" He glanced at his watch "—one hour and eleven minutes. But who's counting?" His gaze trailed over Katherine, and she felt the beginnings of a blush. She had known it was fifty-three days, but she hadn't expected him to keep track.

Jack's brow creased and he urged the horse toward her. Swain dripped foamy sweat and his delicate, cup-shaped nostrils fluttered as he pumped air into his lungs. "Are any of the girls awake? Did they see you come out?"

"No. Well, at least I don't think so."

"Good," he said, brightening. "Things are just getting interesting here."

When he turned Katherine saw a slender rod jammed in the back of his jeans.

"What's that thing?" she called, gesturing at his back.

"What?" Jack had moved almost imperceptibly and Swain picked up an easy canter. "Oh, this. It's my secret weapon." His mouth turned in a wry smile. "Just watch."

She leaned against the rail as Jack and Swain made another gentle circle or two around the ring. Then he turned Swain toward the hog's back set up in the center of the ring—the one Paula had demolished when Swain threw her. A few strides back she saw Jack relax. His legs loosened and his hands fell visibly, giving the horse free rein. Swain dropped his head and one stride away from the fence he gathered himself and slid to a stop.

"Gotcha," Jack said, with a smug grin. He reached around his back and pulled out the rod. It was a short riding crop with a big square of leather at the end. "You stinkpot," he said gruffly. "Now you're gonna get it." She barely saw his arm rise and fall but clearly heard three sharp smacks. The horse snorted in shock and his head flew up. Rolling his eyes wildly he lunged sideways as if trying to leap out from under his rider. Jack sat him as easily.

"Be careful," Katherine called as she clutched the rail.

Jack glanced at her. He was grinning. "Don't worry. Everything's under control."

He turned Swain in a tight circle and headed him back toward the jump. This time the gelding fairly charged at the fence and one stride away from it, he gathered himself and soared over the barrier, clearing it with almost a foot to spare. He landed in a head-shaking gallop on the other side, and the muscles in Jack's forearms stood out as he reined the animal in. For twenty more minutes he cantered Swain around the course. They jumped the stile, the in-and-out, the wall and the hog's back. The horse behaved angelically.

Finally, Jack reined him in to a walk and let the reins fall loose around Swain's neck. "That's better," he said, breathing a little heavily as he walked the horse in a slow circle at Katherine's end of the ring. "He just needed a little special attention, didn't you, you old outlaw. You're not so bad." He patted Swain's neck, and the horse shook his head and flattened his ears. He wore the sullen, irritated look of a naughty boy—caught in the act, scolded and punished.

Jack wagged the short whip right beside the horse's face and Swain rolled his eyes and swung his head away. "You see this?" Jack said and again waved the crop threateningly. "You better be good to Paula at this horse show or you'll really get it. Hear me?" Swain's breath rattled and he shied again.

Katherine smiled at Jack. "So that's what you're doing. Working the meanness out of him."

"Well, sort of. Swain isn't mean, but he's too much horse for Paula. If she had the confidence to ride him aggressively, it would be different, but she's timid. You know, she hangs back. If the animal feels his rider is unsure about jumping, it's a sure bet he's not going to go over the fence." He turned Swain in another circle, still showing him the whip. Swain regarded it with a suspicious, wary eye.

"This little thing," Jack said, holding up the crop, "this is the equivalent of a rolled-up newspaper to a puppy. It's got this piece of leather on the end of it so it makes a loud noise, but it surprised him and hurt his pride more than anything else." Jack reached down and patted Swain's neck again.

"Paula's going to be so pleased that you did this for her."

Jack pulled up and fixed a sudden look on Katherine. "She doesn't know. And you mustn't tell her. And you mustn't tell any of the other kids, either. Once you tell one it always gets back."

"But—"

"Like I said, Paula needs some confidence. If she knows I've been working Swain, it won't do anything but humiliate her. You saw what happened at the lesson last Saturday. I hated excusing her, but she was about to get hurt and she was reinforcing some really bad habits in this horse. I could have hopped up on Swain then, or had Teddie or Judy get on him, but it would just undermine... it would just make Paula feel bad. This way, from now on she's going to find Mr. Swain, here, a little more congenial. If not, we'll just continue his private lessons."

"Won't you get too tired doing this? You know, working all day and then riding so late? You're going to be driving all night to Dallas and all."

He smiled at her. "No, I'm used to it. Besides, I'm too wired to go to sleep for just a couple of hours. I've got to help Hermes start loading up our gear pretty soon." He urged Swain closer to Katherine and she could see the pattern of veins standing out on the sweaty horse's neck and shoulders. "Was there anything special you wanted to talk to me about? Something wrong at the house?"

Katherine shifted from foot to foot. Now that she was with him, all her clever ideas about Teddie's trouble had fled. When he looked at her that way, all she could think about was kissing him and she knew he'd see that thought in her face. Besides, the way Jack gazed down made her feel as if she were being tumble dried. "No," she said. "Not really anything special. But I was wondering if there was anything you wanted me to do while you're gone. Do any of the girls have any standing appointments I should cancel or anything like that? You know how forgetful kids can be. Especially if they're all excited, and this is really important."

Swain shifted restively and Jack's brow furrowed. "There's nothing I can think of."

Katherine made a show of biting her lower lip and frowning. "Doesn't Teddie have some kind of lessons on Saturday?"

Jack's expression grew grim. "Oh, yeah. The modeling thing. But her grandfather will see to that."

"So? Teddie wants to be a model?" Katherine gave her voice a really convincing note of nonchalance. "Isn't that interesting?"

Jack shrugged. "That's what she wants this week. You know how kids are—there's always some nutty idea or other they latch on to. Once she wanted to go to one of those weird camps, you know, where people go and shoot paint guns at each other. Then it was roller blades." He shrugged. "Who knows what's next? Teddie's mother did some modeling and I think that's what got her interested in it." He glanced at his watch. "I better start walking this horse before he gets stiff."

He smiled as he gazed down at Katherine. "I'll be leaving in the small hours and I guess you know you won't get to see me for three and a half days. Think you can handle it?"

Katherine felt a ball of frustration welling up. She wanted to jump up and down and shout, Pay attention! This is important! But instead she just smiled wanly. "We'll just have to pick up the shattered pieces and go on, I guess."

Jack laughed, and at that moment Hermes appeared at the gate, holding a saddled and bridled horse. Although Swain wasn't small, the creature pawing the ground at the end of lead line rose like a black avalanche of muscle and brute animal masculinity.

The Phoenix.

When Katherine looked at the animal, an uncomfortable twinge skittered along her spine and she grimaced at the stallion.

His white, ruined eye was turned toward them, and Katherine knew she saw an assessing, threatening glare. It appeared to her that he was calculating his chances. She could just see the dark wheels and cogs turning. How much time would it take to cover the ground separating him from Swain? Could he do it before Hermes dragged him away or Jack beat him off? The bad eye shifted and its white scar wobbled like a sickle moon on black water while the pale, serpentine stripe sliding down the stallion's face seemed to undulate with a cold life of its own.

When Katherine looked over at Jack, she saw him smiling. He actually seemed pleased to see the brute. She shuddered.

Jack glanced at her. "See you Sunday."

She nodded and turned toward the house. Since Hermes was waiting, there was nothing to do but walk back.

On Sunday, Jack and the girls returned from the show full of good news. Jack had sold two of his prospects for outrageous sums. Teddie had been named champion in her division, and Paula had taken reserve champion honors. Swain had behaved like an angel.

Suzanne Sifara had done so well that her parents decided she was really serious about riding. They decided it was time to buy her a good, gentle horse—so they did.

Pandora.

Chapter Seven

Monday morning Katherine stood looking for her favorite cup at the kitchen cabinet. The tantalizing aroma of fresh coffee filled the room and the mugs rattled and clinked as she pushed each aside. Jack sat at the table behind her, finishing his breakfast. She glanced over her shoulder at him. "It's hard to believe Teddie sold Pandora," she said conversationally.

Jack looked up from the sports page and leaned back in his chair. "I know." He rocked forward and scooped the final spoonful of cereal from his bowl. "I guess since the mare's not leaving the barn, things won't be that different for her, but it sure surprised me." He looked up thoughtfully at Katherine. "Maybe Teddie's more serious about this modeling thing than I thought."

Katherine tried to sound casual—to keep the urgency from her tone. She turned toward him. "It sure seems that way to me. Maybe you ought to talk to her about it."

Jack shrugged. "Maybe so. But the mare is... was hers. I s'pose I shouldn't interfere in her decision." He glanced down at his watch and turned back to the article he was reading.

Katherine pursed her lips in frustration. This wasn't getting anywhere, and she almost decided to go ahead and break Teddie's confidence when Jack suddenly snapped the newspaper, folded it and scraped his chair across the floor. "Well, I better get out there. I need to work Phoenix."

When he stood he turned toward Katherine and gazed at her as if he'd only just seen her. When her cheeks began to burn, she had to look away, back toward the kitchen cabinet. She had seen that look in his eyes twice before: that rainy morning in the loft and again on the afternoon he'd kissed her in the office. When she finally found the mug, she almost knocked two more off as she pulled it out. The back of her neck seemed to prickle, and she glanced back at him. "What is it? Why are you looking at me that way?"

He didn't respond right away, but the corner of his mouth lifted. "Are all the girls outside?"

Fine hairs rose on Katherine's nape. "Mmmm" was the only response she could muster. The butterfly flutter once again erupted just under her sternum, worked its way down and fanned out in quivering waves. "Jack?" She glanced left, then right, to see if someone might be wandering around in the house.

He crossed slowly to where she stood, stopped scant inches away and began to lift his hands. Then he hesitated, squeezed his eyes closed and dropped his palms to the edge of the sink. When he opened his eyes, he stared resolutely out the kitchen window. "I owe you an apology," he said softly.

"Apology?"

"For the other day. For the way I behaved in the office last week." He tipped his head toward her and smiled ruefully. "For the way I'm thinking of behaving right now." He looked at her and his mouth turned up a little. "You just look so gorgeous standing there. I really like your hair down and..." He winced as if in pain and looked out the window again. "I was, uh, overcome. Anyway, it won't happen again." He smiled down. "At least until our situation changes. I hope I haven't... I mean, I don't want to make you feel uncomfortable around me."

Katherine's skin warmed and she had to look down at the cup she held. "Oh, but I don't," she murmured. "Well, not too much. I admit part of me wishes things were different, but I love working here, too. This is a life I never imagined—the kids, the animals. It's so different from anything I've ever done."

He turned around, folded his arms across his chest and leaned against the sink. "And that's another thing. You know, I don't think I've told how much I appreciate everything you've done here—the books, the way you handle the girls. You make life here better in so many ways I...even though I may not say it, I want you to know how much it means having you here. Knowing there's someone I can trust to take care of things. To watch my back." A trace of humor returned to his eyes. "And if I survive this summer, I'd like a chance to court you like a gentleman rather than a crazed caveman."

"You know," she said, as her voice dropped shyly, "sometimes I can hardly wait for fall to get here, and then sometimes I can't imagine going back to that other way of life. You know—offices, suits. All that."

"I know," he murmured. "In September you'll move away and I'll hate that, but then we'll be able to see each other in another way." He laughed. "Funny, isn't it?" he asked with a glint in his eye. "We've been living together for more than a month and I've only kissed you twice."

"Jack," Katherine said, and glanced around in horror, in case anyone might have heard, "will you please behave yourself." She punched him lightly on the arm. When her fingers contacted the warm flesh of his biceps, she felt an almost electric shock. The surge of energy traveled through her arm and when it reached her torso, expanded in waves that made her breath grow shallow and reedy. "Oh," she said. "Oh."

Their eyes locked and Katherine could see he'd felt the same thing. The kitchen seemed suddenly very quiet and very warm and the sound of distant pounding slowly filled the room. Katherine realized it was her heart. She tilted her head back to look into his amber eyes, and the pounding increased until it sounded like booted feet on boards.

It was booted feet on boards.

When the handle of the back door rattled, the cup slipped from Katherine's hand, clattered on the floor and broke. "Oh, damn," she said and stepped to the side. Away from the sink. Away from Jack. She heard him mutter something irritably as he turned toward the door.

"There you are," Judy said cheerfully. "The girls are warmed up in the ring, and I'm through with the beginner lesson so I thought I'd cool off in the pool."

"Great idea," Jack said, with scarcely a trace of aggravation. "How'd the lesson go?"

"Fine," she replied. "No broken bones to report." She smiled at Katherine as she passed through the kitchen. "Well, I'm going to go change."

"Maybe I'll join you later," Katherine said, hoping she wasn't blushing or looking as guilty as she felt.

At the archway leading to the family room, Judy turned around, her face slightly clouded. "By the way, Jack. I saw the Rolls in the parking lot, and Teddie's not in the ring. Do you want me to go find her?"

Jack's jaw tightened instantly and his eyes grew hard and narrow. "No," he said tersely. "I'll find her. You enjoy your swim."

Katherine set the broken pieces of the cup on the counter. She still hoped to find a way to subtly encourage Jack to talk with Teddie. "I think I'll go with you, Jack, and watch you ride."

Jack's expression softened slightly. "Of course," he said, and then the kitchen echoed with the sound of Judy's booted feet thundering up the stairs.

As she followed Jack out of the house and across the porch, neither spoke. He seemed preoccupied and pensive, and Katherine couldn't think of a way to bring up Teddie's conflict that would sound uncontrived. She was walking slightly ahead of him, and when they entered the coolness of the barn she turned to face him. "Which way?"

"Let's try Pandora's stall," Jack replied. "That's where she usually hangs out."

He led the way through the barn, and just as they reached the last aisle, Katherine heard Teddie's laugh, high and musical.

"What'd I say?" Jack asked.

When they turned the corner, Katherine saw that Teddie wasn't alone. Standing with her in front of Pandora's stall was a tall white-haired man. He wore plain soft slacks and a casual sport coat, but even at a distance his clothes looked expensive and impeccably tailored. Despite his white hair he had startling good looks and an aura of power and elegance. Statesmanlike, Katherine thought. Important. She turned to ask Jack if the man was Teddie's grandfather, but the look on his face silenced her.

His expression reminded her of a time-lapse sequence she had once seen on public television—a nature piece about a forest pond caught at the cusp of winter. Ghostly white fingers of ice had darted over the surface, trapping and suffocating the life beneath. The reeds bent into the black water and died. The water stilled.

"Jack?"

He didn't seem to hear her. Didn't see her. He walked stiffly toward Teddie and her companion. A tentacle of fear slithered through Katherine. *He's going to strike that man.* She had never in her life witnessed violence, but it was unmistakably here—shimmering in the air like an evil spirit. Quivering just beneath the surface like bad blood.

The man turned their way, his face grave but impassive. Teddie looked around, saw them and blanched.

"Dad. Hi, Katherine." Her voice was high-pitched and strained.

In the awkward silence, the man looked inquisitively at Katherine.

"Ka—Katherine," Teddie said, her gaze darting wildly between her father and the older man, "this is my grandfather, Brooks. Edwin Grosvenor Brooks. This is Katherine Hanshaw, Granddad."

His smile revealed perfectly even teeth; the faintest twinkle appeared in his hazel eyes. The same color as Teddie's, Katherine thought.

He gave her a firm, warm handshake. "Katherine," he said. "I'm so pleased to meet you. Teddie speaks of you highly and often."

"I'm glad to meet you, Mr. Brooks," she replied, feeling more profoundly awkward by the minute.

Brooks turned to face Jack and held out his hand. "Jack," he said simply.

Katherine watched Jack's icy gaze travel from Brooks's face and down his outstretched arm. From the look he gave the older man's proffered hand, Jack could have been studying a snake he'd just found in his bed. For three slow heartbeats Brooks left his hand extended, then slowly his arm fell back. The expression on his face didn't change, but Katherine was certain she saw the sadness in his somber eyes deepen.

Jack didn't say a word but nailed Teddie with a cold glare, then turned on his heel and walked back the way they'd come. Katherine looked helplessly from Teddie to her grandfather. "I—I don't know..."

Mr. Brooks smiled gently. "I'm awfully sorry about this, Katherine. Teddie, I shouldn't have come back here. I'd better go—"

"Please wait here, Granddad," Teddie said. Her voice quavered and Katherine heard the raw edge of tears. "I've got to go talk to him."

Katherine reached toward her. "Are you sure, Teddie? Maybe it would be better if—"

"No. Just wait here, please. Okay?"

Teddie didn't wait for an answer but ran down the aisle after her father.

For a long, uncomfortable moment Katherine stared after Teddie. Then she turned around. "I don't know what to say, Mr. Brooks."

"Brooks," he said. "Just call me Brooks. Everyone does." Then he smiled at her. A kind, wistful smile. "Actually, I don't blame him at all. I really shouldn't be in the barn. We have an unspoken understanding. Don't look so horrified, dear. I believe he's shown remarkable restraint." Pandora bumped his arm with her nose, and he reached over and absently stroked her neck. "If positions were reversed, I'm not sure I would have been able to resist the urge to hit someone." He smiled ruefully. "Me, of course."

Now Katherine was really embarrassed. She didn't know how to react. How much to let on that she knew. "Brooks," she said tentatively, "this is really hard for me. You see, I've heard that you and Jack had some conflicts."

He laughed quietly. "Conflicts. What a lovely euphemism. I suggest you abandon your career as a chaperon and consider the diplomatic corps." The smile gradually faded from his face. "I'm sure someone here at the stable has told you how I tried to get custody of Teddie. Oh, I see I've embarrassed you. I apologize for my bluntness, but at this advanced age I've learned not to equivocate."

"I'm not embarrassed," Katherine said, and then realized she was wringing her hands. "Not much, I mean."

Brooks turned back to Pandora and smoothed her forelock between her eyes. "Jack and I got off to a terrible start more than fifteen years ago. You see, he was exactly the kind of young man you'd love for a son, but hate for your daughter." He glanced at Katherine. "If you know what I mean."

"Yes, I think I do."

"Anyway, I hope we haven't gotten you too wedged in the middle of our family troubles." He fell silent for a moment, then looked over, his head slightly tilted. "Teddie thinks you're wonderful, you know."

Katherine smiled. "Teddie is a special person. Really... well, spirited."

Despite all that she'd heard about Brooks and the way she felt about Jack, Katherine found it hard to dislike Teddie's grandfather. He had an engaging air of sadness tinged with humor, elegance and kindliness. Katherine assumed him to be in his late fifties or early sixties. The white hair made him appear older from a distance, but up close you could see his skin was still firm and fine, and that most of the hard lines on his face came from knitting his brow—as if he'd spent years in consternation or deep thought.

He smiled down at her. "If you think Teddie's spirited, you should have met her mother. Blaize was the most vital, alive person I ever knew. Hardheaded as a Yankee mule. We fought constantly."

Katherine reached up to pat Pandora's neck. The mare let her eyelids drift downward, blissfully luxuriating in the attention. "Teddie and Jack seem to have their disagreements, too, but I think that goes with the territory when you're raising a teenager."

Brooks nodded thoughtfully. "I certainly hope he does a better job than I did." He looked Katherine square in the eyes. "All this trouble—between Jack and me—it's entirely my doing, you know. I violently disapproved of him for Blaize. Actually, I violently disapproved of almost everything she wanted to do. It always seemed to interfere with the wonderful life I picked out for her. After she died in the accident I still blamed Jack. Stupid of me, but I was demented with grief. I've come to understand that when I was trying to take Teddie, what I really wanted was a chance to rear Blaize again—to do a better job." He grimaced. "I probably would have made another complete mess of things."

For the first time in her life Katherine saw real grief, not the kind of sadness eased by mourning, but the undiminishing kind that becomes part of a person. "I'm sure you loved her very much."

"Oh, I did. I just wanted to make all her choices for her. Actually," he said, giving Pandora a final pat, "I believe my daughter had been . . . gone for about two years when I finally decided to let her grow up."

"Everybody makes mistakes, Brooks."

"So I hear," he murmured. "So I hear." He looked down at Katherine and narrowed his eyes slightly. Obviously considering something. "There is, I believe, something you should know. Jack knows it, or thinks he does." His expression was ironic and sad at the same time. "He is perfectly justified to feel the way he does about me. You see, as far as Theodora is concerned, I still intend to get exactly what I want, and he knows it."

Katherine's jaw dropped open. For the first time she saw something in the older man's level gaze—an iron-willed determination. Relentless, maybe ruthless. "I—I—"

"Oh, don't look so green, dear," Brooks said, and the twinkle returned to his eyes. "I haven't said what it is that I want, have I?" He took a quick breath. "Well, I suppose I'd better wait for Teddie at the car."

"Shall I walk out with you?"

"I think not, Katherine. Consorting with the enemy and all. But thank you very much for offering. I can see you're spirited, too."

They shook hands and Katherine stood by Pandora's stall while he walked slowly down the aisle. Despite what he'd said, Katherine couldn't help but like him. *"I haven't said what it is that I want, have I?"* He walked a little stiffly, she thought. Just like Jack.

At the corner he turned as if he'd just remembered something. "Teddie needs her friends. She's very slow to form attachments, and I know you mean a great deal to her. You, of course, aren't nearly old enough, but you're the closest thing to a mother she's had in a long time." He lifted his hand. "Goodbye, now."

Katherine waited by Pandora's stall. In the large enclosure next to the mare, Phoenix moved restlessly. Katherine stayed away from his door and didn't look through the bars to see him.

When Jack returned he still seemed wary, angry. His gaze darted left and right, almost as if he were inventorying—making sure Brooks hadn't made off with anything valuable.

Katherine smiled. It felt utterly fake. "Hi."

He nodded. "I'm sorry you had to see that."

"I'm not." She stood aside while he entered Phoenix's stall, bridled the stallion and put his halter on again. When he brought the horse out and cross-tied him in the aisle, Katherine sat yoga-style on the tack trunk in front of Pandora's stall. "Can I talk to you about something?"

Jack's jaw tightened and the expression around his eyes grew hard. "Of course, Katherine, but first I'm going to talk to you about something." He brushed the stallion with long, sweeping strokes, and the horse's head nodded with each pass of the stiff boar's hair brush. "I know you've heard plenty about me and Blaize and Brooks. Stable gossip is as common as stable flies, but the truth is Brooks and I hated each other on sight. Sometimes I think Blaize and I might not even have gotten married except for his constant interference. Anyway, our marriage was pretty much of a disaster, but we stayed together—mostly for Teddie's sake."

"Jack, you don't have to—"

He silenced her with a glance. "After the accident, the glue holding the marriage together just, well, just unglued. That was pretty tough. But then Blaize died. I had some setbacks and wound up in a wheelchair again. Hell, I was still trying to learn to walk when that old..." He seemed to struggle for a suitable expletive. "That old *man* tried to take my little girl away. He took her for a visit one weekend and just never brought her back."

He stopped and faced her, gesturing with the brush. "Think about it, Katherine. Months of lying on your back, staring at a water-spotted ceiling and wondering if you'll ever stand up again. Much less ride. Or run. Or make love. You say to yourself, How am I going to make a living when I am like this? Then some old devil tries to use his money to steal away the most important thing in your life. Your little girl. Your baby." He turned back and resumed currying his horse. His voice was more quiet. More dangerous. "Would you just forgive? Would you forget?"

"He's sorry now."

"He lost," Jack spat out.

Katherine could see there was no point in arguing with him, so she watched unhappily while he finished grooming and saddling his horse. When he led Phoenix to the indoor ring she sat on the rail and watched him ride. There were times when she enjoyed the thundering hooves on the sawdust and the faint creak of saddle leather. Jack seemed totally absorbed in his work. In only moments the man and the animal wore the light sheen of exertion.

These moments defined them both, Katherine thought—powerful, iron-willed masculinity at the very apex of strength. Each was scarred—damaged, even—but neither would ever be bowed. Or even really tame.

When they started jumping, Katherine left the ring and walked back to the house. She knew Jack would have Hermes set the fences really high. He always did when he was disturbed about something. Although Jack was the most capable of riders and Phoenix almost supernaturally athletic, something about the way the two of them flew toward the threatening configurations of rails and standards always made her sick with foreboding. She probably would never be able to watch.

At the pool Judy lay stretched out on a lounge chair. Katherine took the seat next to her but didn't speak right away.

"What's up?" Judy asked.

Katherine told her what had happened.

Judy raised her sunglasses. "Don't get in the middle of it," she said. "This is one place where Jack really digs his heels in. He can't stand Brooks."

"I know. It seems so sad for Teddie, though. For all of them, really. Teddie has hardly any family at all and the two people she loves most in the world don't even speak."

Judy sat up and looked at Katherine earnestly. "Not your problem, buddy. I'd stay out of it. Jack really gets wound up if you interfere in his relationship with Teddie or do *anything* that wastes his time. He always says he figured out what was most important when he spent all those months flat on his back."

Katherine gazed out toward the barn. "That whole time—Jack's accident, Blaize's death. The fighting over Teddie. It's hard to think of anything more that could have gone wrong."

Judy nodded. "It was terrible. Jack will never be the same. Physically, at least. It really gets to him, too, so he pushes himself. If he's tired or if he gets stressed out, his muscles seize up and he starts limping."

The younger woman leaned over and picked up a soda can. "Empty," she said and screwed her face in irritation. "Let's go get something to drink."

A music video channel blared on the television set, so they walked through to the kitchen. They took cold drinks from the refrigerator, and Katherine sat next to Judy and traced a pattern in the dampness on the side of her can.

Paula walked into the kitchen and joined them. "What're ya'll doing?"

Judy tugged one of the girl's long red pigtails. "I'm giving Katherine an ancient history lesson, Miss Nosy Parker."

"How did it happen?" Katherine asked. "The accident, I mean?"

Judy shrugged slightly. "Well, Jack was riding Magic Knight in the Austin show. It was a grand prix class."

"What kind of class?" Katherine asked.

"A grand prix. Huge fences, huge money and lots of pressure. They made the first few fences just fine, but the horse was really fighting him. Then, just when they turned toward the wall, the martingale broke." She pointed to her chin. "The martingale holds the horse's head in place. You know, keeps him from throwing his head up high in the air and running away with you."

She squeezed her eyes closed. "When he rounded on the jump he was obviously out of control. He stuck his head out and charged. It was more of an attack than an approach to a jump. When the horse was about four strides back, someone yelled, 'He's getting in there all wrong,' but by then it was too late. He'd already committed himself to jump."

Paula's eyes were huge and she leaned forward as if she were hearing the story for the first time. "They said everything went quiet. Dead quiet."

Judy sighed. "It did. The horse knew what he'd done—the mistake he'd made. He really grunted when he left the ground. He gave it all he had, but he just took off too far back. At the crest of his jump, he started scrambling and then he slammed into the wall. Pieces of it splintered and flew everywhere—the plywood painted to look like bricks, the pole across the top, even the flowerpots at the base of the jump just exploded from the impact." She rubbed her forehead as if remembering an old pain.

"When he was falling, he started twisting in the air. I remember you could see the glint of his steel shoes when he turned over. Someone screamed and there was this horrible smashing noise when they hit the ground. It happened right in front of me. The most horrible thing of all was . . . well, the last thing you heard was this one sickening crack." She shuddered. "Now we know that was Jack's spine snapping."

Katherine covered her mouth with her hand. "Oh, no," she murmured against her fingers.

Judy turned her soda can in her fingers. "Magic got up almost right away. His face was really cut up and there was blood everywhere. I heard later that Jack was conscious the whole time. He knew it was bad. He couldn't feel anything. Of course, they wouldn't let anyone in the ring but paramedics, so none of us could go see him."

Paula's eyes were huge emerald disks and her bright eyebrows formed startled arches. "My mother told me Teddie's mom didn't want to see him. They said she was so terrified when they told her what happened she wouldn't go to the ring."

"I don't know if that's true or not," Judy said skeptically. "Anyway, it *was* horrible. They told Jack he'd never ride again and he'd be lucky if he ever stood without a walker." She gave Katherine a wry smile. "Obviously they were wrong, but it was really awful."

Katherine tried to imagine it as she gazed out the kitchen window at the square of white summer sky, framed by gently billowing curtains. The shattered wood and bone. The shattered lives. She sighed and glanced at Judy, silent and deep in her own memories. "What ever happened to the horse? Did they destroy it?"

Judy's brows knit. "What horse?"

"You know, Magic Knight."

Judy gave her a puzzled look. "Well, the last time I looked he was just fine."

"You've seen him? He's around here?"

"Of course." Realization flickered in Judy's eyes. "Oh, of course you don't know. Jack bought him. You know, no matter what anyone calls him, that horse will always be Magic Knight to me. Actually, Jack used the last of his money..."

Judy's voice seemed to fade and Katherine was almost overcome by dread. *Jack bought him.*

Judy smiled happily as she talked. "So after everything that happened Jack decided to change his name. You know, to the Phoenix."

Chapter Eight

"I can't believe you didn't tell me that Magic Knight was the Phoenix. Why didn't you tell me?" Katherine's voice quivered. She jumped down from the railing into the ring and walked right up to where Jack sat on Phoenix. The stallion flattened his ears and ground his bit between his teeth. Jack's face was impassive.

"I can't believe you didn't know. Everyone knows. Why are you so upset?"

"How can you ask that? That..." Torn between anxiety and disgust, she nodded at the horse. "That *animal* injured you terribly. He tried to kill Ishmael. He tried to hurt me. He's a menace, Jack. You should get rid of him." She shook her head and gazed up into his eyes. "Why would you even want to have him around after what he did to you? After what he cost you? It's... it's unnatural."

The corner of Jack's mouth turned up, but he didn't seem amused. "Funny," he said. "You're not the first person who's said that. Some people seem to think I have some kind of weird attachment to him, like I'm trying to prove something, but that's just not true. I need to keep this horse until the end of the summer so plenty of people can see what he can do. I need every penny I can scrape together to make my note, and if I sell Phoenix prematurely I'd be cheating myself. I might even lose the barn. You've been doing the books. You can see that."

"But he's dangerous, Jack. Something bad is going to happen. I just know it," Katherine said. "There are other horses you can sell, you know, to make up the difference in the note."

"Katherine," Jack said, his voice edgy with irritation, "this is my business. My livelihood. I need to make every bit of money I can to keep my stable and be able to buy horses. It's true that I was riding Phoenix when I was hurt, but it's also true that I bought him very reasonably and I'm going to sell him for plenty." He adjusted his reins and his voice grew softer. "It means a lot to me that you care."

"But wait a minute," Katherine persisted. "The two you sold at Dallas brought in more than you thought and you still have others. You've been buying and selling horses all summer. I'm sure if he's half as good as you say he is, you could get enough for him to make up the note."

Jack shifted in his saddle and winced slightly.

"You see?" Katherine accused, pointing at his back. "You're in pain now. If it wasn't for him you'd be fine." She reached up and rested her hand on his knee. Touching him was probably taking a chance—just feeling the warmth of him seeping through his jeans sent darts of strange fire sizzling through her—but she wanted to make him see. She would plead if she had to. Even cling to him. "Please get rid of him, Jack. I have a bad feeling about this."

He gazed down and gave her a wry smile. "Katherine, just relax. In the first place you're overestimating both this horse and me. I'm not a kid anymore. I'd be sore no matter what horse I'd been riding. And besides, no man who makes his living in professional sports gets to be my age without aches and pains."

There was one more thing she could try. "Jack," she said softly. "I've been dealing with the people at Farm and Home, you know, paying the monthly interest on your note.

They've been awfully nice. I'm sure you could get an extension if you—"

"No," he snapped, his expression hard. "You don't know them like I do, Katherine. They may act like they want to help, but they're just waiting for an opportunity to take the barn. Believe me. I've known them for years. I know how they work."

Katherine took her hand away and fought back tears of frustration. "I guess I'll go back inside, then." She turned to face him. "If you need me in the morning, you can find me in Ishmael's stall. Since Phoenix attacked him he's almost quit eating, but sometimes he'll eat for me."

Jack's face twisted irritably. "Katherine," he said. "You're just not being reasonable—"

She didn't wait to hear the rest of what he said but turned and left. "Stupid man," she muttered as she turned the handle of the back door. She paused. Stupid *man?* Wait a minute. I'm the one who's not thinking. She pressed her lips together in a tight smile. First thing tomorrow morning, she thought, I'm phoning David Wiley and telling him that Jack's best horse is for sale now. If someone makes a big enough offer, Jack will have to sell Phoenix—that is, if he's really serious about keeping the stable. And, of course, that is his number-one consideration. He said so himself.

She smiled, feeling clever and pleased with herself. Of course she'd have to wait until Jack took Phoenix to a horse show. If someone just appeared at the stable and offered tens of thousands of dollars for a horse that hadn't been shown in years, Jack would get suspicious. Still, he was bound to take Phoenix on the road soon. After all, he'd been training the animal all summer. Now she just had to be patient and wait for him to take the monster to a horse show.

"Mr. Wiley, this is Katherine Hanshaw." She gripped the phone tightly and twisted the cord with her free hand.

"Katherine," he said. "What a nice surprise. How are you?"

"Just fine. How was your vacation?"

"Fine. Fine. Since it's August, Cozumel is almost completely deserted, which suited Vickie just fine. She and the boys went snorkeling, and I did some fishing." His voice changed. Grew slightly guarded. "Is there some news out there at the stable? Jack did go to the show, didn't he? I told...I mean, I know the bank is sending an agent to Beaumont with the intention of buying horses."

Katherine listened for a moment, just to make sure no one was standing in the hallway. "That's why I'm calling. Jack just took a couple of beginners with him because Beaumont is not an A-rated show, but he's been working a new jumper quite a bit lately—a stallion named Phoenix. Anyway, the reason I'm phoning is because this is the horse that Jack is counting on to sell to make his note and give him some breathing room. Since I've been doing the books for a couple of months now, I've got a pretty good idea how much Jack needs to get for him." Katherine mentioned the figure and squeezed her eyes shut. She couldn't imagine anyone spending that kind of money for any horse, much less a horrible beast like Phoenix.

Wiley didn't hesitate. "Hmm. Well, I guess I'd better make some calls."

"There is one more thing." Katherine spoke more rapidly, feeling more apprehensive that someone might overhear her. "You see, the word isn't really out that Phoenix is for sale, but I know he's Jack's most valuable horse, even though he hasn't been shown in years. So what I'm saying is whoever makes an offer for him will have to be a little, uh—"

"Discreet," he interjected. "Of course I understand. Well, thanks for letting me know. Oh, and Katherine, before I let you go, I want to tell you that we're very happy with what you've done, your cooperation and your loyalty." There was a long, silent moment. "We're looking forward to having you back at the end of the month, and my directors want me to assure you that your bonus is going to be generous."

"Thanks, Mr. Wiley," Katherine said, feeling more uncomfortable by the moment. "I appreciate that. I'd better go now—most of the girls are here in the house."

After saying goodbye, Katherine sat in the office for a few moments waiting for her nerves to settle. She was torn between an irrational urge to tell Jack everything, and the certain knowledge that he'd be livid with her for not being honest with him. Still, she would feel completely vindicated if she could do something to get Phoenix out of the barn. From the moment she found out that he was the same horse who'd hurt Jack, a sense of dread had settled around her. She wanted the animal gone. The sooner the better. Even if it meant deceiving Jack.

All that day, Katherine watched for Jack's truck to return pulling the horse trailer without Phoenix in it. She practiced what she would say. How surprised and delighted she would be to hear that Phoenix had sold so easily. And for such a large price.

She was standing in the kitchen gazing out the window when Teddie walked in. She wore a man's white T-shirt, loose-fitting khaki shorts and flip-flops. Even dressed so casually, she could have posed for the cover of a New York fashion magazine.

Katherine sighed and resolved to start aerobics again. "Hi, Teddie. Anything new about the contest?"

Teddie shook her head. "Not yet. They're supposed to notify the winner by phone the last weekend in August."

"Just a few weeks. You must be on pins and needles."

Teddie frowned. "Yeah. The only thing is that's the weekend of the Austin Show. I haven't told Jack that I won't be able to go, but I want to be home to get the call."

"Is there something special about this show?"

Teddie's mouth skewed. "Yeah. It's a really important show—the last one of the summer—and Jack'll need lots of help. I hope he's not too upset with me." She shrugged. "But this is probably the most important day of my life. My whole future could depend on this."

Although Katherine felt Teddie was overestimating the impact of the contest on her life, she didn't want to minimize Teddie's feelings. She merely nodded. "I know how you feel about this—what you've sacrificed to get this far." She dropped her voice a little. "You know, I think you've been awfully brave about having to sell Pandora. I know it was probably the hardest thing you've ever had to do."

Teddie's eyes grew huge for a moment but then she dropped her gaze. "Yeah, um, well. She's staying here at the barn, and I can still ride her whenever I like and Suzanne is really sweet to her." She rambled on for a few more moments but never really looked Katherine in the eye again.

Poor little thing, Katherine thought. She's being so grown up about this. When Teddie walked back into the living room, Katherine went outside and sat on the deck. She spent the afternoon trying to read magazines while watching for Jack and the others to return.

Just before dark she heard the familiar crunch of tires on gravel and the intestinal grumble of Jack's truck. Katherine did her best to appear nonchalant as she walked briskly to the large barn. When Jack climbed out the truck, Hermes walked to the back of the trailer to unhook the latch and drop the gangway.

Jack looked up and smiled. "Hi, gorgeous." He pitched his voice low. "You got some sun today, didn't you?"

"A little," she replied, as she crossed her arms. "My boss was away all day, so I hung out by the pool."

He shook his head. "It's hard to find good help."

She faked a swat at him. "How'd it go in Beaumont?"

He grinned. "Great. Lisa and Becky are getting better and better."

Katherine heard the hesitant sound of a horse backing down the wooden walkway from the trailer. She turned to see which horse Hermes was unloading first—Becky's mare, or Lisa's white pony. Instead, a flash of ebony tail appeared, a powerfully muscled neck. A white, ruined eye.

"Oh," Katherine said. "Oh." She looked back at Jack, who was smiling broadly.

"Phoenix was champion in the Open Jumper Division," he said, obviously unaware of how disappointed Katherine was. "We blew them away." He looked down at her. "Well? Say congratulations."

"Oh, of course. Congratulations. I... Isn't that great," Katherine said without enthusiasm.

"Yeah," Jack said. "Just wait until Austin. I'd better help get these animals put up." He gazed at Katherine for a long moment. "Thanks for coming out. It means a lot to me." He stared at her mouth. "I missed you today. Every time one of the girls did something right I found myself looking over my shoulder. Finally realized I was looking for you."

Katherine wanted to put her arms around him and pull his strong mouth down on hers. Since she couldn't she tried to communicate everything she felt through her eyes. He gazed down at her, and she knew he'd understood what she couldn't say. He took a short breath and glanced up as Hermes led Phoenix toward the stable. "If everything goes like I plan at the Austin show, on September first I'd like to take you to Tony's or the Rainbow Lodge. Anywhere you'd like to go as long as it's quiet and expensive and has nice dark corners and no kids or horses."

Though the sight of the stallion shattered the closeness of the moment, Katherine smiled as brightly as she could. "Sounds good to me."

Hermes gave Jack the stallion's lead line, and Katherine waited while Jack led the stallion away and Hermes unloaded the other horses. In only moments the girls arrived in another car with their parents. Katherine visited with them and was properly enthusiastic about their success. Some of the other girls came out to hear the details of the show. As soon as she could slip away without being obvious, Katherine went into the office and phoned David Wiley at home.

"Mr. Wiley, it's Katherine. I'm sorry to bother you at home again, but Jack just came back and he had Phoenix with him. Do you know why your investor didn't make an offer?"

"But he did, Katherine." His voice was sharp. Aggravated. "As a matter of fact, he even offered more than you suggested. Apparently Jack didn't want to sell just yet."

"What?"

"That's right. He said there was one more horse show that he intended to take the animal to. The one in Austin. Apparently the horse isn't for sale until September."

Once again dread settled around Katherine. *Why would he want to keep that animal instead of selling him now? Why would Jack pass up the chance to sell him? Why?* But no matter how much she wanted to know, she couldn't ask. She spent the rest of the evening trying to act attentive to the girls' stories about the show. If Jack noticed that she was pensive, he didn't mention it.

The following afternoon Katherine knelt in the hay next to Ishmael. He was lying down and barely blinked when she reached over to smear the salve on his neck. The long, jagged strips Phoenix had gouged from his neck and shoulders had healed, but the hair had never grown back on the ugly, sickle-shaped teeth marks along the top of his neck. Katherine felt an almost giddy rage building inside her. That monster, she thought furiously. That devil. *You don't understand, Katherine. He's a stallion.* She sighed and shook her head, trying to dispel the frustration she felt. Gently patting Ishmael's bruised neck, she crooned to him. "He'll be gone soon. Gone forever. And good riddance, too."

Ishmael didn't respond to her voice or her hands. His dark, liquid eyes seemed dull and he appeared listless and dazed. The combination of being traumatized by Phoenix and then rejected by his terrified mother had shocked his system terribly. Although Jack assured her he would snap out of it eventually, as far as Katherine could see, Ishmael's body might be healing but his spirit would never be the same.

"Oh, well," she said aloud, gently smoothing Ishmael's wispy mane. "You're safe in here."

She screwed the top back on the jar but felt reluctant to leave the colt. He seemed so desolate. So abandoned. His hay bedding was fresh and smelled sweet, and the barn was still and quiet. Katherine settled into herself more comfortably and breathed in the good clean smell of new straw and liniment. Lessons and feeding were over for the morning and a drowsy tranquillity hung in the air. Her lids grew heavy and she sat back against the wall. This was the time of day the stable dogs napped—stretched out in cool places with their noses and paws twitching as they dreamed their dog dreams. The jays and mockingbirds sat fluffed and sleepy-eyed in their nests until the heat of the day passed, and even the flies seemed to buzz more lazily and loop casually away from swishing tails. Although Ishmael's stall was in the busiest area—by the doors and next to the telephone—the barn seemed deserted. The stillness and calm of the summer afternoon stole over Katherine.

Ishmael stretched out and sighed a shuddering sigh, his gangly colt legs and knobby knees making a dark contrast on the yellow hay. Katherine rested her hand on his neck and let her eyes drift closed. Just for a minute, she thought. Then I'll get up and go finish my filing.

She wasn't certain how long she'd dozed when something woke her. Ishmael stood by his water bucket, his fuzzy tail twitching as he restlessly bumped the float in the water.

"I know, Granddad, but it was the only way, really. You know how important this is to me."

Katherine rubbed her eyes. People were talking just outside Ishmael's stall. Teddie. Her voice was low, urgent. And someone else.

"You know I don't like this at all, Teddie," a masculine voice said. "In the first place I still have a hard time thinking anyone would believe you'd sell your mother's horse—"

"Of course. I can't believe anyone would think I could really sell her, either, but it was the only way I could get the money for my pictures and the composite. You know he would never let you loan me the money."

"I know, sweetpea. I wish he would, but you know I don't blame him. I feel terrible about this."

"I feel bad about it, too, Granddad, but just wait. It'll go just like I said. I'll win the contest and then Suzanne's dad will say he wants to sell Pandora back and buy Megan' pony. Suzanne wanted that pony all along and she wa pretty disappointed when they bought Pandora instead. S Suzanne will be happy, I'll get Pandora back and when I wi the contest my dad'll feel different about me modeling, too He'll see that I'm really serious."

"I hope so, sweetpea."

Katherine sat up slowly and blinked as the implication o their words sunk in. Everything fell into place. No wonde Teddie was so philosophical about selling Pandora.

Teddie and Brooks had faked the sale of the mare. Whe Jack found out he would skin her alive. And what abou Brooks?

"Well, I'd better go now, sweetie. Your dad will be bac soon and we don't want another scene, do we? Do you nee to go saddle up now or can you walk me to my car?"

"I can walk you to your car, Granddad. Don't worry Everything's going to be okay."

As Katherine's head cleared, accusation slid through he conscience. *They don't know I'm here. What I'm hearing* My gosh, she thought, I've got to let them know. She stoo so quickly that she startled Ishmael. He bleated nervousl and darted from one corner to the other of the box stall "Easy, baby," she said in a deliberately loud voice. "It' okay." She patted him briskly and fumbled with the clips o the gait. She heard the sharp intake of Teddie's breath an a muttered oath.

Katherine rounded the corner and faced Brooks and a wide-eyed, furiously blushing Teddie. When the girl sa who it was, her expression changed from horrified embar rassment to resentful anger. Her jaw jutted and she clenche her fists. "You were spying."

Brooks touched her arm and she looked up at him "Teddie, you know better—"

"She was, Granddad." She faced Katherine again. "I you weren't, why didn't you let me know you were hiding i the stall?"

"I wasn't hiding. I was asleep with Ishmael. Your voice woke me."

Teddie scowled. "I'll bet."

"Theodora," Brooks said sharply. "You're being rude. Apologize at once."

Teddie faced her grandfather. "Don't let her tell Jack, Granddad. Please. He'll make Pandora leave the barn. Or shoot her." Her eyes grew huge. "He'll make me drop out of the contest."

"Oh, Teddie," Katherine said. "That's not true and you know it."

Teddie voice rose. "You don't know—"

"Teddie," Brooks said gently. "I want you to apologize to Katherine for your behavior. Although I'm sure she realizes you are very young and very distraught, your actions are inexcusable. Then I want you to leave us alone. Go wait for me at the car."

"But, Granddad—"

"Please, Teddie." Although his voice was calm, Katherine heard the adamancy. The tinge of command. He was a man used to having his way.

Teddie seemed to deflate, then turned toward Katherine.

"I know I'm acting mean," she said, without really facing Katherine. "I'm scared you're going to tell my dad on me and get me in trouble." She did look up then. "Please don't tell Jack, Katherine, please."

Katherine's jaw fell and she fumbled for words. "Teddie," she began, then faced the girl's grandfather. "Brooks, you know I can't just ignore this or pretend I never... Look, I'm sorry this happened. I would give anything not to have overheard your conversation, but I did hear it. I don't know what to do."

Brooks gave her an enigmatic look. "I think it's time we had a talk, Katherine." He turned to his granddaughter. "Teddie?"

She turned and walked out of the barn. As she walked away, Katherine saw that she wiped at her eyes with the back of her hand.

"Katherine, I'm sure you and I can work this out so that you're not thrust into the middle of my family troubles."

Katherine looked up at his patrician face, the eyes identical to Teddie's, the straight, broad shoulders. She felt stunned and nauseated. Just behind her, Ishmael moved restively in his stall. "Brooks, I don't know what to say—"

"Maybe you should just listen for a moment. You see, I believe we are working toward a common goal."

"What do you mean?"

A smile played at the corner of his mouth. "In the first place, I sit on the board of Farm and Home Bank. David Wiley works for me, as does Suzanne Sifara's father. I know how you came to be here and I want you to know that I appreciate the excellent job you've done. For the last couple of years I've done everything I can to offer my help to my son-in-law. He's refused every overture I've made and, as I've said before, I certainly don't blame him."

Katherine knew she must have looked dazed. She felt as if she'd been struck by an air hammer. *"I sit on the board of Farm and Home Bank."* "So it was you? You bought the other horses?"

"Oh, them. Some of them. Certainly. There's no doubt had I not bought them, Jack would have sold them to someone else eventually—everyone knows he's one of the finest horsemen in the state. But you see, this way I could at least feel that I was doing something to help. To make up for what I'd...well, it suited me to be able to buy them. I would have bought Phoenix, too, but apparently he has decided not to sell him until after the Austin show." Brooks shook his head. "Although I must say I find that a bit horrifying."

"What do you mean? Horrifying?"

Brooks tilted his head slightly. "Eight years ago, at the Austin Charity Horse Show, Jack had his accident. The animal is entered in a grand prix event in the same show at the end of the month. I believe Jack sees it as some kind of finale. He plans to win big at the same show and with the same horse that crippled him and ruined his business years ago."

Katherine wanted to sink to the ground. "Oh, no."

"As I said, Katherine," he continued, "I'm one of the irectors of Farm and Home and there are others who are verse to the idea of Blazingbrook functioning as a stable. 'hey feel this is prime land for commercial development." le looked around. "My daughter used the last of her ineritance from her mother for the down payment on this old lace. Jack struggled to make a go of it, and they might have one well if I hadn't interfered."

"Brooks, surely you can't blame—"

"Oh, I don't. I don't." He crossed his arms. "I suppose 'd like to change the past, though, too. Just like Jack. 'hat's why I really must insist that you not tell him what ou've overheard here today. After all, Jack would certinly be as disappointed with your part of this as he would vith mine."

Katherine felt as if she'd been struck. So this was the fist nside the glove. "I see," she said, and looked him squarely n the eyes. "If I tell Jack about Pandora, you'll make sure ack finds out I'm from the bank. And then I'll get a pink lip from Mr. Wiley, too."

Despite Katherine's harsh words, Brooks's expression idn't harden. In fact, he seemed if anything, to grow sad. 'That's not exactly true, Katherine. In the past I've learned very difficult lesson about interfering too closely with my amily members. I wouldn't have helped Teddie with the sale f Pandora, but she cried so. It was so important to her. If weren't for me, Jack would have had the money to give er for her modeling contest, and although I don't want to nterfere, it seemed the least I could do. After all, so much f this is my fault."

"So what are you saying? I can tell Jack? You are going o?" Katherine felt a surge of dread. Jack seemed so hosle wherever Brooks was concerned that he might really do omething in a temper. He might have Pandora removed rom the stable. And he would almost certainly stop Tedie's modeling lessons.

Brooks uncrossed his arms and spread out the fingers of is hand. "First, let the contest run its course. It's only three weeks, and it is so important to Teddie. If she wins, that' be wonderful. If not, well, Jack will certainly see how dis appointed she is and he'll feel inclined to be sympathetic After all, he adores her. Second, let Teddie tell her fathe what she and I did and why. After the Austin Horse Show he should be in a generous mood. It's certain that someon will buy Phoenix. That stallion is a brilliant jumper—inter national potential easily. Jack's barn will be secure, and believe he'll feel generous. Third, you can tell Jack abou your part in this or not, just as it suits you. I won't inter fere."

Katherine could scarcely believe it. "Is that it?" She fel almost sick with relief. "You really want Teddie to tel him—"

"Of course I do." He smiled wryly. "I intend to patch u my relationship with my son-in-law and have some sem blance of a family if it's the last thing I do. I'm a very de termined man."

Katherine looked down and toed a piece of straw. " don't know what to say." She looked back up at him. "Yo see, no matter what, I intend to tell him about how I got sen here," she swallowed. "Even if it means we won' be . . . friends anymore."

A light flickered deep in Brooks' eyes. "Oh, I think you' probably remain *friends*, despite the way events were ma neuvered around you."

"So Teddie will tell him?"

"The last weekend in August, I promise. Right after sh hears about the contest. Now I really must go. Occasion ally, when Jack's away, I come back in the barn to see Pan dora. I'm pretty sentimental about the old girl. I first bough her for Blaize and now for Teddie."

They shook hands, and Katherine watched him disap pear around the corner. There was so much to think about So many secrets to keep. But not for much longer. Just un til September. Then everything would be out in the open Everything would be clear and uncomplicated then.

* * *

Teddie's eyes burned with resentment as she glared at her
her. "You're going to *make* me go? But I don't want to
to Austin. I need to be home to get the call about the
ntest."

Katherine and the other girls sat in awkward silence
ound the kitchen table as they finished breakfast before
rning chores began. The trouble had started as soon as
ddie mentioned she didn't want to go to the Austin show
t weekend.

"I'm sorry, Teddie, but I need you in Austin. You're the
ly one who can ride Penny and Snooks in their classes."
ck pushed his cereal bowl away. "I'm sorry if you won't
here for your call, but there'll be someone here to take the
ssage or they can phone you on Monday." Jack's voice
s cool, determined.

"No," Teddie said, and stood up so quickly that she
nged against the table. Glasses tottered wildly and Kath-
ne and the girls clutched at their wobbling dishes.

Jack stood slowly, his eyes riveted to Teddie's. "Come
th me." His voice was slow. Dangerously controlled.
ddie blanched and her eyes filled.

When they walked out Katherine looked at Judy. She
ook her head and shrugged. "There really isn't anyone
e who can show those horses," she said quietly. "Teddie
ew all along that this is the last show of the summer. It's
important to miss a four-day horse show for one ten-
nute phone call." The other girls stood and stacked their
hes in the sink, or exchanged embarrassed, wild-eyed
nces.

"They'd probably call back, don't you think?" Kather-
asked no one in particular.

"I'd think so," Judy said. "But I don't know anything
out it." She looked up and smiled. "I hear you're finally
ming to a show."

Katherine smiled back. "Yes. It's the last one of the
mmer, so I couldn't miss it. Mrs. Gomez is going to take
re of things here."

"Great," Judy said. "We'll have a ball."

"Mmmm," Katherine said. She'd heard the front do shut firmly and floating down from upstairs came the sou of crying.

Chapter Nine

As Jack pulled his truck into the Austin Fairgrounds, Katherine turned toward him. "I was thinking," she said as nonchalantly as she could, "Judy and I are rooming together and I thought it would be fun to have Teddie stay with us rather than with Becky and her mother. Would you mind?"

Jack gave her a slow look. "Fine with me," he said evenly. Becky, Tina and her mother had one of the cluster of rooms the Blazingbrook group had reserved at the Guadalupe Inn, which was situated directly next to the fairgrounds. Katherine and Judy, on the other hand, were staying at the Austin Guest House, two blocks away. Jack and Teddie were speaking again, but only barely, and Katherine was eager to avoid any more friction between them. Jack obviously knew what she was doing, but either agreed with it or chose to ignore it. "Just make sure she gets up in time for schooling in the morning. You know what a slug she can be."

Katherine nodded and smiled. "Leave it to me."

While Jack and the girls unloaded the horses and set up the Blazingbrook area in the show barn, Katherine drove

Jack's truck to the hotel. After checking in and leaving her luggage in the room, she drove back to the fairgrounds.

As she pulled into the parking lot, she took several deep breaths and rolled her shoulders. This was going to be a tough weekend. Jack intended to win the grand prix and sell Phoenix. Teddie was a nervous wreck about the modeling competition, and she was blazing with frustration and resentment because Jack had insisted she come to the show. Added to the girl's anxiety was the fact that this was the weekend she'd promised to tell her father about deceiving him over the sale of Pandora.

Katherine's nerves weren't much better. She constantly feared she would slip up and tell him what she knew about Pandora and Brooks. Or something about working for Farm and Home. She dreaded she'd reveal the way she felt about Jack. Worst of all, she feared if she didn't get a chance to put her arms around him and kiss him, she'd go completely nuts.

Jack was so preoccupied and edgy about the show that he had little patience for anyone—especially Teddie. Years of agony, hope and determination would culminate in the show ring on Sunday night and his control had fractured more than once. While loading the horses to come to the show, he'd snapped at the grooms and swatted the animals. The girls avoided him when possible and approached him tentatively, which seemed to irritate him even more.

Katherine decided she hated horse shows. She just wanted the weekend to be over.

Pulling up next to the show barn, she set the hand brake and groaned aloud as she ran both hands through her hair. At that moment Jack strode through the barn doors. He wore a white, skin-tight T-shirt and his tan jodhpurs faithfully outlined every hard line of his thighs and the flat plane of belly; knee-high calfskin riding boots traced his strong calves. Every step revealed the bunch and release of ruthlessly conditioned muscle and sinew.

He sauntered up and rested his elbows on the window. "Hello, gorgeous."

Katherine decided she loved horse shows.

Jack squinted against the sun and watched as another van backed carefully up to the show barn. "Do I have a room or am I going to be forced to sleep in a stall?" He tilted his head and grinned at her. "But come to think of it, maybe it wouldn't be so bad if I could roll in the hay with—"

"You have a room, Jack," Katherine said, and tried to keep her emotions from showing. His mouth was scant inches from her, and she felt an almost irresistible urge to drag his face down and bite his lower lip. But that would, of course, be breaking the rules. "Is everyone settling in up here?"

"Phoenix decided to expand his stall space by kicking the boards out. Swain got away from Paula and ran amok for about twenty minutes and I think one of our dogs bit the show chairman."

"In other words—"

"Yeah," Jack said with a grin. "Everything is shaping up normally."

"You seem to be in a better mood."

Jack's brows came together. "A better mood? What makes you think I've been in a bad mood?"

Katherine said nothing but raised one eyebrow in wry accusation.

Jack pressed his lips together. "I suppose I have been a little . . . intense."

"Intense?"

"Well. Maybe *testy* would be a better word."

"Jack," Katherine said flatly, "a cornered wolverine is testy. You've been insufferable."

A dangerous light glimmered in his eyes. "Insufferable? Me? How dare you talk about suffering to me, Katherine? *I'm* the one who's been suffering." He lowered his mouth toward hers. "Shall I show you how I spell relief?"

She gasped and looked over her shoulder. "Jack. Cut that out. Someone's going to come by here and . . ." She turned back in time to see his face split wide in a grin. "You are a complete devil, you know that?" She faked a jab at his torso, but instead of flinching, he merely stood gazing down at her, one corner of his mouth lifted.

"You're getting warmer," he said, and gave her a wink—that sexy, special wink she knew he saved for her alone. Her heart shifted into overdrive and she felt warm blood suffuse her face.

Katherine yanked at the door handle and looked down, afraid he'd see the color rising in her cheeks. His suggestive, half-joking banter was only a hair's breadth away from the truth and she knew it. She knew that Jack felt the same way, and the thought fanned the blush on her face to a higher intensity. "So what's next?" she asked as she stepped out of the truck and slammed the door.

Jack looked back toward the barn. "Well, I'll school the girls this afternoon. Then I guess we'll all meet back at the hotel for dinner and an early night." He dragged a hand through his thick hair. "You know," he said as he looked back at her, "you don't have to stay here all day."

Katherine almost yelped with joy, but just before she did, she thought she saw a glimmer of wistfulness in his eyes. Could it be that he didn't want her to go? Jack? Needy? Maybe even he needed some moral support.

"Nah," she said. "The fun's just getting started. Let's go turn some more horses loose and see what happens."

He smiled. Hugely. "Yeah. Someone else's."

"Yeah."

Jack's jovial mood evaporated as soon as he joined his students in the practice ring. He worked the girls without mercy. It almost seemed that he intended to cram months of conditioning and show-ring savvy into one three-hour schooling session. Even Judy—levelheaded, laid-back Judy—grew waspish and prickly by the end of the grueling day.

After a couple of hours, instead of her customary place beside Jack, Katherine stood outside the ring, grateful that she wasn't one of his students. By four o'clock, three of the younger girls had burst into tears. Teddie remained cool but white faced and thin lipped as she rode horse after horse under her father's scrutiny. After the schooling session, while the girls cooled their horses and polished their tack, Jack rode Phoenix for an hour and a half. Glancing at her watch, Katherine realized he hadn't sat down to rest in more than fifteen hours.

Katherine drove in silence back to the hotel with Teddie, Judy and three of the younger girls. She decided that instead of trying to eat out, she would order Chinese and have it brought to the hotel for everyone. At the desk there was a message for Teddie. Brooks had arrived, had taken the presidential suite at the Harborrow and wanted Teddie to join him for dinner. Katherine said she'd tell Jack, while she fervently hoped she wouldn't have to. They'd left him at the show barn, hobnobbing with the other professionals. Horse shopping. Story swapping. Sizing up the competition.

After the nine-thirty bed check, Katherine took a long, cool shower, put on a gown and turned on an old movie. Judy sat quietly on her bed and painted her nails. "He's in a cruddy mood, isn't he?" she said.

Katherine sighed. "I haven't seen him this way all summer. I guess it's the pressure. The grand prix and all."

Judy muttered something and Katherine didn't ask her to repeat it.

A little before ten Teddie knocked on the door.

"Hi, gal. How was dinner?"

"Fab," she replied. "Lobster."

At last Teddie seemed relaxed and happy again. A few hours away from the show grounds had obviously been what she'd needed. "Oh, yeah," she said. "Granddad asked me to give this to you." Teddie groped in her shoulder bag. "He said he'd talk to you at the show if there's anything you want to ask him about."

Teddie handed Katherine a white, letter-size envelope. One corner was emblazoned with the emerald-and-azure logo of Brooks International Enterprises. There was no addressee on the front.

"Thanks, Teddie."

"Well," the girl said, and smiled brightly. "I'm going to shower now. And no fair saying 'At last.'"

"At last," Judy said drolly.

"Thank heavens," Katherine said with a grin.

"Okay," Teddie said as she walked toward the bathroom, "you know that means toothpaste in everyone's shoes."

When Katherine heard the gush of the shower, she slipped her finger under the flap of the envelope and broke the seal. Inside she found a single key, a folded sheet of Brooks International letterhead and five one-hundred-dollar bills.

Dear Katherine:

Thanks so much for everything you've done for Teddie. I can't tell you what it's meant to her to be able to compete in the Panache contest. She never could have obtained her composite without your loyalty and discretion. You know, of course, how her father would react if he found out that it was me who bought the old mare.

There is a poolside condominium leased for six months in your name at Brookhollow II. If you haven't been there, Teddie and I will gladly give you a quided tour some weekend in the near future.

Also, please accept the enclosed brokerage fee with my sincerest thanks. It's slightly more than the customary percentage but no more than you deserve. Also, I want you to know this will in no way affect your bonus from Farm and Home.

With best personal wishes—

It was signed by Edwin Grosvenor Brooks III.

"Oh, hell," Katherine said.

"What's the matter?" Judy asked.

Katherine folded the letter and shoved it back into the envelope. "Oh, nothing much," Katherine said as her heart squeezed painfully. If she thought she could catch Brooks she'd have run outside right then, nightgown or no. "Oh, well," she muttered. "I can give it back tomorrow."

Friday morning the usual horse-show pandemonium broke loose. After showers and light breakfasts, Katherine took the girls to the barn. By ten-thirty Blazingbrook had four firsts, two seconds and fourth. Two of the first-place ribbons and one second were Teddie's.

Katherine, as usual, was busy holding numbers, riding bats, hard hats, snack money and purses. Although she searched diligently for Brooks whenever she could, there just didn't seem to be any time to drop everything and go find him.

Friday afternoon, Lucy Threadgill took a fall in a Large Hunter class and Katherine spent three hours with her in the first-aid station. The show nurse said she was merely frightened and shaken up, but Jack insisted that Katherine take her to the emergency room. Teddie took another first- and two more third-place ribbons. Judy won both classes she rode in. It looked as if Blazingbrook would sweep all the divisions.

Even Jack seemed more relaxed at dinner. He took everyone to Vaudeville Pizza and sat between Paula and Lucy, his arms draped over the backs of their chairs. They were delirious.

Teddie still hadn't heard the results of the contest and she'd grown steadily more snappish. Brooks had promised her he'd pull whatever strings he could to find out what was happening. He wasn't invited to join them for pizza and Teddie obviously felt miserable.

That night Katherine thought she heard her crying in the shower.

At four-thirty Saturday afternoon, Katherine sat in the bleachers watching Jack school Phoenix over the practice jumps. The sight of them galloping, wheeling and leaping effortlessly over the enormous square oxers and panels filled her with a kind of giddy dread. The jumps seemed impossibly solid and high—the man and horse seemed incredibly agile and powerful.

All the Blazingbrook girls had finished schooling and grooming their horses and sat in the bleachers watching. Evening classes wouldn't start until eight o'clock, and Jack took advantage of the lull in the usual show-ring stampede to give the stallion a workout. He'd given everyone plenty of warning that he'd be schooling an extremely unruly stallion; only one or two of the other professionals were using the ring and they rode geldings. They also maintained a discreet distance.

Katherine sat with the rest of the Blazingbrook girls and listened while Judy, Paula or one of the others kept up a running commentary so Katherine could appreciate the exercises Jack and Phoenix were doing to prepare for the upcoming jumper classes.

"See," Judy said, "Jack really knows how to make Phoenix use himself. Just watch. See that. Right up to base. Watch the horse stick his neck out and curl those forelegs—"

"Gorgeous, isn't he?" Paula murmured.

Katherine smiled. She couldn't tell if the girl meant the horse or the rider. Almost all the Blazingbrook girls gazed enraptured as Jack worked his horse. All except Jack's daughter. Katherine glanced over her shoulder to look for her.

On the edge of the group, her eyes narrowed and her lips pressed together in a sullen line, sat Teddie. Katherine smiled and waved to invite her to join them. The girl barely tipped her head in acknowledgment. Katherine sighed. This had been a difficult horse show. Teddie would probably be champion in her division. She'd definitely take reserve champion if nothing else. The rest of the girls would give almost anything for a third of Teddie's natural ability, and all Teddie wanted was to canter her mother's old mare across the fields at Blazingbrook and be a model. Well, Katherine thought, chalk up another of life's inexplicable ironies.

For a moment Katherine toyed with the idea of once again broaching the subject of Brooks with Jack. But she figured the effort would be hopeless. All it took was the mention of his former father-in-law's name to cause a vein to swell in Jack's neck. There was really nothing she could do until Jack was ready to mend those bridges.

The sad thing is, Katherine thought, Jack is missing out on such an important part of his daughter's life. Teddie's accomplishments would fill him with pride, if she only felt she could share them with him. She couldn't even tell the other girls how nervous and anxious she was. For now, Teddie sat angry and alone on the fringes of the group where she should be happiest; burdened with the need to perform well for her father, waiting for news of the competition, and facing the fact that she'd had a very difficult confession to make at the end of the weekend. Quite a lot for a thirteen-year-old to deal with.

"You're not watching," Paula said. "You're missing some of the best jumps."

Katherine shook her head. "I can barely stand to watch. They look so huge. So solid. Especially that wall. I hate it."

"Just wait until Sunday night," Judy said, her eyes shining. "It'll probably go at least seven feet—"

"Oh, spare me," Katherine replied. "I won't be able to watch."

"You'll have to," Paula said. "We'll all have to cheer Jack on."

"I don't know what would be worse," Katherine muttered. "Watching it or not watching it." Although she said it like a joke, she was completely serious. The wall stood like a horrid, red-brick reminder of everything that had gone wrong in Jack's life. He had an unnatural determination to do well on Sunday. But there was more to it than winning a class and selling a horse. More to it even than getting the money necessary to meet the note and save Blazingbrook. The whole business filled Katherine with a sense of unease.

She knew Jack saw the grand prix class as the moment when he triumphed over his past—eradicated all the old defeats. He'd win the class with the horse that broke him and do it in front of an adversary who'd tried to break him in another way. Katherine also knew plenty of others saw it that way, too. There had been no mistaking the raised eyebrows and sudden whispers every time Jack or Phoenix came into view.

The situation obviously had Teddie's nerves raw. Katherine knew the sheen in the girl's eyes wasn't always caused by flying dust. She and Jack had had more than their usual share of cross words since Thursday. Jack had been utterly preoccupied with his own burdens; he'd been less than patient with Teddie, and Teddie had been more demanding and volatile than usual.

Katherine faced the ring again. Jack was apparently finished schooling Phoenix because he'd slowed the stallion to a walk. Phoenix champed at his bit and tried to walk sideways. Jack reached down and gave his horse an affectionate swat. "Save it for tomorrow, big guy," he said. "We'll kick their, uh..." he said as he gave the girls a mock scandalized look. Then he leaned over and acted as if he were whispering something so only the stallion could hear.

"We know what you said," Paula called, giggling.

Jack winked at her. "No you don't."

Julia Brown, one of the wealthiest, sleekest of the mothers, laughed in a knowing, throaty way. "Well, Jack," she said, "maybe you'd care to repeat it."

He lifted the corner of his mouth in a lazy smile. "Maybe so," he said, as he turned Phoenix in a slow circle. "Maybe not." Once again her throaty laugh floated through the air. Jack smiled and gave her a sexy wink.

Katherine hated that wink. She studied Jack. He sat relaxed and confident on the sweaty ebony stallion as they walked with a loose, muscular ease around the ring. Both of them oozed masculine confidence and athletic prowess. Irritation skittered through her. Suddenly it all seemed so annoying. The competition. The posturing. The winking.

She stood up. "Well, I think I'll go for a walk," she said. Her tone dripped irritation but she didn't care.

From the corner of her eye she saw Jack's gaze snap her way. She pretended not to notice as she stood, grabbed her purse and began to thread her way through the girls sitting around her.

"Judy," Jack called from the ring. "Would you mind seeing what's keeping Hermes. He's supposed to come walk this horse."

"I'm on my way."

From behind her, high in the bleachers, Katherine heard Teddie's voice. "Hermes is probably taking a nap, Jack.

Why don't you let me walk your nag. I promise I won't fall off."

Katherine heard the challenge and sarcasm. The tone was subtle, though, the kind only a parent could recognize and appreciate—the kind you had to be intimately familiar with in order to discern. Katherine swallowed hard and kept walking. She'd had enough of Teddie and Jack right now. Enough of her rebellion. Enough of his stubbornness—and his winking.

Still, she glanced back just in time to see Jack's eyes narrowed in irritation as he glared at his daughter. "The only thing you'll be cooling, little girl, is your sassy heels." Jack swung his leg over the saddle and landed lightly in the saw dust. Katherine knew he didn't see Teddie's cheeks suffuse with color as she stood and stalked away. Nervous giggling rippled through the girls in earshot. Katherine shook her head as she turned back and walked down the steps leading out of the ring.

Let them work it out, she thought irritably. Let Jack learn to get along with Teddie. He was so good at getting along with everyone else. Like Julia Brown. At the thought she squeezed her eyes for a moment and pressed her lips together. He winks at me. He winks at Judy. He winks at Julia. All he has time for are these stupid horses and this stupid grand prix. Well, if he thinks I'm going to put my entire life on hold just so he can go around winking...

An iron grip clamped around her upper arm and turned her around to face blazing amber eyes.

"Katherine, what the hell's the matter? I must have called you five or six times and you just walked faster and faster—"

"Let go," Katherine said, yanking her arm away. "Why don't you go back and talk to Julia."

Jack tilted his head and his eyes narrowed. "Talk to Julia? What do you mean?"

Katherine's frustration poured out in flood of angry words. "I'm sick to death of all this." With a wild flap of her hands Katherine tried to sum up her frustration. "Last June. The things you said then...but the way you act now..." She realized she wasn't making sense. There was so much to say, but so much that couldn't be said. "What's going on, Jack? What do you want from me? If you can't treat me any different than you do everyone else, well, you can just go...jump a horse."

She was almost gasping with emotion and couldn't seem to get her breath. Jack's eyes cut to the right, to the left where a tack room door stood open. Before she had time to register what was going on, he grabbed her arm and pulled her into the room. The door slammed shut and he stood in front of her, his eyes bright and hard.

"What kind of man do you think I am?" His voice rasped. "Would you like to see how I want to treat you? What I want from you?"

His mouth descended. Covered hers. Devoured hers. He moved her backward until she was pressed against the door. He groaned. His arms crushed her to him and a surge of desire rolled through her like thunder that begins in the distance and explodes with sky-searing lighting. His hands pressed her into him—into the rigid planks of muscle of his belly. His shoulders curved around her. Over her. She slipped. Was slipping. Falling deeper and deeper into a well of sensation. Far away there were voices. A horse clopping by outside.

Katherine's mind barely registered the sounds. She was drowning. She clung to him. Passion, she thought. This is what they mean when they say passion.

Jack tore his mouth away from hers. "You see?" His voice was harsh. Guttural. "This is what I want. I want everything. All of you. And I want you now. I want you every minute. But I can't take you in fragments. I can't sneak a kiss here. A touch there. Do you understand that? I'm not that kind of man. I tried that more than once and I nearly drove myself crazy. I can keep to our agreement. I can keep my hands off you until September, but I can't treat you any differently than I do anyone else. Right now it's all I can do to sleep at night knowing that you're in bed somewhere close to me. I'm sorry if you think I'm flirting too much. I probably am. If it bothers you that much, I'll try to cool it.

But I'm not going to treat you any differently than I am right now. I can't. If I start touching you I won't be able to stop. Do you understand me?"

Katherine couldn't speak so she nodded. Weakly.

"Good. Now I've got to go look at a horse. Sonny Sheppeck has a gelding that I might want to bring back. It's not far from here, so I won't be gone more than twenty or thirty minutes."

Another spine-melting kiss and he was gone. Katherine heard the crisp rap of his boots disappearing down the corridor, and she sagged against the tack room wall, against the hanging bridles and lead ropes and halters. The metal snaffle bits clinked faintly together when they swayed. For a moment she stood motionless, hardly aware of where she was. Her hand brushed against a well-oiled leather strap. She touched it absently. What a wonderful smell, she thought as she turned and fingered the bridles and hanging tack: fine oiled leather, saddle soap, freshly laundered sheepskin saddle pads drying on bamboo racks. She breathed deeply, filling herself with the warm, good smells.

Her mouth tingled from the kisses. She touched her lips and her knees wobbled again. What an intense man, she thought. Sighing, she once again counted the remaining days in August. Just a few.

In one way she could hardly wait, and in another way she dreaded September. Somehow she couldn't imagine being anywhere except Blazingbrook. More than anywhere she'd lived, she loved the stable, the rolling fields, the barns, the animals and children. Sighing, she straightened up, fluffed her hair and smoothed her shirt back in to her jeans. She would wait a few minutes while her heart slowed. Will the others be able to tell, she wondered as she again ran her fingers over her lips. Surely not by looking at her mouth, but she knew there would be no hiding the glow she felt. She felt incandescent. Radiant. She wanted to shout and run through the barn.

As she walked along the rows of stalls and back toward where the Blazingbrook horses were stabled, Katherine nodded and smiled at everyone she passed. She stopped to pat strange horses and stable dogs and spoke to everyone she met.

I'll go back to the ring, she thought. Maybe Julia was still there. Katherine liked Julia and felt particularly generous toward her just now. Besides she was learning how to watch the horses and riders work, learning how to see when a rider "drops" the horse or lets the animal get into a fence wrong. She wanted to educate herself, to be able to sit with the others during the classes and make intelligent observations about the riders and horses. She smiled. Maybe she'd even learn how to ride. Jack would like that.

The first thing she noticed when she walked into the arena was that the practice course was deserted, but an unusually large number of spectators still stood in the bleachers. They all appeared to be engrossed by something happening at the far end of the ring. Katherine climbed high up into the stands to get a better view and turned around just in time to see a black shape plunging between the temporary jumps.

Teddie was riding the Phoenix.

Katherine's first urge was to rush out and try to phone Jack, only she didn't know exactly where he'd gone. Besides, she couldn't drag her eyes from the girl and the stallion galloping madly around the ring. Katherine had never seen Teddie unable to control any horse she chose to ride. But Phoenix wasn't just any horse. The contrast between the way he behaved with Jack and with Teddie made him seem like a completely different animal. Without Jack's powerful legs clamped around him, without the knotted and corded muscle of Jack's arms to hold him in, the Phoenix careered uncontrollably around the ring like a loose cannon on the rolling deck of a warship.

The stallion took the bit in his teeth and shook his head, jerking Teddie forward, causing her arms to fly down beside his neck. With an audible snap, the strap of her helmet broke and the velveteen hard hat flew off. White-blond hair spilled out like a pale waterfall against the horse's sweating, ebony neck. Teddie stood in her stirrups and pulley-reined fiercely. Obviously desperate for control, she'd set her jaw and her face was a pale oval stained bright pink beneath her eyes. Katherine swallowed hard. Standing just at the edge of the ring, just even with the high-jump wall, stood Judy, her gaze riveted to Teddie and Phoenix.

When Katherine clambered down the bleachers to stand beside her she saw that Judy's hand, resting on the top rail, trembled. For the first time Katherine felt dread worm through her. Besides Jack, Teddie was the best rider at the stable. She would get control of her father's horse...surely.

"What's going to happen? She can handle him, can't she?"

Judy didn't take her eyes from the ring. "Where's Jack?" Her voice sounded choked—strangled, almost.

Fear slithered through Katherine. "He's...he's gone somewhere to look at a horse."

Judy seemed to suddenly sag, to grow smaller. She clutched the rail with both hands. "Oh, no," she muttered. "Vault, Teddie, vault off."

Katherine turned back toward the ring. Phoenix was galloping by them, shaking his head and showing the whites of his eyes; his harness buckles rattled madly. Just when he drew level with them, Judy called out. "Get off him, Teddie. Bail out. Just jump off."

Teddie appeared not to hear. Her white arms were bare and fine sinew and cords of muscle stood out as she used all her strength to try to rein Phoenix in. At the far corner of the ring, she turned him a tight circle and he grunted in anger, his black legs slashing into the ground and tossing up clods of dirt and sawdust.

Katherine took a sharp breath. The tightness of the circle shortened his stride. He would have to slow down now. Surely. Once Teddie broke his gallop, he'd let her get off. No one would be hurt. Just a little embarrassment; they'd all crowd around Teddie and scold her. Everyone would be furious with relief. Katherine just knew that's what would happen.

A sharp pain in her hands drew her eyes downward. A series of sickle moons were etched in each palm. She hadn't realized how tightly her fists had been clenched. She opened her hands, concentrating on how she'd handle telling Jack—

what she'd say to him when he returned. Yes, she'd just do some thinking and rub away those ugly marks on her hands while Teddie brought the horse under control. She wasn't going to watch anymore. There was no need to. Everything was going to be just fine. Then Judy gasped.

Phoenix had slid to a stop facing the wall. He eyed the jump and his ears, which had been swiveling in agitation, now flew forward as if he'd just received a challenge. His breath clattered in his throat when he snorted angrily. Once again, Teddie yanked hard on the reins. The stallion's head hardly bounced. Then he stood straight up on his hind legs, pawing the air and trumpeting savagely. Someone screamed.

He was one of those rare animals who teeters on that fine line between brilliance and madness.

When his front hooves met the ground again, he threw his head down well past his knees, easily dragging the reins through Teddie's hands. She clawed at them, obviously struggling to recover any shred of control. As if she didn't even exist, Phoenix gazed at the wall with his head thrown up, ears pricked in concentration. Dancing sideways, he pawed the ground once, twice, and his ebony forelock spilled over his eyes. Through the tossing blue-black hair Katherine caught the glint in his eyes. The glint of madness.

At first he only walked forward, great shoulder muscles rippling and glistening with sweat. Then he picked up a trot and his ears whipped backward and flattened hideously against his head. His haunches bunched beneath him and he flung himself forward like some nightmare charger bursting into battle.

Tears streamed down Teddie's white face and Katherine saw that the girl clung desperately to the horse's mane. She no longer even tried to control him. She'd lost both stirrup irons and they hammered against the stallion's flanks, goading him to further madness.

"When he rounded on the jump he was obviously out of control. He stuck his head out and charged. It was more of an attack than an approach to a jump...

About four strides back, someone yelled, 'He's getting in there all wrong,' but by then it was too late. He'd already committed himself to the jump....

"The horse knew what he'd done—the mistake he'd made. He really grunted when he left the ground. He gave it all he had, but he just took off too far back. At the crest of his jump, he started scrambling and then he slammed into the wall. Pieces of it splintered and flew everywhere—the plywood painted to look like bricks, the pole across the top, even the flowerpots at the base of the jump just exploded from the impact.

"When he was falling, he started twisting in the air. You could see the glint of his steel shoes when he turned over.... And there was this horrible smashing noise when they hit the ground....

"The last thing you heard was this one sickening crack."

Chapter Ten

When Jack pulled up to the visitors' barn, he noticed im mediately that none of the Blazingbrook riders were an where around. He frowned. It was too early for everyone have gone back to the hotel. There should have been gir sitting in front of the stalls cleaning tack, checking the horses for loose braids, gossiping. Just before he killed th engine, he noticed the emergency medical service vehic parked by the arena.

A black thought skittered through his mind but he forc it away. His girls were all through schooling for the da None of them would be involved in any kind of acciden Surely. He decided to walk through the barn on his way the arena to see if anyone there could tell him what ha happened. Although he was concerned, he felt it best to l the professionals handle the emergency situations witho the unnecessary distraction of spectators. He also grim acknowledged the part of him that would always dread th sight of ambulances and white coats at a horse show.

As soon as Jack rounded the corner, he saw that the ga to Phoenix's stall was open. For one moment he sto blinking owlishly at the stall, at the webbing gate unclipped and sagging against the door jamb.

The Phoenix was out of his stall.

An ambulance waited outside the arena.

The hair on the back of his neck rose.

Jack ran. Down the swept corridors, heedless of the startled animals snorting and scrambling as he ran past. The crisscross of intersecting hallways took on a nightmarish aspect. He would get lost. He wouldn't reach the ring in time. They would take her away and he would never see her again. His beautiful little girl. Fine, white-gold hair fanned out and trampled in dirt and sawdust. Surgeries. Scars. Wheelchairs.

When he burst into the cavernous arena, he choked back a yell. The tableau before him seemed hideously familiar, only this time seen from a more terrifying perspective. The wall lay in a tumbled, splintered mass in the center of the ring. At least a dozen people stood in little groups with their backs to him, obscuring the figure he dreaded to see.

He yelled his daughter's name and every face in the somber, little knots of people whipped toward him. Their mouths all gaped open in horrified little O shapes like so many startled, landed fish. All of it, every face, every gaily painted rail and pole, every terra-cotta pot of white or red azaleas registered automatically in Jack's mind in photographic detail, but he didn't concentrate on absorbing any of it. He knew that every splintered timber, every startled, pitying face was etched forever in his memory, along with other splintered timbers, other startled, pitying faces. Once again he would spend years seeing the same thing again and again in every waking and sleeping nightmare.

From the wreckage of the jump, he could tell that it must have been set very high, easily over six feet. The knots of people stood motionless and no one spoke. The entire arena was utterly soundless except for the rush and groan of his own breath and the muffled thud of his boots.

He saw no paramedics, no white coats or stretchers. Then he saw Katherine shouldering through the others, moving toward him, her face a portrait of grief. There was some-

thing dark and wet splattered on her hands and jeans. H
nearly screamed.

"Where is she? How bad is it?"

"Teddie's all right, Jack." In the slight pause she too
before starting again Jack's heart soared. *Teddie's all righ*
He'd never felt his heart pound and ache like this. Th
panic. The suffocating terror. But Teddie was all right. The
it began to sink in—the anguish on her face, the choke
thickened sound of her voice. "Judy took her to the bat
room to clean up. She has a cut lip and the paramedics thi
she sprained her wrist...but that's all." Katherine turn
toward where the smashed pieces of the jump lay like th
ruin after a tornado. Jack saw the black swell on the groun
the slowly heaving side. He heard a low gurgling moan. H
took one step. Two more steps. Then he saw the magni
cent blue-black forelegs curl weakly. The back legs didn
move.

Jack recognized Dr. Valdez, the horse-show veterina
ian, standing beside the now motionless form. His case l
open like a fishing-tackle box revealing rows of little via
ointments, shiny metal instruments and rolls of gauze.
one hand he held a long syringe filled with dark fluid. H
eyes met Jack's. He offered no pity; he merely stood the
communicating silently. Horseman to horseman.

The world shifted into slow motion as Jack walk
woodenly to where his horse lay dying. The people shuffl
back, allowing him through. When he knelt down, Pho
nix's eyes fluttered and his lips quivered. With every breat
bloody foam spewed from his nostrils or slid down the v
vet muzzle. Jack wiped it with his hand. He picked up t
massive head and rested it in his lap, heedless of the da
fluid spilling over his arms and running down onto his jea
He unbuckled the bridle and slid it over the ears and dow
the face with its melted lightning streak of white.

His horse knew him. The massive lips worked, showi
the strong white teeth, the wine-colored gullet. Dr. Vald
cleared his throat, knelt next to Jack and held the syrin
where Phoenix couldn't see it. Low, behind his ears and ju
beneath the crest muscle of his powerful neck.

"He's in agony, Jack," he said quietly and smoothed some of the inky mane away.

For an instant Jack wanted to stop him, to smack his hand away and say, Are you sure? Can't we…? Can't he…? But he knew. Someone had taken away the saddle and he could see the grotesque angle of the spine.

Jack nodded.

It worked quickly, evaporating the pain almost instantly and releasing the animal to that place where he would never again feel a bit or a girth or gaze at endless fields through the boards of a fence. But in the final moment before the dullness set in, Jack thought he saw something flicker through the magnificent liquid eyes. A look of betrayal and shock and accusation. It was as if Phoenix knew and asked, Why? Why?

Katherine watched with grief and pity as Jack stood up. Dr. Valdez stood beside him. People drifted away in ones and twos—some glancing with furtive pity at the dark figure on the ground, others pausing to rest a sympathetic hand on Jack's shoulder. He never turned away from his conversation with Dr. Valdez, but acknowledged each offer of sympathy with a slow nod. At the far end of the ring someone was opening the gate to let a tractor in. It pulled a flatbed. Katherine squeezed her eyes shut.

She knew Teddie was with Brooks and the doctor. Thank heaven for Brooks. After she called him, he'd taken less than fifteen minutes to arrive. On his way he'd phoned a doctor who'd been a school friend. The man had rushed from a golf course to come see about Teddie and the paramedics had gladly given way to him. Once he'd taped her wrist and swabbed her split lip, he gave her a shot that calmed her enough for Katherine to feel safe about returning to the ring to see about Phoenix.

Teddie had been completely hysterical from the moment she'd seen what she'd done to her father's horse. Even after the medication invaded her with its relentless lassitude, she still quivered like a violin string. "I've killed him," she repeated over and over. "Daddy's going to hate me."

Katherine realized that was the first time she'd ever hear
Teddie call her father "Daddy."

As she waited for Jack to finish with Dr. Valdez she trie
to gather her courage. How could she possibly console him
She felt completely inadequate. Powerless. Helpless. Sh
wasn't even sure she could tell him what happened witho
breaking down. But of course by now the veterinarian woul
have told him everything. All she had to offer him was h
presence.

Jack's face was turned slightly away from her, and whe
he raised his hand to shove his hair away, Katherine saw th
bloody foam and clinging to it the grime from the show rin
His hands, arms and shirt were all splattered with the gru
some reminder. Her heart constricted.

Like a grunting, mindless scavenger, the tractor ha
pulled up alongside the motionless form on the groun
Katherine heard the clink of a chain as the driver mov
about his grim business. She felt nauseated with dread. Ja
didn't need to watch this. How could she get him away fro
this place?

Then she saw him see her. He nodded, but there was
softening in his stance, no discernable breach of comp
sure. His control knifed through her—to feel so much pa
and be unable to reveal any of it. Tears stung her eyes a
clawed at the back of her throat. I've got to get him out
here, she thought. Dr. Valdez wiped his hands with a clo
and when he finished he offered it to Jack. When Jack to
it and looked down at his arms and clothing, it appeared
Katherine that he almost staggered. Then he stood moti
less for a long moment—staring at his arms, his hands,
dark stains on his jeans.

"Jack," Katherine said as she reached him. "I'm
sorry."

He looked up. His eyes were dry and unnaturally brig
"Who did you say is with Teddie now?"

"Judy. And Brooks. They're at the first-aid stati
There's a doctor with her and they've given her a shot.
has a minor sprain and a little cut on her lip but it's no
rious, won't need to be stitched." What can I say? she w

dered. What do I do? More than anything she wanted to put her arms around him, to offer whatever comfort she had. She *needed* him to accept her comfort. His pain caused her anguish. She rested a hand on his arm. His skin felt clammy.

Jack turned back to Dr. Valdez. "I've got to see Teddie," he said. He jerked his hand toward the tractor and the form on the ground. "I know that I need to see about—"

"You go ahead, Jack," Dr. Valdez said quietly. "I'll finish here."

Jack hesitated, and Katherine reached up and pulled gently on his arm. Don't argue with him, she thought, just act. "It's this way."

They walked from the ring in silence.

Katherine's mind tumbled. She knew Jack wouldn't want to see Brooks. Not now, not in the wake of another accident. Another defeat. Then the full implications of what had happened crashed into her. Since Phoenix was dead, Jack had no grand prix champion to sell. That meant he wouldn't be able to meet his balloon note. He would lose the stable. All his plans for reversing past defeats now lay behind them in a black, silent shadow in the show ring. Just before they entered the tunnel leading from the ring, Katherine heard the snarl of the tractor's winch motor. Jack flinched.

When they rounded the corner outside the first-aid station, Katherine saw Teddie slumped on a bench. Dr. Guiness, Brooks's friend, sat beside her, holding her hand and speaking quietly. When he looked up and saw Jack and Katherine, he stood. Teddie swayed and looked up at her father through red, bleary eyes. Her mouth formed the word "Daddy," but no sound came out. She pushed herself up and tottered unsteadily. The doctor wrapped his arm around her shoulders and she sagged against him.

Just before Jack broke into a run Katherine heard him choke out Teddie's name. He reached his daughter in a dozen or so strides, and she flung herself at him with a sob.

Katherine couldn't understand what Teddie was saying. Her words were spoken against Jack's shirt and garbled by sobs and the injection she'd been given. When Katherine came up beside them, she covered her mouth with her hand. Teddie's arms were wrapped around her father's waist, and he awkwardly patted the top of her head. His eyes were riveted to the dark globs clinging to his arms. His gaze wavered helplessly between the ugly mess and the white-gold fineness of Teddie's hair.

He doesn't want to get it on her hair. He knows if she sees it she'll get hysterical all over again. Katherine exchanged a look with the doctor, who stood by as helplessly as she. Teddie rolled her head away, and for one instant her words came out clearly. "Hold me, Daddy," she said. Over and over. "Hold me."

Jack's breath came in uneven gasps. Katherine could see he was raw with emotion—an almost sickening relief that his little girl was unhurt, grief for his horse, dread for all the losses that lay ahead. He licked his lips, and the magnitude of devastation crashed through Katherine. If only she could help him take some of it. If only there were something she could say. Or do.

Even with the tranquilizer working its dull magic, Teddie appeared to be growing more upset. Her words, though thick, were spilling rapidly. Tears coursed down her face.

"Where's Brooks?" Katherine asked the doctor.

He glanced quickly at Jack, then back to Katherine. "When he heard Jack had arrived, he thought it best that he wait outside." He looked at Jack. "He suggested if you had...things to take care of that he could take Teddie back to his hotel to spend the night with him there. Under the circumstances, Mr. Fitzpatrick, I think it might be best if Teddie spend the night away from her horse-show friends. I know everyone will be extremely well-meaning, but the questions, the explanations..."

Katherine held her breath. What would Jack think, she wondered. How would he take Brooks's offer? When she looked at him, she could barely believe what she saw in Jack's eyes—instead of gratitude or even grudging acceptance of the kindness of an adversary, Jack's eyes blazed with resentment.

His words were civil, though. "I suppose you're right, Doctor," he said. The words rasped out through Jack's hardened jaws. "Would you tell Brooks I'd also appreciate his giving Teddie a ride back to Houston. We'll wrap up here and leave in the morning."

Then he looked at Katherine and slowly raised his arms up in a helpless gesture. Obviously if he tried to extricate Teddie's grip, the horrible reminders of what had happened would smear through her hair and on her clothes. He leaned down as best he could with Teddie clutching at him so desperately.

"Go with the doctor, baby," he said quietly. "I love you. Everything will be all right. Your grandfather is going to take care of you tonight. There's a good girl."

Katherine gently pried Teddie's arms away. "Come on, Ted," she murmured. "Brooks is waiting. It'll be all right. Come away from here."

Teddie allowed herself to be led away by the doctor, but her shoulders slumped pathetically and she never looked back. Jack stood watching with his fists on his hips. When they rounded the last corner, he looked at Katherine. "There are some people I need to phone," he said quietly. "But first I want to wash this off."

Katherine knew she needed to be strong. "There's a sink just inside." She pushed open the door to the first-aid station. A low couch took up the far wall facing a stainless-steel basin. When Jack saw his reflection above the sink, he stopped and stared for a moment.

Katherine wondered what he saw. As if he were studying a stranger's features, Jack turned his head slightly, presenting a better view of the old scar that slid like a tentacle over his cheek bone. He took a deep breath, and closing his eyes, he leaned heavily against the sink. He remained that way for several long heartbeats, then he shook his head and turned on the faucets until steam rose from the gushing spigot.

Katherine stood behind him with her arms crossed, hugging herself while he washed and rewashed his face and hands and arms. A helpless misery gripped her all the while she waited for him to finish. When he turned around, she almost sobbed. His eyes were dry; his face composed. Where did it all go? she wondered. Where is his grief?

"I need to make some phone calls now," he said quietly. "I'm sure Judy will be waiting for us back at the stalls. It would be better if someone else told the younger girls."

"I'll do that. I'll do... anything I can, Jack."

He smiled sadly. "How about a hug?"

She fell into his arms and let her tears come. She cried for the Phoenix and for Teddie and for Jack, who couldn't cry for himself. He held her close but not hard. His hands traced a slow trail over her shoulders, down the curve of her spine and over the sharp angles of her hip bones. Then back up, over the swell of her shoulder blades, up under her hair and into the little hollow at the base of her neck where the hair grew wispy and fine. His fingers moved lightly over her, like the hands of a sightless man reading braille.

Katherine fought for composure. For the first time ever, Jack's touch seemed hesitant. Tentative. Almost wary. The thought arrowed through Katherine that now he might be afraid to care too much for her—afraid that she, too, would disappear from his life the way so many other things he cared for had disappeared. She knew her face was a ruin, but she threw her head back, clutched at him fiercely and gazed into his dry and desolate eyes. "I'll always be there for you, Jack. And I'll be strong, too. I can—"

His lips silenced hers. He had been comforting her, and now he took comfort. She submitted joyfully. His hands, no longer tentative, demanded every part of her. She could feel what he said with his hands and lips and arms. He would have everything or nothing. Better to lose all at once. Here and now. Once and for all. Say it now, he demanded, tell me now.

Katherine melted into him. She tangled her fingers in his ragged hair and stroked his temples with her thumbs. She pressed her body into his, against the rough fabric and knotted muscle. Their breaths mingled, rushed in and out of each others' mouths. Their fingers traced eyelids, lips—invaded and shared the kiss.

She would have made love with him then. On the narrow couch in the little room outside the show ring. On the floor. She was ready to make love with him, eager to share more with him. Their first love would be desperate, aching—a dance of anguish and comfort. She knew he sensed all she thought. Her kisses and the way she touched him held nothing back, offered all she had to give. He knew.

Jack groaned again and cupped her face in his hands. His kisses slowed, soothed. Slower still. Not so desperate, not so breathless. She knew it then. This is not the place. Not the time. He trailed a slow kiss down the side of her neck and into the hollow where the skin grew thin and sensitive over her collarbone. His breath, warm and powerful, slowed while he held her and pressed her against him.

"We have to go, Katherine. Everyone will be waiting for us," he said quietly into her hair.

"I know." There were others who would want to help, who would need the chance to offer a hand or a sympathetic word. They would need to see Jack, to be reassured that he was all right.

As they walked back down the aisle through the arena, Katherine couldn't keep her eyes away from the place where Phoenix had fallen. The broken pieces of the jump had been removed and replaced, and the ring had been freshly raked for the evening classes. The high-jump wall stood challenging and silent as it had before. The ring was deserted. Soundless. For Katherine, it was like facing the empty, quiet room after the nightmare passes.

They walked the rest of the way without speaking, and when they turned the corner to where the Blazingbrook contingent was stabled, Katherine stopped. There must have been thirty people milling quietly about in front of the Phoenix's empty stall. His gate was clipped shut, and his blanket had been folded neatly and hung over it.

She almost started crying again at the sight of his fine, polished leather halter with its glistening brass nameplate hanging empty by his stall door. As soon as those in the waiting group saw Jack, they grew quiet. Judy had been sitting on a tack trunk, and when she glanced up and saw them she stood and walked toward them.

"How's Teddie, Jack? I've been phoning the room, but there's no answer."

"She's fine. She's going back to Houston with Brooks."

A lean sunburned man in jodhpurs and a black turtleneck strode forward and offered Jack his hand. Katherine recognized Dale Justiss, one of Jack's toughest adversaries in the show ring. They had both been scheduled to compete in the grand prix event.

Jack would have been Dale's most serious competition.

"Sorry about your stallion, Jack," he said. "Anything I can do?"

Jack took his hand and shook it thoughtfully. "Well, Dale, if you're serious, I guess you could give me your horse."

All the murmuring stopped, and Dale stood transfixed for one awkward moment. Then he threw his head back and laughed and clapped Jack hard on the shoulder. "You crazy son of a gun. I was worried about you, but I should have known—"

"Yeah, you were scared that I was going to kick your tail Sunday night."

As they talked, the others in the group came forward, all wanting to offer sympathy or ask about Teddie. Someone pressed a drink into Jack's hand and Katherine waved one away. The crowd closed around him, and Katherine, feeling profoundly out of place hung back on the fringes.

Utter control, she thought with a pang. Jack was obviously in complete control of himself and the situation. One or two of the older girls stood around awkwardly, and Jack hugged each of them, patting away their fears and offering his consolation to them. Katherine watched in confusion as he moved easily among his friends and associates.

What's happening? she wondered. What does he feel? How can he act as if nothing happened? Then she noticed that no matter whom Jack spoke with, whose hand he clasped, or whose head was inclined toward him, he always, without fail, faced away from the empty stall.

She had to turn away to keep from bursting into tears. He won't share his grief, she thought. He's got to appear strong, in control of everything, no matter what. He can't let any of them see how he feels. Why? These people really care, she thought. Why can't he let them give him something? Instead he has to hang on to this stupid control. She finally accepted a canned drink from one of the girls and sat down on a folding chair.

For the next hour she spoke quietly with Paula and some of the other Blazingbrook girls, offering consolation here, a shoulder there. She tried to keep Jack in sight, though, thinking that somehow, no matter how collected he seemed, in truth there was part of him that needed her. He had his arm around Elaine O'Neile, one of his students. Elaine swiped at her eyes and nodded when Jack whispered something in her ear. He gave her a rough hug and said something that caused her to raise her brows and then laugh weakly.

People drifted in and out of the barn. Activity was gearing up for the evening classes and grooms came to feed and brush horses, polish tack and tighten loose braids. The crowd in front of Phoenix's stall thinned; many of those who had stopped to see Jack were exhibitors and had to prepare to ride.

Judy's face appeared utterly ashen and blotchy from tears. Katherine reassured her time and time again that there was nothing either of them could have done. Teddie had been determined to take Phoenix out, and no one except her father could have stopped her.

Teddie had been scheduled to show in classes that night, and Judy had taken Katherine aside to explain that someone needed to scratch Teddie's horses ahead of time in order to get the entry fees refunded. After the initial awkward moments had passed when Jack appeared, Katherine noticed that no one seemed to want to bring up the subject of Teddie's whereabouts or what she had done.

Jack leaned against the wooden boards of a stall with one calfskin booted foot crossed casually over the other. He appeared to be listening intently to Sonny Sheppeck's theories regarding bandaging a horse's legs for shipping. Had it not been for the grayness around his eyes and the stains on his clothes, thought Katherine, he'd appear the picture of masculine athletic poise and confidence. She crossed to the tack trunk and stood next to him.

"Jack," she said tentatively, "do you still want to show Duck Soup tonight? Teddie was down to ride him in the hunter classic, but if you'd like I can go to the secretary's office and scratch..." She let the offer drift off.

Jack took a deep breath and ran a hand through his hair.

"Let's see," he replied. "I guess I could ride him. Or I could put... Well, I'm not going to decide just this minute, Katherine. I'll let you know." He folded his arms across his chest and resumed his conversation with Sonny. He didn't even look at her.

He'd never brushed her off before. For the first time ever he seemed remote, preoccupied. Almost cold. Then he moved his arms slightly, and Katherine noticed again the dark blotches staining his shirt and jeans. His eyes were red rimmed and something in his stance struck Katherine as dangerous. He simply couldn't ride that night. Something horrible would happen—she just knew it.

She remembered how he'd looked right after he'd held Phoenix, when he stood up and for the first time saw the ugly stains on his clothes. *Don't argue with him, just act.* She stood and took his arm; he looked down, almost as if surprised to see her. "Jack," she said. "We need to get back to the hotel now. Judy says she can ride in Teddie's place. Mrs. Lockhart will see that the rest of the girls get to and from the hotel. We have to go now."

He looked down and nodded, then turned back to Sonny. "We have to go now."

Sonny shook his hand. "See you later, Jack. It's a damn shame. If you need to leave early, I'll be glad to take some of your horses back with mine."

Katherine felt all the pairs of eyes on them as they walked from the show barn. She tried to speak lightly and cheerfully without seeming nervous. Dr. Valdez had seemed a wonderful vet; Judy had taken it all very hard but had, as usual, been mature and dependable; and weren't the girls all behaving well?

Jack murmured answers in monosyllables if he answered at all. Nearly all spent, Katherine thought. Now if I can just get him to his room without running into anyone else.

Back at the hotel, he opened his door then walked in and tossed the keys on the little table, then sat down and dropped his face into his hands. "Thanks for... for everything, Katherine," he said slowly. "I know I'm acting pretty weird right now, but I don't want you to think that I'm not noticing everything you're doing...."

A dart of pain slid through her and she crossed and sat next to him on the bed. "Don't thank me, Jack. I haven't done anything. I want to be there for you. I want to do anything I can to... to help you."

He looked up. "You know what I'd like? I just wish we could—"

The phone jangled noisily. A double ring. An outside call. Jack picked up the receiver. From listening to one side of the conversation, Katherine could tell that someone else had just heard. Someone else needed to offer commiserations. To find out details. Katherine struggled with a slow boiling anger. They would phone all night, she was sure. The well-meaning friends. The morbidly curious.

As soon as Jack hung up, Katherine sat on the bed, picked up the phone and called the desk at her hotel.

"This is Katherine Hanshaw. Yes, Hanshaw. That's right. Could someone please leave a message for Judy Tuttle in room 119. Tell her that Katherine won't be back at the room tonight, but not to worry. Tell her Jack is taking his phone off the hook. Yes. Fine."

When she hung up the phone and looked at him, a tremor shook her. Gratitude flickered in his tired, golden eyes. Something warmer, too. He didn't even try to kiss her but merely stretched out facedown on the bed, rested his head in her lap and wrapped his arms around her waist. Katherine stacked the pillows behind her and leaned against the headboard, content to hold him, content to know that he was safe and not grieving alone.

"I'm tired, Katherine," he murmured.

"I know," she said softly, smoothing his hair away. "I know."

Chapter Eleven

Katherine watched the red digital numbers on the clock flicker and change configuration. Minutes and hours burned away, each marked with its own bleary numeral. Several times during the long night, Jack's ragged breathing became regular, but just when Katherine thought he'd fallen into a deep sleep, he would groan or ball his hands into fists. Sometimes he clasped her so tightly that he hurt her.

She hadn't been able to convince him to change clothes, and dark stains stood out in ugly contrast against the paleness of his shirt. Stubble roughened his cheeks, and his hair was matted with sweat and sawdust from the show ring. Just when Katherine thought his resistance burned low and his spirit was too battered to fight her, she leaned over and murmured, "Let me take your shirt off, Jack. Just your shirt." He didn't answer but took her hand and kissed her fingers, then pressed her palm against his chest and held it there.

Time crawled. Helplessly, Katherine tried to smooth his hair from his forehead or gently massage the knotted tightness at the base of his neck. All through the night it was the same. His mouth would open as if he meant to speak. Then close. He would clamp his lips tightly and his brow would furrow as if in pain.

She knew he was dreaming—dreaming the same dark dream over and over. A black horse slamming into a wall. The sound of a bone breaking. Running and running in heavy sawdust. A broken figure spinning into endless darkness.

Katherine felt she could offer so little comfort to him in the face of such devastating loss. As the hours crawled by, she snatched fitful moments of sleep. Phoenix had been more than a valuable animal to Jack. All along she had seen that his attachment to the horse went far deeper than economics, deeper than competition—beyond even his burning drive to succeed. Even the animal's name, the Phoenix, revealed his expectations—his hopes. This was how he had intended to redress the past. To rewrite the end of a terrible story. But worse of all, having those dreams destroyed by his daughter—the one person he loved most in the world—must make the loss bitter beyond endurance.

For both of them.

Katherine's thoughts often flitted to Teddie. What was she feeling? Crushing guilt? Horror at what she'd done? Terro of a future filled with subtle accusation by her peers? An then there was the painful irony of knowing how much he father loved her—it would make the reality of what she' caused even more difficult.

Pale light glimmered at the corners of the window whe Katherine finally eased out of Jack's bed. Her eyes wer grainy from lack of sleep and her shoulder ached from cra dling his head. The day hadn't even begun and she alread felt drained. Besides physical exhaustion, emotion wreckage from the previous night lingered oppressively lik a dirty fog.

When Katherine unlocked the door to her room, Judy s up and rubbed her eyes. "Hi. How is he?"

"Bad," Katherine murmured.

Judy winced. "Pretty rough on you, huh?"

The tears were welling up, but Katherine didn't want to ive in to them. If she started, she wasn't sure she could :op. "I'll be okay, but I need to keep moving." Rubbing her yes, she walked to the vanity and took off her earrings, ıen her watch. As long as she kept moving, she could stave ff her grief. "I just want to grab a quick shower, get packed p here and go back and see if there's anything I can do to elp him." Katherine glanced at Judy. She regarded Kath-rine with a wistful, knowing look—a look that spoke vol-mes.

Katherine stopped what she was doing and leaned against ıe vanity. "You know, don't you?"

Judy nodded and smiled. A sad but hopeful smile. Yeah. You can't fool me, I've been around him for years. Vhen you came to work I thought he seemed to like you a ɔt, but then it was so unlike him. He's never gotten, well, *ıvolved* with anyone as long as I can remember."

Katherine squeezed her eyes closed and rubbed her tem-les. "I thought we'd been completely discreet. We decided ıonths ago to wait until after the summer so nothing would ɛ inappropriate. So there wouldn't be any cause for gos-p."

"Oh, don't worry," Judy said, leaning forward. "You ren't the subject of rumors or anything like that. It's just ıat I know him so well, and I've seen the way he acts when ɔu're around. To tell you the truth, as soon as anyone sees ow he looks at you . . . I mean, you'd have to be blind not see it." She tilted her head. "Are you in love with him, o?"

"Madly."

Judy stood and crossed the room. "Wonderful. It's what ɛ's needed for a long time." She hugged Katherine, then ood away. "Don't take any bull from him. Guys can be al pills, you know. Especially Jack."

Katherine struggled again with her tears. "I wish he ould be a pill. I just can't stand to see him this way."

Judy's face clouded. "I know. But if you really—"

At that moment someone knocked softly at the door.

"Brooks," Katherine said when she opened the door. . behind him, looking ashen and deflated, stood Teddie. eyes were vacant; she hadn't even brushed her hair.

"Hi, Ted."

The girl barely nodded. She flicked a glance at Kath ine. "Have you talked to my dad? I think the phone is the hook in his room."

"It is, sweetheart. So many people were phoning night and the hotel people didn't know who to put thro so I... he just took it off."

"We just stopped by to get her things," Brooks softly. "We're heading back for Houston now. She c ride today, and she's just not up to a lot of explanati and... all."

Katherine nodded. "That's probably best."

"Has he asked about me?" Teddie blurted out. A br darkened her mouth, and her lip was swollen and puck around a thin scab. "He didn't phone me."

The anguish in her voice tore at Katherine. "Of cours asked about you. You're the most important thing in his You know that. He was just so exhausted last night... Th all."

Katherine crossed to Teddie and pulled her into her a "Try not to worry so much. I know this is awfully to but your dad loves you more than anything in the world. all work out."

"We had a call from Houston last night," Brooks quietly. "Teddie won the modeling contest."

"Teddie won the modeling contest."

Katherine smoothed Teddie's tangled hair away from face. "That's wonderful news. Congratulations, Teddie we have a real cover girl among us."

Teddie gazed up vacantly. Tears spilled from her eyes ran down her cheeks in wobbly rivulets. "I don't care al that anymore." She didn't sob, and that made her s more dangerously tragic than ever. "I wish I was ugly," said. "Then none of this would have happened."

"Theodora," Brooks said, his voice stern but anguished. "Don't say such terrible things. It was an accident. If your father knew all you went through to be able to—"

The girl suddenly stiffened and turned a panicked gaze up at Katherine. "Today's the day I'm supposed to tell Daddy about Pandora and the money, and all." Her eyes widened. Grew wilder. "I can't tell him." She pulled out of Katherine's arms and backed away. "He'll hate me forever."

"Oh, no, Teddie. You're wrong," Katherine said. "Your father loves you more than—"

"No!" Teddie shouted. "I can't tell him." Her voice rose, tinged with hysteria, and she glanced frantically from Brooks to Katherine. "Please don't make me."

"Of course you don't have to tell him today," Brooks soothed.

Katherine was certain neither Jack nor Teddie could take any more right then. There seemed little to be gained at that point by Teddie's confession. "Don't even think about it, Teddie. Now look here, Judy's got your things packed. I'm not sure what time we'll be back in Houston, so why don't you plan to spend the night with your grandfather. Don't you think that's best, Brooks?"

He nodded gravely and tried to smile. "That's a good idea. Come to my house, sweetpea."

Katherine patted her gently on the shoulder. "I promise I'll ask your dad to phone you as soon as we get home. Okay? Is it settled, then?"

Teddie's head drooped. "Okay." She didn't look up again.

"Shall I help take your things down?" Katherine asked.

Brooks shook his head. "Thanks, but it's just the suit bag and an overnight case. We can manage."

Katherine mouthed the words "I'll phone you."

Brooks nodded and picked up the luggage. As Katherine watched him follow his granddaughter down the corridor, she thought for the first time that Brooks looked stooped. Old. A dark thought slithered through her mind. What would Jack do when he found out the part Brooks had played in this whole situation? She shuddered as she closed the door.

After the Sunday morning classes, Katherine got all the girls checked out and the bills settled. Jack and Hermes, who stopped by briefly from their hotel, drove the van back to Houston, while Katherine and Judy went together in the station wagon. The horse van was nearly empty because so many of the girls had made prior arrangements to have their horses shipped directly back to their home stables after the show. And of course, one space in the horse van was conspicuously vacant.

Hours later Katherine stood in the driveway and waved goodbye as Mrs. Philbin's sedan rumbled away. Most of the girls had gone directly to their homes from the Austin show. Paula's family, however, lived just outside Houston, so she'd returned to Blazingbrook to gather her things and walk through the barn one last time. Jack had loaded Swain into the little horse trailer and had followed them to the Philbin's farm.

Now the parking lot was empty. Quiet.

Katherine walked to the front porch and sank into the glider. She toed the gray boards of the porch until the swing moved on its creaking chains in the still, hot air. She needed to sleep, and she needed to pack, but she felt too drained tc tackle any of her chores.

The dust had long since settled back onto the powdery white gravel when Katherine saw a familiar beige Rolls pul up. Teddie got out and walked toward the house. When she looked up and saw Katherine on the porch, she lifted he hand to wave. She didn't smile. When Katherine saw Teddie up close, she nearly gasped. The girl's beautiful face seemed haggard, washed out. "Is everybody gone?"

Katherine nodded, trying to keep her concern fron showing. "The Philbins just left. Your dad is taking Swai out to their farm."

Teddie nodded. "I wanted to say goodbye to Paula bu I—I—"

"It's all right, sweetheart. Everyone was in such a hurry."

"I need some stuff from my room for tonight, and Brooks thinks it would be best if he wasn't here at the same time...with my dad, you know."

Katherine sighed. "I guess not. Why don't you go get your things and I'll go keep him company." Without another word Teddie crossed the porch, and soon Katherine heard her footsteps on the stairs. She turned back toward the parking lot. Brooks stood leaning against his car with his arms crossed as he gazed away from the house. Wearing his customary slacks, loafers and patched sweater, he looked urbane, elegant and wistful.

Katherine needed a few minutes alone with him to return the key and money. She could have mailed them, but this was something personal. She'd left her purse on the table in the foyer, and it only took a moment to grab the envelope.

As she walked outside and across the front lawn she noticed the unmistakable signs of the approaching fall. Fading leaves. A dryness in the air. A slow quiet as if everything were settling down to sleep. Three months ago she had thought she'd be looking forward to this fall as a new beginning; instead, so many things were coming to an end.

Brooks must have heard Katherine approaching, because he turned and smiled broadly. His smile didn't reach his eyes, though. They looked tired and sad.

"Katherine." He walked toward her with his hand extended. "How was your ride home? How is Jack?"

"As well as can be expected," she replied as she took his hand. "He's gone to take Swain to the Philbins'."

He tilted his head, his brilliant blue eyes cloudy with concern. "So he's holding up all right?"

Katherine shook her head. "I really can't tell. It's been so busy. He's going about his work. Moving the horses. Making the phone calls. But it's as if there's something gone out of him." She sighed. "I suppose that's to be expected after everything that happened."

"I suppose so," Brooks murmured. He sighed and crossed his arms. "Katherine, I've been thinking and I'm afraid I have another favor to ask you. I was wondering if you would consider being the one to tell Jack what happened. With Pandora and the other horses, I mean. I want to, but I think it would be too bitter coming from me. I can't tell you how much I regret my part in this. It seems now that every time I try to help, things just seem to get worse." He pinched the bridge of his nose as if he felt pain. "Teddie simply can't endure telling him," he said quietly. "She's almost incoherent with misery. I'm afraid she'd do something...foolish if she thought she had to face her father with this. I was hoping—"

"You don't have to say any more," Katherine replied. "I've been thinking about it, too. It would be best coming from me, and actually I want to be the one to tell him." She gazed around at the empty paddocks, the quiet fields, and took a deep breath. "And now, Mr. Brooks," she said briskly, "what in the world is the meaning of this?" She presented the envelope toward him, held gingerly between her thumb and forefinger.

If a man as elegant as Edwin Grosvenor Brooks could look sheepish, he did then. "Ah, yes," he began. "Well, Katherine, you see...I thought you might have a question about that." He took a short breath. "The truth is there are so very few people in the world who mean anything at all to me. I lost my only child. My wife. And with things the way they are between Jack and me, I get to do so little for Teddie. Do you know how frustrating that is? I spent my life accumulating a fortune, and now I have no one to share it with."

"But this is completely inappropriate. You know I can't take it." She extended the envelope.

Brooks held both hands up in a gesture of rejection. "I'm sorry, Katherine. I refuse to take that back."

"Well, I certainly can't keep it. What would..." She paused and let her voice drift off. She'd been going to say, *What would Jack think?* but the thought seemed out of place. Before she could say anything else, her thoughts were interrupted by the bang of the front door.

Brooks waved and smiled, and then, in a quiet, urgent voice he said, "I wish you would reconsider, Katherine. That condominium has been empty for at least a year, and the money is only slightly more than the regular brokerage fee we pay. Please accept this. It would mean a lot to me."

He glanced over her shoulder toward the house again. "Teddie's almost here. Please keep the money—just in case of emergencies, and feel free to use the condo. If only for a few months. Here she is. We mustn't let her see—"

"But, Brooks, I just can't—"

"Enough," he said firmly. "I won't hear of anything else. Teddie," he called and smiled broadly. "All set, sweet-pea?"

Katherine folded the envelope and jammed it into her hip pocket, then turned around. Teddie walked up, put her arms around her grandfather and buried her face against his chest. Her shoulders quivered. Brooks gave Katherine a pained look and patted Teddie's back. "It's all right," he said softly, his own voice trembling. "It'll all work out. I promise."

Teddie straightened, and looked up at him. "It'll never be all right again, Granddad. Never."

Katherine stepped forward and rested her hand on Teddie's back. "It's going to be tough, Teddie, but we'll all come out on the other side of this. You'll see."

Teddie faced Katherine and looked at her through eyes swimming in tears. "Will you tell Daddy I'm sorry I didn't get to say goodbye to him? Will you tell him I'll be back tomorrow night?" She looked at her shoes. "I won't phone, though. I'll just talk to him when I get back."

"Of course I will. I know he's sorry he wasn't here to see you, but he had to move Swain—"

"I know, Katherine," Teddie said softly. "He's trying to stay busy."

Katherine looked up at Brooks. He didn't meet her gaze but turned and busied himself settling Teddie's canvas bag in the front seat of his car. When they left, Katherine stood and watched the cloud of dust until it disappeared in the distant avenue of trees.

Jack would be back soon. Katherine folded her arms and walked in the house.

It seemed unnaturally quiet. She left the front door open to listen for the returning truck while she checked her reflection in the foyer's mirror. I look so tired, she thought. When she smoothed her shirt into her jeans, her hand brushed against paper tucked in her jeans pocket. The envelope. She drew it out.

The azure-and-green waterfall logo on the envelope looked cool and elegant. The thought of living in Brookstone III was definitely tempting. Her apartment could only be described as, well, efficient. Small. Fairly close to the bank. Still, there was no way she could accept Brooks's offer. Jack would be livid. She jammed the envelope back in her pocket.

He would consider her living at one of Brooks's developments as consorting with the enemy—even if she paid fo it with her own money. Ha. What a laugh. As if she coul afford a place like Brookstone. Monday she would have t phone Mr. Wiley and tell him about the horse show and tha Jack would, of course, be losing the barn.

Katherine thought again of Jack. Once he found out th way Brooks and Teddie had tricked him, he was going to b furious. Teddie was his daughter whom he adored, and he remorse and heartbreaking vulnerability would soften hir toward her, but Brooks? This would probably sour their re lationship even more. It seemed so sad. Brooks had onl wanted to help.

There was nothing left to do now but go upstairs and be gin sorting through her things. Packing, she thought. I can think of anything I'd rather *not* do.

She glanced at her watch. Jack should be back soon. T day might have been a wonderful day for them. Alone last. All the girls had returned to their homes and Tedd would be with Brooks. They'd have hours to spend alo together. Even now, after all that had happened, that image sent a swirl of sensation through Katherine.

Her thoughts were cut short by the sound of a car pulling into the driveway. She walked to the front door and looked out and her heart leaped. Jack stepped out of the pickup and glanced toward the house. Katherine raised her hand in greeting. He nodded and waved.

As he walked toward the house, Katherine nervously smoothed the fabric of her blouse and patted her hair. She wore it down, the way he liked it. What if he had decided to simplify his life, to eliminate any possible source of pressure. She squeezed her eyes closed for a moment.

"Please let him still care for me," she whispered. She licked her lips and waited. As he crossed the lawn toward her, his eyes never left hers. He didn't speak, and when he reached the porch, he jumped up the low steps and without hesitation he folded her into his arms.

He does care. He does.

Katherine pressed her face against his shirt and shivered at the feel of his warm breath moving through her hair. When he kissed her temple, her heart quickened. With the tenderest roughness he tangled his hands in her hair and teased her head back.

"Are you all right?" she asked.

"At this moment I'm better than I've been in the last couple of days," he said.

Then the past, with all its fractured dreams, faded into nothing. Katherine felt the hand at her waist move downward, pressing her hips into his. His tongue flicked down the side of her neck to the hollow just beneath her ear, and a fire low inside her roared to life.

Her lips parted in a sigh of desire. He caught it in his mouth and breathed it back into hers. She held him to her, memorizing the feel of his body pressed against hers. His lean legs. The deep furrow of his backbone and his straight flanks and hard ribs. She pulled him closer. He groaned.

"So long," he murmured. "I've wanted this for so long." He lifted a hand and gently stroked her hair. "But everything is so...so—"

She raised her hands to his face. To be able to touch him this way, to finally comfort him, was a sweet agony. She wanted to take his troubles and make them disappear. She wanted time to stop. "Don't think about it," she said. "Just hold me."

They stood pressed together, exploring and learning—stoking a passion she knew would take hours to exhaust. There was no hurry now. The torture of waiting seemed almost sweet. Thoughts of the stable, of livelihoods and horses and futures faded to irrelevance. This place and time were all that existed. All that mattered was his hard stomach pressing into hers. The fire from his hands and lips. Her eagerness to explore him and make him hers in every way she knew.

The wind sighed through the willow trees and somewhere in the house, old wood moaned in return. His mouth left hers for a moment. "It's time to go upstairs," he murmured.

She gazed up at him and lifted the corners of her mouth. They moved like sleepwalkers, like dancers—each movement a caress, a surrender.

The bedroom seemed so far away. She wanted to stop in the entryway where the sunlight would wash over them—where the dappled light through the willow would play across his shoulders and his furrowed chest. The heels of his boots thumped faintly on the parquet, and a breeze slid through the door and around them. She stopped, faced him and tugged his shirt free. His skin quivered under her touch. So firm. So warm. Sweet air, heavy with the smells of cut grass, bruised pine needles and rich earth swirled and cloaked them.

Katherine wanted to drift away with him, to immerse herself in touches and kisses and all of love's tender indignities. First, though, there was something she had to do.

Part of her would hold back until he knew the truth, and she wanted no hesitation between them. No barriers.

"Jack," she said softly as his teeth grazed the side of her neck. "We have to talk."

Maybe he hadn't heard. His arms enclosed her and his fingers slid down gently and caressed her rib cage, her waist and back up to brush tantalizingly close to the sides of her breasts.

"Jack, please. We have to."

He stopped. Sighed. Stepped away and brought his hands up to cup her face. "What? What can there possibly be to say that we haven't said without words? You aren't afraid, are you?"

The tenderness on his face pierced her. He was a good man. A man who endured terrible loss without self-pity. A man who struggled hard against devastating burdens to keep what he loved intact. He deserved honesty. Loyalty. Love. She had to clear away every shred of deceit between them so that she could come to him without reserve. Without regret.

"It's about Teddie. And Pandora. And I suppose it's about Phoenix and me and everything that's happened since I came here. And before."

A pained look crossed his face and he tried to smile. "You want to talk about horses now? Now?"

She pressed her hands against his chest. "Please, Jack. We have to." She wanted her voice to stay strong, but it betrayed her and fell to a whisper. "Brooks played a part in this, too, but I didn't know about it until a couple of weeks ago."

Had she not been gazing directly into his eyes, she would have missed it, but at the mention of his former father-in-law, a flash of animosity kindled in his eyes. He let his hands fall. "What is it, then? What's this about?"

Katherine didn't try to recount every detail, and she deliberately omitted the things that would cause Jack more pain, but she spoke with quick intensity as she recounted everything starting with the day at the bank when Wiley called her in. The way Wiley coerced her. The modeling contest. Teddie's portfolio. Pandora. Suzanne Sifara's father.

"And then in Austin Teddie gave me this. It's from Brooks." She took the envelope out of her pocket and handed it to him.

His hands were steady as he took it, but his eyes narrowed as he flipped the envelope over and withdrew the letter. As he counted the one-hundred-dollar bills his eyes grew wide again.

Katherine cleared her throat, but he didn't look up. "I tried to give it back to him today, but he wouldn't take it." She told him what Brooks had said. That he was behind the purchase of most of the horses over the summer. That he had intended to buy Phoenix.

Jack smoothed open the paper and began to read. Katherine had memorized the words.

> ...Thanks so much for everything you've done for Teddie and me. We would never have been able to accomplish this without your help...
>
> I'm getting rather used to buying Pandora now...

Although his face was tilted down to read, Katherine saw his brows knit and his mouth open slightly as if he couldn't breathe well. When he looked at the crisp bills, his face darkened.

Katherine shifted uncomfortably. Why didn't he say anything? Ask questions? Rant? "Today he told me Teddie was too torn up to face you with all of this. He asked if I would tell you about his part as well as Teddie's." She paused. "He feels horrible about everything, Jack. I know he does."

His silence began to unnerve her. Why didn't he talk? Curse Brooks? Threaten to punish Teddie?

"Now I see," he said very quietly.

Something in his voice sent dread sliding down the flesh of Katherine's spine like a cold finger. Slowly, with obvious deliberation and care, Jack tucked the money back into the letter, folded it once, twice, three times and replaced it in its envelope.

"I expect this sort of thing from Brooks. And it doesn't really surprise me coming from Teddie. But you, Katherine. You, too?"

Then he raised his eyes, and all the air left the room.

Chapter Twelve

Katherine's heart labored, each beat squeezing a universe of agony through her body. "Jack, I can explain—"

"Can you?"

She could barely stand to look at him. The betrayal and pain in his face seared her. Not even when the Phoenix died had he seemed so devastated. "Can you really?" His voice was toneless. Dead. For the space of five slow heartbeats he stared at her without moving. Then something stirred in his eyes and altered the pallor of his skin. Katherine had seen his anger before but nothing like this creeping rage. A giddy dread sawed through her as he focused his gaze on her. He took a hard, shallow breath. "I'd be interested to hear what you have to say. But then there's no telling what you'd leave out, is there, Katherine?"

The expression on his face hardened and set. *My God,* Katherine thought, *that's not rage. It's loathing.* She reached out to touch his arm. "Jack, please. It's not what you think." He recoiled.

"Don't." The word rang dully like metal dropped on concrete. "So it's true? You knew all along that Brooks fronted the money to buy Pandora?"

"Yes, but—"

"And you were really working for Farm and Home when you came here?"

"Jack, if you'll just listen—"

He took an ominous step toward her. "Were you?" he shouted.

Katherine flinched. "Yes, but you see, they were going to—"

He looked down at the letter and his mouth twisted. "You and Brooks," he said quietly, but the accusation roared in Katherine's ears as if he had bellowed the words. "You and Brooks... and Teddie."

He looked squarely into Katherine's eyes, and in that moment she watched his love for her gutter and fail. She saw it die as unmistakably as if it were a fire being drowned by a rising tide of cold, filthy water. "Jack, please..." She heard rather than felt the sob in her own voice. "Please give me a chance to explain—" She took him by the arms. She would hold on to him. Force him to hear her.

He glanced down at her hands as if they were snakes twined around him. Then his eyes found hers. "You've interfered in my relationship with my daughter," he said, his voice intoning the words like a verdict. His right hand closed over Katherine's wrist and pulled it away. "You deceived me," he said, and rotated his other arm, forcing her to release him. "And now," he continued, as he leveled a look of utter contempt at her, "you're wasting my time."

She reached up one last time, desperately fighting a rising tide of despair. "Jack, give me a chance..."

"Get away from me," he ordered, as he shoved her arms away. His voice sounded strangled. "Get out of my house."

Hot tears poured down Katherine's face. "Don't do this to us, Jack. You're making a mistake. I love—"

He grabbed her wrist. "Don't," he said, and the word cracked like a pistol shot. He dragged her forward until their faces were almost touching. "Don't *you* dare ever say that to me." He turned Katherine's hand over and slapped Brooks's letter into it, then folded her fingers around it. He grinned at her—a tortured, death's-head grin. "I'll say one thing for you." His voice sounded eerily jaunty. Mad with grief. "You don't come cheap, do you?"

Then he turned away. He must have moved his body awkwardly because a spasm of pain racked his face. As he walked toward the door, he limped so badly that it seemed that he almost dragged one leg. Before going out he turned to face her. "On the other hand, I guess cheap *is* the right word, after all."

He was gone.

Katherine's legs wouldn't hold her, and she collapsed to the floor, her arms wrapped around her body. She cried silently, her hair curtaining her face and plastered against her wet cheeks. Crushed under the weight of her own guilt, Katherine bowed her head until it met the floor. Soon the hardwood felt clammy against her forehead and she couldn't seem to breathe. She sat up and dragged a hand across her face. Convulsive sobs still shook her, bubbling up like poisoned water and filling the empty hallway with the sound of grief.

He would never forgive her. Never. She had betrayed him. She should have gone to him immediately about Pandora. She should have told him about the bank. She should have. She should... Her mind reeled. How could she explain it? How would she make him understand? She remembered the look on his face. The contempt. The loathing. "No," she groaned. "I didn't mean to... I didn't mean..." She buried her face in her hands.

When her sobs subsided to shudders, she grabbed the edge of the table and dragged herself up. The house seemed unnaturally quiet. Waiting. The room closed around her. Reminded her of what she had done. Accused her. Stared.

She had to get out.

She wanted to wash her face. She had things to pack. None of it mattered. He had ordered her out and she had t get away. Grabbing her purse, she fled through the house and out the front door. She didn't even want to walk out the same door he had. If she saw him something would tear loose inside her. Her spirit would hemorrhage.

As she ran across the lawn, the trailing fronds of the willow trees seemed to reach for her and drag at her. She was running. Getting inside her car.

With a roar of outrage the engine came to life. White fence boards blurred as she fled down the drive and out of the stable. Out of Blazingbrook. Out of his life. Again she saw his face. The disbelief. The pain undiluted by hope or mercy. He would never forgive, never forget.

Katherine realized she was driving dangerously fast. It didn't matter. She had helped destroy the spirit of the only man she would ever love. The Phoenix was dead, killed because of his daughter. He had lost his chance to redeem his business. The woman he loved had betrayed him with his bitterest enemy. His daughter had conspired with both of them to trick him. Katherine thought she would go mad from the magnitude of it all. She pressed the accelerator harder. And what about Teddie?

Dread sawed through Katherine for Jack's daughter. What would he say to her? She envisioned one hideous scenario after another. Teddie would feel this same devastation. And she was still just a little girl. She would carry a horrible burden of guilt and remorse for years. She would never pursue her dreams; she'd feel unworthy of ever having a happy moment, knowing the pain she'd caused her father. Brooks would never be allowed to spend time with Teddie again. And the poor horse. Since Jack knew Pandora really belonged to Brooks, he'd probably turn her loose on the highway. Katherine took a tremulous breath and swiped at her eyes with the back of her hand. So many lives were ruined and she could have prevented all of it.

The insupportable weight of her guilt settled around her. There would be no escape from it. Ever. Behind her she left the wreckage of so many ruined lives and all of it was her fault. All of it.

Or was it?

The ghost of an accusation wormed through her ravaged conscience. Teddie or Brooks shared some of the responsibility for what had happened. Teddie could have been honest with Jack about her aspirations. If her father wanted something else for her, well, that was something she'd have to face. And Brooks might have at least tried to approach Jack with the idea of loaning Teddie the money. After all, even if she didn't win the contest, she was bound to make enough money to pay back the cost of her portfolio. The car lurched on the gravel and Katherine eased back on the gas pedal.

She sighed. A long, quivering sigh of resignation. How could people who are supposed to love one another treat each other in such a way? Jack would never even know how important modeling was to his daughter. He hadn't been given a chance by Brooks or Teddie, but then he probably wouldn't have listened if either of them *had* tried. Yet, who knew how he might have felt about his daughter's ambition? He might even have been proud. Someone should have told someone. Katherine had been caught in the middle of their old quarrels. Old hurts. Old unhealed wounds.

Then the memory came crashing back. Jack's face. A wasteland. Ruination. He'd lashed out at her in his own pain and despair. His "cheap" comment had been a little strong. After all, that entire summer she'd been loyal, patient and supportive. She'd been there for him when he needed her, and she'd put her life on hold until the timing was better for Jack and his business. She'd tried to smooth the way between Brooks and Jack and Teddie. If Jack hadn't been so rigid and unforgiving, Teddie could have told him what modeling meant to her. If he'd only been willing to accept the apology Brooks so often offered, then the older man could have given his only grandchild the money openly. The poor kid wouldn't have been forced to either sell the only remnant of her mother, or sneak behind her father's back to borrow money he couldn't spare.

Katherine sighed. Jack would never see it that way. He'd been irrational in his pain—like an injured animal that lashes out blindly in agony. Yes, just like an injured animal.

But Jack wasn't an animal. He was a man. A thinking, intelligent, rational human being. Someone with the power to weigh facts and come to conclusions. A mature adult with plenty of time and information to make considered decisions. Katherine let the car coast.

The anger started somewhere at the base of her spine and roiled up her backbone in a white hot wave.

Cheap? She slammed on the brakes.

Jamming the automobile into reverse, she whipped the convertible around in the narrow lane. She remembered the fear on Teddie's face when she insisted that Katherine not tell Jack about the modeling competition. She remembered the resignation on Brooks's face when Jack had scorned his handshake. Her knuckles whitened on the steering wheel. She had supported every one of his decisions, bitten back her deepest misgivings, swallowed her pride and waited patiently. Everyone had tiptoed around him and accepted his word as the last word.

Even if it was a word like cheap.

"Well, not this time, buster," Katherine said. "Nobody calls me names." Once again she recalled the contempt in his face, in his voice. She pressed her lips together. "I'll give you cheap, you...you..." She couldn't bring herself to voice any of the words that sprang to mind. Instead she pressed the accelerator down, and sneered at the Caution sign. Gravel rattled against the car's undercarriage and peppered the fence boards when she careened around the corner.

She remembered the first time she'd pulled into that lane. Cars had taken up every available space. None were parked there now except Jack's battered red pickup, parked in almost the same place it had been that day. The memory fanned her anger even more. From day one he'd been the same. "Arrogant, hardheaded, unforgiving... bossy," she muttered.

There was no doubt where she'd find him, and she parked as close to the barn as she could. Leaping out, she slammed the door so hard that the car rocked. Stalking toward the barn as quickly as she could, she flung her purse down and broke into a run. He might physically throw her off the property, but he was sure going to get an earful before he did.

Her emotion must have been apparent in her body language because Ishmael first pricked his little ears forward when he saw her, then flinched and leaped backward. He'd been turned loose to wander through the barn, and the warm nicker that started deep in his throat turned into a squeak of alarm as he shot out the barn doors and galloped toward the outside ring.

Katherine ignored him as she rounded the corner and ran up the stairs to the loft, taking them two at a time. Even though she was wearing sandals, her feet echoed loudly on the steps. The loft was dark.

Just as she thought, he stood silhouetted against the open hay doors. His arms were crossed and his back was to her. He'd probably been there since he stormed out of the house, standing and staring out at the view he'd lost forever, she thought. The view he'd thrown away because of his own stubborn ego, she amended.

"Jack," Katherine said and she strode between the hay bales. "I've got something to say to you."

He turned and Katherine almost chocked on her words. His face seemed so haggard, so hard. Then she remembered. *Cheap.*

"In the first place, I don't appreciate being called cheap by you, and I'm telling you now, don't you ever call me names again. Ever. And secondly, it's about time you realized that everyone here has tiptoed around you for months—years even—because of what happened. Only instead of putting it behind you and getting on with your life you've been carrying around a grudge and waving it like club. It's like you're saying, 'I can act any way I like, say anything I want, be rude, demanding and unforgiving be cause I got hurt. Life kicked me around.' Well, let me tell you something. None of the rest of us has it easy, either. Everyone gets kicked around, and you're just going to have to get over it."

Something dangerous flickered in his eyes and he uncrossed his arms. The beginnings of alarm fluttered through Katherine, and she thought she might not have too much longer to finish what she had to say, so she blurted out the story about overhearing Teddie's conversation with Brooks and everything else she'd left out earlier. "And another thing. Teddie hates horse shows. She has for years. More than anything she wants to be a model, but she's so scared that she'll disappoint you she's been too scared to tell you. And as far as being forced to sell Pandora—"

"That's ridiculous," he interrupted. "You think I don't know how my own daughter feels? Teddie knows how much I love her. If she felt so strongly about wanting to model she would have come to me and—"

"Oh, no she wouldn't," Katherine snapped. "She can't come to you because she's afraid you won't love her anymore if you know how she feels. The only reason she rides competitively is so she can please you, be close to you. But she's afraid if you find out how she really feels you'll freeze her out. That's your doing. Maybe all that icy determination and single-mindedness got you through when you were hurt, but now you're so determined to do things your way that you freeze anyone out who dares to oppose you. You insist on having everything your way with no questions asked. You want to carry your stupid grudges around without anyone telling you how... how stupid you're acting—"

"You don't know what you're talking about. Anyone here—Teddie, the hired grooms, the students—any of them can come to me any time with—"

"Oh, yeah?" Katherine shot back with an angry toss of her head as she gathered momentum. "Tell me this. When was the last time someone disagreed with you about anything important? You can't, can—"

"That's enough, Katherine. I think you'd better—"

"And another thing," she interrupted, talking even louder. "You say you despise what Brooks did to Blaize, controlling her with money. Dangling clothes and cars and...and whatever in front of her so she'd do just what he wanted her to do and withdrawing all of it when she didn't please him. Well, you're doing the same thing to Teddie. Only you're even more cruel because you control her with fear. She's afraid you won't love her. She's afraid she'll disappoint you. She can't even tell you when she misses her mother because she's scared to death you won't love her anymore. She's just a little girl, Jack...."

He was definitely walking toward her, stalking her almost, with an unmistakable glint in his golden eyes. Katherine pressed herself against the hay. "You're turning into what you hate, Jack. You've been obsessed about Brooks for years and now you're doing exactly what you accuse him of doing." Her voice was faltering, and the fire she'd felt before had almost expended itself. She felt drained, and the lump that had formed in her throat made her words sound strangled. She stood as tall as she could and looked at him through eyes swimming with tears.

"There is one last thing, Jack. I love you. Did you hear that? I love you, and nothing and no one can stop me from saying that now." Her lips had begun to quiver, and though there were still things she wanted to say, she knew her voice would fail her. "This is one time being scared of you is not going to prevent someone from speaking out. You can't stop me." She dropped her gaze and swiped at her eyes with the back of her hand. "I can say what I like. I don't work here anymore."

He towered over her and she tried to shrink away, but the hay trapped her in front of him. The sun had fallen low enough to blaze through the open hay door. The fiery backlight obscured Jack's face, and Katherine couldn't make out his features, but she didn't really want to. She remembered the coldness she'd seen in his eyes. Lethal coldness. Enough to freeze even love. He raised both his hands and she flinched, squeezing her eyes closed.

His hands closed around her shoulders and pulled her forward. Katherine stiffened. Surely he wouldn't push her bodily down the steps. Or out the... She sucked in a huge breath and gathered herself to struggle, but instead of handling her roughly, he pulled her to him and closed her in his arms. With one hand he stroked her hair and ran his fingers beneath it to press against her neck. His heart thundered against her breasts, and she hesitantly folded her arms about his waist. He sighed into her hair. "You're right."

Katherine's mouth fell open. "Wha...what did you say?" she murmured against his shirt.

She felt him take a tired breath. "I said, 'You are right.'" Then the strangest thing happened. He laughed. "But I don't have to like it."

Katherine arched her back to look up at him. "What did you say?"

"You're repeating yourself."

"I—I don't understand," she said. "Turn this way so I can see your face." She tried to step away, but he wouldn't let her. Instead he held her tightly, pressed her close. Closer.

"Not yet. Just let me hold you for a minute."

She melted into his arms, hardly daring to believe the glorious feel of the hands tenderly tracing the curve of her spine, the nape of her neck, the angle of her shoulders. He sighed. "Do you know what hurt the most?" he asked quietly. "I thought you didn't love me. Losing the barn seemed minor. I know someday I'll get over what happened to my horse. I've gotten over some tough things before. And Teddie and Brooks...well, I'll admit that'll take some getting used to. But you...if you didn't love me. I don't think I'd ever get over that. The wheelchair seemed trivial compared to not having you."

"You mean you're not...you don't hate me?"

He sagged against her and his breath rushed out with a sound halfway between a sigh and laugh. "Hate you? *Hate you?*" He pulled back and turned sideways so that they were both half lit by the setting sun. "Katherine, you're the only woman I've ever loved."

The words thundered through her like a torrent of joy. *"You're the only woman I've ever loved."* She pulled back and looked up into his face. "But what about—"

He pressed his fingers to her lips. "Be quiet for a minute. No, don't interrupt me. Now you listen." As he spoke he tenderly pushed away the tendrils of hair from her face. "Blaize and I were a lot alike—two wild, rebellious kids who saw something similar in each other. If I were really being honest I'd say we probably married as an act of defiance. We were attracted to the wildness in each other, but it was never love. I didn't know anything about love."

His hand fell to her cheek, her collarbone, reverently traced the outline of her breast. "We were married before either of us grew up, and then we were struggling to stay afloat. You know the rest. After my accident I didn't have love to sustain me, so hate just had to do. It did pretty well, too. I hated what happened to me. I hated losing my future, my family, my legs. After a while I just hated. It made me strong and maybe even scared me a little. Still I couldn't let go of it."

He closed his eyes as if remembering the old pain. "Even after I started walking again, after I got Teddie back, there was still some part of me that said I needed that...that strength I got from hating so many things, fighting so many things. I was afraid that if I let go of it, everything would fall apart again. But then you came along, and it seemed that everything had finally fallen into place. I got my life back. I had a family again, and as soon as I sold Phoenix that whole time would be gone forever—something would be completed. I would have the woman I loved, my barn, my beautiful little girl and there was nothing that ol' bast...nothing that Brooks, my enemy, could do about it." He closed his eyes and shook his head. "But then it all unraveled so fast. I should have known it wouldn't be that easy."

"Jack, there are some things you're not saying. Brooks isn't really your enemy. It's just that back when you were dating Blaize he just thought you wanted—"

"You think I don't know that?" He gave Katherine a wry look. "Every time I see some hormonal sixteen-year-old ogling Teddie I know exactly how he felt about me. I want to either fire up a chainsaw or maroon Teddie on an island until she's . . . oh, thirty-five or so."

"Then why didn't you ever . . . ?"

"Katherine, I'm not a saint—I'm just a man. That mean old devil gave me hell and I wanted my chance to give it right back. Things didn't work out like he planned, so he comes here, waving wads of dough in Teddie's face—in my face—and saying all's forgiven and he's ready to play Happy Families again. Well, let me tell you—"

"Jack, you're working yourself into a state again. And besides that—" Katherine took a shaky breath "—besides that, you're wrong."

Jack's mouth snapped shut and he narrowed his eyes. "What do you mean by that?"

"You know exactly what I'm going to say, and you're not going to like it. You and Brooks are just alike. You both react like cavemen when you think something's threatening your family. But you're just not taking into account that Brooks loves Teddie and she loves him. And you know what? That's not so bad. How many people do you get in your life who really love you? Do you think he's going to take all of Teddie's love? Believe me, there's plenty of Teddie to go around. If the two of you could just strike some kind of happy medium between overindulging her and overcontrolling her . . ."

Jack raised his hand. "Enough about Brooks. I've had it with his interference. But if he did what he did because of some...some modeling thing for Teddie. Well, I'll let it go. We'll just call it a loan and Teddie can—"

"Jack!"

"Okay," he said, rolling his eyes toward the ceiling. "It's a done deal. Brooks gave Teddie the money for this...this..." He looked at Katherine and for the first time she saw a flicker of something new in his face. Confusion. Regret. "What kind of modeling thing was this?"

Katherine smiled tenderly at him. "It was a contest sponsored by a teen magazine to find new faces—a talent search for models."

"And Teddie did well?"

"She won."

Katherine saw the words slam into him. His brows drew together. "Was there any kind of, you know, pageant or something? Anything I should have gone to?"

Katherine squeezed his arm. "No. No pageant. But you could see the composites and the bio she sent in. That's what the money from Brooks went to pay for—professional photography. She won enough money to pay back what he gave her, though. It's really a very prestigious award . . . as modeling goes."

He stared at a place just above and beyond her shoulder. "I didn't know." He sighed. "I guess I didn't want to know." Then he brought both his hands to Katherine's shoulders. "Why didn't you tell me?"

"I promised not to. I tried to get you to talk to her, but you were so preoccupied with the horses. And then I overheard her conversation with Brooks and she thought I was spying on her. She was going to tell you about Pandora, though. Today, actually. But then there was . . . well, Phoenix and all, and Teddie was terrified you'd hate her."

His mouth dropped as if he were going to protest, but the words never came. Instead Katherine saw once again the play of emotions trail across his face. She wasn't going to lie to him, though, even to soften the impact of what had happened.

"I guess it's been pretty bad," he said. "For everybody."

"Pretty bad," she echoed. Jack looked away, and she almost saw the thoughts fleeting across his mind. Regret for the time lost. Anger. Disgust. Acceptance. Then something else clouded his face and he dropped his arms. Katherine felt bereft without that touch. He turned and walked back toward the open hay doors. Katherine followed. "What is it?"

He leaned against the jamb and pulled her toward him. Katherine wrapped her arms around his lean waist and gazed up into his face, but his eyes stayed fixed on the paddocks and rolling fields. A bitter smile curved his mouth. "This would be pretty hard to swallow at any time, but now... I'm not going to be able to make my note, you know. I'm going to lose the stable. And I wanted to ask you to..." He shook his head. "What do I have to offer you now? I don't have a barn or even a place to live now that I'm going to lose Blazingbrook." He glanced down at her and his mouth quirked. "I think that's a stupid name, don't you. My next stable is going to have a better name—something that reflects the real me. Hammerhead Farms or Obstinate Acres or...or something." He looked back out the door. "I am going to miss this place, though." Once again he looked out over the paddocks and hunt field. "I'm really going to miss this place."

Tears stung the back of Katherine's throat. Jack loved Blazingbrook and now he'd lost it. If only I had something to sell, she thought, or huge piles of money or a fabulous credit rating or a friend with huge piles... Katherine stiffened so suddenly that Jack peered down at her, his brows drawn in concern.

"What is it?"

"You don't have to lose the barn, Jack."

He quirked his mouth into an indulgent, incredulous expression. "What do you suggest? We could knock over a few convenience stores...maybe hit the train on payroll day."

Katherine's heartbeat quickened and she gazed earnestly into his face. "Borrow the money."

For one moment he stood still, his face blank. Then he smacked his forehead with the heel of his hand. "Why didn't I think of that. I'll rush right down to First National with some feed sacks and bring back a load or two of fifties. That should do it. Now let's see, what shall I use as collateral? There's my high school letter jacket, my collection of indian arrowheads—"

"Jack," Katherine said, and punched him on the arm. "You wouldn't need collateral if someone wealthy co-signed the note for you."

His eyes narrowed. Katherine counted the breaths he took. One. Two. Three. "Katherine," he said quietly. "Don't even think of it. Maybe Brooks and I can come to some kind of understanding someday, but if you think—"

"But it's the only way, Jack." Katherine interrupted, and as the words left her mouth, she knew they were true. "Brooks would leap at the chance to help you and Teddie keep Blazingbrook...and not because he wants any kind of leverage over you. You know that." Her voice grew quicker, more urgent. "And this would prove to him once and for all that you forgive him . . . if you let him help you this way."

His face hardened but she forged ahead. "Jack, you know I'm right. You said there was something from the past that needed to be completed. Finished somehow. Well, this would do it. In fact, this is the only thing that would really do it. If you had sold the Phoenix and made a huge amount of money, you'd just be trying to prove something to Brooks. It could go on forever with Teddie being jerked back and forth between you. Don't you see, Jack, Brooks is tired of this. He regrets terribly everything that happened and he wants it to be over. Can't you forgive him? And Teddie?" She reached up and touched his check. "And me. Can't you forgive all of us...including yourself? Brooks wants so much to be part of your lives. Won't you let him? If you do this—I mean, if you allow Brooks to help you this way—it'll be saying that you're putting the past behind you Forever."

She could see that her words were eating away at him eroding his bitterness like waves dissolving a sand castle.

Jack grimaced but hauled her to him. "I hate it when you're right."

Katherine felt joy bubbling up, spiraling higher and higher. Any minute it would erupt like a fountain. She searched his face. "You mean it? You'll ask him?"

Katherine saw him fighting a smile. Unsuccessfully. "Yes, I'll ask the miserable, rotten, old son of a—"

"Jack!"

He threw his head back and laughed. A long, healing laugh. "I feel so strange. My horse is dead. I'm broke. My daughter has run to the house of my worst enemy, whom, I have to add, I'm going to hit up for a huge unsecured loan." He glanced around as if trying to get his bearings. "Why do I feel so good? Why do I feel so... lighthearted?"

Katherine tilted her head to the side and she smiled. Through his shirt she felt the steady throb of his heart, the powerful pumping of his lungs, the heat from his body. "Of course you feel a ton lighter. There's nothing heavier to carry than a grudge."

His head snapped down and he gave her a long, slow look. "Think you're pretty smart, don't you?"

She almost preened. "Well, actually, yes, I do."

He folded her in his arms again. "By the way, love," he murmured into her hair, "I know it's none of my business, but I have to ask. You plan to give that money back to Brooks, don't you?"

Katherine pushed him away and tried to pull a cold face. "You're absolutely right, Jack. It *is* none of your business."

He grinned and pulled her close again.

Behind them the sun was falling, bathing them in vermilion and gold. Jack's hair was ablaze with the light. Looking up at Jack, Katherine was awed by the love and tenderness she saw in his eyes. It warmed her even more than the heat of the falling sun. He slid his hand under her hair and brought his lips down to hers and pressed her to him. He tasted like sunshine and summer air, and the heat from his hands seeped through her clothes and swirled inside her.

"Well, love," he said as his fingers worked slow magic at her waist and neck. "I guess we'd better go see my new business partner and tell him you won't be needing that condo he's holding for you."

Katherine smiled at him. "Darling, as much as I want to, you know I can't stay here. It wouldn't be right."

His brows knit. "What do you mean, it wouldn't be right? What isn't right about a man's wife living with him?"

The barn fell silent. No horses rustled or kicked in the stalls beneath them. No branch scraped against the walls. It seemed that even the sun stopped where it was to listen. Katherine knew he could feel the waves of love radiating from her. She felt certain he could hear the pounding of her heart.

"I take it this is a proposal?"

"Certainly not," he answered. "Darling, we've been living together all summer. What are people going to say? We've got a business to run here, so you can't consider this a proposal at all. I'm insisting. And you know how I am about having my own way."

"Ah," she said. "I see. Well, do you mind if I ask your favorite date for weddings?"

He shook his head incredulously. "I'm surprised a smart woman like you doesn't know this sort of thing. I'm afraid I'm only prepared to wait until September."

* * * * *

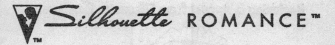

NURSE'S RISK WITH THE REBEL

KARIN BAINE

HARLEQUIN
MEDICAL ROMANCE

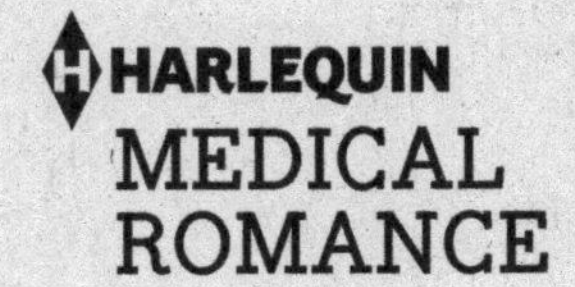

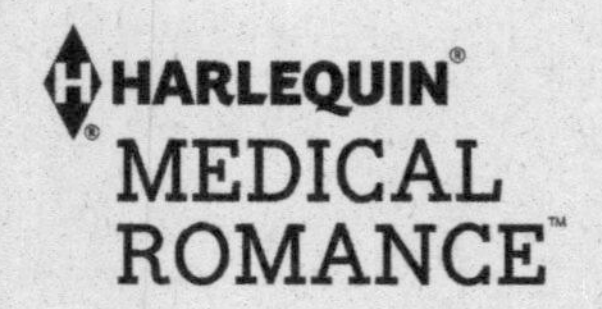

Recycling programs for this product may not exist in your area.

ISBN-13: 978-1-335-59501-0

Nurse's Risk with the Rebel

For questions and comments about the quality of this book, please contact us at CustomerService@Harlequin.com.

Harlequin Enterprises ULC
22 Adelaide St. West, 41st Floor
Toronto, Ontario M5H 4E3, Canada
www.Harlequin.com

Printed in U.S.A.

Karin Baine lives in Northern Ireland with her husband, two sons and her out-of-control notebook collection. Her mother and her grandmother's vast collection of books inspired her love of reading and her dream of becoming a Harlequin author. Now she can tell people she has a *proper* job! You can follow Karin on Twitter @karinbaine1 or visit her website for the latest news—karinbaine.com.

Books by Karin Baine

Harlequin Medical Romance

Carey Cove Midwives

Festive Fling to Forever

One Night with Her Italian Doc
The Surgeon and the Princess
The Nurse's Christmas Hero
Wed for Their One Night Baby
A GP to Steal His Heart
Single Dad for the Heart Doctor
Falling Again for the Surgeon

Harlequin Romance

Pregnant Princess at the Altar

Visit the Author Profile page
at Harlequin.com for more titles.

This is Jennie's fault!

Praise for
Karin Baine

"Emotionally enchanting! The story was fast-paced, emotionally charged and oh so satisfying!"
—*Goodreads* on *Their One-Night Twin Surprise*

CHAPTER ONE

HEAT BURNED JAY'S eyes as he watched his new life go up in flames.

'I guess you didn't need to get here in such a hurry after all, huh?' Marko, the taxi driver who'd given him a ride from the landing strip, stood beside him watching the fire service battle the inferno engulfing the house he hadn't even got to set foot in.

'I guess not.'

'If I'd known you were having a barbie I would've grabbed a few snags.'

Although he'd been working in Australia for over two years now, Jay wasn't sure he'd ever get used to that dry sense of humour.

'Now what do I do?' he said to no one in particular. His move to the Outback in Victoria was supposed to be an adventure, but he had hoped to just climb into bed tonight and sleep. Not look on, helpless, as the accommodation he'd been provided with as part of the package for his new flight doctor position went up in smoke. The red and gold tongues of the fire illuminating the dark night sky would've been pretty if it didn't represent more loss.

'There are no more scheduled flights out of Dream Gulley and goodness knows when the Royal Flying Doctor Service will get alternative accommodation sorted out for you. You know anyone else out this way, mate?'

'No.' He hadn't seen much sign of civilisation flying in, but he supposed that was why he was here. The flying doctor service was to give the rural community medical services they couldn't easily access because of the location. Unfortunately, until he got to know anyone out here there was no one he could ask for a sofa for the night.

Marko shrugged. 'You could try the pub. They have rooms there.'

'Okay, thanks.' There didn't seem to be any other option, especially since the only person he'd met since getting off that plane was now high-tailing it back to his pick-up truck before he could ask him for a bed.

Jay spotted a police car pull up and went over to speak to the officer who got out. 'Hi. Er…can you tell me what happened?'

'That's not a local accent.' The cop eyed him with some suspicion.

'No, I'm from London, England. Jay Brooke. I was supposed to be moving in here tonight.'

The furrowed brow soon morphed into something friendlier.

'Ah, you're the new doc? Didn't know you were a pom.' He shook hands with Jay.

'Nice to meet you.' He didn't take offence at the affectionate nickname—he'd heard it a lot in the time he'd been in the country.

'Sorry it isn't in better circumstances. Too early to tell what caused the fire, but it's been hotter than hell lately and it doesn't take much to start a fire out here when everything is dry as dirt. It's a tinderbox and one spark could set the whole town on fire. On top of that, we don't have the emergency services on tap out this way, but I guess you know all about that.'

'I guess so. Do you need me for anything, or can I go and find somewhere else to stay the night? Marko said the pub might have a room?' He was too tired to get upset about the fact he was standing here in the middle of nowhere with all his worldly possessions in a couple of bags, watching the life he was supposed to share with Sharyn go up in flames.

It was probably fitting when this had been

her dream. She'd been the one who'd talked him into coming out here with that stupid tick list, and without her he was struggling to complete it. They'd moved to Melbourne to start a new life together, never in a million years expecting she would be dead just over a year later from a heart condition she didn't even know about.

Those three years they'd spent saving and planning for their epic adventure seemed so long ago now. That sense of excitement he'd uncharacteristically felt as they'd made their list of things they wanted to experience was now replaced with an unending feeling of loss. This was supposed to be his freedom from the troubled childhood that had leaked into his adulthood, leaving him tied to his job and his home, afraid to venture too far from the places he felt safe. Sharyn had rescued him from that life, forced him out of his comfort zone on their crazy dates taking pottery classes, visiting animal shelters to volunteer, or just jumping on a train and seeing where they ended up. She'd shown him how to have fun, how to live life without being afraid of what was coming next.

Coming to Australia to explore more of those crazy adventures had been her idea and he'd been happy to go along with it because he loved her and wanted to be with her.

It had been great in those early days, visiting new places, doing things he could only have dreamed about when he was that frightened little boy locked in the closet, waiting for his father to take out his drunken temper on him.

Then one morning he'd found Sharyn dead in their bed and his whole new world had shattered, leaving him stranded without a purpose or anyone to lean on for support. They'd been planning on working for the RFDS, training in Melbourne so they could make the transition, anticipating so many more adventures in Victoria. Sharyn was going to be the flight nurse, with him as the flight doctor, so they'd be working and living together. Without her, he didn't know who he was, or what he should be doing.

He'd finished his training and taken the post out here because that had been their plan, but he wasn't even sure if he wanted any of this any more without her.

Perhaps this fire was a sign that he should call it quits and go back to his old life. Except that life had been without colour before Sharyn came into it, and he was afraid to go back to that dark place now she was gone.

Reason enough, he supposed, to carry on with the adventures they'd planned together. At least it gave him a reason to get up in the morning, a purpose for the foreseeable future, though he didn't know what he'd do once he'd ticked everything off that worn piece of paper he kept in his jacket pocket close to his heart.

'We'll probably need to get a few details from you, but we can do that tomorrow. I'm sure Barb will find you a bed for the night. Probably hers.' The cop gave a hearty laugh and almost winded Jay with a slap on the back. He managed a feeble smile in response.

'So, the pub?' Without wanting to seem rude, he wished someone would simply point him in the right direction before he was forced to spend the night sleeping under the stars, along with whatever dangerous beasts lived out here in the Aussie wilds.

'Yeah, it's back there. Can't miss it, mate, just follow the noise.' The officer tipped his head back in the opposite direction to the burning wreckage that was supposed to be Jay's new life.

'Thanks for your help,' he muttered, hoping this wasn't a sign of things to come. The community hadn't exactly been falling over themselves to make him feel at home so far.

'No problem. Just don't leave town.'

'As if I have a choice.' Jay lifted his bags and turned his back on the fierce heat, walking towards the town lights, and the aforementioned racket echoing through the night.

The Buchanan Arms was an imposing brown brick building standing on the edge of town. Jay imagined it was a leftover from the gold-mining days of the early nineteen-hundreds, when towns built up around nearby goldfields during the boom period. Each floor was punctuated with white trimmed arches which reminded him of those Mark Twain era ornate paddle steamers. He couldn't help but wonder if the interior had been updated at any stage in the last hundred years or so.

Jay opened the doors. All eyes turned on him, and the room went silent.

He stood there like a roo in the headlights. Pub-goers froze mid-drink, watching him suspiciously over their glasses. He hovered, deciding whether to stay or flee, contemplating taking his chance sleeping al fresco after all.

'Yes, love, what can I get you?' Thankfully, the brunette behind the bar shouted over at him, her acceptance apparently enough for the patrons to lose interest in him and return to their conversations and beer.

'Lager, please.' Whilst he didn't particularly feel like drinking, his throat was dry from the smoky atmosphere outside, and he thought he should attempt a conversation at least if he was going to make friends around here.

He perched on a barstool at the counter and set his bags on the floor, facing the mirrored backdrop displaying the large selection of spirit optics available. The barmaid set his pint in front of him, the condensation sliding down the glass making him lick his lips in anticipation of the cold brew slaking his thirst.

'I'm looking for Barb. Can you tell me where I might find her?'

'You've found her.'

'Great. I need somewhere to stay tonight and Marko said you might have a room available.'

'Oh, he did, did he? I don't let rooms any more, more trouble than it's worth. He knows that. Then again, Marko doesn't usually heed anything a woman has to say around here.' She glanced over at the corner, forcing a curious Jay to swivel around to see what was going on behind him.

Marko, who must have come here when Jay was talking to the police officer, was standing with a beer in his hand, pressing himself up against a blonde bending over the pool table trying to take a shot. Jay thought he was the woman's boyfriend until she batted him away.

'Knock it off, Marko. I'm not interested.' She stood up, brushed down her thigh-skimming skirt and walked around to the other side of the table.

Jay took a swig of his beer, still watching the interaction now it had become clear they weren't a couple. Although he'd only spent a car ride in the man's presence, it was sufficient to know the sweaty, dirt-smeared taxi driver wasn't exactly a prize catch. Especially for a woman who looked like that.

'I was good enough for you last month,' Marko boasted, proving Jay wrong.

He went back to his beer, realising there probably weren't a lot of options for single, attractive women out here in a town of not much more than two hundred people. It wasn't like the city, where dating was available at the swipe of a screen and people could pick and choose a partner based on their outward appearance. Not that he had any experience of dating out here, when he and Sharyn had been an established couple when they'd arrived. Together five years, she'd been his world, and he'd planned on proposing to her once they'd settled. When he'd been with her, no other woman had even been on his radar, and now he was grieving her loss too much to even contemplate meeting someone else.

'Yeah, well, I must've been desperate. I'm not interested, Marko.'

Jay was trying to block out the conversation. It shouldn't have been hard with the cacophony of sounds carrying on around him. Even Barb had lost interest, leaving him to go and serve someone else, conversation about possible accommodation seemingly over too. At this rate he might as well get on the first flight back to Melbourne and try to get his old job back at the hospital in the emergency department.

'Aw, come on, Meadow. You know you want me really.'

Out of the corner of his eye, Jay saw the man who'd brought him to town trap the pretty pool player in the corner of the bar whilst the rest of the patrons appeared oblivious to what was going on.

'I think the lady said she wasn't interested,' he said, loud enough to be heard above the general chatter, setting his beer back down on the counter. Jay wasn't the sort to get into fights or drama, but neither was he the kind of man to sit back and let a woman be publicly harassed without doing anything. It was that culture of being passive through fear of making a scene which let men like Marko think they could get away with that disgusting behaviour.

He felt all eyes on him, the atmosphere thick with tension, everyone apparently waiting for someone else to make the next move. Marko slowly turned around to face Jay, finally giving his prey some space to breathe.

'Who the hell do you think you are, telling me what to do? You've only been in town five minutes.'

'Long enough to realise what a piece of work you are, and that this lady doesn't want to know you.'

'This is none of your business, mate. The *lady* is capable of making her own decisions.'

'I think she already made it, but you appear to be hard of hearing, *mate*.' Jay slowly rose from his barstool, sick of this place already, and the stench of Marko's body odour problem still fresh in his nostrils.

'What, do you think you're in with a shot, big guy? You think you can sweet-talk my girl with that fake British accent and find yourself a bed for the night? I don't think so.' Marko fronted up to him and, after the day he'd had, Jay was ready to knock him out just to shut him up.

'Hey, you two, I'm still here, and very capable of defending myself as well as making decisions! Marko, rack off, and you, whoever you are, I'm not into macho morons either.' The woman who'd been fending off Marko's advances wedged herself between them, clearly not afraid to make her opinions known.

Close up, Jay could see why Marko had become territorial. She was beautiful, and feisty. He could see by the tension in her body and the fire burning in her blue eyes that she'd been holding back, and Marko was lucky she hadn't shoved that pool cue somewhere very personal. It was clear to Jay she could fight her own battles if she chose to, so he backed off. Marko clicked his tongue against his teeth before he stood down.

'I'm sorry. I didn't mean to—' Jay attempted an apology but the petite firecracker grabbed her coat and bag and shoulder charged them both on her way out of the door.

'Making friends already?' Barb set another beer in front of Jay before he could refuse it.

'Looks like it.' He drained the first bottle and set to work on the second.

'Don't mind our Meadow, she's got her daddy's temper. As for Marko, he's harmless, if a bit too handsy.'

The source of the evening's unpleasantness

was sitting in the corner nursing his beer, glaring daggers at Jay. He was sorry he'd given him a tip now.

'I was only trying to help.'

'I know, don't take it personally. We wouldn't have let it go too far, but we know from experience not to offer Meadow any help unless she asks for it. She's a spitfire, that one. But it is nice to have a real gentleman here and I think we could find you a bed for the night at least.'

'Thank you. You have no idea how grateful I am after the night I've had. I just watched my new home burn to the ground.' As soon as he finished his beer, he'd say goodnight and disappear upstairs. Hopefully, tomorrow would be a better start.

'You're the new flight doc?'

He supposed he'd have to get used to everyone knowing his business now in a town this small, a world away from the anonymity of the city, where he'd been able to grieve Sharyn without getting dragged into other people's drama. Tonight had taught him one lesson and that was to think before he acted. The opposite of everything Sharyn had taught him.

When they'd met in London, he'd been working all the time, his life completely devoted to helping others, leaving no time for himself. Relationships up until that point had been brief physical affairs because he hadn't been in the right head space to share his life with anyone. Sharyn had shown him how to have fun, how to live, and persuaded him that moving to Australia would be a great adventure, leaving behind the trauma of his childhood to embrace the endless possibilities available in a new country.

Although it had given him a few sleepless nights, he'd been excited for the move. Melbourne was supposed to have been the start of their new life, the base for everything they wanted to do, all the adventures they were going to experience. Neither of them could have known that all of their plans were going to come to a premature end.

Now, moving to the Outback without Sharyn, he was just going through the motions. It no longer felt like an adventure, just something that was expected of him. Instead of more big plans for working together and exploring the countryside, he was here alone, grieving for the woman he loved and the future they would never get to have. Getting himself into trouble in the meantime.

'Yeah,' he conceded eventually, resigned

to the fact that everyone would know who he was and why he was here soon enough.

Barb tipped her head back and gave a chesty laugh, the kind that came from years of hard smoking and living.

'What's so funny about that?' He'd had a good reputation back home, a steady job, and he'd given it all up to gamble on a better life out here. So far, it had been a nightmare. He had hoped this would be his new start, but now it seemed he was simply making enemies. Neither Marko nor the lovely Meadow were likely to buy him a beer any time soon. That left him another one hundred and ninety-eight residents to try and befriend or risk complete alienation.

'Meadow is the flight nurse you'll be working alongside. Good luck with that.' Barb bit back another laugh as she walked away, apparently to share the news with the rest of the bar, a raucous chorus of laughs sounding soon after she spoke. With that final humiliation Jay decided to call it a night. It sounded as though tomorrow wasn't going to prove any more successful than today if he'd just ticked off his new colleague.

Maybe he'd get lucky and she wouldn't recognise him once he'd had a shower and a shave…

* * *

Meadow stomped into the flight base, ready for her shift. Hopefully, she'd be kept busy enough to get out of this funk she'd been in since last night.

'What have we got?' she asked Kate, the base manager who co-ordinated the calls providing healthcare for communities which didn't have a local medical facility to call on. As well as emergency aeromedical retrieval they provided patient transfers, primary healthcare and fly-in, fly-out general practitioner clinics in rural areas.

'We've got that vaccination clinic for the kids out in Whitley today. Other than that, it's pretty quiet so far. Touch wood.' The older woman, who'd been here long before Meadow came to work, rapped her knuckles on her head so as not to tempt fate. Although if there was one person whose head was certainly not wooden, it was Kate. She was the hub of the service, if not the building. Sometimes Meadow wondered if she ever left work at all when she always seemed to be here, organising everything and everybody.

'As much as I don't wish anyone ill, I could do with a distraction today, before I go and give that bogan Marko a piece of my mind.' She dropped the file Kate had just given her with a thump on the desk, wishing it was Marko's head.

'Oh? What's he done now?'

'Just Marko being his usual obnoxious self. I was very restrained, if I do say so myself. He didn't go home with a pool cue embedded in his skull.' She shouldn't have encouraged him last month and given in to his attentions. Now he had false hopes for something more between them.

In her defence, she'd been feeling particularly low when he'd asked her to dance and bought her a couple of beers. It had been a while since her last relationship, and there weren't a lot of viable options out this way. She'd grown up with most of the men her age out here and none of them were the reliable type, including Marko. No one stayed for long in Dream Gulley and those who'd been born here left as soon as they could because there were no prospects in the old Outback mining town. She was only here because it was the place her father had last settled and he was the only family she had left, bar her mother, who had remarried and started a new life in Queensland.

Meadow didn't worry so much about her, she had a job and a partner. It was her father's life that still lacked stability—her father's and hers.

Kate reached across the desk to pat her hand. 'It's about time you found a nice man to settle down with.'

Meadow's laugh was completely devoid of mirth. 'Don't you think I've tried? All I want is someone with a good job who wants to get married and have kids. That's all. It's not such a big ask, is it?'

Kate tilted her head to one side and gave her that sympathetic look everyone had when they found out Meadow was single and over thirty. Meadow had known plenty of girls who'd married young and whose partners cheated on them, or ran off because they were too immature to deal with having a family. So she'd taken her time, and apparently been left with the dregs, but she still wasn't going to settle. If she was expected to make compromises she'd rather stay single. She was used to doing everything on her own anyway.

'Don't take this the wrong way, but maybe you're being too picky?'

She snatched her hand from under Kate's. It was all right for her; she'd found her nice guy with the steady job and they'd been together for ever. And yes, she was jealous, but that didn't mean she was going to lumber herself with the first sweaty ape who showed an interest in her. Not again, anyway.

'I most definitely am. I'm not going to be my mother.'

'Your mother's lovely.'

'I'm not denying that, but she waited until we left Dad before she made any sort of life for herself. We were so unsettled, with Dad chasing his fortune all over the country. Gold-hunting isn't as glamorous as everyone thinks it is. It's an obsession, an addiction, which cost him his family, and does he have anything to show for it after all this time? No.' It was a touchy subject for her. Although she looked out for her father, they didn't have much of a relationship. His choice. After years of traipsing around the country with him on a whim, all their money ploughed into whatever sure thing he'd found, it wasn't surprising her mother had eventually had enough and issued him an ultimatum.

He'd chosen the gold, or rather, the pursuit of it, rather than settling down in a nice house in town. But he had made an attempt at compromise, buying land and finally putting down roots. It had come too late for her mother, who'd left him anyway. Meadow still held some resentment over that. Her father had tried, her mother hadn't. She'd moved out anyway and rented a place for her and Meadow in the town. It had seemed cruel to her to live so close but give up on their family as a whole and she'd tried to keep a relationship with her father over the years because he had no one else, but it wasn't easy.

A few years later, when her mother had met someone else and planned a new life in Queensland, she'd tried to get Meadow to go with her, but she hadn't been ready to give up on her dad. At eighteen, she'd been old enough to make the decision to stay, to train as a nurse and have a life of her own. Staying close by for her father if he ever needed her.

Once in a while they saw each other in the pub, or she called in to make sure he was doing all right. It felt like a one-sided relationship when she was the one making all the effort, but she was fighting a losing battle against the one true love in his life. Gold. Meadow didn't think it was about making his fortune any more, it was the buzz he got from it that kept him going. Like a gambling addict always chasing the win, even when he made any money he put it back in, hoping for a bigger pay-out at the end.

'Not everyone's like your dad, hon.'

'You reckon? I've dated a few feckless wasters in my time, unwittingly, I might add.

They always start out attentive and reliable but it's not long before you find out they're still using multiple profiles on every dating app that exists, or they're living at home with their mother because they've gambled every last cent they ever had.' That last one had come as a shock. Shawn had seemed perfect for her, but she wasn't prepared to be around another man who lied to her or who had the potential to sacrifice her for his vices, as her father had done. She was going to have to be more vigilant than ever when it came to her love life or she'd end up with someone like Marko and convince herself he would change. Like her mother must have done a hundred times before she'd plucked up the courage to walk away from her father.

'You've just been unlucky.'

'I'm beginning to think I'll have to move to the city if I'm ever going to meet someone.'

'I don't know… That new doc is here and he's a bit of a hunk. He's already been in this morning. I sent him over to the hangar to meet the engineering crew. I hear he's single too.' Kate gave her a wink and Meadow knew she'd been giving him the third degree already.

'Yeah, well, looks aren't everything,' she grumbled, her mood not improved by Kate's mooning over the new doctor's arrival. After her disastrous dating life so far, she was tempted to just surround herself with stray cats and dogs for company instead of burdening herself with another disappointing man. Even handsome strangers thought they could wade in and she'd fall at their feet, grateful for the attention.

She thought back to last night and the man at the bar who'd made a show of her. As if she couldn't handle Marko on her own and needed someone who looked like an action figure to save her. Perhaps he'd thought playing her white knight would've earned him a place in her bed instead of Marko, unaware it took a lot more than a pretty face and smouldering grey eyes to impress her. Like every other new face around town, he'd probably only been passing through anyway. They got a lot of strangers stopping off for a drink or supplies on their way to more exotic locations. No one came here on purpose and it wasn't easy to attract staff. That was why the RFDS offered incentives like accommodation and attractive salaries with the positions.

After the fire last night, she assumed the new doc had spent the night in a fancy city hotel, counting himself lucky. With nowhere to live, he wasn't likely to stick around anyway, so there was no point in getting doe-eyed over him like Kate. Meadow was more concerned with having someone here long-term to pick up the slack and ease her work-load.

'Oh, yeah? See for yourself,' Kate whispered before sitting up in her chair and plastering a great big smile on her face. 'Morning, Dr Brooke.'

'Just call me Jay.'

Upon hearing the English accent, Meadow pivoted to see who had come in. It seemed to happen in slow motion—the sun creating a halo effect around his head, illuminating that buzzcut she recognised from the man who'd annoyed her even in her dreams last night. He offered a bright white smile in response to Kate's as he removed his mirrored sunglasses, and a pair of familiar grey eyes homed in on her.

'Oh, for goodness' sake…' It was just her luck to get some macho moron as her new workmate, who'd be bossing her around in no time. He'd already made it clear he didn't trust her to do things without his help.

'Hello again, Meadow.' He acknowledged her with a tip of his head. 'And you, of course, Kate.'

The manager's coy giggle did nothing to

alleviate Meadow's irritation. Neither did the way Dr Jay Brooke said her name, as though he was mocking it, mocking her.

She told herself it wouldn't be for long. His house had just burned down, there was nothing left for him here.

It was only that thought that would get her through a day spent in close quarters with him.

CHAPTER TWO

'I KNOW WE got off on the wrong foot last night…' Jay's voice was tinny over the headset, distorting that English accent that she already found jarring. Mostly because it reminded her of the scene in the pub last night and some behaviour she'd rather forget.

'Greg, can you isolate our headsets please?' If Jay was going to talk about private matters, she preferred their pilot not to overhear. At least this way the conversation would remain between the two of them. Greg wasn't known for tact or discretion when it came to other people's personal lives, or his own.

'Are you two having a lovers' tiff already? You work fast, man.'

'I'm not… We're not…' Jay looked flustered.

'Ignore him. He thinks he's funny. Greg, headsets, please.' She was not in the mood for another smartass man.

'I was just saying I know I was out of line last night.'

Meadow might have been tempted to ignore Jay altogether, but since there were only the two of them seated in the rear of the small craft it would've been petty. The inside of the shiny new plane was sleek, modern and well equipped for medical emergencies. However, that meant there wasn't much room to avoid people, their seats facing one another to leave space for injured patients and gurneys.

She settled for flashing him a sarcastic smile. 'Just a bit.'

'I was only trying to help.'

'I understand that, but, for future reference, I can look after myself.' She wasn't going to pretend to be grateful and reinforce his delusional saviour complex.

'I heard, and duly noted. The next time one of your exes tries to take liberties with you, it's none of my business.' He held his hands up in surrender and she had an irrational urge to slap him.

'You're right, it's not, but, for the record, Marko is not an ex.' Damn, now she wanted to know who had been talking to him and what exactly they'd said about her. She hadn't realised she had a reputation for being trouble. If anything, she went out of her way to avoid it, which was why she wasn't happy about being with old grey eyes here every day. He was trouble in rolled-up shirtsleeves and butt-hugging slacks. Hopefully, by tomorrow he'd be in regulation uniform and look like everyone else in the crew.

'Okay, one-night stand, or whatever he is…' He seemed to lose interest in the conversation, looking out of the window rather than at her when he was making her fit to be tied.

She supposed the vista was stunning, but she'd become accustomed to the vast desert planes, taking the warm red and gold lands stretched out before them for granted. Still, she thought the English were supposed to be famed for their manners.

'I have not had, and never will have, a one-night stand with Marko, or anyone else.' This was not an appropriate conversation to be having during working hours, but she'd be damned if she was going to let him think she was the kind of woman who slept around. She had high standards and, for reasons she currently didn't understand, it was important for this new doctor to know that.

'It was just that he said—'

'We had one kiss. I was drunk and lonely, we all make mistakes, but that was it. Now, can we drop the subject?' She wasn't proud of herself and would be content to erase the whole ordeal from her memory if everyone would let her.

Jay shrugged, as if it didn't matter to him if she slept around or was a virtual nun. 'So what's the score today? I mean, what will I be doing out here?'

His turn of phrase, along with the accent, was new to her. It wasn't the cut-glass, posh tone of the upper-class gentleman she'd heard on TV and in films, but something grittier, earthier. Something she associated more with English gangster films, or Victorian street urchins. If he called anyone *guvnor*, she'd lose it. Although he was probably expecting her to say *fair dinkum* every two minutes if stereotypes were to be believed.

'Getting to know some of the locals. It's primarily a vaccination clinic for the preschoolers, but we'll have walk-in patients who've been waiting to see a doctor.'

'That doesn't sound very organised.'

'You'd better not let Kate hear you say that. It's as organised as we can get out here. People take medical advice where they can get it and it's our responsibility to make sure they get it, wherever and whenever we can. It's a bit like a GP practice, only more...informal.' She didn't know how to prepare him for the long chats about family and the personal questions, of which there would be plenty for an out-of-towner like him. For some people their visit was the only chance to socialise outside of their own little community and they liked to make the most of it. Usually, it turned into some sort of impromptu party, with food and drink provided by their attending patients. She just hoped Jay showed his appreciation and accepted whatever happened in the spirit in which it was offered. Or that it was so far out of his comfort zone it would make him yearn for a more formal arena, away from her.

It wasn't just that they'd had a run-in last night, or that he was devilishly attractive, which unnerved her about her new colleague. Years of living on a knife-edge, her home life dictated by her father's obsession, had built up a defence mechanism which she very rarely disengaged. Even less so since she'd been lied to and let down repeatedly by men who'd sworn they loved her. All she wanted was a stable relationship and it had eluded her since birth.

There was something dangerous about Jay which set alarm bells ringing in her head. A warning that he was someone she should stay away from. Whether it turned out he was on the run from a life of crime in the UK or he was just another man who wouldn't last five minutes out here, she didn't think it was a good idea to get close to him. Not that she had any intention of getting to know him outside of work.

He arched an eyebrow in query. 'You mean I won't be limited to ten minutes per patient in between phone triage and home visits? How will I ever cope?'

The sarcasm didn't do anything to endear him to her. Neither did knowing he wasn't a regimented English doc who apparently wouldn't be put off by the lack of structure in the job after all.

'Why did you take this job?' She hadn't meant to say it out loud but curiosity had got the better of her. For someone to travel halfway across the world and take a position in what must be completely alien territory to him, there must have been a strong motivation. It wasn't as though they weren't looking for doctors in Melbourne or on the Gold Coast, where life seemed much more glamorous and touristy. Where they had sun, sea and probably sex, on tap. All this place offered was dry heat, dirt, and despair.

She only stayed here because it was the one place she'd ever felt really at home. The place her father had finally settled down and they'd lived in long enough for her to get to know people. She'd been fifteen when her parents had split, eighteen when her mother had met someone else and decided to move away to Queensland. Old enough to decide she didn't want to uproot her life again. The three years she'd had living in Dream Gulley with her mother had given her a sense of security, even if their family had been broken. Leaving her life there to start somewhere new again simply hadn't appealed to her.

Her father had been working on the same claim for fifteen years now and, to her knowledge, had never found anything more than a few nuggets of gold which barely kept him afloat. She checked in on him from time to time but it was more of a welfare visit to a vulnerable man than anything. He'd let her down too many times for her to ever fully trust him again.

Jay adjusted the belt around his waist and couldn't seem to meet her eye. 'I like a challenge.'

'Oh? So you get bored easily?' This sounded promising. Not that she wanted to be stuck with the majority of the workload again, but if he tired of life out here pretty quickly he'd be moving on elsewhere and out of harm's way.

Next time she might get lucky with a married, elderly female doctor who posed no threat to her peace of mind.

'Not exactly. Life should be an adventure, shouldn't it? What is it if we aren't always seeking that thrill of discovering something new?'

She gave a triumphant 'hmph', knowing she'd pinned him exactly right. Jay Brooke was just a younger, more attractive version of her father. Never happy with what he had and always looking for something better. It was all about the chase for him and she was glad she'd found that out straight away instead of when it was too late and she'd actually begun to expect anything from him. At least now she could cling on to that fact to prevent herself from liking Dr Brooke.

'Er…it's safe. Just how I like it.' Even as she said it she knew it made her sound boring, but she'd rather be that than carry on the family's unreliability gene.

'Meadow, you need to learn how to love life.' He shook his head and clicked his tongue like someone who had all the answers instead of the new fish in this backwater pond.

'Ladies and gentlemen, please put your trays up, make sure your seats are in the upright position and hold onto your butts. This is gonna get bumpy.' Greg interrupted their conversation to tell them in his own unique way that they had arrived, giving her the perfect excuse not to have to explain herself. Or listen to Jay telling her how she should behave when he knew nothing about her.

The plane landed with a bump, kicking up a dust cloud of dirt and debris in lieu of a proper runway.

'Looks like we're here. I hope you put your sunscreen on.' She unbuckled her belt and got out of the plane as fast as she could, inhaling a lungful of the warm air when she stepped outside. Born and raised here in the Outback, she was used to the oppressive heat and seemingly relentless sun. For those who'd grown up with more inclement weather, she hoped the novelty would wear off. Especially when there wasn't much in the way of air conditioning in these parts.

She looked across at Jay now, opening his top button and fanning himself with a patient file. Sweat was already beading on his forehead.

'Are you going to be okay? I know you're probably not used to the temperatures.'

'I'll be fine. I've already worked out here for a couple of years.' He headed towards the farmhouse, set his bag and files on the porch steps and walked around the side.

Meadow watched as he ran the outside tap, cupped his hands under the water and splashed it on his face. He scooped another handful over his head and the back of his neck, the water soaking through the thin fabric of his white shirt to leave it translucent and clinging to his torso. She could see the outline of his chest and the ripple of muscles below. All she needed now was some sexy music and a stripper pole to enjoy the floor show even more.

'Aren't you coming in? Everyone's waiting out back for you.' Noelle, one half of the couple who owned the farm, called her from inside the main house.

Meadow hadn't realised she'd been staring until Jay looked up and smirked. This was not good at all. The last thing she needed was to encourage another meathead into thinking she was interested just because he looked good. She was usually more professional than this, more sensible, and she totally blamed Jay Brooke for the distraction.

Jay could have sworn he saw a flicker of something more than irritation in Meadow's pale blue eyes before she flounced off into the house. Wishful thinking, he supposed, when she'd shown nothing but contempt towards him. Oh, so far, she'd been professional and efficient around him, but he hadn't exactly made a good impression on their initial meeting.

He'd had a slight advantage this morning, coming in knowing they were going to be working together. It had obviously come as an unpleasant surprise to her. In the short time he'd been with her, it was clear she wasn't someone who hid her emotions well. If only he hadn't got involved last night, they might have managed to get along. As it was, he was always going to be trying to make it up to her. He'd read the situation wrong, but he couldn't be sure he would do things any differently now, even knowing Meadow was not the helpless damsel he'd mistaken her for.

He followed her into the house, seeking shade from the punishing sun, if not a reprieve from the heat. It was an old-fashioned farmstead, a world away from the modern city life he'd been enjoying until recently. He walked through the hallway, lined with family photos on the walls, to the kitchen, which seemed to be the hub of activity. Meadow was already laying out the medical supplies on the large wooden dining table.

'We're doing this here?'

Meadow looked up at him with that frown she only seemed to wear for him. 'Yes. It's where we've always done it. The Bright family very generously let us use their house so we can see everyone at once.'

There was something in her tone that said, *Be gracious, just shut up and get on with it.* So he did, not wanting to offend their hosts, or anyone else if he could help it.

'Do we have appointments, or a list?' Surely they needed something to work from.

'Well, I know everyone and, as far as I can tell, they're all here. Just work your way through the queue.'

He hesitated for a moment, until Meadow sighed and waved him away. 'They're all waiting for you on the porch.'

True enough, there was a queue of people snaked around the corner and out into the garden, with the Bright family supplying chairs and drinks to those waiting. It was an unusual set-up but obviously one that worked well for the people in the area and he wasn't about to rock the boat.

'Who's next to see the doctor?' he asked the assembled crowd as he hung his stethoscope around his neck and prepared to run his first Outback clinic. Sharyn would've been proud.

* * *

Jay had been working flat-out in his makeshift office in the Brights' front room, whilst Meadow took care of the vaccination clinic in the kitchen. Once he'd got over his initial surprise it had pretty much been like any other day in a practice managing minor ailments. The notable difference being the time he got to spend with his patients. He'd already been invited to dinner with at least five families, provided marriage counselling, and had several offers to set him up on dates. Despite the distance separating most of the people he'd seen today, there was a real sense of community and he was sure that was because of the service the RFDS and the Bright family provided.

He'd heard a fair share of gossip among the attempts at matchmaking on his behalf. Most had already heard about his run-in with Meadow and dispensed their own advice in accordance. It was obvious she was well respected and liked by the locals, most of whom had known her for years. The consensus seemed to be that she'd had a rough time growing up and it had made her…spiky. Also, that he should definitely apologise because he would need her onside. Something he'd already decided, but he thanked everyone for their advice regardless.

'Would you like a glass of lemonade, Dr Brooke?' Mrs Bright knocked on the door in between patients and he jumped at the chance for a cool drink. Although he'd brought his own water bottle with him, he'd drunk most of it and the little left was now warm.

'That would be lovely, thank you.'

'There's some food here too if you want to take a break?' Meadow appeared at the door too, munching a sandwich. Jay's stomach rumbled before he could respond.

'I'll take that as a yes,' she said with a grin, holding out a plate of sandwiches for him to choose from.

'Why not?' He helped himself to a tuna mayo and stepped out of his makeshift office to join everyone else outside. Several trestle tables had been set up in the grounds and were groaning with food, no doubt provided not only by the Brights but the people who'd come to see them today. He already had more plastic tubs of casserole and lasagne he'd been gifted than he could hope to use. Especially since he didn't even know if he had a bed tonight, never mind a fridge or an oven.

'They like to make a day of it.' Meadow

smiled at him from the other side of the table and handed him a paper plate.

'It is a lot of food.'

'Everyone wants to do their bit and show their appreciation. Besides, what use is a doctor who faints from hunger or dehydration?' She poured him a glass of water, looking very at home amongst everyone here. Despite the fact she was working, she seemed more relaxed than he'd seen so far.

Last night he'd been too absorbed with his own problems to really pay attention, but standing here, with the sunshine gilding the dark blonde waves of her hair and bringing out the freckles on her button nose, he could see she was a real *beaut*, as the locals said.

'This is the happiest I've seen you,' he said, when he realised he'd been staring too long.

Meadow popped a cherry tomato in her mouth and bit down. 'I love it out here. It's very family orientated.'

'Do you have family out this way?' It occurred to him he knew nothing about his new colleague, other than she had a temper and played a mean game of pool.

'My mum moved to Queensland over ten years ago. Her and my dad split up and she remarried, but I stayed here. It's all I've ever known.' She shrugged as though that was the beginning and the end of the tale, but Jay was sure there was a lot more she wasn't saying.

'And your dad?'

He could sense the shift in her demeanour immediately.

'He's not too far from here, but we're not close.'

Jay decided not to probe any further. He got it, and wasn't in the mood to share details of his messed-up relationship with his father either.

'Well, everyone I've met today only has lovely things to say about you.'

'Really? I've had every one of your patients come out and tell me to be nicer to you.' She laughed and Jay was sure it was the sweetest sound he'd heard in days. A real salve for his spirits after all the upheaval he'd been through since his arrival, and more welcome than another scolding.

'I didn't say anything, I swear.'

'I know, they just seem to really like you. Goodness knows why.'

He knew she was teasing and he was relieved she was comfortable enough around him now to do so, even if it had come from other people's opinions rather than her own.

'I'm sorry about last night—'

'I'm sorry—'

They stumbled over their apologies, only to end up grinning at each other like loons. Jay stuffed half of a chicken salad sandwich in his mouth before he said anything stupid enough to ruin their truce.

'You just caught me at a bad time. I'm getting over a break-up and Marko was being his usual drongo self…'

He swallowed down his food and took a sip of water, almost choking at her admission. 'I shouldn't have got involved. I'd had my fair share of the *drongo* too, having just endured a ride over from the plane with him. You really kissed him?'

She laughed again. 'Don't. I wish I could erase it from my memory. I hear your place burned down too, so I guess you weren't having a great night either?'

'You could say that.'

'I take it you found alternative accommodation? You don't look as though you've slept in a ditch.'

'Thanks… I think. Barb let me stay at the pub last night. I think she took pity on me after you publicly humiliated me.'

Meadow winced.

'Don't worry, you did me a favour, but you might have to come back and do it again if

I can't persuade her to let me stay another night.'

'They haven't offered you somewhere else?'

'Nowhere local. There isn't an abundance of free housing here, as I'm sure you can appreciate.'

'I'm sure you could bag yourself a room for the night with some of your patients,' she said with a glint in her eye.

'I have been offered a few numbers, and I don't think it's just for phone consultations, but obviously, as a professional, I had to decline.'

'Obviously…'

'Hopefully, the service will find something for me or I don't know what I'm going to do.' Not only did he want more time to get to know the people here better, but he hadn't planned his next challenge beyond this one yet. There were only a few things left to complete and without Sharyn's list guiding him he would be a rudderless ship. At least they'd planned this step of their journey together, and he didn't want to fail her memory now.

Meadow opened her mouth to speak, then closed it again, as if she'd been about to say something and changed her mind. Given their short history, he imagined it was probably a suggestion to relocate somewhere far away from her. He hoped she'd decided against another sly dig because they seemed to be making progress in their working relationship today. This relaxed atmosphere was certainly more conducive to a happy work life than being stuck inside four walls.

His background had already made him more than a tad claustrophobic, and though he'd enjoyed the short stint in general practice he'd done as part of his training, he'd struggled with the conditions. Being cooped up all day in a small room reminded him too much of those traumatic days when he'd barely got to see sunlight, often locked in his bedroom by his father in one of his frequent alcohol-fuelled rages.

For some reason, Jay's father had blamed Jay for his mother leaving, when it had certainly been his own abusive behaviour which had seen her off. Jay could hardly remember what she looked like when he hadn't been more than four or five at the time, but he did recall the tears and rows. Not an environment anyone would've wanted to remain in, yet he couldn't forgive her for not taking him with her. For leaving him there to endure years of physical and mental torture until he was old enough to make his escape too.

Jay's nightmarish journey back into the

past was punctuated by screams. He thought he'd imagined them, that they were remnants of that life come back to haunt him, crying out with every lash of his father's belt across his body. Then he saw all of the adults around him running towards the group of children who'd been playing nearby. Even Meadow had joined the concerned party racing across the grounds.

Among the screaming and crying he heard the word 'Snake!'

The children, bar one little boy who was lying on the ground, were running and emitting ear-piercing shrieks as the mothers tried to guide them back to the house.

'What happened?' he asked Meadow, joining the melee. She was already kneeling down beside the boy, who was shaking, his face deathly pale.

'Snakebite. Did anyone see what kind of snake it was?' she yelled to those who'd been present.

'King brown, I think,' a father carrying his toddler out of harm's way shouted back.

'Can someone get my medical bag, please?' Meadow shouted to the crowd and Mrs Bright came running back a short time later with her kit.

'Is Brodie going to be okay?' a woman

holding the boy's hand asked, tears welling in her eyes.

'He needs to get to the hospital as it's the best place to keep an eye on that bite, but we're going to stabilise him first. I'm going to use a pressure bandage around the bite site to prevent the venom from getting any further into the bloodstream. We need to immobilise the limb but I want to get him into the house out of danger first. What do you say, Dr Brooke?' Meadow pulled out a bandage and wrapped it around the child's leg as she spoke, deferring to him for the last word, but he knew she had more experience in this area than he did.

'Whatever you think, Nurse Williams. I'll radio through to base and tell Greg to stand by for hospital transfer.' He relayed the situation and requested antivenom and tetanus to administer on the plane.

'Brodie, mate, you're going to be okay,' he reassured the boy, who was clutching onto his mother's hand with all of his might.

Jay had done enough training to know this was a highly venomous snake they were dealing with and although it might not be as potent as other snakes, there were still dangerous side-effects from a bite. It could cause paralysis from muscle damage and affect blood clotting, along with extreme pain and swelling. Although they could administer some antivenom en route, they needed to get the child to hospital in case he needed more. As long as they moved quickly, he should be all right.

'We should get him into the house,' Meadow added.

Jay scooped the child into his arms and hurried into the house. Meadow rushed ahead and was clearing the table when he arrived so he was able to lay the child out to take a better look. He checked their patient's pulse and breathing and, once he was satisfied that he was out of the woods, began looking for a makeshift weapon.

'Did anyone see where the snake went?' Jay didn't want Meadow, or anyone else, to suffer too.

A couple of the kids pointed towards a pile of brush and branches.

'What are you doing?' Meadow asked.

'Get him ready for transfer to hospital for observation. I'm going to make sure no one else gets hurt.'

'What? Jay, don't be crazy.'

Ignoring her pleas, he grabbed an old potato sack lying by the back door and a rake he found lying out front. He ran over to the wood pile and poked the debris until a small brown head hissed back at him. Although he wasn't a snake wrangler, he'd seen it done before. All he had to do was get the creature into the bag without getting himself killed, then they could call someone to get rid of it. He held the bag open with one hand, and with the other he tried to hook the rake prongs under the snake. It lunged at him, forked tongue flicking, trying to reach its prey.

Despite wearing long trousers, Jay wasn't confident that covered legs would prevent him suffering injury. The snake flicked its tongue, its beady eyes locked onto Jay. A couple of metres long, it could cover the distance between it and Jay in a split second if it chose to attack. If it launched itself and managed to clamp its fangs into Jay's leg, he'd have a job trying to unclamp it again. King browns were known to bite repeatedly to envenomate their prey. If Jay lost focus and gave it a chance to strike, he was facing considerable pain and swelling at the very least.

He took a step back as the snake slithered across the ground, agitated now and coming for him. Holding the rake at arm's length, he tried again, scooping the beast up into the air. It was caught between the prongs, trying to wrap itself around the shaft, as Jay carefully placed the opened sack beneath it. He placed his captive inside, using the rake to close the bag over until he was able to pull the draw-string tight around it.

'I've got it. Someone call the snake catcher, and for goodness' sake keep away from this area.' He wiped the sweat from his brow and took deep breaths as the snake in the bag writhed and hissed its irritation at being trapped. It was quite a feat for a non-native of the country and he was feeling quite proud of himself when Meadow came running out shouting.

'Are you out of your mind? You could have been bitten too. It's the number one rule to stay away from a snake if you see it, not chase after it.'

'I… I just wanted to make sure no one else got hurt.'

'There are people who do that for a living. People who know what they're doing.' She was standing with her arms crossed, lips drawn into a tight line, a deep frown across her forehead, looking every bit as angry as the snake.

'I didn't think.' He'd acted on pure instinct, wanting to protect her and the children.

'Clearly.' There was almost steam coming out of Meadow's ears and Jay lamented the fact he'd upset her again when they'd been making progress.

'Well, there's no harm done and I'll know for next time not to try and impress you with my snake charming skills.'

'You're an idiot.' Despite her unrelenting hard stare, Jay was sure there'd been a slight tilt to her mouth.

'Why do you care anyway? I would've thought you'd be glad to see the back of me if I got bitten and died.' It was an improvement in relations that she didn't apparently want to see him expire, after last night when he was certain she would've killed him with that death stare if she could.

'Too much paperwork,' she said and turned on her heel. 'Now we need to get Brodie to the hospital. We can come back again tomorrow and finish the clinic. They'll understand.'

Jay followed her lead. It was going to take him a while to learn the ropes and Meadow had more experience of the best working practice out here, even if she was a reluctant teacher.

Although her concern for his safety, demonstrated via that infamous temper, only made him want to get to know her a bit better.

CHAPTER THREE

MEADOW'S STOMACH WAS still roiling and it wasn't anything to do with the bumpy take-off as they headed towards the nearest hospital. Brodie seemed fine, thanks to the antivenom and the quick actions of everyone involved, and snakebites were common enough in their line of work out here. It was Jay's reckless actions which had left her shaken.

The last thing she'd expected him to do was chase after a venomous snake. It hadn't been bravado or a need to show off, he was one of that particular breed that terrified her—the reckless kind. Her father had been selfish in his actions, seeking his gold without thought for his family. Although Jay had acted in everyone else's interests, disregarding his own safety, the two men had one thing in common. They didn't give a thought for the worry and distress their actions might have caused those around them. Jay was much like her father in that way, acting without thinking. Doing what he wanted and disregarding anyone else who didn't agree. Exactly the type of man she tried to avoid. Except she had no choice now they were working together.

Up until the moment he'd scared the life out of her, and come close to losing his own in the process, they'd been doing well. He'd been attentive and supportive to the patients, and to her when she'd needed any advice for her junior attendees. The families had certainly taken to him and he was definitely easy on the eye. He'd taken a good-natured ribbing about his accent from some of the locals and earned respect in return. People liked him and that was half of the battle working in some of the more remote areas. Gaining everyone's trust wasn't always an easy task for outsiders but he'd worked hard today, gaining acceptance. She'd even mellowed, and had briefly considered putting him in touch with her father, who often rented out the old shearers' quarters on his land for extra income.

In the end she'd held back, uncertain if she wanted to offer a solution to his accommodation problem and keep him around. His action hero behaviour, taking on a snake without any regard for health and safety, had further deterred her from mentioning anything. She had one hare-brained male wreaking havoc in her life and she didn't need a second one.

'Well, I guess I can add snake wrangling to my CV,' Jay eventually said to break the silence, with Brodie sleeping soundly on the trolley between them.

She refused to laugh at his feeble attempt at humour when the thought of what could have happened was still making her feel sick. What if he'd been bitten and had an adverse reaction? He was the one who was supposed to be treating the patients, not leaving her to deal with everything because he'd acted thoughtlessly.

'You were lucky,' she said in the end, not wishing him to know how worried she'd been about his welfare when he'd only gloat about it. It wouldn't do any good to let him think she cared; it would only encourage him to be more reckless in future.

'That was one thing we should've had on our list. Sharyn would've got a kick out of that one.' The wistful smile on his lips and the mention of another woman awakened something ugly inside her that felt almost territorial, like a feral cat wanting to attack anyone who dared encroach on her space. If she'd been at home she'd have gone for a cool shower to wash away these inappropriate, and frankly baffling, feelings.

'Sharyn? Is that your wife?' she ventured, though she didn't see a ring on his finger or understand how a marriage would work with one half working out here on his own.

He shook his head. 'My girlfriend. She…um…she died last year, not long after we moved out. Sudden Arrhythmic Death Syndrome.'

Meadow immediately regretted the jealousy which had prompted her to ask, when he was clearly a man still grieving his loss. She knew the term was used for heart conditions which had no recognised cause and that the death must have been unexpected and traumatic in someone so young.

'I'm so sorry, Jay.'

Now she felt bad about the hard time she had given him from the moment they'd met, when he must have been going through hell. She might not know how it felt to have a loved one die but she knew a thing or two about loss. Her family had disintegrated long ago, her father merely another elderly member of the community she kept an eye on, and her mother too far away to have a proper relationship with. She could only imagine the void left in Jay's heart, losing someone he'd planned to start a new life in Australia with.

'It's okay, but you should know she's the one who encouraged me to act first and think later.' He laughed and she could tell he was lost in good memories of times they'd spent together, long before Meadow had known he even existed.

'Oh? You mean she would be happy with you risking your life to catch a snake?' She didn't think she'd ever get over that one.

'Yeah, probably,' he chuckled. 'She was the adrenaline junkie. Believe it or not, I was the cautious one, but she showed me excitement and spontaneity, and how to really live.'

All the things Meadow fought against when it reminded her too much of her unreliable father and the uncertainty of the life her mother had endured for far too long.

'She sounds like a wonderful person. You must miss her.'

'I do. It was her idea to come out here, to spread my wings. We had this tick list of all the things we were going to do. I had no idea it would literally kill her. Ironically, she had the cardiac arrest in her sleep, not during one of our crazy stunts, but I'm sure it was those adrenaline-rushing events that triggered it. It's silly, given the circumstances, but I still want to keep on with the list. It gives me something to focus on.' He pulled out a tatty piece of paper with a list of adventures written on it, most of which had tick marks beside them.

To-Do List:
Take a cooking class
Stroke a koala
Surf on Bondi Beach
Sky dive
Pan for gold
Swim with sharks
Dive on the Great Barrier Reef
Work with the RFDS
Eat some Bush tucker
Bungee jump off the Sydney Harbour Bridge

'That's a lovely way to honour her memory. Do you have many still to complete?' Meadow could only imagine the tragic circumstances of finding his girlfriend dead like that and understood his need to continue with the journey they'd started together. Though she was itching to know what was on it, she also didn't want to intrude on such a personal memento.

'There are still a few—bungee jumping off

the Sydney Harbour Bridge, swimming with sharks, diving on the Great Barrier Reef… Although I reckon snake wrestling tops a few of those.'

'Is there anything a bit safer on there? Even thinking about doing any of those is making me shudder.' If someone paid her a million bucks she couldn't imagine wanting to do anything on that list, never mind doing it for fun.

'Panning for gold, stroking a koala, going to Bondi Beach—they were things Sharyn just wanted to do because she'd seen them on TV when she was younger.' He tried to flatten the crumpled piece of paper on his leg and Meadow could see the handwriting on it had already started to fade. She wondered how many hundreds of times he'd read it or lovingly stroked the words of the only link he probably had left to his girlfriend.

Although he was obviously broken-hearted over his loss, at least he'd had a great love. Her relationships had all ended in disaster, with no one meeting her expectations. It was difficult for her to trust anyone when the people in her life had always let her down.

That lack of security early on in her childhood, moving from one plot of land to the next according to her father's whim, had been followed by her mother's decision to end their marriage when they had eventually settled somewhere. She was always afraid that everyone was going to leave, or do something to ruin any feeling of security. It didn't make relationships easy when she couldn't let herself fully trust her partner. Not helped when her instincts had been proven right thus far, and past boyfriends had validated that need to protect herself first. She couldn't imagine any of them carrying out her wishes once she was gone, when they hadn't managed during her lifetime. Jay must have loved his Sharyn very much and she felt bad that he had to do the rest of this on his own.

Meadow yawned as she poured herself a cup of coffee. The early night she'd planned last night had eluded her, her mind and conscience keeping her awake long into the night. Neither she nor Jay had left the hospital until Brodie's parents arrived to be with him. Since there was no room on the plane and they had their other children to see to, they'd had to arrange childcare and make the drive to the hospital themselves. It had begun to get dark by the time Meadow and Jay had returned to the base.

With Greg and Kate both having plans,

Kate's date night with her husband, and Greg hooking up with whoever would have him, it had been left to her to drop Jay back at the pub. She'd stopped in long enough to plead his case for another overnight stay, but the noise and hubbub of the place had guaranteed he wouldn't have had any better night's sleep than she'd had. After the day they'd had, she reckoned they'd both needed it too.

She took her coffee into the living room and tried to distract herself with a magazine, but she was flicking through the pages without really taking anything in. Her mind was still locked on yesterday, and the personal information Jay had shared with her. He'd had a bad run since moving from England and it was in her nature to try and make him feel better. As someone who'd grown up never fully comfortable in her surroundings, always waiting for the rug to be pulled from under her, she empathised with other people's struggles. She didn't like watching anyone go through a bad time, remembering how it was to feel so alone and wanting someone to notice, to do something about it. If she could help people in need, she did. Whether it was checking in on her father, donating to foodbanks or giving someone a lift when they needed one, she did it to try and make people feel better.

Jay had left her with a moral dilemma. He was clearly someone who was suffering, who needed help, and she could offer a solution to one of his problems at least. There was nothing she could do about his grief, or the list he wanted to complete in Sharyn's name, but she did know somewhere he might be able to stay after his home had burned down before he'd set foot in it: the shearers' quarters on her father's land. The trouble with that scenario was two-fold. Firstly, she would have to speak to her father and he wasn't answering his phone. Part of the reason she'd gone into the pub was to see if he was there before she said anything to Jay. The second problem was that inviting Jay to stay on her dad's land would mean moving him further into her life when every instinct was telling her to keep him at a distance.

In the end she knew she would have to do the right thing, if only so she could sleep soundly in her bed at night without her conscience bothering her.

Jay might have scared her half to death with his snake antics but everyone else seemed to love him. It was clear he'd been through a lot and she didn't want him to feel unwelcome, even though they'd got off on the wrong foot. His house burning down on top of his grief might explain him losing his temper with Marko that night, though it didn't excuse hers. She'd taken her bad mood out on him at a time when he'd needed some understanding. There was one way she could try to make amends, even if it would make her life a little more complicated than it already was.

Jay was mourning his girlfriend, clearly not in the market for another relationship, so she had no reason to worry that he was somehow going to hurt her. Romance wasn't on the cards at all. He was a work colleague, one that infuriated her at times, but she would get used to him the way she had with Greg, the party animal. Greg often regaled her with tales of his debauched nights out and, though she didn't agree with his lifestyle, he was good at his job so they muddled along. It certainly didn't keep her awake at night, anxious about getting involved with him and the repercussions if it did happen, when she was the one single woman in town who hadn't been out with him. She didn't know what made Jay Brooke special, but she was hoping that if she did this one thing for him she could stop him from invading her thoughts.

* * *

It took her all day to pluck up the courage to broach the subject, and only then because she knew it would be dark again soon and Jay was worried about asking Barb for another night at the pub. Although he'd been professional and courteous to the patients they'd transferred to the hospital today, she'd seen him yawning when he thought no one could see. It was clear his current accommodation wasn't ideal and it wouldn't do for the flight doctor to be deprived of sleep when he had such an important job to do for the people of Dream Gulley. Therefore, she had no choice.

Meadow cleared her throat, the words seeming to stick in her throat as though her body was trying to stop her from saying them. 'I think I know a place where you can stay. Until you get something else sorted out at least.'

'Oh?' The hope in his eyes told her she was doing the right thing, though it went against her desire to keep him at a distance. A man who had a tick list of adrenaline-fuelled activities to work through and clearly thought nothing of launching himself at a venomous snake was not someone she needed around her. That was pain just waiting to happen for both of them.

'My dad has a place, a gold claim called Rainbow's Walk. There's an old shack there that used to be for shearers. He sometimes rents it out to other gold hunters.' There were a few who still passed by this way and tried their luck in the old mines. Ironically, though this was the place her mother had finally decided she'd had enough and left him, Meadow's dad had settled here after having some success. He'd bought the land, convinced this would be his big pay-off. Fifteen years later he was still waiting, so he had to raise money to pay the bills somehow.

'Are you serious?' Jay looked delighted. 'That would be great and maybe I can tick that gold panning thing off my list too.'

'Don't hold your breath. I can't promise gold or a happy home. If I could, I might still have a family,' she muttered, drawing a quizzical glance from her colleague.

'Anything is better than what I currently have, which is nothing. When can you speak to him?'

'I…er… I suppose I can take you out to see him after work.' She should check in on her dad, she thought. It had been a while since they'd last spoken, and then there was this business with him not answering his phone. Not that he was great about staying in touch at the best of times. He only had a mobile phone because Meadow had insisted on it when he was often working in extreme temperatures and dangerous conditions. She fired off a text to let him know she'd be stopping by, but there was no guarantee he'd read the message or even had the phone turned on. Still, Jay was in urgent need of a place to stay and after everything he'd been through he deserved a break.

She would simply have to set aside any awkwardness on her part and accept that Jay was going to be in her life from now on.

Jay leaned so his head was partially out of the car window, trying to take in some fresh air. Easier said than done with the dust cloud the wheels of Meadow's Jeep was kicking up. He hadn't realised he got travel sick until he'd been bouncing over this dirt track in the heat. Neither he nor Sharyn had accounted for the lack of air con in these more remote places. He'd had to sleep in the buff at the pub last night, very aware there was no lock on his door and that there had been a full house. It hadn't been the most relaxing sleep he'd ever had, sweating his bits off and keeping one eye on the door in case an inebriated customer mistook his room for the toilets.

Although Barb might have been persuaded to let him stay another night, he was glad Meadow had come up with an alternative solution. And surprised. Up until then he was sure she'd have done anything to get rid of him. Especially after the snake debacle. He'd acted without thinking, he knew that, but Meadow had really freaked out about it. It was possible she'd thawed towards him after he'd opened up a little bit about Sharyn, something he didn't usually do but he'd been trying to explain his behaviour. Sharyn was the one who'd dragged him out of his shell and made him want to experience all life had to offer instead of living as though he was still trapped inside his childhood home. Although even she would have drawn the line at something so dangerous.

It had taken Meadow some time to tell him her father might have somewhere he could stay. Waiting until they'd finished their shift and he was getting ready to go cap in hand to Barb again because it seemed his only option. Meadow had said her relationship with her father was strained, and it did make him wonder more about her private life. She hadn't shared much with him other than her parents' separation, and after the other night's events he assumed she was single—but that was all he really knew.

'Thank you for doing this,' he said, fighting to be heard over the noise of the engine as Meadow floored it across the scorched earth, taking any bumps in the road at full speed.

'I said I would make enquiries. I'm not promising anything. I told you I haven't been able to get hold of him. It's not unusual, he doesn't always have his phone on him, but we'll go and see if he's about.'

'So...your dad is a gold hunter? That must have made for an interesting childhood.'

'You could say that,' Meadow muttered through gritted teeth and forced the car into the next gear. All signs that he should leave the subject alone but he wanted to get to know her better, even if just to make their working relationship a little easier.

'Are you sure he'll be all right with me staying?' Despite his dire need for somewhere to stay, he didn't want to be the cause of any family drama, or indeed end up in the middle of it either.

'Well, he hasn't answered my text, but if you've got cash I'm sure he can be persuaded to take in a lodger.'

It wasn't the effusive invitation he would've hoped for, and now he was imagining some dirty, curmudgeonly, stooped figure snatching his wallet off him before sending him to stay in the dunny.

'Hopefully, it won't be for too long and the service will be able to rehouse me somewhere close to work.' It was becoming clear that there wasn't going to be public transport to get him from A to B near her father's land and he'd have to rely on other people, namely his workmates, to get him to work. Less than ideal, but at least it should be quieter than the pub.

'Maybe you should see the place first before you commit,' she said ominously as they drove past several *No Trespassers* signs and pulled up outside what looked as though it had started life as a static caravan but over the years had had a lean-to and porch added on at some point. Jay wasn't sure it would still be standing after a strong gust of wind and it made him wonder where the hell he'd be staying. This place certainly wouldn't be in the tourist information offered by the service when trying to entice doctors from abroad.

'Dad? Are you in there?' Meadow knocked on the screen door before letting herself inside. It appeared security wasn't a big factor here, which was concerning for someone who made his living from finding gold. Either he didn't get many people trying to steal off him or he never found anything worth anyone coming out all this way for in the first place. Given what sparse information Meadow had shared with him, he suspected the latter to be true.

Jay hovered on the porch, waiting for a signal that he should set foot inside, but instead Meadow came back out with her phone to her ear. 'He's not here. Must be out digging in the dirt. That's how he got his nickname. No one calls him Derek, it's always Digger.'

She hopped down off the porch and Jay followed her out onto the property. It was a vast, sparce area, the dusty red vista occasionally broken by spiky scrub. It put him in mind of an old Western and he half expected to see an old saloon with swinging doors and grizzled old gunslingers the further they walked out onto the land away from the main house.

'It seems quite a lonely existence,' he noted, thinking he wouldn't want to live out here on his own. At least not permanently, and not if he had to work here too, with no chance to speak to anyone. Although he'd had a brief period after Sharyn died of not wanting to see or speak to anyone, generally he enjoyed being with people. It hadn't been easy at first, after years of seclusion, but the foster family who'd taken him in, after his father's abuse had been discovered, had supported him and encouraged him to join all sorts of clubs to socialise. He'd been behind in his education because he'd missed so much school, but caught up thanks to their dedication. If it wasn't for them, he wouldn't have found the courage to go on to medical school, even though he'd spent more time studying than indulging in the full student experience of pubbing and clubbing.

It was meeting Sharyn that had forced him out of his comfort zone and gave him a life worth living. Being around people was a good tonic and he'd come to need it since Sharyn had gone and life had become all too quiet.

'I guess that's how he likes it.' Meadow shrugged, yet again giving off the vibe that their relationship was strained.

'It's not healthy though.'

'Don't you think I don't know that?' Meadow snapped, throwing him a deathly glare over her shoulder. 'None of this is healthy. It's an obsession which has completely taken over his life, but does he listen? No.'

She stomped away and though he knew she'd probably prefer it if he disappeared, Jay had no choice but to follow her. It was a mystery to him how anyone ever found their way out here with no landmarks to navigate by and he knew he'd never find his way back to the house without a guide. He took his medical bag just in case.

'Dad? Are you out here?' Meadow called out every few steps to try and elicit a response, but not even the sound of digging could be heard anywhere.

'Mr Williams? Can you hear us?' Wanting to be of some use but not venturing too far from his companion, Jay called out too.

They walked for some distance, calling out and searching behind every piece of brush to no avail. He could see the panic begin to set in with Meadow, who seemed more worried than annoyed about her father's disappearance now.

'His truck's outside the house so he's here somewhere...'

'We'll find him,' he assured her, determined to stay out here looking for as long as they had enough light. At some point, though, they might have to consider calling in extra help if Meadow was absolutely certain he was out here and in trouble. He'd gone through a traumatic loss and he wouldn't wish that on anyone. Especially not someone who was going against her instincts and trying to help him rebuild his life.

* * *

Meadow inhaled deep breaths to keep her heart regulated in her effort to keep the rising panic at bay. It wasn't going to do anyone any good for her to lose it, though she was worried her father was lying out here somewhere, unnoticed perhaps for days. He wasn't the only one who wasn't great at staying in touch. They mightn't have much of an emotional relationship these days but he was still her father and she didn't wish any harm to come to him.

She was glad she had Jay with her in case something had happened. It was clear he was a good doctor with excellent people skills when he'd even managed to win her over after she'd blasted him in the pub that first night. More than those things, she suspected he was a good hugger and that might be something she'd need before the end of the day.

Perhaps it was the fact that he was mourning his girlfriend, added to spending more time with him, that made her lower her defences. As though she didn't have to be on her guard so much around him, that he wasn't a threat to her peace of mind. An attractive man with an apparent death wish could have tested her when they were going to be in such close proximity all the time. If she'd been drawn to him his reckless attitude would have been very difficult for her to reconcile with, but now she knew she was safe, that he wasn't interested in her or anyone else whilst he was lost in grief. It might not be so bad after all to have someone around who could do their job and be the sort of man she might be able to rely on in the midst of a crisis without worrying there would be a price to pay later. She'd be sure to keep some distance, though, when he had a list of risky escapades still to work his way through.

'Wait.' She put a hand out to stop Jay where he was, thinking she heard a noise somewhere nearby. They stood still and she tried to block out the sound of the wind and the birds overhead. She even held her breath so as not to contribute any sound.

Eventually she was sure she heard a faint cry coming from over beyond the ridge, where the land dipped down towards the boundary.

'I can hear something,' Jay confirmed.

They both ran to where she was sure there'd been a low moan. Sure enough, they found her father rolled into the ditch on the other side, dirty, bloody and scorched by the sun.

'Dad!' She dropped to her knees and felt for his pulse. It was weak, but he was breathing.

'I'll phone it in.' Jay got straight onto the phone to relay their co-ordinates, though their colleagues knew where her father's place was located, before going to aid Meadow's father too. After a preliminary exam, there didn't seem to be any major trauma, the cut on his head likely occurring as he'd fallen into the ditch. Although he might have suffered a concussion too.

'I think he's dehydrated.' Meadow took the water bottle which was attached to her belt and lifted her father's head to pour a little onto his dry, cracked lips.

'How long have you been out here, Mr Williams?' Jay fished around in his bag for an ice pack, broke it to activate the cooling ingredients, wrapped it in a cloth and placed it around his neck.

'Don't…know…' he mumbled, seeming confused and disoriented.

'Dad, it's me. You're going to be all right,' Meadow reassured him as she lifted her father's legs up to rest them on her knees to lower the risk of him going into shock. Even though she was afraid he'd been out here since last night at least when he hadn't answered his phone. If he didn't recover from this, the guilt of not coming out here sooner, of worrying about her own petty fears instead, would haunt her for ever.

'It looks a lot like heat exhaustion, though it looks as though he's hit his head too.' The man's skin was clammy, his pulse racing, and when Jay put a thermometer under his tongue he found he was running a temperature. All signs that he'd been exposed to the punishing sun for too long, although it was difficult to tell if the heat or the fall had overwhelmed him first. Either way, they had to get his temperature down or there was a possibility of damage to his internal organs. Meadow was already taking off his socks and shoes and Jay swiped the water bottle to pour some on a cloth. He laid it across her father's forehead.

'What have I told you about coming out here without your phone? It's got to be forty degrees and no water bottle I can see.' Even in Meadow's scolding, Jay could hear the concern in her voice for the father with whom she apparently didn't have a relationship worth talking about.

He knew what it was like to be estranged from a parent, not having seen either of his in nearly twenty years and with no desire to rectify that situation. Despite Meadow's protestations, he thought there was still love there, but he could understand her not wanting to get hurt. With a little time, and some repentance from her father, he was sure this parent/child relationship might be salvaged after all. They just had to make sure he was okay first.

'Sorry,' her dad mouthed, as a tear dripped down Meadow's face.

She swiped it away and gave him a watery smile. 'You will be if you do this again, you silly old coot.'

'Is he on any medication?' Jay asked, in case it should exacerbate the problem.

Meadow shook her head.

'I think we should get an IV set up. We don't know how long they'll take to get out here.' He pulled out a saline drip from the emergency supplies, to replenish the fluids lost before the organs began to shut down, and inserted a canula into her father's arm.

'No…hospital…' he gasped, apparently as stubborn as his daughter.

'You have to get proper treatment. We don't know how long you've been out here exposed to the elements, or how long you were unconscious. They'll need to do blood tests at the hospital to make sure your organs are functioning properly, check that head injury and get that temperature down before they'll even think about letting you go home.' Meadow helped him sit up for another sip of water and wetted the cloth for his forehead again.

'I…need…to…work…'

'You need to rest.'

'Bills…'

'They can wait. It could take days or weeks before you're ready to go back to work and even then you're going to have to be more careful, Dad.'

Her father made an attempt to sit up. 'Can't afford…to…sit…around…'

'You could get some help in.'

'Yes, Mr Williams, we'd actually come to see if I could rent a room from you. Maybe I could help out somehow with your work?' Jay was willing to give his assistance in return for the lodging and it might even earn him some Brownie points with Meadow.

Or not. She shot him an unimpressed look. 'You'd get yourself killed. You don't know the first thing about working this land and I don't need another fool out here who won't listen to me.'

'You do,' her father croaked out to draw back her attention.

'I do what?'

'Know the work, Meadow. I'll agree to go to hospital if you help out on the land until I get out.'

'That's blackmail, Dad,' she sighed.

The old man gave a croaky laugh and Meadow knew her fate had been sealed.

CHAPTER FOUR

'THANKS FOR THIS,' Jay said for the hundredth time as he set his bags inside the old weatherboard cottage.

'Well, it's too late for either of us to go anywhere else tonight. Besides, it looks like I'll be moonlighting as a gold hunter in whatever spare time I have.' Meadow was leaning in the doorway, still wearing her uniform, which was more red than blue now, covered with dirt and blood from their earlier drama.

'Surely he doesn't expect you to actually dig?' If it was the kind of work which could render an experienced man almost to the point of death, it was inconceivable to Jay that Meadow's father would expect his own daughter to do it. Especially when she was already working in such a demanding role.

She arched an eyebrow at him. 'Clearly you don't know my father. Gold comes before everything. You saw how he was willing to put his life on the line today and all he came up with were a few tiny nuggets to show for it. He claims he's found a patch, and that's why he didn't want to leave.'

'A patch?'

'It's a small area with a concentration of gold deposits. The reason he bought this land was because he was convinced there was still gold to find. It was thought there was an ancient dried-up riverbed on site, a prime source for undiscovered gold deposits. This has only spurred him on more, thinking there's more to be found, and he doesn't trust anyone else to work it for him. Except for me.' She let out a sigh which seemed to come from the very depths of her soul, as though she was used to dealing with his idiosyncrasies and was bone-weary from it. Jay couldn't blame her if she didn't get any form of love or thanks in return.

'You know I'll help if I can.'

She shook her head. 'No. If he thought there was a stranger digging his patch he'd discharge himself from hospital and run us both off his property. Besides, I'll be quicker doing it myself than trying to stop you from killing yourself again.'

'Whatever you say.' It was in Jay's nature

to protest and offer to help rather than stand by and expect her to do such hard manual labour herself, but he left it alone for tonight. They'd been through a lot over the course of these past twenty-four hours and there was no point in starting another argument. If he annoyed her any more there was a very real chance he'd end up with nowhere to stay tonight.

'Give me half an hour to shower and find something to wear, then you can come up to the house for something to eat.'

'You don't have to—'

'It's been a long day. We're both tired and hungry. You'll be lucky if there's hot water in this shack, never mind food in the cupboard. Call it an act of mercy.' She turned and walked out into the falling darkness before he could stop her, or thank her.

Despite their differences, and though she might have done so begrudgingly, Meadow had been the only one who'd helped him since he'd arrived. For someone who claimed to want a quiet life, she seemed to be smack in the middle of other people's dramas and Jay couldn't help but admire her plucky spirit and kindness. Meadow was unlike anyone he'd ever met and he was looking forward to getting to know her better.

* * *

This was one of those times Meadow wished her father had a proper house, with a real bath so she could relax instead of hopping under a slow trickle of cold water trying to shower. They'd never had any luxuries when she was young, but since earning her own money she'd become accustomed to simple pleasures such as a functional bathroom, mains electricity and air conditioning.

At least her father should be comfortable in hospital with a decent bed and nutritious meals until he felt better. He'd put up a bit of a fight when the plane had arrived to airlift him away but he'd soon conceded, which was all the confirmation she needed that he wasn't himself. She and Jay had gone with him and once he was settled and reassured that she wouldn't let trespassers raid his patch, they'd bagged a lift back. It had been easier for her to stay the night than to come back first thing to pick up where he'd left off, and Jay needed someone to show him around. She couldn't very well dump him out here and expect him to fend for himself. That was tomorrow's plan.

Tonight, she'd be a polite host and rustle up something to eat to thank him for his assistance with her father. Although she could have managed on her own it was nice to have that backup and someone to share the responsibility for once. Since her mother had gone it had been solely down to her to keep an eye on her dad, even though they weren't close. Today proved why she could never completely sever all ties. Despite everything he'd done, or how he'd treated them, she'd never forgive herself if something happened to him and she could have prevented it. She didn't even want to think about what could have happened if they hadn't called by today.

A shiver crawled over her skin and she didn't think it was from the tepid water trickling over her.

She shut off the shower and grabbed a threadbare towel to dry herself. Her uniform and underwear were in the wash so she could wear them tomorrow, so she had no choice but to use her father's robe, hanging on the back of the door, to preserve her modesty in the meantime.

She padded down the hallway towards the kitchen and leapt a couple of feet into the air when she saw a figure standing in front of her.

'Sorry, I called out but you must not have heard me.' Jay was standing at the cooker fry-ing something which smelt good enough to make her stomach rumble.

'I was in the shower. You didn't have to do this.' She gestured towards the table, which had been laid with plates and cutlery and the evidence of his cooking was strewn around the tiny kitchen.

'It's just a stir fry. There was chicken and veg in the fridge so I hope that's okay? I just wanted to say thank you.'

'You didn't have to, but I'm glad you did. I'm starving.' She was too tired and hungry to fight him, especially when he'd made such a lovely gesture. It made a change to have someone cook for her, and to even have someone to share dinner with. Most nights it was a rushed affair and cooking for one seemed so depressing that when she did make something from scratch she made a batch to freeze too. A fresh, nutritious meal prepared by a handsome doctor was a treat indeed.

'I could only find beer in the fridge. I hope your father won't think I've been raiding his supplies. I'll pick some up tomorrow when I'm in town.' Jay added some sweet chilli and garlic sauce along with some noodles before serving, by which time Meadow's mouth was watering in anticipation.

'It's fine. I think he'll be in hospital for a

couple of days at least. That gives us plenty of time to restock.' She smiled as she took her plate to sit over at the table on one of the mismatched chairs her father had gathered from the roadside hard rubbish over the years.

Jay came to join her and she noticed him glance at her a little closer. When she looked down she realised that her father's robe was gaping, giving him a clear view down her cleavage. Meadow quickly pulled the sides of the dressing gown closer and tied the belt tighter around her waist.

'Sorry, I don't have a change of clothes with me. I haven't stayed here since I was a teenager.'

'It's fine. I don't think there's a strict dress code for whenever someone breaks into your house and cooks themselves a meal,' Jay joked but Meadow could swear he blushed before he looked away. As though he'd been caught red-handed doing something he shouldn't.

Strangely, the thought of Jay trying to cop a look didn't make her want to throw her beer over him, as she might have done with someone like Marko. She reckoned it was payback for her staring at his backside all day in those tight trousers. They obviously found each other attractive, but it didn't have to make things awkward. It was clear they both had too much emotional baggage to even think about getting romantically involved. No, it was better to think of him as a colleague and forget all about his cute butt, and how thoughtful he'd been to her today, for both of their sakes.

'This is so tasty.' She turned her thoughts and attention back to dinner, which was a much safer topic for tonight.

'I took a cookery class last year. Sharyn thought I should expand my repertoire from spaghetti bolognese or beans on toast to something a bit more adventurous.'

'Was this part of the tick list?'

'Yeah. I started with a nice easy one. It's a shame she won't be around to see me swim with sharks. She was looking forward to that one.' His smile this time was dimmed by the sadness in his eyes which always appeared when he talked about his past with Sharyn. They'd clearly had something special and Meadow was sorry that it had ended so tragically.

'She sounds really special.' Someone full of fun and daring, everything Meadow wasn't.

'She was. She brought out the best in me.' He raised his bottle of beer in a toast and they fell into a companionable silence as they finished their meal together.

'So...what's your long-term plan? I mean, are you planning on staying in town indefinitely?'

'I haven't thought that far ahead. I guess maybe when I've ticked a few more things off my list, or when something else comes up that I think will challenge me.'

The idea of him moving on was already something that didn't sit well with her when she was just getting used to having him around. Suddenly she was hoping this list would take a while to get through.

'You don't have to complete it though. If you find somewhere you're happy, surely Sharyn would want that for you too?' She couldn't imagine that kind of transient life again at their age, never knowing what was coming next. One childhood of that was enough for a lifetime.

'I guess...but right now I don't see any future beyond that list. Thank you, by the way, for letting me stay.'

'Well, it's not my house and my dad probably doesn't remember the conversation we had about you staying so your gratitude might be premature.' She popped the last piece of chicken into her mouth nonchalantly, whilst making Jay almost choke on his dinner he was laughing so much.

He had to take a swig of beer to wash his food down before he was able to speak again. 'I'm sure I'll find out what he thinks about squatters once he gets out of hospital.'

'I'd sleep with one eye open if I were you,' she teased.

'I'm not sure I'll sleep at all. It's so dark out there you can't see your hand in front of your face.'

'You were expecting floodlights? I'm sure there's a torch in the drawer so you can find your way back.' She kind of liked the absolute darkness away from the town lights, the stars shining so brightly it was as if someone had spilled diamonds over the black velvet sky. It gave her a sense of peace, a familiarity, when the sky was the one constant she'd ever had on their travels with her father.

Jay winced. 'The lights don't work. I think the bulbs need replacing.'

'Oh. Sorry. It must have been a while since anyone stayed there. I'll pick some up tomorrow when I'm at the shops.'

Jay stood, collecting the plates to take them over to the sink to wash. 'Do you think there might be some spares in the cupboard? I don't really want to wait until tomorrow.'

There was an edgy air to him she hadn't encountered before, he was usually so assured in his actions, and she wondered what had caused the shift in him.

'It'll be fine. I told you I'll find you a torch. What, are you afraid of the dark?'

He dropped his gaze to his feet, embarrassment radiating across the kitchen to where she sat, and she knew she'd hit a nerve.

'I'm not afraid of it…uncomfortable would be a more accurate description.'

'Sorry, I didn't realise.' This land, as much as she resented it when it represented everything that had gone wrong in her life, was familiar to her. She forgot that not everyone treated a remote, desolate spot like home. This would all be alien to someone who'd grown up in the big city without an inch of space around him unoccupied or lit by fluorescent lights.

'I just had some bad experiences when I was younger.'

'I'm sorry to hear that. There are just some things you never get over, I suppose.' Although she was curious to know what had happened to make this strapping bloke 'uncomfortable' in the dark, Meadow wasn't going to ask him to relive his trauma. It wasn't going to solve anything other than her curiosity and that would be selfish. She had her hang-ups and didn't share them with anyone either. Jay had a right to his privacy and his pride, even if she did bear ill will towards whoever or whatever had caused him such obvious distress.

'Some things. Others you have to try and work your way through before they can stunt your growth.' He could easily have been talking about her, when her past still dictated how she lived her life—cautiously, with order and structure so no one could hurt her again.

It hadn't been completely foolproof, when her disastrous love life had still left a mark on her. Though none of her relationships had been serious enough to be devastating when they'd ended, each breakup had left her thinking that she couldn't trust anyone except herself. If anything, it had made her more wary about inviting anyone else into her life.

She wondered if things would've been better if she had ever thrown caution to the wind and lived the same nomadic existence as her father, even for a short time. Simply stopped worrying about the consequences of her actions to live in the moment. Although the thought of doing something spontaneous or potentially dangerous brought her out in a rash. She couldn't understand why certain people seemed to get a kick out of it. Jay included.

'That's what the tick list is about? Do you think it has enhanced your life in any way, or is it just something you've committed to doing and now you have to see it through?' She was genuinely curious and hoped this line of questioning wasn't impinging on his grief or past traumas when it seemed such a big part of his life.

He was silent for a moment, contemplating his answer, but thankfully didn't appear upset by her interest in the matter. 'It definitely broadened my horizons and pushed me so far out of my comfort zone at times I think it has made me stronger as a person. Now… I don't know. I guess I'll just keep going with it until my life has a new direction.'

Meadow pitied his aimless existence but only because he seemed so forlorn and lost at present. If he'd been happy alone doing whatever thrilling adventures they'd planned she might have envied him. Now it just seemed as though it was a chore he had to carry out because he had nothing else to do with his life. She was happy in her job, settled in her own home, but sometimes she had a sense that she might be missing out. Certainly she'd never experienced the rush her father got from gold hunting, or that Jay and his girlfriend had once enjoyed from chasing the next thrill.

'What did you do before you lost Sharyn? Anything you really enjoyed?' Meadow wondered why there'd ever been a need for him to have such a list. Perhaps his childhood trauma had been so great it had affected all aspects of his life, much like hers. If that was the case, perhaps she should get some tips on how to move past it. Scary though that idea was, she didn't want to stay angry at her father her whole life and end up some bitter, twisted old spinster who never left her house.

Jay smiled and she noticed a dimple peeking out at the corner of his mouth. 'I did enjoy the skydive, even though I had to be pushed out of the plane.'

'Oh, my goodness! I know we're up in the air all the time, but actually jumping out of a plane for fun is beyond my comprehension.'

He laughed at her horror. 'I was strapped to my instructor, and I don't think I'd be in a hurry to do it again, but it was a real buzz.'

'So is sticking your finger in an electric socket, but I don't think I'd be in a hurry to do that either,' Meadow mused, a little in awe of the bravery it must have taken to go through with such a feat.

'You have to try these things,' he said with a shrug.

'Er, no, I don't.'

'I thought that way too, before Sharyn.'

'I don't mean to sound rude, but was this really for your benefit, or was she simply an adrenaline junkie?' Meadow knew she was treading on perilous ground saying something like that about the woman Jay loved, but if she'd ever had a boyfriend who'd forced her to put her life in danger like that, she was pretty sure someone would've staged an intervention on her behalf. That kind of coercive control was part of the reason none of her relationships had ever worked. The moment they tried to persuade her to do something she wasn't happy about was when she got the hell out of there. She knew her own mind, what she was comfortable with, and spontaneity to her was simply a way of trying to force her to do something she didn't want to.

Like the time Shawn had sprung a surprise white-water rafting trip on her for her birthday, trying to make out it was for her when he was the one who wanted to do it. She hadn't been prepared to drop everything and travel halfway across the country to drown herself in the name of fun, so that had been the end of that.

'A bit of both, I suppose. She enjoyed her extreme sports and I needed to live a little. I wasn't just some lovesick puppy trailing around doing everything she said, in case that's what you think.'

'No, I didn't mean—' She tried to back-pedal but Jay clearly wanted to put the record straight.

'I loved her and I was willing to try different things but I had my limits too. I drew the line at base jumping. Despite any previous evidence to the contrary, I do not in fact have a death wish.' He leaned across the table and held her gaze, his dark eyes reminding her that he was very much his own man, strong and independent, and captivating.

'So…your turn.' Eventually he shifted back into his seat, leaving her blinking as though she'd just come out of a hypnotic trance.

'What…what do you want to know?' There was a knot in her stomach tightening by the second, waiting for him to extract information from her. She had no desire to be pitted against the ghost of a woman whose idea of a good time had only been when there was a risk of death or serious injury involved, because she would be found sorely lacking. The most adventure she ever had was letting the fuel in her car go lower than the halfway mark before filling up. There was nothing to write home about when it came to relationships either. She was beginning to regret quizzing him on his if she was about to be subjected to the humiliation of sharing the details of her boring love life.

'Meadow's a curious name. Especially out here.'

The breath she let out was one of relief. 'Mum was originally from Brisbane. My dad met her out there when he was working in construction. They moved here to the gold fields so he could pursue his dream.'

'Are they hippies? It's a lovely name, but very unusual.'

Meadow's relief was short-lived, knowing she was going to have to share at least one piece of embarrassing information. 'You know how some celebrities like to name their children after the cities they were conceived in... Well...'

She let the silence fill in the blanks, Jay's raucous laughter signalling the very second the penny dropped.

'I'll never look at you the same way again. That's priceless.' He dissolved into fits of laughter again and she was glad they'd brought some levity back into the situation, though it had come at her expense.

'I suppose I should be thankful it wasn't in the dunny or somewhere equally glamorous. At least Meadow sounds pretty.'

'It suits you. A floral oasis in the midst of the desert.' He clinked his bottle to hers and it was her turn to blush. It was the nicest compliment anyone had ever paid her. After a lifetime of teasing at every school she'd ever briefly attended, she thought she might actually start to like the name her parents had inappropriately explained during the awkward enough teen years.

'I think it reminded Mum of home.'

'Do you get to see much of her?'

'Not as much as I should because she lives so far away, but we stay in touch.'

'You could take a trip some time. It does the soul good to blow away the cobwebs once in a while.'

'I'm good here. Not really one for travelling.'

'Meadow, you're in a plane every day. Everyone needs a holiday every once in a while, is all I'm saying. You could go see your mum and kill two birds with one trip.'

'What about your family? Aren't they missing you?' She turned the question back on him, the best way she knew to get herself off the hook and stop him asking any more questions about her background. After everything he'd told her about his life with Sharyn it would've sounded tragic to him that she never left town because she needed that safety of the familiar. This dirt town was the equivalent of a tatty old security blanket that she couldn't let go of, even at thirty years of age.

'I doubt it.' Jay's expression changed at the mere mention of his family, his thunderous frown a clear indication that he did have a chequered history there too. At his reaction she would hazard a guess that his parents had something to do with the issues he was still dealing with. Unlike her, he'd chosen to escape the place which had caused him pain, and she had to wonder if emigrating was a more extreme reaction to the trauma than never leaving town. If they found a happy medium there might be a chance of real progress for both of them.

'Mum left when I was about five, so I don't remember much about her, and haven't heard from her since. Dad was an abusive drunk who should never have been allowed to raise a child, but I guess that's why she left in the first place. To cut a long story short, I was taken into care when I was fourteen. I had one foster family who were really good to me, but they have their hands full with all the other kids they've taken in since. I check in with them every now and then but I don't have any of my own family to go back and visit.

None who I have a wish to ever see again, at least.' There was a hardness to him whenever he spoke about his parents that Meadow was sure came from a place of pain. It hadn't gone unnoticed that he'd skipped over the details, the brief synopsis of his life enough for her to realise he'd had a difficult time growing up too. The fact that he'd become a doctor, helping others, and in a different country, was to be commended.

'I suppose this is a clean slate for you. I mean, I know it's not the one you'd planned, but you can build a whole new life for yourself.' It would be nice to leave the past far behind, but it was clear time and distance hadn't managed to erase Jay's troubling memories either. The most either of them could hope for was to eventually move on and not let the past encroach on their present or future any more than it already had.

'Our move out to Melbourne was so full of hope for the future. As though the world was ours for the taking. Coming out here, no offence, felt more like a chore. Something I had to do because it was on the list. Don't get me wrong, I know I have to create a new life for myself. It's just knowing where to start.'

'I don't know about the future, but for now you've got a room at least.'

Jay drained his bottle and tossed it into the overflowing recycling bin. 'I think that's my cue to leave. Early start in the morning.'

He started towards the door and Meadow rushed to catch up with him, grabbing a bulb from the lamp sitting in the lounge area, and a torch from the drawer in the kitchen.

'Here, take this with you. I want you to be comfortable. Although I can't guarantee what the mattress on the bed is like. It's probably been there since the first gold rush.'

'It's fine. Everything seems new enough and there were clean sheets in the cupboard. Thanks for the bulb.'

Meadow was surprised that her father appeared to have been taking care of the place when he couldn't seem to do the same for himself. Every time he cleared a new plot to work on, he had to hire earthmovers and some locals to do the heavier lifting for him. She supposed he had people staying more than she'd thought. Perhaps he realised he was making more from renting out the room than his prospecting.

'If there's anything you need just let me know and I'll see if I can sort it for you.' It was the least she could do until her father was back to keep an eye on things here. Jay had been great helping her get him to hospital, brushing off any insults or resistance from her father, who'd fought against the idea at every turn, often physically, but Jay had managed to get him onto the stretcher and talk him down from the various threats he'd made during his disoriented episode. Being dehydrated and concussed, along with his prolonged exposure, had made him more belligerent than usual.

The interaction between the two had made her wonder more about Jay's childhood. It was sure to have brought back memories, none of them pleasant, when he'd had a combative parent of his own. More than that, he'd called him abusive. Her father might have been neglectful, emotionally distant, but he'd never raised a hand to her when she was a child. When she put the information he'd shared about his father along with his fear of the dark she was sure there was a tragic tale behind it all that was even more unbearable than her own.

He'd been so sweet today with the patients at the clinic, and cooking for her tonight, and he didn't deserve to have had someone treat him so badly. The calm, reasoned way he'd spoken to her father made her think he'd had experience of dealing with someone who was out of control. It hurt to imagine what situations he'd been in for that kind of survival instinct to kick in, that need to placate someone so irate before they caused damage. Although it sounded as though it was too late for Jay, who was already scarred by whatever his father had done.

If this was his new life, his new start, Meadow wanted to help make it better for him. Even if it was only by giving him a lightbulb for now.

'Thanks. You made today a better day, Meadow.' His sad expression made her heart break all over again.

Careful to make sure her robe was tightly fastened first, she stood up on her tiptoes to kiss him on the cheek. 'Thanks for a lovely night, Jay.'

She didn't know what happened in that moment, but she delayed moving back from that slight contact when her lips touched his cheek. Their eyes met, their hot breath filling the space and silence between them as they both seemed to contemplate their next move. She felt his arms move around her, resting on her hips briefly before he pulled away from her again.

'Any time,' he said, his voice deeper and gruffer than she'd heard before now. Regret probably—she was feeling it too for almost acting on that growing attraction.

She had never been one to jump into a fling, or act on impulse simply because she liked the look of someone, or related to them more than anyone she'd ever met. A lot of factors came into play before she even thought about getting involved with someone. Usually. Especially with a man who represented everything she was afraid of in the world. He lived his life on a whim, thriving on change and a challenge. Jay Brooke was not the one who could offer her the stability she'd been craving her whole life. So why did it feel so good to have her blood pumping this hard around her body?

She put her feet back down on solid ground, doing her best to come to her senses.

'Don't say that. I'll be expecting you to cook for me every night.' She forced out a shaky laugh in an attempt to cover her awkward goodbye.

'Any time,' he repeated with a grin on his face before he walked out into the night.

Meadow watched the light from the torch bobbing across the darkness until he reached the shack. Once she saw the light in the bedroom go on she smiled to herself, happy he was safe. She closed the door and leaned against it, the blood in her veins fizzing with adrenaline, and she wondered if it was this kind of excitement which caused her father's addiction. And if it was hereditary.

CHAPTER FIVE

'HOW'S YOUR DAD TODAY?' Making small talk on the plane flying into a medical emergency was necessary to keep him sane. Jay needed something to take his mind off the scene of the traffic accident awaiting them at the end of the flight and it was better than sitting here with Meadow in silence after last night. After the way they'd left things, that almost-kiss on the doorstep, he needed to prevent things from becoming weird between them.

They'd shared a moment on her doorstep. Likely one born out of tiredness and loneliness, perhaps with a dash of chemistry upping the ante. It had been a nice way to wind down the evening, sharing a meal in good company. Though he'd overshared, talking about his childhood, something he'd hardly ever talked about with Sharyn, never mind someone he'd only known for a matter of days. He put it down to the situation, working closely together and dealing with her own difficult parent. Plus he'd been feeling vulnerable opening up to her the way he had, and having to admit his fear of the dark, even if he'd omitted his reasons.

Giving him a bulb so he would feel safe and comfortable in his new, strange environment, without any hint of ridicule, had lowered his defences. Meadow had understood his need for the simple gesture and done it without asking any questions.

As much as he'd loved Sharyn, she had always pushed him to tell her more, to delve deeper into those memories and share his pain. He knew the abuse he'd suffered was something he needed to get off his chest, but once he'd told her what had happened he hadn't seen the need to revisit it. She'd been something of an amateur psychologist, always seeking the reasons for people's behaviour, perhaps to better understand her own desire to take risks and live on the edge. Whilst speaking about what his father had done to him as a boy had given him the freedom to move on with his life, talking about it opened up old wounds that never got a chance to fully heal. Meadow seemed to understand his boundaries, his need for personal space, even without knowing the circumstances. That was a connection he didn't want to throw away with one stupid act of recklessness.

Of course there was an attraction. She was a beautiful woman, but they were colleagues and anything more than that would be a complication neither of them needed. He certainly wasn't ready to get into another relationship, and Meadow was the kind of woman who needed something more than he could ever give her. It was clear that her father's lifestyle had been the cause of their conflict in the past and staying here long-term was not in Jay's plans for the future. He would only be in town until he could figure out the new path he wanted to take. Although he was a little lost at the minute, he was sure it wasn't one on a red dirt track leading to nowhere.

'He seems to be getting back to his old self. I spoke to him on the phone this morning and he was bending my ear about getting out in the field to do some digging.' Meadow rolled her eyes, seeming more eager to attend this accident scene than have to do her father's bidding.

'He really couldn't leave it for a few days? It doesn't seem fair to expect you to do that kind of manual work on top of the day job, as well as entertain his new lodger.' The reference to last night made him think of those few seconds on the doorstep when he'd forgotten about his parents, Sharyn, the fire, even the list. His entire being had been focused on Meadow and the feel of her lips on his skin, the fresh smell of her hair and the need to hold her in his arms. He'd been tempted to do just that before common sense had kicked in to remind him who she was and what they were doing. Today he hoped to get back on track as co-workers who occasionally rubbed each other up the wrong way, figuratively speaking.

'Every cent counts, or nugget in my dad's case. He won't be able to settle if he thinks there's gold sitting out there, waiting for someone other than him to find it. I suppose I'm the next best thing since I'd actually give it to him. It's not totally alien to me. There was a time I used to enjoy going out with him, using the metal detector and my little trowel. Except I wasn't efficient enough and once I got older I realised it was mainly a waste of time, effort and a life.' The bitter tone matched the frown line blighting her forehead as she spoke about their toxic relationship.

Jay wondered that she maintained any contact with the man when he'd clearly caused her so much emotional damage. He'd chosen to never set eyes on his father again, to completely remove the source of his pain. Whilst he admired Meadow for trying to maintain some sort of connection, he couldn't help but think it came at a huge cost to her wellbeing.

'Hopefully it won't be for long, eh?' If her father's condition was improving it would take some of the pressure from her shoulders, and it might also lessen the chance of temptation. Once her father was ensconced back in his own home Meadow wouldn't feel as though she had to stick around and spend time with Jay out of hours.

'I was thinking I'd move into Dad's place for a couple of days, until he gets home at least. I don't want to be driving back and forward all the time.' Perhaps seeing the look of concern on his face that they would actually be spending more time together for the foreseeable future, she added, 'Plus, it means we can car share to work.'

'Great.' Jay forced a smile. It would solve the problem of how he was going to get to work until he sorted out his own transport, but it also entailed being with Meadow most of the working day. He was going to have to keep his wits about him, have the tangible plan of his future close at hand at all times, holding the list close to his heart instead of Meadow.

'We're coming in to land. Brace for impact,' Greg notified them over the intercom. The terrain, as Jay was finding out, didn't always provide a smooth landing. They often had to set down in less than ideal locations, making it a bumpy experience as the wheels met the rocky landscape. It certainly wasn't the flight experience he'd been used to on his journey from the UK to Oz.

He and Meadow both made sure they were buckled in to their seats and prepared to launch into full medical emergency mode once they hit the dirt. Their kit was ready to go in their bags so they could get the patients stabilised as soon as possible before transferring them to hospital.

'You ready for this?' Meadow asked as the plane bumped along the ground.

'I hope so.' This was his first emergency call as a flight doctor, and whilst he'd had plenty of experience dealing with those, he was used to having more facilities at his disposal. At an accident site all of the emergency services would be more readily available, with local hospitals nearby to provide all the latest medical equipment and technology, not to mention the best surgeons, to treat whatever life-changing injuries might occur.

Out here, they were the first responders, the nearest hospital miles away, with probably the most basic facilities to treat the casualties. Responsibility was going to be primarily borne by him and Meadow and they had no real idea what they were walking into.

As soon as the plane stopped moving, they unclipped their belts and grabbed their medical bags. The territory still unfamiliar to him, he followed Meadow as she ran towards the main road, and thanked modern technology for getting them to this exact location when it all looked the same at eye level.

The crash involved an articulated lorry and a heavy loader. With those kinds of large vehicles, and depending on the speeds involved, the impact was huge. He hoped the drivers had been wearing seatbelts at least, to give them a chance. The anticipation of what they would find always gave him that feeling in the pit of his stomach of impending doom, but it was his job to get there as quickly as possible and minimise the severity of potential injuries.

Meadow too was rushing to the scene without a second thought, and he wondered what had prompted her to work in this field when they did have to walk into the unknown like this. She certainly didn't seem to like her father living his life that way. Although there weren't that many options available out here for people who wanted to work in the medical field, so she might not have had a choice if she'd wanted to pursue her nursing career. Even more reason to admire her when she was willing to face whatever fears she had to help others.

'You check the truck driver's vitals. I'll go to the other guy.' Jay moved towards the heavy machinery; the front of the vehicle had obviously taken the brunt of the impact and spun across the road. It was half off the road, the window smashed and arcs from the tyre marks scorched into the road.

He swore when he realised the driver hadn't been belted in. Though he was lucky not to have gone through the windscreen, his head was bleeding profusely from where he'd obviously hit the glass.

'Hello. Can you hear me? You've been in an accident. My name's Jay, I'm with the flying doctor service. Open your eyes if you can hear me.' The man was unconscious, unresponsive and hanging halfway out of the vehicle. He had a pulse but there was a chance the collision could've caused him spinal injuries and they needed to stabilise his neck so as not to exacerbate any damage already done.

'Can you give me a hand?' he called to Greg, who'd brought the stretcher and back board so they could immobilise the patient ready for transit. Between them, they managed to gently manoeuvre him out and lie him flat on the board.

Jay checked his pulse and his breathing to make sure the move hadn't caused any deterioration in his condition. Once he was satisfied the patient was stable enough to be transferred, they began pushing him back towards the plane.

'Jay? Come here, quick.' An anxious-sounding Meadow beckoned him over to the truck, where the driver was lying on the ground, fitting.

'What happened?'

'He was conscious, and insisted on getting out of the cab, against my advice. Then he just dropped to the ground.' Meadow was already down beside him, loosening the top button on his shirt to help him breathe easier.

'Did he mention being epileptic? Maybe that's what caused the crash.' It was difficult to tell without having a medical history to hand, or diagnostic tools. All they could do was wait out the seizure and get him to the hospital for tests.

'Wait!' Meadow stopped Jay just as he was about to move him into the recovery position. 'His tongue's rolled back.'

With one hand on his forehead and one on his chin, she tilted the driver's head back to open his airway and move the tongue forward again. Although it wasn't physically possible for the man to swallow his tongue, it had blocked his airway, preventing oxygen from getting to his lungs, but with Meadow's vigilance it had been a quick fix.

Jay brushed away the bits of rock and glass littering the ground around them so the patient wouldn't injure himself further. Thankfully, the seizure didn't last long, and they were able to move him into the recovery position, after which he began to regain some consciousness.

'Hi, I'm Meadow from the flying doctor service, remember? You were involved in an accident and have just had a seizure. We're going to have to get you to hospital to check things out, okay?' Meadow talked to him calmly as she held his hand, the man still disoriented and drifting in and out of consciousness.

Once Greg returned with another stretcher,

they were able to lift him onto it and all make their way back to the plane. Hopefully, the injuries the men had suffered were superficial and there was no internal bleeding or broken bones to complicate recovery. They would only find out for sure when they reached the hospital, by which point Jay and Meadow would be handing over the responsibility and treatment to the staff there.

They made sure the patients were secure and ready for transporting before securing their own seatbelts. Only then did Jay relax some of the tension from his body with a sigh. He saw Meadow grinning out of the corner of his eye.

'It's full-on, isn't it?' she said.

'I feel like I've just run a marathon. I'm used to the adrenaline rush working in emergency departments, but actually being out in the field, or the desert, brings a whole new dimension to the job.'

'Is that a good or bad thing?' She cocked her head to one side, waiting for his answer as though she genuinely cared whether or not he was enjoying his new role.

'It'll never be boring I suppose. Sharyn would approve.'

'It's definitely challenging at times, but rewarding too. You'll get to know most of the community doing this job. They're like an extended family.'

'It's a surprising career path for someone who professes not to like the unpredictable nature of life out in the sticks.'

'I didn't want to move to the city, this is my home. If anything, life with my dad, on the move, out in the middle of nowhere, gave me some understanding of what people need in the way of medical services out here. I wanted to help, it's as simple as that.'

'I think you're more of an adventurer than you care to admit, Meadow Williams.'

She'd proved to him again today that she was as brave as she was kind-hearted. A dangerous combination, even to someone who didn't think he'd want to share his life with anyone ever again.

'Are you coming round to mine later? I'm having a few birthday drinks and firing the barbie up.' Greg approached Meadow and Jay some time later, back at the base. They'd safely delivered the victims of the accident to the hospital and finished their open clinic for the day. Meadow was hoping to finish up the paperwork and drive her stuff over to her dad's place.

'I don't think so. I have a lot to do tonight.'

Jay gave her a nudge. 'Oh, come on. It'll give me a chance to get to meet some new people. Or would you rather keep me all to yourself?'

Meadow rolled her eyes. He was surprisingly perky after the day they'd had, whilst she was barely managing to stifle a yawn. 'Knock yourself out, Party Boy, but I have work to do if my dad's going to keep a roof over his head.'

'Surely you're not going digging out there tonight? You can do it tomorrow when you're off. I reckon we need to let off some steam and it'll save you from having to make me dinner. I think it's your turn to cook, isn't it?'

'I don't remember saying that.'

She thought about the possible evening ahead, when they probably would end up spending it together, alone, and came to the fast conclusion it wasn't a good idea. They'd come close to doing something stupid last night and another cosy dinner together, getting to know each other even more in a repeat of last night, wasn't going to help her avoid temptation.

'Well, we haven't had time to grocery shop and barely got to eat lunch. We could get something to eat, toast Greg a happy birthday, and leave. No offence, mate.' Jay clapped

Greg on the back in apology for the assumption they'd only stay long enough to fill their bellies.

'None taken. Meadow doesn't usually come to any of our shindigs, so it'll be a birthday treat to have you there. Make sure you both bring your swimming togs.'

'No way.'

'Not a chance.'

Meadow's protest was quickly followed by Jay's as Greg walked away from them. The last thing she needed was to see him parading about in his swimwear as if he were participating in a beauty pageant for hot doctors. It would be no contest when he'd surely take the tiara anyway.

'Dinner and one drink. That's it.'

'It's a date.'

'Not a date,' she corrected, knowing full well he was teasing her.

'Dinner, a drink, back to your place… I'd call that a date.'

'I'd call that wishful thinking. Now, do you want a lift home or not?' Meadow wondered how he'd react if she actually said yes to a date. Now, that would give him something to think about. Unfortunately, it also put more thoughts in her head that she definitely shouldn't be having about a co-worker.

* * *

'Why don't you socialise with the rest of the crew?' Jay asked as they drove back towards the town.

'I socialise. I'm just choosy about what events I attend.'

'Like playing pool in the pub with people like Marko?'

Oh, he knew how to push her buttons!

'I told you I was having a rough time. I'd just broken up with someone and I was a bit vulnerable and lonely.' She didn't know why she was explaining herself to him, other than to make sure he knew that wasn't her usual behaviour. Every time she thought of Marko and their drunken antics she cringed. She had a similar reaction when she recalled the way she'd been with Jay that first night. In hindsight, he'd only been looking out for her, calling Marko out for being inappropriate, and something she should have appreciated when everyone else let him get away with it. It seemed to have done the trick at least; Marko had kept his distance since Jay had stepped in to protect her.

'Sorry. Your personal life is none of my business, as is who you play pool with, or kiss in a moment of weakness.' The playful tone drew the side eye from Meadow.

'I don't make a habit of it.' In case he got any idea that he was next, especially after last night's near-miss. Hopefully, she'd learned her lesson and wouldn't make another embarrassing mistake she'd live to regret. It was the main reason she'd agreed to attend this party, regardless that she'd rather crawl into bed for an early night. Jay had a point about meeting other people and making new friends. If he managed to do that, they might not spend so much time together. He might find someone else to give him a lift to work, to find a room for him or that he could cook meals for. Then she could get back to her quiet life in her own house, with no distracting Englishman around to annoy her.

'Hey, guys. Grab yourself a few snags before they're all gone.' Greg greeted them wearing a pair of bright yellow board shorts and a white vest that almost blinded Meadow when he opened the door.

'Happy birthday, mate.' Jay leaned in and gave their co-worker a manly hug with lots of back-slapping involved.

'We brought you a case of beer as a present. I hope that's okay?' They'd stopped off on the way for the joint purchase, realising they couldn't turn up empty-handed to a birthday party.

'You can never go wrong with the old grog, can you?' He took the beer from Meadow and tucked it under his arm before leading them out towards the backyard.

Like most of the houses around the area, hers included, it wasn't a vast property but Greg had managed to squeeze a small pool into the backyard where everyone was currently congregated.

He directed them towards the cloud of smoke coming from the barbecue. 'Grub's over on the table, there's a few stubbies in the fridge, and towels on the decking if you fancy a swim.'

'We won't be staying that long, sorry. I'm staying at my dad's place at the minute so I have to drive back out there.' Meadow made her excuse early so she could duck away as soon as possible without having to go through the rigmarole of saying goodbye and him trying to persuade her to stay. Greg had enough family and friends, not many of whom she was acquainted with, to keep him busy. Given the stories she'd heard of the drunken antics that went on at some of Greg's pool parties, she wasn't tempted to stay until the inebriated masses decided it was a good idea to go skinny-dipping. She tried not to let her mind wander towards Jay getting involved with such abandon in case she was tempted.

'Sorry, mate.' Jay made his apology too, even though he was free to stay on if he wished. Although with Marko the only local taxi driver as his alternative means of transport, perhaps she wasn't giving him any option but to leave with her.

'Wait…' Greg looked at Meadow then back to Jay. 'Are you two together?'

'We're living together,' Jay casually replied, lifting a bottle of beer from the bucket of ice under the table.

'No, we're not.' Meadow huffed out a breath through gritted teeth.

'I mean, you don't seem a likely couple, but fair play to ya.' Greg clinked the bottle of beer he was now holding in his hand to Jay's.

'We're not together, and why would we make an unlikely couple?' It was ridiculous to be outraged by the comment when she was taking pains to make sure Greg knew they weren't a couple, but Meadow knew the comment was sure to be an insult against her. Greg and Jay had hit it off immediately, whereas it had taken her and their pilot some time to build up a good working rapport. He was another man who took risks; sometimes he had to when it came to getting to their patients. By no means was he reckless, but some of the hairy situations they'd found themselves in over the years had caused some friction. They had different ways of doing things, and though they didn't always agree, they both wanted the best for their patients and muddled along. A bit like her and Jay, except they'd never had a cosy dinner for two or nearly pashed on the doorstep.

Greg held his hands up in surrender and she knew it was because he was expecting her to go ape at him after what he was about to say. 'It's just…don't take this the wrong way, but you can be a bit uptight sometimes, Meads. Jay's more laidback, like me.'

Meadow opened and closed her mouth but words refused to come and fight against the character assassination because she knew it was true. She couldn't help being the stickler for rules she was because it was how she protected herself and others around her. Safety was a big issue for someone who'd grown up without it, emotionally and physically.

'Was that the doorbell? I'll have to go and let more bogans in if we're really gonna get this party started. Whoo!' With his beer held aloft, Greg disappeared back into the house, giving her no further chance to defend herself.

'Don't let him upset you. He is like me, sometimes he doesn't think before he speaks. Being cautious isn't a bad thing. It's what I like about you.' Jay's words managed to alleviate some of the pain Greg had clumsily inflicted upon her.

He liked her.

'You like that I'm boring?' Okay, the tail from the sting was still embedded somewhere under her skin.

'I never said you were boring. I said you were cautious. After being with Sharyn, who was always pushing me to do something out of my comfort zone, it's nice to be around someone who'll just let me be.' Jay gave a little chuckle to himself.

She knew he wasn't disrespecting his cherished girlfriend but perhaps now, with a bit of time and space, he realised that he didn't have to be constantly challenging himself.

'Some peace and quiet now and again can be good for the soul.'

'As can doing something exhilarating and breaking out of the norm,' Jay added, giving her pause to think that it didn't have to be one way or another.

Once again, that niggling feeling that she

should let loose and do something spontaneous, just to see what happened, was creeping into her thoughts. Although the only reckless thing she'd imagined doing recently was kissing Jay, and the fallout from that would have been a price too high to pay when they'd still have to work together. She knew she'd be in danger of liking him too much, and getting romantically involved meant being invested in his welfare, his safety. Something he didn't appear to value. Falling for Jay proved a risk too far if it entailed having her heart broken when he left her for the next thrill elsewhere.

'I'm here, aren't I?' She took a bottle from the ice bucket, cracked the lid on the edge of the table and chugged back the beer in defiance.

'Yes, you are. Maybe for your next venture you could go shark swimming with me.' He didn't take his eyes off her as he took a swig of lager, as though watching for her reaction. As much as she wanted to prove a point, she wasn't going to put herself in danger simply to try and get one up on him.

'If I won't even get in the pool here, what makes you think I'd even entertain that idea? I'm thinking more along the lines of stroking a koala. One step at a time, Jay.'

'It's a date,' he replied, walking away.

'Not a date,' she corrected, looking forward to it already.

'Hey, you.' Kate wandered over to her at that moment, or at least Meadow hadn't noticed her until she'd spoken.

'Hey. I didn't think you'd be here.' Meadow pulled her into a one-armed hug, holding her beer with the other.

'Well, Bob thought hanging out with you kids would keep us young at heart.'

'You're not old, Kate.' And she'd a much busier social calendar than Meadow could ever hope to have.

'No? I've only had one glass of wine and I'm ready for my bed. Not that Bob would complain about that.' The usually reserved manager giggled, suggesting it might have been a very large glass she'd had.

'You're lucky to have each other.'

'I guess so. Speaking of romance, you have a glow about you tonight.' She peered closely at Meadow.

'Really? Must be the wine goggles.'

Kate wagged a finger. 'Nope. I've known you a long time, Meadow Williams, and I can tell when something's changed. I haven't seen you this happy since that Shawn left. Is there a new man on the scene I don't know about?'

Meadow inadvertently cast a look at Jay,

who was over talking to some of the guys from the base.

'No,' she said, the high-pitched denial unconvincing even to her own ears.

Kate's jaw dropped. 'The doc?'

She whistled, then raised her glass in a toast. 'I'll give it to you, he does have a peachy bum, love.'

Meadow couldn't argue on that point, but she was perturbed by the fact she was so easy to read. 'Why does everyone think there's something going on between me and Jay? We're just colleagues, like you and me, Kate.'

'Uh-huh. Yet you came here together, according to Greg.' Kate narrowed her eyes at Meadow over the rim of her glass.

Meadow huffed out a sigh of frustration. 'He doesn't have a car. I gave him a lift. He's going to be staying at my dad's old place until he gets sorted out with somewhere else so I guess it'll become a regular thing. It's no biggie.'

Kate set down her glass. 'No biggie? I've known you to have entire relationships without introducing your significant other to your father. You've known Jay for a matter of days and he's living out there? Girl, you've got it bad.'

Meadow tutted and rolled her eyes at the

insinuation but felt as though she'd just been slapped. It had taken her some time to convince herself that she should do the right thing and offer Jay the place to stay, that there was nothing more to it than doing him a favour. Now Kate was calling her out on it there was nowhere to hide. She was right, Meadow had kept introductions with her dad to a minimum when it came to romantic partners. Not that Jay was anything of the sort, but even her colleagues only got to meet him if they ran into him by accident at the bar.

She didn't like her family business, and the mess it was, to intersect with the life she'd created for herself in Dream Gulley. In case it somehow contaminated everything she had achieved. Back on Rainbow's Walk were the bad memories of her family splitting up, of leaving her dad behind, but her adult life in town was settled and safe. She had friends and colleagues, a sense of belonging in the community, and didn't like to be seen as Digger's daughter. They knew the sort of person he was, unkempt, irascible and unpredictable. At times she was embarrassed to be associated with him, but she already knew Jay wasn't the sort of person to make that judgement. He'd been through a rough childhood too and understood the importance of keeping a personal life private.

That was the only reason she'd let her defences down and agreed to Jay crossing that line from their working relationship. That almost-kiss had just been a blip. Absolutely no reason for her to panic.

She knocked back the rest of her beer.

Jay stopped teasing Meadow long enough to go and fill a plate likely to give him the meat sweats later, with a green salad on the side to salve his conscience. He'd had no more interest in coming here than she had, but he reckoned it was safer for them to be in a crowd after last night.

By the time they'd had a bite to eat and a drink it would be acceptable for him to head on to his accommodation and leave with Meadow to go back to her dad's. They wouldn't feel obliged to spend more time together once it got dark. Basically, he was using Greg as a buffer to prevent him from crossing a line. It wouldn't go down well if he'd called Marko out for making unwanted advances, only to do the same himself. Although, judging by the way she'd been looking at him and the hitch in her breath when their lips had been a whisper away from touching on the doorstep, the idea hadn't been totally abhorrent to her. Making it even more dangerous.

Deciding to come to the party instead brought its own problems. It was one of the rare occasions when he'd seen her out of her uniform, if he didn't count almost naked bar her dressing gown at dinner. She looked relaxed tonight in her rust-coloured gypsy-style skirt and cropped white top that showed off her tanned, flat belly. Her hair was free from the usual ponytail, the golden waves perfectly framing her heart-shaped face. She'd even put on a little make-up tonight, the pink lipstick making her lips look even more delicious than usual.

He swallowed down his lustful thoughts with another mouthful of cold beer, though he wondered if he'd been at the back of her mind at all when she'd got ready tonight. After another cold shower he'd pulled on a clean shirt, even ironed it first, in order to make a good impression on her. He certainly hadn't taken that level of effort for Greg's sake, whose idea of dressing up was to wear a shirt at all.

They hadn't spent the whole night joined at the hip; after all, he'd told her he wanted to make new friends. That didn't mean he hadn't always had her in the corner of his eye when he'd been shooting the breeze with Greg's friends, and taking a ribbing over his accent. In fact, he could see her now, making her way back to him with a plate of food in her hand and stifling a yawn.

'Too much excitement?'

'Sorry. I didn't sleep well last night, too much going on in my mind.'

'Yeah, me too. I mean, I need to find somewhere permanent to stay and I have an extreme to-do list to complete.' He didn't want her to think he'd been replaying that moment between them in his head over and over again and trying to convince himself he didn't regret walking away.

'No word back from the service?'

'They're looking into it, but I guess the way they see it is I'm already here, doing the job, so they're probably not in a rush to rehouse me. Especially when I'm staying at your dad's place.' Something that wasn't going to be ideal long-term when it meant being around Meadow twenty-four-seven whilst actively trying to avoid getting close to her.

'Tell them they need to compensate you if they're not going to give you the agreed accommodation, that should get them moving.'

'I'll do that. I was wondering if I could accompany you tomorrow for a while when you're digging. That's one more thing I could cross off…'

He didn't like the idea of Meadow doing that kind of dangerous task out on her own when her own father had succumbed to the heat and terrain, despite her having experience, and Jay being a total novice. She probably wouldn't need his help but he wanted to be around to make sure she was okay, and could do so under the pretence of completing another of his challenges.

'I'm not sure…' Meadow was trying to formulate a response which wouldn't hurt his feelings too much when there was the sound of a splash and a scream.

Jay had been watching something unfold over her shoulder and he took off in the direction of the pool. Before she knew what was happening, he'd dived into the pool with a crowd peering down into the deep end. It seemed an age before he emerged with a young woman in his arms. He swam on his back, guiding the woman, who was clearly unconscious, to the edge of the pool, where everyone worked together to get her out of the pool and lay her on the ground. Meadow set her plate down and rushed to help.

'She's not breathing.' Jay was kneeling by the woman, his wet clothes clinging to every hard inch of his body like a second skin, which made it hard not to stare.

Meadow tilted the woman's chin up to try and help her breathe as Jay wiped the water from his eyes. 'She has a cut and a bruise on her head too. She must have knocked herself out.'

'I saw her slip just before she went in the water, but it happened so quickly there was nothing I could do,' Jay said worriedly.

'I think you did plenty,' Meadow told him as he started chest compressions, his interlocked hands pushing down on the middle of the woman's chest in an attempt to bring her back to life.

'Someone call an ambulance,' Jay shouted at the assembled crowd. A blanket was thrown over his shoulders but he shrugged it off, his only concern for the woman at the mercy of his ministrations.

Meadow admired his dedication and determination, but saw him begin to tire, the physical exertion taking its toll on him. 'I can take over for a while.'

He nodded his agreement without argument, a sign not only of his exhaustion but his trust and respect in her capabilities too. In the end they took turns with the chest compressions whilst Greg cleared the rest of the partygoers away from the area, probably to prevent any further distress if they couldn't bring her back round. It was an intimate yet tense scene, with the two of them working together to save a life. As medics, it was something they encountered every day but here, now, Meadow felt the pressure more. They were at a friend's house, on his birthday, with everyone relying on them to perform a miracle.

Meadow glanced up, feeling Jay's eyes on her as she pumped the woman's chest.

'It'll be okay.' That look, that promise, gave her the strength to keep going, and she was rewarded when their patient spluttered, exhaling some of the water which had filled her lungs.

Between them, they moved her onto her side in the recovery position. She coughed up what was left of the pool water and opened her eyes.

'Hey,' Meadow said softly, stroking the wet hair away from her face. 'You slipped and fell into the pool but you're going to be okay. The ambulance is on the way.'

Jay took the blanket which had been offered to him and covered her shivering body just as they heard the sirens approach. The three of them sat in silence until the paramedics came through, led by a happier-looking Greg.

'Am I glad you guys were here for Junie. I'm not sure I'd have been in any fit state to perform CPR.'

'Next time maybe keep the pool covered if you're going to be drinking. Alcohol and swimming don't mix.' Jay's admonishment seemed to take Greg as much by surprise as it did Meadow. Perhaps he wasn't as reckless with others' lives as he seemed to be with his own and it showed a level of maturity which their colleague had yet to reach.

Jay had acted heroically, and though Meadow didn't know if she would've reacted the same way, she was glad he had. They made a good team, their different ways of doing things working together to get the right outcome. She couldn't help but wonder how that would translate into a more personal relationship. There would never be a dull moment, undoubtedly, but that was also what terrified her when she thought about a possible life with Jay.

Once the paramedics took the patient away Greg called everyone to attention. 'Okay, ladies and gentlemen, I've been assured that Junie is going to be all right, so I think we should get this party back on track. Everyone inside for beer pong!'

Slowly, the partygoers began to filter back inside, leaving Meadow, Jay, Kate and Bob standing outside.

'Never one to let the party stop is our Greg,' Meadow said with a laugh, shaking her head.

'I think that's enough excitement for one night. I'll see you two at work tomorrow.' Kate hugged both of her colleagues before taking her husband's hand and walking away.

It always made Meadow yearn for the sort of relationship they had when she saw Kate and Bob together. Being happily married with a family was something she'd aspired to for a long time. Probably because she hadn't had much experience of it herself. But she was beginning to think it wasn't on the cards for her. She hadn't met anyone who fitted the bill, or who she would trust enough to let that close to her. Okay, so she'd let Jay into her private life, but an adrenaline junkie like him would never be satisfied with someone who simply wanted quiet nights in and a partner to hold hands with.

It didn't stop her from wishing for it.

Once she was alone with Jay, she noticed

then that he had begun to shiver, still soaked to the skin.

'You need to get out of those wet clothes before you end up with hypothermia.' Her nursing instincts kicked in and she began to unbutton the shirt presenting his body like a gift to the watching world. The almost transparent fabric clung to the ripples of his stomach, the taut muscles of his chest, pinching around his tight nipples to show her just how cold he was, and Meadow lost herself to the unwrapping of Jay's spectacular form.

He made no move to stop her as she peeled away his shirt and let it fall to the floor, but his eyes never left her face. She could feel that grey steel gaze locked onto her as she concentrated on disrobing him, for his own benefit. The fact that she got to see him like this up close and very personal was merely a bonus.

She barely resisted sliding her hands down the smooth lines of his body, glistening in the moonlight. But when she moved to undo his belt, her fingers refused to obey, fumbling over the simplest of tasks.

'Let me,' Jay insisted, working deftly to undo the fastening before slowly, torturously, to unbutton his fly.

Meadow was watching, mesmerised, and when he let his trousers fall, the belt hit-ting the tiles with a thud, she had to fight to breathe. His boxers were moulded intimately, and impressively, around his hips, and she couldn't look away.

'Hey, eyes up here. I'm not a sex object, you know.' He laughed and tilted her chin up to look at him.

Her cheeks were burning at being caught out ogling under the pretence of regulating his body heat. Yet embarrassment wasn't the main emotion she was currently feeling. Just looking at him, knowing he was letting her, had awakened that deep need inside her for more. She was unbelievably turned on.

'Sorry. I was just wondering if you needed to take everything off in this situation.' She decided it was better to play along with the flirting than admit she was enjoying the view.

'I will if you will. They do say that skin-to-skin contact is better to produce body heat.' He hooked his fingers into the sides of his underwear and she was sure she was about to get the full Monty when Greg came rushing back, carrying towels and clothes.

'I thought you might need a change of clothes…'

He took one look at them and tutted. 'And you're not together? Pull the other one.'

'It's not what it looks like.'

'I was just taking off my wet clothes.'

They protested their innocence in vain as Greg dropped everything and backed away, holding his hands up. 'Whatever you say.'

'Grow up, Greg,' Meadow pouted, though she couldn't figure out if she was more annoyed at the insinuation or the interruption.

CHAPTER SIX

THE SUN WAS high in the sky when Jay eventually woke. It had been a late night after all. Later still when he'd lain awake into the early hours, going over the events at the party in his mind. Not only on a high after saving that woman's life with Meadow, but also because of the sparks between them which were dangerous so close to a body of water.

Even though they'd been out in the open, he'd been freezing cold and wet and the circumstances anything but sexy, those few seconds of Meadow staring at his partially naked body had been the most erotic thing he'd experienced in a long time.

He didn't know what would have happened if Greg hadn't walked in on them, probably nothing since there was a houseful of people still there. However, the interruption had managed to bring them both back down to earth. So much so they'd barely spoken on the journey back. Meadow hadn't even taken the opportunity to tease him about the neon board shorts and cerise vest top Greg had provided him with in place of the wet clothes he'd carried home in a bag.

They'd said their goodbyes and gone their separate ways as soon as they'd pulled up on her father's property. It was clear she regretted whatever had gone on in her mind as he'd performed his impromptu strip tease, but he hadn't missed that flare of desire she'd briefly allowed to burn before it had been extinguished. In those few seconds he'd got to see a more uninhibited Meadow, a woman who knew what she wanted and wasn't afraid to show it. Then those barriers had popped up again, stealing that light from her eyes, and making sure he redressed in double quick time, the intimate moment obviously over.

Then he'd tossed and turned until dawn, wondering if he'd wanted things to go further and not liking the answer. Yes. He'd been tortured by the thought of going over and knocking on her door to see if she wanted to carry on where they'd left off. Then he realised if she had, she would've come to him. Meadow was a woman who knew her own mind, knew what she wanted, and what she didn't. There had obviously been something, other than

Greg's untimely arrival, which had caused her to rethink her interest in him as more than a colleague.

He should be relieved her aversion to spontaneity had saved him from betraying Sharyn's memory. Yet it had been that 'what if?' fantasy which had kept him from sleep, not guilt. Since Sharyn's death he hadn't thought about being with another woman, the grief too raw to let him form any sort of emotional attachment to anyone else. He hadn't even wanted a purely physical hook-up because it would've been empty, meaningless, and would have made his mood sink lower, disgusted with himself for doing it.

Sharyn would have wanted him to meet someone else. She would never have expected him to lock himself away from the world again. In fact, she would've been angry at him for waiting so long before even thinking that getting involved with someone could be a possibility.

As he lay there debating the issue, he realised the whole thing was futile anyway when Meadow clearly didn't see him as relationship material. He knew she was still reeling from a breakup, and whatever issue had caused it was perhaps preventing her from moving on too. Or maybe she just wasn't that into him.

And yet… He considered briefly that lustful look in her eyes as he'd let his trousers drop to the floor.

'Nah,' he said aloud to his empty room, pleased with himself at managing to get Meadow to at least recognise she found him attractive.

After another period of convincing himself he could catch forty winks, only to find himself lying staring at the ceiling again, he had to concede it was time to get up. After a quick wash and a bite of toast, he dressed and headed over to see her.

'Meadow? Are you up?' After getting no response he let himself in—security was noticeably absent and he hoped she was more conscious of it in her own house.

There was no sign of her in the living room or kitchen, though there was an empty cereal bowl and a half-finished glass of orange sitting by the sink. She was another one who'd risen early.

Since she hadn't come out of the bedroom to accuse him of breaking and entering, he deduced she'd already gone out to dig without him. To be fair, she hadn't actually agreed to his request to join her; events had overtaken them. But he had registered his interest so it was jarring to find she'd chosen to ignore his suggestion, knowing it was on the list.

He'd made sure to bring some water with him, along with his phone and a hat. It could be she'd decided she didn't want to encourage his company all the time in case it gave him any ideas about the nature of their relationship. He didn't want to be another Marko so he would respect her boundaries there, but he also wanted to make sure she was safe. Surely she wouldn't mind too much if he stopped by to say hello and check in with her?

Jay wandered out towards the spot where they'd found her father a few days ago, ensuring he kept one eye back on the house to maintain his bearings. Of course Meadow wasn't answering her phone because it had been sitting on the kitchen table where she'd left it. He hoped she hadn't done so intentionally, knowing he'd been keen to go out this morning with her. If so, she really wasn't going to be pleased to see him.

'Meadow?' he called out into the vast expanse in case she'd ventured off track to somewhere new. There was no point in him walking aimlessly into the bush with no idea where she was or where he was going. That was just asking for trouble, and a repeat of what had happened to her dad, which was the last thing she'd want, or need. He wouldn't be very popular if she had to waste her day off getting him airlifted to hospital.

'Meadow? Are you out here?'

'Jay? Be careful. I'll come to you. Wait there.'

He heard her but couldn't see her, and ventured towards the edge of the ditch where her father had come unstuck, careful not to lose his footing too. Peering over the drop, he saw her crouched down in the dirt. With her hair tied up under her wide-brimmed hat, showing off her tanned limbs in khaki shorts and camo shirt, dirt smeared on her cheek, she looked even more gorgeous than last night.

'I told you to wait,' she sighed, standing up to brush the dust from her clothes.

'I'm not going to do anything stupid. I'm just standing here.' He didn't want to be a liability or a source of irritation, he only knew he had to come out here this morning to be with her.

Another hefty sigh. 'I'm busy, Jay.'

She was shielding her eyes with her hand, the sun already blazing down on them at this hour. That, combined with the amount of flies he was constantly having to bat away, made Jay wonder what the attraction of this was, apart from the obvious hope of finding a fortune. He could think of easier ways to make money. It began to make sense why she was so risk-averse and in need of stability. Perhaps why she didn't want to contemplate the idea of being with him when he was always talking about that stupid list. Although it had been important at the time for him and Sharyn, a way for him to break out of old habits, he didn't want it to get in the way of the future.

'Any luck so far?' Even though she would probably be more welcoming if she'd uncovered some gold, it was the only question which came to mind for now.

Meadow frowned. 'Nope. So there goes the patch theory. Give me a hand up.'

She reached up and he hauled her, the detector and pickaxe out of the ditch.

'Are you done for the day then?' Maybe they could take a drive out for some lunch, or spend the afternoon together at a wildlife park for that talked about koala experience.

Meadow gave a shrill laugh. 'No. I'm not going to go back to my father empty-handed if it kills me. If I can find something decent it could keep him going for a while, and hopefully he won't try and kill himself finding money for next month's bills.'

'So how do you find a good prospect? Where do you start?' Whilst Jay admired her determination to provide for her father, it seemed like relentlessly hard work for very little gain. Unless she did something her experienced father hadn't managed, and uncovered a boulder-sized nugget of golden goodness.

'Well, I thought my dad's finds would've been a good place to start. He always maintained there was a motherlode waiting to be found in the ancient dried riverbed that supposedly ran here. Gold deposits are often transported by rivers, but I've scanned the area and there isn't a signal to be found.' She waved the metal detector in the air and he got the impression if it hadn't been worth a small fortune on its own, she would've launched it into the stratosphere.

'How long have you been out here?'

'Since daybreak. I need to find something, Jay. He'll be so disappointed if I don't, and he'll be straight back out here rather than resting.'

'Okay. So do you have any idea where it would be a good spot to start over?'

'I don't have his map grid of places he's searched before, or intends to search. There are some old gold mines around. Although they're largely mined out, they didn't have the same equipment in the eighteen-hundreds as we do now. I guess that's as good an area as any to try.'

'Can I tag along? I won't get in the way, promise.'

'You're happy to stand out here in near forty-degree heat, plagued by flies, to just watch?' She was standing with one hand on her hip, detector slung over her shoulder, and she'd never looked more Aussie.

It was tempting to front it out and say yes, that was enough, but they both knew it was a lie. He was dying to try it.

'I'd love to have a go on your bleepy stick thing.'

Meadow rolled her eyes and walked off, calling behind her, 'You ever call it that in front of my dad and you'll be homeless again.'

Jay grinned, knowing he'd got her approval to tag along after all.

Meadow should have insisted that he go back to the house out of harm's way, but the truth was she liked the company. She'd thought she could do this on her own but her frustrated attempts in the heat had left her seconds away from a teary breakdown before Jay had arrived. The sight of him had made her glad he'd ignored her obvious decision to leave without him this morning, despite his request to accompany her.

Things last night had got too hot and steamy, too wet and wild, for her to take any more chances of being alone with him. Yet here they were again, and only time would tell if she'd have the strength to resist another wave of sexual tension capable of turning her into a voyeur. The way she'd watched him undress last night, she might as well have tucked dollars into his jocks and asked for a lap dance, and she was sure he would've obliged. It was only Greg, and the knowledge they'd both regret it in the cold light of day, which had stopped her from asking him for a private show when they'd come home.

Even that notion of this place as being home was skewed, when she'd never seen her dad's land as anything other than something she had to bear. It was only Jay who'd made it feel somewhere safe. Ironic, given that thrill-seeking nature and the current threat to her peace of mind.

After spending most of her adult life looking after herself, her parents off exploring their own lives, it was nice to have someone with her. She knew part of the reason Jay was here was to make sure she didn't get into difficulty. If he'd really wanted to cross something off that damn list, he could've used his day off to go and do something more exciting than digging in the dirt. He couldn't fool her. The sort of man who'd dive into a pool fully clothed to save someone was also the kind who wouldn't be content to stand back and let a woman do hard manual labour alone.

If it was anyone else, she might be offended that he thought she couldn't manage on her own, but that wasn't it with Jay. Despite his risky behaviour at times, she got a sense that he wanted to keep her safe, and that was something she hadn't had from anybody in a long time. Certainly not from her parents, and not from any of her past partners who, now she looked back on it, might be considered weak. Men she knew couldn't hurt her because she didn't love them enough, so she wouldn't be too broken-hearted when they invariably let her down.

She'd always thought it was stability she wanted in a relationship, but she knew there was part of her that craved the sort of excitement someone like Jay brought into her life. Except she needed care and kindness with it, not risk. Her father and Shawn had got their kicks at her expense and inviting Jay further into her life was the ultimate gamble. In this case, instead of risking her family and finances, she would be putting her heart on the line in the hope of winning her prize. Only time would tell if that adventurous streak would win out over her desire for self-preservation. But for now she was glad she had someone to talk to other than herself out here in the wilds.

'What's the story with the mines? I mean, why aren't they still in operation if it's thought there's still gold in them thar hills?' Jay's insistence that he wasn't going to get in her way was already in dispute when it seemed he wasn't one for companionable silence for the journey.

'The gold rush in the later eighteen-hundreds and into the nineteen-hundreds meant every man and his dog was out trying to find gold. They stripped whatever they could, then the mines were simply abandoned and they made their way to new promising sites, until the price of gold crashed. People like my father are convinced that there might still be gold waiting to be found that modern-day equipment can help discover. Trust me, if my father had the money, he'd have these back in operation.'

'But you don't believe there's a fortune still to be made?'

She shook her head. 'I don't think those men would've walked away if there was a sliver of gold left. I mean, I know he's found a few nuggets round about, but nothing that justifies the money and effort he's put in to find it.' Nor the family he'd traded for it.

'I take it he can't be persuaded otherwise?'

'No. I think at this stage he's too pig-headed to admit defeat. It's an obsession, the mistress that took him away from us.' Meadow couldn't help but be resentful. It might've been easier for her to reconcile events in her mind if it had been another woman who'd stolen his time and devotion when she'd been younger. Then she would have had someone else to be angry at other than her father. It made their relationship complicated when she still bore a grudge, yet loved him too much to simply walk away. If he'd had another woman, at least there would've been someone else to look after him too. As things stood, she was the only one he had in his life. Not that he was grateful, or had ever felt the need to say sorry.

Perhaps if he'd ever apologised for neglecting her and her mother, admitted he'd made a mistake, she could have let go of some of that resentment and got on with her life, minus the fear that another man could inflict the same damage. But he hadn't, and so she hadn't found the courage to open up her heart and share her life with anyone capable of breaking her again.

'Yet you're out here, keeping your father's mistress happy in his absence.' Jay was teasing her again but she didn't mind the gentle ribbing when she knew it came from a good place.

'Yes, well, it doesn't mean I'm ecstatic about it, but needs must. Okay, do you want to try?' She turned on the detector, deciding it might take his mind off asking questions for a while, and stop him probing too deeply into her past. It wasn't something she talked about usually, but Jay had a way of making her open up that she wasn't particularly comfortable with when it left her feeling exposed. As if talking about it would allow him to break through her brittle shell to the soft, vulnerable girl behind it, and she'd protect that child as much as she could because no one else ever had.

'I thought you'd never ask!' Jay rubbed his hands together like an excited child waiting to open a Christmas present. With all the other stuff he'd done in his life, the thought that this should give him a similar rush was amusing rather than concerning. It was difficult to tell if this was for her benefit or if he really did get a thrill every time he did something different. If that was the case, it was adorable that he became an excited puppy with every new discovery.

'You need to keep it low to the ground and sweep from side to side, like this.' She did a quick demonstration to show him. 'We're listening for a change in pitch, a sign that it's picking up something metallic underfoot.'

Meadow handed over the detector, hoping he didn't break it or her father would lose his mind.

'Like this?' Jay swung the device wildly, making her twitch.

'You need to go slow and steady so you don't miss anything.' She stood behind him and put her arms around him to rest her hands on top of his and control the motion of the detector.

'Like this?' He turned his head to check he was doing it right, and they were so close it took Meadow right back to that moment on the doorstep when they'd almost kissed. As much as she still wanted that, she couldn't be sure she'd be able to put the fire out if they did light that touch paper.

She released her hold and put some space

between their warm bodies again. 'Yeah. I think you've got it now.'

He held her gaze for another few seconds before he finally looked away and she got her breath back. Thankfully, as he got more invested in his detecting, Meadow was able to keep her distance and didn't feel the need to continue a conversation. She followed his slow, steady steps, letting the birdsong fill the silence. And when the detector screeched a sudden discovery her heart nearly pounded out of her chest.

'Is that…? Have I…?' Jay's eyes were wide, his body frozen to the spot, and he so clearly thought he'd found his treasure, Meadow didn't want to burst his bubble.

'It just means there's metal content present. You could've found a rusty old nail or a bottle top. We need to dig and keep searching for the source.' She took a small trowel from her pocket and dropped to her haunches where he'd picked up the signal.

With a scoopful of earth in her hands, she waved it over the detector and listened for the indication that she'd lifted the metal and it wasn't still in the ground. She repeated the process several times, discarding some of the earth with every pass. This morning had unearthed nothing but useless debris already and though she'd be delighted for everyone involved if this was something shiny and precious, she had her doubts.

'What's that?' Jay was kneeling down beside her now, pointing at the contents of her hand. She poked through the mound of dirt to unearth a small lump of metal. Unfortunately, not the one they were looking for.

'Iron ore. Sorry. But it's often thought that where you find a concentration of iron ore, gold could follow.' Meadow vaguely remembered being told that the deposits were often formed in the earth at the same time, but Jay already seemed to have lost interest. He handed the metal detector back over to her and got to his feet.

'I think I'll let the expert take over. Whilst I can definitely see the attraction, I can only imagine the toll it would take on a person, being disappointed time and again to come away empty-handed. And this is how your father makes his living?'

Meadow nodded. 'That's why he needs the extra income.'

It hadn't taken long for Jay to realise what she was up against with the emotional roller coaster of gold hunting. The precarious nature of the work took a certain type of person to want to do it full-time. Clearly that wasn't her and, surprisingly, not Jay either. She supposed he was someone who needed instant gratification in his adventures and he wouldn't find that here unless he was extremely lucky.

'It's not really suited to family life, is it?'

Meadow tossed away the dirt and stood up. 'Tell me about it. I don't know how my mum coped as long as she did, moving from one place to another. Money was tight, schooling wasn't easy, and it's lonely out here in the Outback if you don't have a good support system of friends. But she made the choice to embark on this life with my dad and there's a big part of me that wishes she would've tried harder to make things work. To give Dad credit, he stopped drifting, bought Rainbow's Walk and made an attempt to settle down. Perhaps it was too little, too late for my mother by then, but I can't help thinking if they'd communicated better they could have salvaged their relationship. That we all could have benefitted from a more stable life if she'd stuck it out a little longer.'

As much as she loved her mother, Meadow believed she should shoulder some of the blame for the breakup of their family too. Her father had made an effort, invested the money he'd made in a plot of land to give them that security, only for her mother to walk away anyway. At fifteen years old, Meadow hadn't been given a choice. If she had, she would've stayed and tried to create a family of sorts with just her and her dad. She hadn't even managed a proper relationship with her mother. They'd only had a couple of years of normality before she'd met someone else and decided to move to Queensland. Her father wasn't the only one with a wanderlust and Meadow had been trying to make up for her mother's actions ever since. Instead of welcoming her back into his life with open arms, he'd seemed to retreat further. As though he was afraid she would leave him eventually too. It was a vicious circle they couldn't break free from.

'I probably would've loved life out here. The open space, the freedom, the fresh air…'

'I know I shouldn't ask, but—'

'When my father wasn't beating me in a drunken rage, he'd lock me in the house so I wouldn't leave him, like my mum.' He anticipated her question and answered it before she asked. It didn't make the moment any easier.

Meadow thought of the young Jay, the boy cowed by his father's temper and rules, abandoned by his mother, and there was only one reasonable reaction. She dropped the metal detector, stood up on her tiptoes, threw her arms around his neck and hugged him as tight as she could.

'I'm so sorry.' She screwed her eyes shut, trying to force away the terrible images pushing their way into her mind, and tried not to let the tears fall.

'It's okay.'

She could feel him smile against her cheek, trying to put her at ease when he was reliving the horror that had been his childhood. It made her want to squeeze him tighter. To discover her prison was his freedom was a difficult thought to process. Both had suffered in different ways at the hands of their parents. Jay had clearly suffered physical and emotional abuse, and knowing that he'd gone on to become a doctor, healing others, made him all the more remarkable. Not least because he'd worked through his personal trauma and pushed himself every day to be someone else instead of that frightened child who'd been caged like an animal, his spirit broken. While she remained trapped in her past, too afraid to break out. Perhaps she should take a leaf out of his book if going against the familiar made for a stronger character.

'I wish I had your bravery,' she sighed.

Jay pulled out from her embrace, the expression on his face making her aware he wasn't comfortable with her choice of words.

'I'm not brave. I'm a survivor, that's all. If it wasn't for Sharyn's encouragement I'd still be cocooned in my own safe little world, having swapped my father's imprisonment for one of my own creation. I spent my time going from the hospital and back to my house, with little else in between. It was Sharyn who pushed me out of my comfort zone and encouraged me to explore life around me.'

'It's not surprising after what you went through. Being in your own home, in familiar surroundings, was your security blanket. Don't be so hard on yourself. I still think you're brave to be here. I've never even left the country.'

At times, Meadow found herself envying Sharyn, who'd got to share so much with Jay and had claimed a huge part of his heart, but she was also thankful to her. If not for Sharyn, Jay might never have left the confines of his home and travelled all this way to become an important part of her life. She couldn't imagine not seeing his face at work, or having him accompany her on trips like this, or to parties she didn't really want to attend. He was becoming her link to the world she'd been avoiding for too long, pushing her to do more, the way Sharyn had done for him. Albeit in a less death-defying manner, which she was thankful for.

'Well, you've enough to do here, haven't you? Bravery doesn't have to come in the form of travel or hair-raising stunts. You go to work in a plane every day, flying into the unknown, and it takes courage to maintain a relationship with a parent who didn't always have your best interests at heart.'

Meadow screwed her nose up at that. 'I'm not sure if that's courageous or stupid. I just couldn't make the break. I think I'm still clinging on to that hope of having some sort of family life.'

'And that's okay.' Jay rested his hands on her shoulders. 'Perhaps you can still salvage your relationship and that's amazing if you want that. I just couldn't.'

That familiar darkness clouded his eyes again when talking about his relationship with his father, and despite opening up to her about some of what had happened, Meadow suspected there was more to the harrowing story. It was up to Jay if he wanted to tell her what that was and she hoped some day he would trust her enough to share so she could understand him better.

Even that insight into his home life, and

the part that Sharyn had played, explained the importance of that list more than ever. It had been her way of freeing him from the confines of those memories. The security of home had been too tempting to leave, and she knew something about that. At least Jay had been willing to tackle that list when presented with it. Meadow would've laughed in the face of anyone who'd suggested it to her before lighting the barbecue with it.

She offered him a lopsided smile. 'There are different levels of forgiveness and I think your father was beyond it.'

'If he'd even want it. He never showed any remorse, or expressed any regret.'

'I can't say mine ever has either, but I suppose I still have a flicker of hope he will some day, to validate my reluctance to walk away.'

'It might come quicker if I stop blathering and let you find his gold. I promised I wouldn't get in your way.' Jay held his hands up and backed away.

Meadow would've stopped him and insisted he wasn't bothering her, that she appreciated he was able to share the details of his life with her. Except she thought he needed a time out to compose himself and gather his thoughts after unloading that emotional baggage. She knew it wasn't easy and talking about it brought those memories and feelings back. That was why she needed a quiet moment too.

'Don't wander too far,' was all the advice she could dispense for now, because her head was too full of thoughts about what it had taken for that abused child to become the man who stood before her now. About how much she admired him, and how much trouble she was in…

CHAPTER SEVEN

JAY NEEDED A bit of space to regroup. He hadn't intended to visit that dark time with Meadow, she just had that way of making him feel comfortable enough to share. She never forced anything, or advised, she simply listened. Perhaps that was all he'd ever needed.

He'd always felt a certain guilt about finally admitting what his father had done to him. It was a teacher he'd confided in on one of the days his father had let him go to school. Unlike most children, he looked forward to school. It was where he got a hot meal and he didn't have to be afraid that anyone was going to hurt him. That morning he'd been allowed to attend because his father was entertaining someone he'd met at the pub the night before and he'd wanted him out of the house.

His teacher had seen the bruises on his arms, and where he'd usually explained them away, he'd been too tired and broken to hide what was happening any more. Things had happened quickly then—social services, police, the foster home. He'd blamed himself when his father had been arrested, as though he'd been the one in the wrong for setting events in motion. There'd been limited contact since, until he'd eventually realised he had to sever all ties if he ever hoped to move on.

Jay hoped Meadow could get the apology she was owed and save her relationship. Then perhaps she could let go of some of that hurt and drop her guard a fraction more.

In sharing some of his issues, she'd been able to do the same, and he'd like to be able to help her break free of those memories, the way Sharyn had done for him. Maybe then she would consider him as more than an inconvenience.

She'd made it clear she hadn't wanted him with her today, but that was in stark contrast to the way she'd looked at him last night. Although he never thought he'd find anyone after Sharyn, he was beginning to wonder if he and Meadow could have a chance of a future together. They clearly enjoyed each other's company and had a lot in common. He didn't know where exploring the chemistry they had would lead, only that he wanted to try. That was enough to tell him he was moving on from Sharyn and it took someone pretty special to even make him think about doing that.

Jay had been so busy contemplating the past and the future he'd wandered away from the spot where Meadow had been detecting. Although he could still see her, she was little more than a dot in the distance. He wasn't going to go any further, but then he spotted the entrance to the old mine.

Although the wooden framework to the opening had rotted in places and had partially collapsed, there was still enough room for him to go inside. Curiosity and his sense of adventure overtook regard for his own safety and he ducked inside.

It was dank and dusty but the tunnel and the old tools lying around spoke so much of the past he couldn't resist venturing in for a closer look. He felt along the stony walls, imagining the sound of the men who'd come here before him, hammering and digging, all hoping to discover their fortune. He'd seen something of those who'd failed and how it had affected the quality of their lives and those around them. Sadness and disappointment permeated the rock all around him, echoes of the past continuing to haunt this place.

Wooden runners lined his path, where miners had ferried out loads of rubble during their excavations. Darker and deeper, Jay continued his exploration into the cavernous unknown, using the light from his phone to guide him. The air began to thin and he knew he'd have to turn around soon, before he became another casualty.

Eventually he found his path blocked, a mound of rubble preventing him from venturing any further. By the way the rocks were piled high, he thought there'd been some sort of cave-in rather than it being the natural end to the tunnel. Jay attempted to dislodge some of the debris so he could take a look further back and climbed the pile. That was when the glint of something high in the walls caught his eye, a layer of glitter sandwiched in the rock.

He held his phone up for a better look and traced his fingers over the sparkle. A long, steady ribbon of gold threaded through the red walls like a pretty Christmas party dress. Gold. He had no idea why it had been left untouched, or how to get it out, but he was sure this was what they were looking for. He took a couple of pictures for reference before heading back out.

'Meadow!' he yelled, forgetting how far

away she was in that precise moment. It was only the echo calling back to him which reminded him where he was, and it wasn't with her. Against everything she'd told him not to do, he'd wandered off. Though he was sure another scolding would be put on the back burner if he managed to line her father's pockets after all.

He scrambled back outside, having to defend his eyes from the blinding sun as he emerged from the dark depths of the earth.

'Meadow!' he called again, running back to where he'd left her, keen to share his discovery as soon as possible and be hero for the day.

'Jay? Where the hell did you go?' Meadow stomped towards him, metal detector over her shoulder, pick in her hand, face like thunder, and he knew he was in for it.

'I know, I know, I'm an idiot for wandering off, but come and see this.'

'What?' Her exasperation was palpable, no doubt because she'd wasted valuable digging time trying to locate him. Jay hoped she'd be appeased once he showed her the wonders waiting in the mine for her.

'I've found something.' He was bursting to tell her but he wanted to see her face when she saw it for herself. To be the one who put a smile on her face was his reward.

'Just tell me what it is so I can get back to work.'

It was clear he'd really ticked her off but, risking her wrath, he pulled her towards the mine. 'You need to see it for yourself.'

'I'm not going in there. Are you crazy? That's condemned.'

'Trust me,' he said, fixing her with a determined stare until she huffed out a breath and stopped resisting.

'Fine.' She dropped her tools and prepared to follow him in, even if it was begrudgingly.

'Did your father ever excavate in here?'

'I'm not sure if he had more than a cursory look because it had already been mined out and it's not fit for purpose any more.' She emphasised the last point loudly so he was in no doubt that she thought this a fool's errand. He was willing to let her think that until he proved otherwise. It was still possible he hadn't found the riches he hoped, and remembered there was something about fool's gold which could still apply.

'It's fine. I've already been inside.' From the outside it looked precarious, the wooden slats had rotted but the walls still seemed sound to him.

Meadow tutted. 'Of course you have. Show me what it is you think you've found, then I can get out of here and do some real work.'

Jay ignored the scepticism, looking forward to the forthcoming apology. Though he was sure there was much more real work to be done before they had any gold in their hands.

'It's down this way.' He led her further in with the light of his phone, though it seemed a longer walk in this time around.

'Jay, it's really not safe in here. The timbers are rotten and the walls need shoring up properly again. We don't even have hard hats. Just tell me what it is, we can take proper safety measures, then come back out when we know there's no risk of a cave-in.' Meadow wasn't keeping pace with him, holding back enough to let him see she was worried, that cautious nature blazing bright, despite current appearances. He loved the adventurer look on her, that image of her looking up at him from the ditch, dirt smeared on her face, a world away from the smartly turned-out nurse he was used to seeing.

'It's not far, I promise. I just want you to see it for yourself, then we can get out again.' They'd come this far now, it seemed a pity not to let her see the gold in situ too. He kept the photographs to himself for now.

'It had better be worth it,' she grumbled, picking up the pace again.

Jay was bursting to tell her. He was the sort of person who got equally excited at giving a gift as the recipient, often blabbing the contents before they got to open it. His joyful enthusiasm was the result of not experiencing the whole gift culture for himself growing up. The first year his foster family had bought him Christmas presents he'd burst into tears, not used to such a display of kindness. Then he'd spent the next year saving to return the favour. Although this wasn't something he'd saved for, or picked out specially, he figured this was still a gift. His present to her, and something he was sure she'd appreciate. Doing this for her might also help her see him as more than an inconvenience. Jay wanted her to think of him as a potential partner.

He mightn't always be the safest bet, but he wanted what was best for her and would do everything in his power to show her that. Some day she might decide he was worth taking a chance on and they could venture into this next unknown chapter together.

Eventually they came to the section he recognised where the trail narrowed and evidence of previous mining wasn't so abundant, as though they'd given up before reaching this point. He kicked away some of the loose rubble from Meadow's path.

'It's just up here.' He held up the light and waited for her to stand beside him.

'Is that…?' Standing up on tiptoe, she reached up and trailed her fingers along the wall as he'd done.

He nodded, grinning as he saw the realisation dawn in her eyes and the smile spread across her face as though she'd swallowed the gold and its glittery beams were shooting straight out of her mouth.

'Gold.' Jay kept his voice low, as though afraid that by saying it too loudly it would attract would-be thieves who'd loot the place before Meadow and her father saw the benefit of the find.

'Okay.' Meadow was trembling but he could see her fighting the urge to scream and shout like he wanted to. 'We need to take a note of the exact location and board up the entrance so no one can get in until we can secure the structure. Dad will need a lot of equipment to extract that seam of fine gold.'

'But we found it.' Nothing was going to take away from his pride and excitement at having found the gold her father had spent most of his life searching for, all because he'd taken a risk.

'Yeah. We did it.' She could no longer hold back her excitement, it seemed, as she high-fived him.

'Come here,' he growled, wanting to celebrate properly. He grabbed her up and swung her around. Meadow was laughing, her hands wrapped around his neck as they spun.

As they slowly came to a stop his head was still spinning, with thoughts only of Meadow and how much he wanted to kiss her. He couldn't take his eyes off her lips, and when she kept her arms around his neck even when her feet were back on the ground, Jay knew this time they were both ready.

Her lips were soft and welcoming against his and when she leaned her body closer into him, he was completely undone.

Meadow was still floating on air even though Jay had stopped whirling her around as though she weighed nothing more than a feather. The gold was undoubtedly the treasure they'd been looking for, but kissing Jay was the ultimate prize. Waiting all this time, fighting against her feelings and all the untimely interruptions, made it all the sweeter. This was what she wanted. His hands on her waist, fingers brushing the bare skin at the bottom of her back, was almost as erotic as watching him strip by the pool. She'd cursed herself for not following up on that moment last night and denying herself the chance to taste the excitement for herself. Now she'd braved the unknown she was content that the reality of the fantasy hadn't disappointed.

Jay was confident and assured in his touch, his mouth demanding on hers, and she was happy on this occasion she'd taken a risk when it had given her such rich rewards. She didn't want to think about future consequences and potential heartbreak and for once simply enjoy some spontaneity. This wasn't planned, probably wasn't a good idea in the long run, but it was the most passionate encounter she'd had in for ever, and they hadn't even taken their clothes off. She gave a little shiver at the thought of taking that next step. If Jay could make her feel this reckless, provide so much excitement in one kiss, she knew there were further riches still waiting to be discovered.

Jay was sliding his hands up her bare back now, pulling her ever tighter to his body as though he couldn't get close enough. That skin-to-skin contact sent ripples of pleasure rushing to every erogenous zone, and puckering her nipples into tight peaks. She knew it was turning him on too when she could feel the hard evidence pressing into her belly. It was insanity and she knew they'd have to put a stop to things soon, but she didn't want to in case that cautious, vulnerable side of her stepped in again with a wagging finger.

She was distracted by a small thud, followed by several more. Jay pulled away from her to check out the disturbance. That was when she felt something drop onto her head. It took her a moment to realise what it was and in that short space of time pieces of the roof were raining down on them both.

'We need to get out of here now, Jay.' She grabbed his hand and started towards the exit.

There was a loud rumble and the earth seemed to rise up to meet them. She felt the full force of Jay's body slam into her and the air was forced from her lungs.

'Meadow? Can you hear me? Squeeze my hand.'

The darkness was drawing close but the sound of Jay's voice was the greater pull.

'Speak to me. Please tell me you're all right. I'm so sorry I brought you in here. I'm so stupid.'

She heard the desperation in his voice and

wanted to reassure him she was okay but she couldn't find the strength to say the words or open her eyes.

'I should have listened to you. I'm so sorry I put you in danger.'

She felt something on her cheek, a tender caress which was much more pleasant than the pounding going on in her head.

'Jay?' she eventually managed to croak, her lips dry with dust.

'Oh, thank goodness.' He gathered her up and the warmth of his body encompassed her. It was tempting to fall back into that deep sleep when she was in his arms, safe and secure, but she had a nagging feeling there was a reason she shouldn't.

'What happened?' she asked, struggling to sit up unassisted, trying to process what was going on.

'A cave-in. I can't see any way to get out. The exit's blocked. Here, take a sip of water. You took a nasty hit.' He held a bottle of water to her lips and poured enough just to wet them.

'I think that was you tackling me to the ground,' she tried to joke, knowing that he'd put himself between her and the roof of the mine. He must've taken the brunt of the hit, trying to protect her.

'Sorry. I acted without thinking, as usual.'

'It's not your fault. I think we both got carried away.' She tried to smile but the pain from her throbbing temple prevented her. When she reached up to touch the spot her fingers were coated in sticky red blood.

'You hit your head when you fell, but it's stopped bleeding. Let me clean it up for you.' He moved to pour more water on her, but she put out a hand to stop him.

'Save it. We might need it if we can't get out of here.' Her head was a bit fuzzy but she knew she'd need her wits about her if they were going to make it back out of here alive.

She looked around as she wiped her shirt-sleeve across her forehead. They were backed up against the section of the mine which had caused all the trouble, and though the air was thick with dust and debris, she could see they were completely surrounded by rubble and broken timbers blocking the path. It looked as though whatever ancient structure had been keeping the roof supported had finally given way. Whether it had been bad timing on their part or they'd inadvertently caused the rock-fall they'd probably never know. The important thing now was to figure a way out of this mess.

'I don't suppose you've got a phone signal?'

She was only half joking, praying there was still an easy way to fix their predicament.

'Sorry. I think it's buried somewhere. Even if it wasn't smashed to bits, I'm not sure I'd get a signal. On the positive side, we do seem to be trapped in an air pocket so we won't suffocate just yet.'

'No, we might die a slow death from thirst or starvation first.' Meadow wasn't one to panic but she knew the chances of anyone finding them out here were slim. Her father wouldn't be home for days and wasn't likely to come straight to the mine, and whilst they would be missed at work she doubted they'd ever guess they'd managed to get themselves trapped down an old gold mine. Judging by Greg's comments, they'd probably suspect they'd run off somewhere exotic together. Chance would've been a fine thing.

She steadied herself against the wall as she got up, causing a few more displaced rocks to fall in the process. Then she began tackling the rocky obstruction blocking their way home, removing one stone at a time.

'Don't waste your energy, Meadow. There's no way we can shift all that by hand. It goes way back. I've already looked.'

Refusing to believe they couldn't dig their way out of this mess, she removed a few more rocks, only to cause an avalanche raining down on her from the top of the pile.

'Meadow, for goodness' sake! You're going to get yourself killed.' Jay rushed at her again, pulling her away from the rockfall and forcing her to toss the one still in her hand back onto the pile.

'We need to get out.' She was trying to keep her cool but the fact remained they were trapped in an old mine, miles from anywhere, with no one likely to come looking for them any time soon.

'I know that. Don't you think I know that? But it's not going to help if you hurt yourself.'

It was only when she turned her head to look at him that she could see the panic in his eyes. She was about to apologise for worrying him when she realised he had his hand on his chest, seemingly gasping for breath.

'Jay? Are you okay?' Caught up in her own panic, she hadn't bothered to check and see if he'd been hurt during the melee. After all, he'd thrown himself at her, using his body to shield her from the walls collapsing all around them. He could've suffered blunt force trauma, broken ribs or internal bleeding, and they'd both been more concerned about her knock on the head.

'Do you have any chest pain?' She checked

his pupils the best she could without any light, and his pulse. His heart was racing, probably causing his sudden shortness of breath since there weren't any obvious injuries.

'Can't...breathe...'

It took her a fraction of a second to realise he was having a panic attack. She'd forgotten his fear of the dark, but circumstances appeared to have triggered that response.

'Just look at me, Jay.' She got him to focus on her instead of his fight for breath. 'You're okay, I'm okay, and we'll get through this.'

Meadow took his hands in hers. 'Take a deep breath, in...and out. That's it. In through the nose, and out through the mouth. I'm here and I'm not going to let anything happen to you.' She took long, slow breaths, encouraging him to do the same, until that initial panic subsided and he was no longer gasping.

Jay eventually let go of her hands and rested them on his knees, doubled over, trying to regain his composure.

'It's fine. Is it the dark? I'm here for you, Jay. You're not alone.'

'It's not just the dark.' He swayed a little and Meadow was afraid he was going to pass out on her.

'Why don't you sit down and have a drink of water?' She helped him over to a corner and sat down beside him, waiting until he was ready to talk.

'Sorry for the drama,' he said eventually.

'Admit it, you were just afraid I was getting all the attention.' She bumped his shoulder with hers to make him smile again.

'I wish that's all it was. At least when I thought you were hurt it stopped me from dwelling on other things.'

'Your dad?' she asked quietly, not wanting to spook him any more. His extreme reaction suggested something more traumatic than she'd even imagined, but she resisted swamping him in another hug. For now.

Jay nodded, scuffing the toe of his shoe into the dirt, focusing on it rather than looking at her. Even though he had nothing to be ashamed about.

'It wasn't just the house he locked me in. Sometimes it was my bedroom, other times in the wardrobe. It depended on his mood or how much he wanted to punish me. Most of the time I hadn't done anything wrong other than ask if I could have something to eat. He'd go off and get drunk, forget I was there for hours, even days on occasion.'

The horror of what he'd experienced brought tears rushing to Meadow's eyes but she willed them away, knowing if he saw she was upset he wouldn't continue and she knew he needed to get this out. Locking a child in a cupboard for days on end was intolerable cruelty and Meadow could only imagine how terrified the young Jay had been, not knowing if he'd ever see daylight again.

She looked around and understood what had triggered his response. They were completely shut off from the rest of the world with no possible escape, light or even food or water. He was effectively reliving that trauma all over again.

'This was an accident, not a punishment, and I'm sure once Greg and the others at work realise we're missing they'll come looking for us.'

He cocked his head to one side. 'You don't believe that any more than I do.'

'We have to believe it. I'm sure there were many times when you thought your dad would never come back and let you out, but he did. I know it's frightening but it's just an obstacle we have to overcome. Like losing a house in a fire.'

He was still staring at her, enough to make her eventually ask, 'What?'

'You're amazing, that's all.'

'Hardly,' she snorted, flicking away the

compliment as though it were another annoying fly.

'No, really. The way you deal with things—work, your father, a big galah like me, afraid of the dark—you take it all in your stride.'

'Not always. I have my moments too and I don't make for an easy person to live with. Ask my ex-boyfriends.' She thought of the men who'd called her high maintenance, and hard to please. None of them had thought her 'amazing'.

'Maybe they're "ex" for a reason.' Jay shrugged.

'Well, Shawn lied to me about the kind of person he was, so that's why he's not in my life any more. Though perhaps he felt it necessary to pretend to be someone who had his own home and was financially stable because nothing less would do for me.'

'That doesn't sound like too much to expect in a potential partner. Although not all of us are ready to sign up for a mortgage just yet.' He was teasing her but it was also a reminder that Jay didn't meet all her requirements either. Maybe, just maybe, she'd been too picky in the past. After all, none of those who'd had their own homes and had plans to settle down had held her attention long enough for her to want to do the same.

'That didn't bother me as much as the gambling of all his wages and the bad credit history, which meant he was still living at home with his mother. It was the secrets and lies I couldn't deal with.'

'Understandable. Although it could be argued that the problem I had was the complete opposite. Until Sharyn, I didn't do long-term relationships because I didn't want anyone to dig too deeply into my personal affairs. She kind of forced the information out of me, wanted the truth so she could help me move past it.'

'Do you think you'd still be with Sharyn if you hadn't lost her like that?'

Jay considered her question for longer than she'd really expected.

'Honestly, I don't know. Not so long ago, I would undoubtedly have said yes, but that was when I was still in mourning. Sometimes when you lose a loved one you only want to remember the good times, like looking back wearing rose-tinted glasses. Don't get me wrong, she's the reason I'm here in Australia, living a life I never thought possible, but now I'm not sure we would've lasted.'

'Oh?' It seemed such a turnaround from the man who'd clearly still been in love with his recently deceased partner and Meadow wondered what had brought about the change, igniting a little spark of hope that it had been her.

'I loved her, I really did, but so much of our relationship was based on that list and going on adventures, I'm not sure it would've lasted for ever. Now, I can't picture what it would've been like for us as we got older. I don't imagine I'd still be wanting to dive off cliffs or go backpacking in the Himalayas, and Sharyn wouldn't have been one for sitting in an armchair with a blanket round her knees playing board games. I appreciate everything she did was to help me move on from the past, but it also made me a different person to the one she met. I'm sure there'll come a time when I just want to put my feet up.'

'There's a lot to be said for playing board games. Same adrenaline rush without the imminent threat to life.' Meadow was only partly joking. Board games weren't her thing, neither were extreme sports, but she'd take a quiet life over being stuck in here, not knowing if they were going to live or die.

'That's beginning to sound appealing.' Jay's wonky smile made her heart lurch. She knew she was privileged to see this vulnerable side of him when he was such a happy-go-lucky character on the outside. It was likely he only divulged this valuable personal information to people he trusted, and though it seemed they'd known each other longer, they'd only been acquainted for a few days. From what she'd gathered, he'd waited years before opening up about the abuse he'd suffered. Sharing it with her suggested the bond between them wasn't all in her head.

'As soon as we get out of here, I swear we're having a games night so you can see what you've been missing.' And so they could spend more time together if he wasn't sick of her by then. Despite everything she'd expected him to be on their first run-in, Meadow was beginning to think Jay wanted to settle down somewhere. Maybe she could persuade him to do it with her. If their earlier kiss was anything to go by, they certainly had a chemistry that was worth exploring, and if he was planning on sticking around she might be willing to take a risk after all.

'If we get out.' He stood up, his stress manifesting again as he paced the small area that had escaped the rockfall like a caged bear.

She understood now that the claustrophobia of their situation was equally as triggering as the dark. That feeling of being locked in, fear of the unknown, was just as real for him now as it had been then.

'What can I do to help you, Jay?'

'I don't know.' He rubbed his hands over his scalp as he walked, clearly agitated and building up to another panic attack.

'Okay, what's making you uncomfortable? I know we're stuck here, but what would give you peace of mind in the meantime?' It wasn't something he could easily answer when he was visibly uncomfortable, but at least it would give him something to think about other than the past.

He ducked his head. 'It sounds stupid, especially given our current circumstances, but I need to see the outside. At least have the illusion of fresh air coming in so I can breathe properly. What I remember about being locked up was the stale air. The windows in my room were nailed shut. My dad didn't want me climbing out or shouting for help. Of course, when he threw me in the wardrobe and tied the doors shut I couldn't even see out of the window. It was like being buried alive. Ironic, really, when that's exactly what's happening now.'

Meadow could accept that, but there was no point in both of them panicking, at least until they'd been in here a while longer and it was clear rescue wasn't coming. Instead of asking him more about the conditions he'd been in then, Meadow wanted to suggest something to make him feel more positive.

'A lot of that rubble came from the roof. Maybe there's a gap somewhere up there that we can reach?' If not to get out, at least to give them both some fresh air and a view of the outside world.

'It's not safe, Meadow. We could bring the rest of it down on top of us.'

Oh, how the tables had turned, when Jay was the one advising caution. It just proved how much his past had impacted on him and how far he'd come, trying to shake it off. Meadow didn't want to court disaster, but she also knew they needed to explore all avenues if they had any hope of getting out of here.

'I'll be careful. I can at least look. Now, help me up onto your shoulders so I can get up there.'

Jay huffed out a sigh, unamused by her suggestion, but he did hunker down to enable her to climb on board. She didn't know if it was because he trusted her judgement or that they were out of options, but he was going along with her idea for now. Meadow hooked one leg over his shoulder and used his head to balance her as she brought the second one over, hanging on for dear life as he stood. It was all very ungainly but there was no room for vanity or pride when their lives were at stake.

She was sure they were a comical sight as they moved, with her perched on Jay's very broad shoulders, feeling her way along the top of the roof, trying to find a chink of light in the darkness. Every now and then she accidentally dislodged a loose piece of earth, which bounced off Jay's head. After the third time he let loose with a stream of expletives.

'Sorry,' she said, stifling a laugh, glad that this distraction was preventing him from getting lost in his traumatic childhood memories at least.

'The last thing I need is a brain injury, thanks,' he muttered.

'Hey, I'm the one risking a nosebleed or worse up here.' She was trying not to think about another possible cave-in when she'd be the one to take the brunt this time, or the height of the fall from Jay's shoulders. For a few minutes she was willing to risk her personal safety if she could do something to ease his anxiety in here.

'And I appreciate it.'

She hadn't expected his gratitude, or the softness of his voice, both of which almost toppled her. Meadow had to steady herself again, thankful he had a hard head for her to lean on.

'We must add tunnelling our way out of a collapsed gold mine to that list of yours.'

'Let's hope we actually get to tick that one off and mark it as done.'

With a seemingly renewed determination Jay shifted beneath her and held onto her shins to secure her. Meadow continued her exploration until she found a tiny crevice up behind one of the few timbers still in place.

'I think there's something up here. Do we have anything I can use to try and push through?'

Meadow's head was spinning as Jay turned, looking for a suitable tool for her to use, then he slowly lowered to the ground, careful not to unseat her.

'I think this is the handle off an old pick-axe or something. Try it.' He handed a long wooden shaft up to her and Meadow carefully poked it into the crack in the roof.

She had to stretch up, relying on Jay to keep her supported, but she trusted him with her safety. Something she'd never thought she'd do.

'I think it's giving way,' she said, pushing the blunt object into the recess and watching the loose dirt fall away.

'Just be careful.'

With one more thrust she broke through, piercing the earth's crust just enough to let a beam of light shine down on them. Unfortunately, the movement knocked her off-balance and Jay struggled to stay on his feet. Before she knew it, she was tumbling back down onto the dirt.

'Ouch.' This time it was her backside which hit the floor, which had more padding than her head but still hurt all the same.

'Sorry.' Jay was lying beside her, clutching his back as he sat up.

'It's not your fault. Anyway, we've got light. Ta-da!'

Regardless of her joking, Jay was stony-faced as he reached out to her, cupping her face in his hands and searching for signs of injury.

'I've told you I'm fine, Jay.'

'I said I wouldn't let you get hurt. You wouldn't even have been up there if it wasn't for me.'

She stroked the side of his face, trying to ease the tense set of his jaw. 'We're in this together, remember?'

He turned his face into her hand and kissed her palm, and when he looked at her again she saw the concern and genuine affection he had for her right there. Despite her triumph, she knew there was a possibility they wouldn't get out of this and she couldn't help but feel as though she'd thrown away a chance at happiness. She'd wasted too much time worrying about the future and had neglected the present. Much like her father, she hadn't appreciated what she had until it was too late.

Jay had appeared in town and shattered that cosy world she'd built around herself, making it infinitely better. She'd found someone who understood her. Well, he'd found her, but she'd been stupidly resisting these growing feelings towards him. Now it might be too late to do anything about it.

'Kiss me, Jay.' For once, she wanted to do something reckless without worrying about the consequences. Especially when they weren't promised tomorrow.

Jay could have questioned why she wanted this now, if it was a knee-jerk reaction to the situation they'd found themselves in or if she simply wanted some comfort. But he only cared that he wanted the same thing.

They rushed at each other like starved lovers, mouths crashing together, hands clinging to one another, desperate for that connection. If they weren't going to get out of here alive, at least they were going to make the most of the time they had left.

He was sorry he'd brought her here, put her in danger, then freaked out on her because the claustrophobic circumstances triggered those awful childhood memories. Most of all, he was sorry that he might have cost them a future together. It seemed so stupid now to have wasted time when they so obviously wanted one another, pulling at each other's clothes and kissing as though their lives depended on it.

Being with Meadow gave him a very different thrill to those he'd had when he and Sharyn had been together. They didn't need to be doing anything life-threatening to enjoy each other's company—today's events notwithstanding—but this hadn't been planned. In fact, he'd prefer it if they were in a nice cosy bed, preferably in a house. Perhaps he'd finally found a home here, the life he'd probably been searching for his whole life, with a woman who brought out the best in him. He could only hope it wasn't too late.

'If anything happens to me, I just want you to know I really enjoy being with you, Meadow.' He wanted their time together to be special, for however long they had left, and didn't want to shuffle off this mortal coil with any regrets. Since the day he'd arrived in town he'd been fighting his feelings for her because of his loyalty to Sharyn's memory, and his fear of getting close to someone again. There was nothing like facing his own mortality to put everything into perspective. Here, now, nothing else mattered except Meadow.

She stopped kissing his neck and sat back, smiling. 'I'm glad to hear it. I'd hate to think this was some sort of chore.'

'Oh, it's definitely not that. It's all pleasure.'

She purred as he gently lowered her to the ground, using their discarded shirts as a makeshift blanket to protect her from the stony ground. Even as the light outside had begun to fade gradually, Jay had stopped being afraid of the dark. If Meadow had been with him in that house, that room, that cupboard, he wouldn't have suffered as much. When he was with her the part of him who was still that lost little boy seemed as though he was finally finding his peace.

Meadow too needed someone to show her how cherished she was, and he was determined to be the man to do it. If this was their last night on earth, they both deserved to know a little love.

She reached behind her back to undo her bra, whipping it away to reveal the small mounds of her breasts. He palmed one firmly in his hand, plucking the rosy tip between his fingers, and captured the gasp on her lips with his mouth. She was every bit as beautiful as he'd known she would be. Her toned, tanned body, so small beneath him, made his heart weak, and every other part of him hard with desire.

Meadow flicked her tongue along his bottom lip, tasting and teasing, and testing his resolve. He wanted to stay in control, to put her pleasure before his own, but she was fighting against his intention, her hands straying to the fly of his trousers.

'Not yet,' he whispered against her neck and felt her buck against him. When he realised how sensitive she was he dotted wet kisses just there behind her ear, and she shivered when he blew on the damp skin to cool the heat.

Meadow pressed her body ever closer to his, her nipples teasing his skin, begging for his attention. Then she slid her hands down and roughly opened his fly, reaching in to stroke his erection. Jay closed his eyes and groaned. This woman was literally going to be the death of him.

'I said not yet.' He grabbed her hands and pinned them above her head.

'But—' She was pleading with him to stem that ache inside her, he could see it in her eyes, feel it in the arch of her body against him. He wasn't completely without mercy.

Still with her hands caged so she couldn't intervene, Jay took his time kissing every inch of her body. She tilted her head back so he could nuzzle her neck, groaned when he gently nipped the skin along her collarbone. He was driving himself insane as well as Meadow by delaying that bliss he knew was waiting for them.

Lower and lower he dipped his head, using his mouth and tongue to map her body whilst his hands were otherwise engaged. The soft swell of her breast yielded under his mouth until he reached the hardened peak and teased it with his tongue.

'Jay, please—'

Though he wasn't ready to bring them to that ultimate release yet, he drew her nipple greedily into his mouth, tugging gently with his teeth until Meadow was gasping and close to the edge.

He moved so he had one hand still holding her captive and used the other to pull away her shorts and underwear. As he'd expected, she was wet when he dipped a finger inside her, filling her where they both wanted him to be soon before they lost their minds. He circled that sensitive nub, pushing and stroking until she cried out and shuddered against him. His smile was one of triumph and relief as he let go of her wrists.

'Look at you, all proud of yourself,' she said as she stretched lazily beneath him, her body fully on display for him to enjoy.

'Shouldn't I be?'

'If I had a trophy I'd give it to you.' Even in the throes of passion and the most dangerous of circumstances she had the ability to make him laugh.

'But you'll get my name engraved on it first, right?'

'Of course.' With her hand on his cheek, she lifted her head to kiss him. It was a tender touch of her lips against his, a softer display of desire overtaking them, and Jay could wait no longer to make love to her.

He stripped off the rest of his clothes and entered her quickly, both of them emitting a contented sigh as they joined together. This was his safe place. Meadow was all he needed to find his peace.

They moved slowly together at first, savouring each other, getting used to the fit. If they were together a thousand years he didn't think he'd ever tire of this feeling every time he withdrew and plunged back inside, of filling her and being encompassed by her tight, wet heat.

It was Meadow's time for some payback, nibbling at his earlobes, wrapping her legs tightly around his waist and thrusting up to meet his hips. Doing everything she possibly could to demolish his restraint.

'I don't want you to hold back,' she whispered into his ear and snipped that last thread.

Jay thrust his hips against Meadow's, again and again, that increasing pleasure sensation overtaking all thoughts. Every time she gasped or clenched tighter around him drove him harder, faster to bring them both to that much anticipated final destination. Her hot breath and cry of ecstasy in his ear as she voiced her orgasm spurred his own release. His body shuddered and it seemed as though he was pouring his very soul into her as he climaxed.

Jay knew he was falling for her. What he felt for Meadow was so different to anything he'd ever known that he was beginning to think that even the relationship he'd had with Sharyn had been based more on friendship. It had been fun and exciting and she'd taken away his loneliness, but he didn't remember this kind of high, of almost floating on a cloud of happiness when they were together.

'Are you okay? You're very quiet.' Meadow was watching him intently as he lay down beside her.

'I'm just wondering if I've completely shredded my kneecaps on this ground.'

Her laughter at the injuries he might have sustained whilst in the throes of passion echoed around the mine.

'It's okay, you're worth it.' He leaned over and dropped a long, leisurely kiss on her lips.

'Why, thank you. I'm surprised we didn't bring the whole ceiling down—we weren't exactly quiet.' She placed the flat of her hand on his chest as she snuggled against him.

'At least we're going out with a bang.'

Meadow groaned. 'I'm sure we'll be fine. Have faith.'

'Meadow, if you really believed that you wouldn't have slept with me.' He was challenging her to admit that, or at least that she had some feelings for him. Every time they'd come close to a kiss, she'd run a mile. If they did make it out of here, he wanted to know that they might have a future together.

It was early days but he thought they could have something special together. He knew Meadow had been holding back, probably afraid he was a version of her father, who'd always be looking for the next thrill. That might have been true at one time, but if Meadow was willing to give them a shot he could be persuaded to stick around. If he was going to take a chance, he hoped she would too.

She moved away from him, sitting up and hugging her knees. 'I might not have chosen this time or place, but I can't say I haven't thought about it.'

'There's nothing to be afraid of. I mean apart from dehydration and our impending doom.' Jay managed to raise a smile on her otherwise worried-looking face.

'I don't want to get hurt,' she said so softly he wasn't sure if she meant for him to hear.

He scrambled up into a sitting position, put an arm around her shoulders and shuffled closer. 'I would never do anything to upset you. I know this is all new for both of us, and we're both carrying baggage from relationships and our childhoods, but I like being with you, Meadow.'

'For now. We'll see how you feel when the cavalry arrives.'

He wasn't going to argue with her, even though he didn't think his feelings would change, no matter what tomorrow brought. There didn't seem any point in wasting time debating the issue if they really might not see another day.

'Well, we have to make it through the night first. It'll get cold down here soon. I think we'll have to cuddle together for body heat.' Jay lifted one of her arms and hooked it around his neck before lifting her off the ground and onto his lap. If he was going to die, he'd prefer to do it with a smile on his face.

Meadow knew he was trying to distract her and he was doing a stand-up job of it. It was hard to think about anything except his touch. She didn't want to fret about getting rescued, or if he'd still want her if they were. For once in her life, she just wanted to live in the moment and act on her instincts. Right now, they were telling her she needed Jay to satisfy this pulsing ache for him.

She shifted round so she was straddling his strong thighs, his equally substantial erection nestled between her legs. He claimed possession of her with his mouth on hers, and his hands clamped on her backside. Meadow was already slick with need, her body clearly anticipating round two. This was the one chance she had to really throw caution to the wind and she was going to enjoy every single moment. Deep down, she'd been fighting this because she knew making love with Jay would be intoxicating and something not easily forgotten, just as he was.

Using his shoulders to brace herself, she slid down onto his shaft, letting that feeling of being complete blot out all her worries. Jay buried his head between her breasts and groaned, and she knew it was the same for him.

They worked in tandem, their bodies matching each other's rhythm perfectly, stroke for stroke. That desperate need for one another drove their frantic pace until they were both gasping for breath and that final release. Jay rolled them over so he was on top and with one last hard thrust he cried out against her neck. Little tremors seized his body as he continued to rock against her, and she was so close to the edge that when he pushed his thumb inside her, filling her to the brim, she spilled right over.

This hadn't been the way she'd planned things but being with Jay was something special. Even if they did make it out and Jay decided he wasn't suited to a boring life with her, Meadow knew one night with him had changed her life for ever.

CHAPTER EIGHT

MEADOW WOKE WITH a shiver. When she opened her eyes and saw they were still in their rocky prison that sinking feeling in her stomach came back. Closely followed by a rumble of emptiness loud enough to stir Jay behind her. He tightened his arms around her and buried his head in the crook of her neck.

'Morning.' His sleepy greeting, combined with that comforting cage of his body, helped her relax a little.

'We're still here,' she said, hoping as they'd fallen asleep last night that their enthusiastic lovemaking might somehow have magically transported them into the comfort of her bed.

'It's enough for now.' He threw one leg over the top of hers, the shift behind her letting her know his body was wide awake even if he wasn't.

'At least we have some light again.' Her stomach groaned its disapproval again.

'Breakfast?' He stretched over to reach the bag he'd brought with him and produced what was left of the bottle of water inside and the remnants of the cereal bar they'd found tucked away in one of the pockets last night.

'What I wouldn't do for bacon and eggs, pancakes and orange juice. Mmm...' Her mouth was watering at the thought, but she had to make do with a sip of water and some crumbs. They were trying to ration out their meagre supplies when she would have happily devoured a steak, she was so hungry. With their exertions last night, she was sure Jay had the same hunger gnawing away at his insides in search of more sustenance.

'Soon,' he promised, bit the small piece of the bar in half and popped the other one in her mouth before she could stop him.

That small act of kindness—dare she hope, love—melted the last of her defences. She was in deep. Meadow cared more about this man than any of her previous partners and it would be a cruel irony if they perished in here before she was given the chance to carry on the adventure with him.

'Thank you.' She kissed him full on the mouth, trying to lose herself in that sensation of being safe, despite their current predicament.

Another shiver claimed her body and she had to gather some of the old hessian sacks they'd found last night to use as a blanket.

'We should probably get dressed. As much as I'd be happy to spend my last hours making love to you, we are running the risk of hypothermia.'

Although the sun had risen, it wasn't warm enough to justify lying here unclothed. Whilst the sight of Jay's naked form was pleasing, and detracted attention from the destruction around them, she didn't want her propensity for ogling him to come at the expense of their health.

'Hopefully, the afternoon sun will warm us up again.' She was watching Jay as they dressed in yesterday's clothes, wishing they could simply step into a nice warm shower to get clean again. Unlike her father, she wasn't one who usually enjoyed scrabbling about in the dirt.

'Meadow Williams, you're insatiable.' Jay pulled on his shirt without undoing the buttons and came to her again.

'Only with you.' She stood up on tiptoe and threw her arms around his neck, kissing him as if there were literally no tomorrow.

Lost in that sweet, all-consuming taste of Jay on her lips, on the tip of her tongue, she managed to block out everything else around them. All the devastation and the uncertainty of the outside world was nothing but a distant memory. Until the earth began to move around them.

'What's that noise?' Jay ended the kiss abruptly, leaving her dizzy and bereft at the loss.

It took her a moment to compose herself again. That was when she heard a dull roar sounding from somewhere outside. 'There's someone there.'

Jay immediately climbed up to the small hole they'd previously made in the ceiling and began yelling. 'Hello! Is there someone there? We're trapped in the mine!'

'Be careful!' she warned as some of the roof began to fall again, and the pile of rocks blocking their exit appeared to tremble, knocking some loose so they bounced at her feet.

'Meadow?' A voice sounded beyond the obstruction and for a moment she thought it sounded like her father, then dismissed it as wishful thinking.

'We're in here!' she shouted in response, hoping the voice at least was a real chance at escape.

Jay too climbed back down to start yelling.

If someone was out there, she didn't know what else they could do other than scream and shout and make their presence known.

'Stand back. We're coming in,' the disembodied voice instructed, and since Jay pulled her out of the way she came to the conclusion it hadn't been a figment of her imagination after all.

He hugged her close but his eyes were still firmly on the blocked path towards their exit, only venturing forward to grab his battered phone when it reappeared with the shifting of the earth. Meadow clung to him, afraid to breathe, or hope, in case it somehow caused the apparent rescue mission to fail.

They watched the pile of rubble gradually topple from the top, and stood as far back into the cave as they could as the bucket of a digger ploughed forward towards them before retreating back into the cavern. As soon as they had a clear space ahead, and a view of the path they'd taken yesterday on their journey here, they began to climb over the mound of earth. They followed the reversing digger into the light, having to shield their eyes against the blinding sun.

Meadow was still blinking when she was practically rugby tackled at the entrance. 'Dad?'

'I thought you were a goner, love.'

'What are you doing out of the hospital?'

'I'm no use lying there doing nothing, thought I may as well be working here. It's just as well, isn't it?'

'But how did you know we were here?'

'How did I know? You've left a bloody trail of my equipment out here.'

Meadow threw her arms around her father and hugged him tightly. She'd never been so glad to see him. When she finally let go, she could see tears in his eyes.

'I was afraid I was too late. I've never felt so helpless, but I knew I couldn't help you on my own and had to call in a few favours to get the heavy equipment out.'

'It's fine. I'm just glad you got here.' She'd never thought she'd be happy that he'd defied everyone's advice to come out here and work again but if he hadn't, she and Jay would be facing another cold, hungry night in there. Or worse.

'So am I. I knew something wasn't right when you didn't phone to check on me last night at the hospital. I missed not speaking to you on the phone.' Her father hugged her back in an uncharacteristic display of affection. 'I know I haven't been the best dad, or showed you enough love, but I wouldn't want to be without you, Meadow.'

The words, though she'd waited a lifetime to hear them, were an instant balm to her soul. 'You were here when it mattered.'

If a childhood of being overlooked in favour of her father's expensive hobby was what it had taken to reach this moment and save her and Jay from their fate trapped in a mine, she would take it. It seemed her possible demise had been sufficient for them all to rethink their priorities.

'I'm sorry if I've been distant all these years when I know you could have left a long time ago. I think that's what I was afraid of, that you'd go and leave me like your mother.' The pain of the past was still there in every groove of his forehead, but Meadow could also see the genuine remorse and worry for her in his teary eyes.

'Never, Dad. I just want us to be a family. That's all I've ever wanted.' She gave him another hug because she could without fear he would push her away. He'd been hurting all this time, just like her, and perhaps now they could finally put it behind them and move on together.

She reached back and took Jay's hand. He'd made these past hours more than bearable and she had high hopes that they could capitalise on their progress. It would be nice to have some time together with him too, in a normal setting without the constant threat of death hanging over them. She'd surprised herself by taking a chance on him and letting fate take control for once and, going forward, she planned on doing that more if she was promised the same rewards.

The world hadn't ended because she'd risked her heart and enjoyed herself. In fact, she was hoping her life was going to be more enriched now that she had a new relationship with Jay and her father to look forward to. It was apparent to her now how important she was in both their lives, as they were to her, justifying that need to spend time with them, even when her heart told her it was probably a bad idea.

'I don't know if you remember, but this is Jay. He's the doctor who helped me that day when you were ill and he's lodging in the shack.' She pulled him forward to make the introduction.

'Hello. Thank you so much for coming to our rescue. We thought our days were numbered,' Jay said.

'The pom. I remember you. Are you the reason my daughter nearly died?' Meadow's father took a step towards Jay and Meadow intervened, placing her body between the two men.

'I guess I am—'

'There's a good reason though, Dad.' Meadow put her hand on her father's chest before he could advance any further towards Jay, who she knew could knock him flat on his backside if he chose to. In a way she was touched her father was so riled about the threat to her welfare, but she also wanted the two men to get along. After all, she was hoping they would all be seeing a lot more of each other, especially if Jay was staying on at the shack for a while.

If they had a chance at a future together, and if she had a chance to share her life with a man as exciting as Jay, she was going to defend him, regardless of his occasional irresponsible sense of adventure. Without that, they might never have been brave enough to act on that chemistry they had, or express the feelings she was still too afraid to admit.

'Thanks for your help, guys. If you want to go up to the house, I'll get everyone some drinks and snacks.' Meadow was aware there were still a few local men who'd come to assist her father hanging around and, whilst she and Jay would be eternally grateful to them, she knew her father wouldn't want strangers to hear what she was about to tell him.

He was already looking at her as though she'd lost her marbles, offering to host the gang when she'd just suffered a near-death experience. Not least because he wasn't one for entertaining on the premises.

'Are you sure you're up to that? I think you'd be better having a shower and getting forty winks. Your English friend can do the same. Over at the shack.' Ironically, he was eyeing Jay with the suspicion of an over-protective father who didn't trust him with his daughter's honour. Well, it was too late for that, but the news Meadow had to share would probably redeem him, and save him from immediate eviction from the property.

'That's exactly what I think we should do, sir, but I think you'll want to hear what your daughter has to say,' Jay said quietly.

The tense stand-off between the two men in her life made Meadow antsy enough that she just had to say it. 'Jay found gold in the mine.'

'What?' Her father's eyes lit up and she could almost see the dollar signs shining on the surface.

'It's true. There's a seam running along the roof of the cave. I made a mistake dragging Meadow in without making the site safe first, but you can take our word for it that it would be worth your while excavating in there again.'

'How? I mean, I've been in there many times over the years and I haven't seen a speck of gold. I wouldn't have missed a whole bloody seam.'

'It's at the very end of the tunnels and there's evidence of previous cave-ins. Perhaps it was uncovered when a chunk of the wall was dislodged during an earthquake or something.' Jay shrugged.

He'd done the hard part and found the gold when Meadow's dad had spent years of hard work and money with limited success. It was a lucky break, despite an uncomfortable night for them both, and maybe it would not only see her father set up for a while longer, it might also endear Jay to him a little more. That was if he didn't resent him for finding it instead of him.

'I'm going to need to get earthmovers and extra hands and equipment in. We'll need to blast it and set up a wash plant to extract the fine gold from the rock.'

Meadow could see her father's mind working overtime, and though it would be an expensive initial outlay she had a feeling it would be worth it. 'It should keep you busy for a while, at least.'

'It's really true?' Her father hugged her again, clearly struggling to process everything that had just happened.

'Yes, it's true, and it's all yours, Dad. Isn't that right, Jay?' Meadow wasn't staking any claim on what had been discovered and she doubted Jay would, but they both looked to him for confirmation.

Thankfully, he nodded. 'Of course. I merely stumbled on it and, strictly speaking, I wasn't even supposed to be here.'

His generous offer to back her prompted her father to shake his hand and would hopefully put an end to hostilities between them.

'Right, well, I need to make a few calls. I suggest you two go back to the house and get cleaned up and get some food on the go for the guys. I'll have to secure this place as best I can in the meantime.' Her father rolled up his sleeves and began clearing some of the debris away from the entrance.

'Don't do too much, Dad. You're only just out of hospital and I don't want to have to book you a return flight.'

'Listen, I'll go back, get washed and have a bite to eat and then I'll come back and help your dad get this boarded up.' It was Jay who was able to give her peace of mind about leaving her dad out here all alone again so soon after his own accident. At least with Jay he'd not only have an extra pair of hands and get the work done in half the time, but he was someone with medical experience who would intervene if her father showed signs of a relapse. She'd do it herself except she'd promised her services elsewhere to a group of hungry, thirsty workers. It wasn't the quiet, private homecoming she'd been hoping to have with just Jay, but as soon as everyone had gone and her father was safe in his own bed, she would go to him over at the shack.

They had a future to discuss and lost time to make up for, and she couldn't wait for the evening to hurry up and arrive.

'Let me help you with that.' Jay bounded down to help Meadow's father with the thick planks of wood he was hauling in front of the entrance to the old mine.

He'd had his quick, cold shower, and stopped by to make sure Meadow was all right on her own with the men who'd come for their promised refreshments. Thankfully, once they'd been fed, they were keen to get back to their own places. He wondered how many of them were farmers or, like Meadow's dad, obsessed gold hunters who couldn't get their next fix quick enough. However they made their income, he was glad to see them go and leave Meadow in peace. She'd protested when he'd insisted on staying but he didn't care if she knew them or not, he didn't want to leave her on her own with them.

He'd had to fulfil his promise to her father, though, so he'd left instruction for her to take a long, leisurely nap and he'd catch up with her later. Tonight, he wanted them to have a nice romantic time together, just the two of them and some home comforts. After last night he was going to appreciate everything he had here, and that started and ended with Meadow.

'Thanks. I don't want anyone else getting their hands on whatever's in there. I mean, I wish I'd seen it for myself but I don't want to risk another cave-in when it's already going to be difficult to get back to the right spot.'

'Oh, I did take these. Sorry, I forgot all about them in the excitement. The screen's cracked, but it's a miracle it's still working, to be honest.' Jay pulled out the phone he'd spotted in the rubble on the way out and scrolled through the pictures until he found the couple he'd taken of the gold in the cave. 'They're a bit dark but it'll give you some idea of what you've got in there.'

Mr Williams set down the armful of wood to look at the photographs, his eyes growing wide. 'That looks promising, son. It'll take some digging and we'll have to filter it out… but I think we're onto a winner there. I can't thank you enough for finding it, and for looking after my daughter.'

Jay cringed, not comfortable with the praise, given the circumstances. 'It was my fault she got trapped in there. I'm not sure you've anything to thank me for.'

'My Meadow doesn't do anything she doesn't want to. If I'm honest, this is the happiest I've seen her in a while. She acts tough but she's got a soft heart, you know.'

He handed Jay his phone back, which was now displaying a candid pic he'd taken of her before the mishap, capturing that image of her digging in the dirt, her hair in a ponytail and the sun highlighting the freckles on her nose. She looked adorable.

'I know.' Jay had seen it for himself. Meadow gave everything to those around her, sometimes neglecting her own needs in doing so. Jay knew both he and her father were guilty of taking too much and giving too little in return. Which was probably why she'd been so wary of getting involved with him. She'd given him a place to stay, been his chauffeur and a shoulder for him when he'd needed one. All he'd done was nearly get her killed and take advantage of her when she was most vulnerable. It put what had happened last night in a different light and he knew she likely wouldn't have slept with him if they hadn't been in such a precarious position, not knowing if they'd live to see another day. If her father knew, he'd probably have sealed him inside the mine for good.

'She doesn't always act in her own best interests.' He fixed Jay with his unnerving icy blue stare, which said he had more than a suspicion that he was going to hurt his only daughter. Yes, he'd be lucky to get out of this one alive too.

'I mean, she should have ditched me years ago like her mother, but that girl wants a family so bad she couldn't cut me off. I know I'm lucky, and nearly losing her has made me think about what my life would be without her. She's the only person who comes to see me, who cares about me, and it's my turn to be the father she needs. That starts with making sure no one waltzes in and breaks her heart again. She deserves more than to be a passing fancy.'

'Yes, she does.'

Deep down, Jay had known that too, he'd just been too selfish to acknowledge it. He wanted her, he felt good when he was with her, but he couldn't be the man she needed. Meadow wanted someone who could give her that family she'd been denied, but how could he be part of that when he had plans elsewhere? The list he'd started with Sharyn had been their way of helping him move on from the past but he still wanted to complete it, maybe even add to it in the future. He certainly didn't think he was anywhere near ready to settle down, to put down roots and resign himself to a life looking at the same four walls again.

Lecture over, cogs whirring in Jay's brain as to what he was getting himself into, the duo fell into silence as they finished the job at hand. Jay knew he had a lot of things to think over, to be clear about what a relationship with Meadow would entail and if he was ready for it. The worst thing for them to do now was rush into something based on a night of good sex at a vulnerable time, and come to regret it later, to resent one another for being trapped in a relationship they knew could never work out. Meadow was still a home body who wanted a family and security. He was a nomad with adventures ahead of him.

It was becoming clear to him he should only make promises about a life together when they were sure that was what they both wanted. Otherwise, they should call it quits now.

Meadow had been watching the clock, wishing away the time all day, waiting for the hours to tick by until it was time to see Jay again. She'd had her shower and made sure she'd had something to eat to sustain her energy levels in anticipation of tonight.

In other circumstances, she would have found Jay's insistence on staying with her to feed the troops irritating, perhaps even condescending to think she couldn't look after herself, but she'd made that mistake before. It was his way of saying he cared about her and he wanted her to be safe. That sort of affection was something she'd been searching for her whole life. Even the hint of jealousy she'd thought she detected as he'd hovered around her gave her heart a lift that he cared enough about her to make his claim. Of course, if he overstepped the mark she wouldn't be long in putting him back in his place, just like that first night, but it was nice to be part of a couple again. Hopefully, tonight would cement that idea and they might even go official so everyone would know and his patients could stop flirting with him. Okay, so he wasn't the only one to get a little possessive when it came to members of the other sex getting too close for comfort.

'Are you sure you're going to be all right if I go out for a while?' She popped her head around her dad's bedroom door to make sure he was settled before she left. He'd been exhausted after the manual labour he and Jay had carried out earlier on so she'd insisted he get an early night and rest up. She'd left some snacks and drinks on his bedstand and put the TV on to keep him company.

Despite living on his own all this time, in her mind he was still a vulnerable man, as his accident had proven. His apology for the past, combined with his emotionally charged hug once he knew she was safe, had only made her want to take care of him more. It was clear he still needed someone to look out for him and for once in her life she was glad she hadn't severed all ties with him. He was the only family she had around her and she knew they loved each other in their own way. It was enough to know that now.

'I'll be fine. Have a good night,' he said, waving her away.

'Okay. 'Night, Dad.' She closed the door and checked her reflection in the hallway mirror. It was technically her first date with Jay, since the other times they'd spent together had happened organically and hadn't been preplanned. So she wanted to look her best. She'd taken the time to dry her hair and put some product in it so she didn't look as though she'd just rolled out of bed for once. If anything, she was hoping to roll back into one.

The thought of sharing one with Jay tonight put a smile on her lips as she dotted them with pink gloss. With a little make-up and a white sundress to show off her tan, she was hoping to make an impression when he opened his door to her.

Meadow hadn't counted on the backward flips her own stomach would do upon the sight of him.

'Hey,' he said casually and opened the door for her to come in.

She followed him inside the shack, which now smelled of his cologne and with the evidence of him living in it, his shoes by the door and his jacket hanging on the wall, she knew she'd never think of the place again without Jay in it.

'Thanks for helping Dad out earlier. I know he thinks he can do everything himself, but he's getting older and I worry about him.'

Her nerves were causing her to ramble a bit as she took a seat on the old sagging couch. Jay had sat in the single armchair, immediately creating some distance between them, and it had thrown her. In her imagination, she'd pictured them being reunited tonight like two long-lost lovers who hadn't seen each other in years, kissing each other senseless and not making it to the bedroom before ripping one another's clothes off. This was quite a different scenario.

'I know you do. You worry about everyone.' Jay set his beer down on the table and she realised he hadn't asked her if she would even like a drink.

'Jay, is everything all right? You seem a little…off this evening.' There was something in his body language, in his abrupt manner that was setting her on edge. It wasn't the behaviour of the same man who couldn't keep his hands off her last night and who'd talked about a future together. Something had shifted between them and she wasn't sure what that was, how she could fix it, or if he even wanted her to.

Jay cleared his throat and shuffled further

on his seat so he was almost sitting on the edge, elbows resting on his knees, head in his hands as though he was about to say something he knew she really didn't want to hear.

Her stomach stopped flipping and simply plummeted instead, as though she'd been enjoying a fun roller coaster ride and the wheels had suddenly come off. She had the urge to put her hands over her ears and block out whatever he was going to say next because she knew what was coming and couldn't stop it. He was going to break her heart.

'We didn't use any protection last night. You'll have to take the morning-after pill.'

'Yes, I suppose so. Thanks for the reminder.' She didn't know what else to say when none of this was how she'd expected the evening to go. Not only was he being distant and weird, but there was a coldness to him tonight she'd never seen before.

'I mean, I know we got carried away in the moment, and neither of us really thought we'd have to deal with the consequences, but you know we can still fix our mistake.'

'A mistake? That's what you think it was?' Meadow's brain was firing with memories and feelings from last night and not once had he given her the impression that he hadn't wanted any of it. Now she was wondering if she'd been too caught up in the moment to see he wasn't one hundred percent into her. All of those feel-good endorphins which had been coursing through her body as she'd got ready tonight died instantly from the blunt force of his words.

He scrubbed his hands over his face before he spoke. 'What I'm saying is we didn't act on whatever feelings we may have for each other before last night and maybe there's a reason for that. We've both held back because, deep down, we know we're not right for one another, but last night was an exceptional circumstance. The danger we were in made us reckless, not least forgetting about contraception, and I can't afford to take that kind of risk.'

'I can take the morning-after pill. It's not like I was trying to trick you into having a baby, if that's what you're insinuating. I'm not so desperate to keep you in my life I'd do something like that.' She didn't know where any of this had come from. Yes, they'd been careless, but they could take steps to fix that, and to avoid a similar occurrence in the future. Except she got the feeling there was no longer a future involved.

'I know that, Meadow, but the possibility of a pregnancy got me thinking long-term.

You want a family, a man you can settle down with, someone who will give you the stability you didn't have when you were younger. I'm not that man. I can't promise you I'll never have the urge to move on somewhere else or want to do something reckless, and that's not the sort of person you need in your life.'

This sudden turnaround was giving her whiplash when only a few hours ago they were looking forward to being together and having some fun. Now he was basically telling her he wasn't the marrying kind.

'Has my dad said something to you?'

'What? No. I've just had some time to think about what we're getting ourselves into.'

'You make it sound like I'm part of a dodgy business deal. I was just looking forward to us having some fun together, not expecting a lifetime commitment, or a judgement on my morals.' She got up out of her seat, forcing herself onto slightly unsteady legs to try and walk away with some dignity when he was gearing up to tell her they were over before they'd even begun.

'I'm sorry, Meadow. None of this is your fault. We're merely guilty of acting without thinking. Something which is completely out of character for one of us and proves what a bad influence I am.' Jay was doing his best to make light of the situation, to take the blame for things suddenly going awry, but Meadow couldn't find the funny side to it. Not when she'd already thrown her heart into the ring, not expecting to have it kicked around in the dirt.

'So, that's it then? Wham, bam, thank you, ma'am, but if we're going to live after all I don't want to tie myself down?' Meadow could hear the shrillness in her voice and hated herself for getting so emotional, but she'd really thought they'd moved past their differences. Loved up and anticipating another night with Jay, she'd convinced herself this was the start of something special. All the time he was probably thinking of a way out. Perhaps it was only last night's jeopardy which had pushed him over the edge into wanting her. Without that adrenaline-pumping threat of almost dying, she wasn't such an attractive prospect.

'I'll thank your dad for letting me stay and pay him rent for the month, but I think it's better for both of us if I move on. There are other places I want to visit, and things I want to do.'

'I thought you were done with the list?' She was clinging now to the last vestiges of her dignity, close to begging him to stay, if not for his benefit, for hers. Jay had come into her world and shown her everything she was missing. Without that excitement he'd brought into her day she didn't know if her old life would ever be the same again.

'I don't know. I don't know what I want right now.'

'But it's not me. That seems pretty clear.'

Jay didn't argue with her. He didn't even follow her to the door. Those simple inactions told her everything she needed to know as she stumbled back out into the night. The darkness hid her tears. If anyone had been watching her they wouldn't have been able to see her doubled over, the pain of losing Jay a physical wound which was going to take a long time to heal, if it ever did.

Jay was leaving her, felt no responsibility or desire to have her in his life in any capacity, and that was a difficult notion to come to terms with. She'd only ever been herself with him and that had proved insufficient for him to want to be with her. There was clearly something lacking in her personality which drove people away. The only person she still had in her life was her father, and that had been at her insistence, not his. It was becoming increasingly apparent the only person she could rely on was herself, and even that was in doubt, given her most recent decisions.

With past breakups she'd taken some time out for self-reflection, to try and figure out what had gone wrong in the relationship as she came to terms with it ending. Ultimately, as she'd usually been the one to call things off, she'd figured it was for the best, that things simply weren't working.

This was different. She'd known from the start Jay wasn't the safe option. That was why she'd kept her distance. Partly. Subconsciously, she thought perhaps she'd known she would be attracted to the danger he represented, that she would fall hard for him. She'd been trying to avoid this pain, the same feeling of rejection and being alone that she'd experienced through most of her childhood.

Except Jay had managed to break her heart as well as her spirit, and she didn't even have a catalogue of memories to keep her company. They'd only had one night. Not enough for her, but sufficient for Jay to know he didn't want any more. It was impossible not to take that personally.

The things she'd shared with him about her childhood and how it had affected her she'd only told him because he'd made her feel safe. She'd given him her trust, her body, her love, only to have it all thrown back in her face. It was a betrayal, yet she couldn't blame Jay for what she was feeling. He hadn't asked for any of it. She was the one who'd taken the risk, thinking she should be more like him and live in the moment. The mistake had been in believing it could last longer than that.

She had forgotten about using protection last night, but the idea of carrying Jay's baby would not have been the same disaster to her as it was to him. He was right, she wanted a family, the settled life she'd never had. But more than that she wanted to be with Jay.

Now, not only had she scared him off the idea of being together, he was leaving her dad's place, and it sounded as though she was losing her co-worker too.

She must have walked into the house in a daze since she didn't remember how she'd got there. It was only minutes ago she'd left, gliding out of here on a cloud of happiness as she went to meet her lover. Now that naïve version of her had been replaced with a devastated Meadow who was cursing her previous self for not being more wary.

When she went to close the blinds in the front room she saw car headlights outside the window. Before she got nervous about who would be out here at this time of the night,

Jay emerged from the shack with his bag over his shoulder. Clearly, he'd made his decision to leave as soon as possible and in desperation had clearly phoned Marko for a taxi out of here. Perhaps he'd even done it before her visit, it seemed to happen so quickly, meaning nothing she could have said would have changed his mind about leaving.

As the car pulled away, plunging the room into darkness once again, she noted he hadn't even cared about her enough to say goodbye. It was then she allowed the tears to fall, knowing she was watching the love of her life drive away.

She could admit that now. She was in love with Jay, and probably had been from the moment he'd waded in to defend her honour in the pub that night. The knowledge that those feelings weren't reciprocated didn't make it any easier to see him leave. It only emphasised how much she'd lost when he was taking those unrealistic expectations of a happy family with him.

Jay got into Marko's car and looked back at the house until it was nothing more than a dot in the distance. He'd seen Meadow at the window watching him go and felt as though a crushing weight had been dropped onto his heart. If this had been a movie she'd have come running out barefoot after him, he would've stopped the taxi and met her half-way, swinging her around in the air and kissing her through his apologies for being an idiot. But this was real life and that wouldn't have fixed anything, only set them up for more devastation when he failed her again in the future.

He couldn't blame her father for this departure when he'd only told him what he already knew to be true. Meadow needed someone safe, who could be a good husband to her and a father to her children. Jay couldn't promise any of that when he still had things he wanted to do, places he wanted to see. It didn't mean he loved her any less, that this pain in his heart wasn't killing him. He'd grieved for Sharyn for a long time, and though it was only a relationship with Meadow he was mourning, those feelings were just as intense. It was still a loss, leaving his love with nowhere to go. That was why he had to leave now. If he stayed here, saw Meadow at work and on her father's property, he'd realise what he was missing and want to stay. He had to do this for her. No matter the pain it caused him.

His reward would be her future, and knowing she would find happiness with a man who could give her children and the family she needed around her. The only thing he knew about parenting was frightening and dark, and to his mind pretending that was what he wanted would only end up with him hurting Meadow. He'd be as guilty of trapping her in a nightmare as his father, and that was the last thing he wanted.

Though she might never know it, it was his love for her that was setting her free.

CHAPTER NINE

'DON'T YOU THINK we should just fly on up to the fair? I mean, we can still go if we get a shout, and we'll be on site should anyone be in need of medical assistance, but we could go and enjoy the carnival atmosphere while we're waiting,' Meadow asked their new flight doctor with the thought they might as well enjoy themselves along with the rest of the town while they were waiting for the next callout.

She hadn't had much fun in the two weeks since Jay had gone. Her father had been busy trying to get equipment in place to start mining the gold seam they'd found. He was in his element and totally rejuvenated by his new venture but she had stayed on in his house to make sure he didn't overdo things. It also made her feel closer to Jay, especially looking out on the shack which reminded her of him so much. That last night in particular, when he'd driven away.

She'd done her fair share of crying over him and for the first time in her life she found herself restless, her life here suddenly not fulfilling enough. As though Jay had taken a very big part of her away with him and she didn't know how to fill that void left behind.

'I don't think so. We have paperwork to do and we need to be at the base for any emergencies coming in.' Henry, Jay's temporary replacement until they found someone permanently, was a stickler for the rules. Even more so than Meadow. She'd done her best to get along with him, but after Jay she found him very dry and boring.

He unbuckled his seat belt and exited the plane as soon as the engine had completely stopped, keen to get into the hub and file a report.

'Is it just me, or is he a bit of a jobsworth?' she asked Greg in the cockpit, annoyed that she couldn't spend the afternoon at the fair, away from the house and thoughts of Jay.

Greg laughed. 'That's rich coming from you, Miss By-the-Book.'

'What? Am I really that bad?' She liked to do her job well, but she hadn't realised it had earned her a nickname for her fastidiousness.

If that was the case, it was a wonder someone like Jay had ever taken a romantic interest in her, and less surprising that she hadn't been enough to keep him here. To someone who'd travelled the world and experienced so many adrenaline-fuelled adventures, she too must have seemed dry and boring in comparison. Perhaps he'd simply seen her as a respite from the excitement, the human equivalent to a duvet day. The thought didn't improve her current mood.

'Not so much now, since Jay was on the scene. I think he had a positive influence on you.'

'You think?' She hadn't been able to find any positives since his departure, only negative feelings and space where he'd once been.

'You're not as uptight as you used to be, or defensive. I think he brought out your fun side. I hear he's in Sydney now.'

'Oh?' She'd been curious about what Jay had been up to and where he'd gone, but he hadn't made any contact with her since he'd left, and she hadn't wanted to look desperate by texting. Even if there was a message for him still waiting in the draft folder of her phone. She missed him, and she had hoped he would miss her too.

'Yeah, I think Kate was talking to him recently. He needed some paperwork or something for his new job. Anyway, talk to her, she knows all about it.' Greg unbuckled his seatbelt, set his headset down and climbed out of the cockpit, clearly ignorant of her thirst for more information.

'Thanks. I'll do that.'

Greg stepped out on the tarmac and helped her out of the back of the plane.

'I thought you made a good couple.' He shrugged.

'Me too, but I guess I'm just not his type.' It was all she could do to even give a half smile when all she still wanted to do was curl up in a ball and cry for everything she'd lost. They might only have known each other for a few days but it had seemed like a lifetime when they'd come to know each other so well, or at least she thought they had.

That instant explosive chemistry they'd had on the first night in the pub had always been fizzing away in the background but they'd shared so much more than physical attraction. The connection they'd had working together, the bond they'd shared over their difficult childhoods, and the simple pleasure of being in one another's company were things she doubted she'd ever have with anyone else. She couldn't believe she'd got it so wrong by putting her faith in him not to fail her when she'd spent most of her adulthood trying to protect herself. It proved just how quickly, and deeply, she'd fallen for him to give him that trust so easily.

'I don't believe that. I saw you two together, and the way he looked at you. Believe me, you were his type for the whole time he was in town.'

'Ah, but he's not in town any more, is he? I'm sure there's a much bigger dating pool in Sydney for him to dip his toe into and find his real type instead of his only option.' Meadow was well aware there were very few single women in town, just as there was a shortage of single men. It was the reason she blamed for hooking up with Marko that one time, and maybe Jay realised after their one night together that he'd settled too. She was fine as a passing fancy but anything more serious had never been on the cards.

'I don't believe that for a second. I saw you two that night at the pool playing doctors and nurses when you thought no one was looking.' Greg whistled a breath out through his teeth and Meadow blushed at the memory of being caught ogling Jay in nothing but his pants.

'Nothing happened. Not that night, anyway,' she muttered, half hoping he wouldn't hear her admission.

Greg chuckled. 'I'm a man, Meadow. Just because you didn't act on it doesn't mean he didn't want to. I can tell when a man is interested and when he's just grabbing the nearest chick for a good time. Jay likes a challenge, we both know that, and they do say opposites attract. Otherwise, why would our Miss By-the-Book have fallen for the pom with the danger streak?'

'What do you mean? I don't understand...' If what Greg was telling her was true, it didn't explain how easy it was for Jay to simply drive away that night after he'd ground her heart into the dust.

He took her by the shoulders. 'Meadow, you've a lot to learn about men. We run when we're scared.'

'But Jay wasn't scared of anything.' Except the dark, but he'd been able to get over that when she was there to distract him. She wondered who was there to hold him now.

'A man like that, always on the move, is running from something. I'm guessing this time it was his feelings for you. We're a skittish bunch, you know. One whiff of commitment and poof, we're gone.'

'But he was in a relationship before me. I don't think he had commitment issues per se.'

'Then you've got to ask yourself why else he would walk away from a woman he clearly had feelings for if it wasn't for his own sake.' Greg dropped that bit of wisdom and walked away, leaving Meadow to contemplate Jay's motivation from a different perspective. If it wasn't his feelings in question, as she'd believed, then it had to be something to do with hers. The sort of man Jay was, he wouldn't have wanted to cause her any problems and though her father insisted he hadn't said anything to influence his decision to leave, she wondered if that was true. After all, she'd told him she couldn't be with someone who wouldn't stay in one place, someone like her dad.

These past two weeks had told her that wasn't true. She'd been afraid to trust her heart with a rebellious soul like Jay, but it wasn't losing him that had made her so restless. It was not going after him and taking another risk that had made life so boring here now. The least she owed herself was to take one more chance and see where it led.

Jay stepped to the edge of the structure and made the mistake of looking down. Bungee jumping off the Sydney Harbour Bridge would have had any normal person's heart racing, but even with the wind whistling around him and only a safety harness preventing him from hurtling towards his death it wasn't the experience he had hoped it would be. It wasn't blocking out thoughts of Meadow, just as the swimming with sharks, moving to the city and starting over hadn't managed to erase her from his mind either. This was the last thing on the list and once he'd done this he didn't know what came next.

'Are you ready?' the instructor shouted against the wind as he adjusted his straps in preparation for the jump.

'Give me a moment.' Jay was only having second thoughts because he knew launching himself off here wasn't going to change anything, other than his perspective of the landscape.

He'd started his life over, something he'd done time and again on his travels with Sharyn, and something he'd had to do when she'd died. Yet since leaving Meadow he hadn't been able to settle. Ironic when he'd told her that was what he didn't want. Now it felt as though the only real excitement he'd experienced was when he'd been with her and everything else was boring and pointless in comparison. With Sharyn, he'd needed that buzz of jumping out of a plane or surfing giant waves to bond them together and get the adrenaline flowing. He hadn't needed to force anything with Meadow, except an excuse to leave.

With a deep breath and a glance back down, Jay tried to psyche himself up to take the leap. Like the whole list, he was only going along with this because he didn't know what else to do with his life or where to go, doomed to drift for ever. All because this big, brave man had been too afraid to tell Meadow how he really felt.

'Don't do it!'

At first, he thought he'd imagined the sound of her voice. Then he saw Meadow walking towards him on the platform, wearing a helmet and safety pads and picking each step very carefully. When she reached him she grabbed hold of him and hugged him tight, but he wasn't sure if it was because she'd missed him or that she just needed something to cling onto for safety.

'At least not without me.'

As Jay was attempting to figure out what was happening, the safety instructor began to strap her into a harness.

'Hey, you're not actually going to do this,

are you? You don't just jump and hope for the best, you know.' He didn't know why she was here or what she was attempting to achieve, but he wasn't going to let her put herself at risk because he was the idiot who'd thought this was a good idea.

'I've had the safety talk and instructions. Kate told me you were planning this and I thought I would come and surprise you.'

'Why?' As glad as he was to see her, he couldn't understand what was going on, other than Kate having a big mouth. He hoped there wasn't a crowd from the base down below waving banners for him and turning this into a community event instead of a distraction from his lonely life. This had been his choice, even if he'd left Dream Gulley for Meadow's benefit.

She looked up at him with those big blue eyes he'd still pictured in his dreams at night. 'I missed you. Perhaps I'm being stupid, but I thought we had something special.'

'We did, but—'

'Thank goodness I got that right, at least.'

'I just didn't want to let you down, Meadow. You need someone who'll be there for you, who wants to settle down and have a family. Someone safe.'

'Well, it turns out that's not what I need.

Apparently, it's an Englishman with a death wish that's missing from my life. Who knew?' She was smiling up at him and, for the first time since he'd climbed up here, Jay's heart began to race.

'So where do we go from here? I mean, other than off this bridge.' He was afraid to believe that he could still have Meadow in his life when her sudden appearance didn't mean the things that made them incompatible would immediately evaporate. To go back again now would simply delay the inevitable again. That was why he'd ripped the Band-Aid off in the first place.

'This is the last thing on the list, right? I thought you might want some company to mark the occasion, so I took some time off. I know, I know, it's so unlike me, which is why I did, and flew here to be on this bridge with you. I want us to spend some time together and I'm willing to change, to do crazy stuff like this if that's what you need from me.'

'I wouldn't ask you to change, Meadow. I'm not even sure this is the kind of life I want any more. You changed me.' Jay laughed, knowing he'd rather be playing board games together or trapped in a cave, or making love, or doing anything as long as it was with her.

'I think we changed each other, huh?

Things are kind of boring without you around. So, what do you say we spend some time just hanging out and see how we feel?'

'Hey, guys, are you two jumping any time today?' The young instructor was standing with his arms folded, clearly still an adrenaline junkie who hadn't been tamed by love yet.

'I'm ready if you are,' Jay said, putting his arms around Meadow's waist now it appeared they were doing a tandem jump. This was the end of one chapter of his life and, hopefully, the beginning of a new, happier one.

'Yeah, let's get this over with so we can go do something fun,' she said with a grin. 'Now you've finished your list, we might even make one of our own.'

Jay couldn't resist stealing a kiss when she looked so adorable kitted out for her mission in trying to win him back. Not that it would take much persuading for him when he was missing her more than he'd ever thought possible. If Meadow had the courage to leave her safe place and stand here on the precipice with him, then he needed to take the plunge too. She was right, some time together without any pressure would soon let them know if they wanted to carry on past their adventures. Jay had a feeling that life with Meadow, whether they were working together, gold hunting or making dinner out of leftovers, would never be boring.

As they clung to each other and took that huge step into the unknown, Jay knew they were doing so with their eyes and hearts open. The biggest risk he'd ever taken.

EPILOGUE

'I REALLY THOUGHT you would have been better at DIY.'

Meadow was watching Jay attempt to put up shelves to house their growing collection of board games and photo frames of their madcap adventures. They'd even framed his completed list and added one of their own.

'Why? Because I'm a man?' He sucked on the thumb which he'd just hit with a hammer instead of the screw in the wall.

'No, because it involves dangerous things like hammers and drills and potentially maiming yourself.' She took his hand and kissed it.

'It's probably just as well we've hired people to do the essential repairs or this place would be in worse condition than when we started.'

After she'd followed him to Sydney and they'd decided they did want to be together,

Jay had made the decision to return to Dream Gulley with her and start back at his old job. She'd spent so much time at the shack and on her father's land, he'd eventually told them they were welcome to live there permanently as a thank you for locating his long-sought-after gold. It had become their project to renovate the house into a home and with the place so busy with contractors and work going on at the mine, it no longer resembled the vast empty space she'd resented in her youth.

They'd found a happy middle ground, working and living together like any other normal couple, but every now and then they took a spontaneous trip to do something fun and exciting. She was happy and Jay seemed pretty content too. They had an agreement that if either of them wasn't enjoying their life together they would discuss it rather than let things fester. So far, so good.

'You can't be good at everything. You have many other more useful skills.' She danced her fingers up his chest, the sight of him attempting to make his mark on a home for them apparently her new kink.

'I don't like to boast, but I have been known to wrangle deadly snakes and discover gold in abandoned mines.' Jay set down his tools and put his arms around her waist, pulling her close.

'Hmm, I was thinking about the more fun, less deadly things you're good at.'

'There is still one thing I haven't tried. I don't know if I'll be any good at it, but you know I'm up for a challenge.'

'Oh? What's that?' Meadow's heart began to sink as she anticipated the bad news that he wanted to move on after all. Even if he wanted her to go with him, it wouldn't be the same as the life they'd made for themselves here and she would be reluctant to let go of it.

'Being a husband.'

Before she could process what he was saying or doing, Jay let go of her and went down on bended knee.

'Meadow Williams, I love you with every fibre of my being. Will you please do me the honour of marrying me?' He was holding out a black velvet ring box with a marquise cut diamond ring nestled inside.

Even if it had been a rusty old ring-pull he'd found outside with a metal detector she would have given the same answer. 'Yes. I love you too, Jay.'

Jay was reflecting the big grin she had on her face as he slid the ring onto her finger. 'I had it made specially, with permission from your father. The band is made from the seam of gold we found in the mine. A real piece of home to show you how much I love you. Maybe some day we'll even fill this place with a family of our own.'

Those simple words finally made her feel complete. Jay would never enter into a decision about getting married and having children if he didn't feel he could offer a stable home for everyone. It showed his conviction in his love for her to make such a commitment and Meadow loved him for pushing through his own issues for the sake of their relationship. He was letting her know she was loved and had a home where she was safe. It was everything.

* * * * *

If you enjoyed this story, check out these other great reads from Karin Baine

Falling Again for the Surgeon
Single Dad for the Heart Doctor
Festive Fling to Forever
A GP to Steal His Heart

All available now!